PadMad

Sex, drugs, rock & roll and much else besides
… being the life and memories of
The Padiham Don

by

Haydn Woollard

RB
Rossendale Books

Published by Rossendale Books

11 MowgrainView, Bacup,
Rossendale, Lancashire
OL13 8EJ
England

Published in paperback 2010

ISBN 978-1-906801-37-3

Memoirs & Life Story

Chapters & Verse

Chapter 1. To blindly follow the light.

Striving to be a millionaire.what a farce,
I ended up broke on my britches' arse!
Down on my luck without a penny to my name,
To run Padiham club was now my new aim.

Chapter 2. Doubtful situations.

Smack, pills, drugs of all kinds,
Enough to confuse and boggle the mind.
All kinds of scams behind the scenes,
Yet not one punter would spill the beans.
Many attempts to fleece me and pull the wool o'er my eyes,
With con tricks, thieving and various lies.

Chapter 3. A glimmer of hope.

I almost wilted as my spirit started to wane,
But decided instead to play them at their own game.
Rumours spread quickly about a very funny fable,
Of a couple who'd been screwing on the pool table.
I won most of them over and they toe'd the line,
No more con tricks or thieving, it suited me fine.
At this time, Yogurt, Ernie and others emerged on the scene,
My club was now running like a well-oiled machine.

Chapter 4. The sun breaking through.

Yog's sister, Nicola, also came into my life,
I loved her dearly despite all the strife.
These newfound friends with personalities second to none,
Disperse all my past tensions, they'd vanished and gone
Whenever in trouble and in need of a base,
People always congregated at Ernie's place.
Unlike the money people with whom I'd had to deal,
My newfound friends were truthful, loyal and real.

Chapter 5. Fun and laughter.

Yogurt loved the outdoors and taught me the meaning of life,
Whereas Nicola, his sister, acted more like a wife.
Between them they lifted my spirits so high,
I became vibrant alive and felt I could fly.
Dwarling, Hillis and others appeared on the scene,
Characters in their own right if you know what I mean.
The punters now treated my club as a base,
On the grapevine it was voted their favourite place.
A fun place to be without any trouble,
I felt secure now in my own little bubble.

Chapter 6. In unison with the law.

Punters enjoyed themselves being ever so cool,
No bother, no fighting, they stuck to the rules.
Padiham police came into the frame,
To maintain peace was their main aim.
The Inspector was fair and of good tact,
Between us both we came up with a pact.
If I use tactics to allay many a fear,
He promised for pecadillos, he'd turn a deaf ear.

Chapter 7. Anxious moments.

Special parties, fiestas, everything was great,
But alas, something happened to alter my fate.
An armed robbery I encountered without my knowing,
But the twits hadn't a clue what they were doing
A fire destroyed part of the ground floor,
But I decided to cope a little while more.
With the aid of friends we struggled and strived,
The club came together and my hopes were revived.

Chapter 8. A kind of magic.

A couple moved in whilst I was away,
Trying to take over the place, when I arrived home that day.
But their plans were fouled because of a friend,
And fortunately for me, it all worked out well in the end.
Yogurt spent some time in jail,
The police were pleased, he'd been hard to nail.
That New Year's day on reaching my goal,
Was given the title of Godfather and all.

Chapter 9. Accepting the inevitable.

But something more traumatic than any fire,
Occurred in the guise of a new inspector so dire.
He hated me and made it plain from the start,
By imposing a personal vendetta.....what a fart.
New regulations quickly spread around the town,
Leaving me no option but to close the club down.
Hillis and Yog were left with nothing to cheer,
Needless to say they went on the beer.
Hillis took it bad and just faded away,
Yog didn't last much longer, about a year to the day.

Chapter 10. That final day.

Prior to his funeral I went to the moor,
For sadness inside me I needed a cure.
On reaching the moorland I gazed all around,
A rustle of cans but no other sound.
This was the spot where Yog loved to be,
I could feel his presence enveloping me.
In my mind, together, we had one final beer,
Then he departed forever giving a cheer!
Looking to the heavens I instinctively knew,
Never again would the sky be so blue.
But something within told me this was not the end,
Somewhere, sometime in eternity I'll meet my true devoted friend.

Acknowledgements

Roseanne Barr once portrayed the main character in the film, "She Devil", where the lady in question had to revert to an alternative way of thinking and acting, brought upon by the situation she had been forced into, to obtain revenge on her husband, who was an accountant and had run off with Mary Fisher.

Based on the fact that nobody, no item and no situation is perfect, she balanced his assets against his deficits. This way, she could estimate the correct degree of action to be taken in the right direction to obtain the required results.

Watching this special film so impressed me that I also started to live my life by the same rules, with extraordinary results.

Hence, this true story reminds me of a modern version of "Forest Gump" portrayed by Tom Hanks, where totally unorthodox decisions seem to pay off.

I would like to take time in thanking all the folks in Padiham, who eventually allowed me into their company as a respected friend, and because of them made it possible for me to write this unforgettable, down to earth record of seven years of my life there. No insults are intended to anyone.

I would also like to thank Mr. John Cowell, a close friend of mine, and the author of, 'Elephant Grass, 'Broken Biscuit', and 'Cracks in the Ceiling,' for proof reading my manuscript.

God bless you all

Haydn

Dedications

I dedicate this book to the late Mr. Robert Coulson (Yogurt) the main character who was once my best friend. And offer it as a keepsake to my dear friend, Nicola Coulson and her two sons, Brandon and Callum.

Contents

Introduction: PadMad - The Reason Why.

The year 2007

Running about in circles all day. The sort of day that to me was every day. It was a good feeling to arrive home after work to my small, comfortable sanctuary, tucked away from the entire world for a few precious hours. It was the time to gather my thoughts together before settling down for the night. Simple comforts like food, television, warmth, and most important of all, a time to rest. Time to unwind, to relax and think. Time to build up my strength to face yet another day.

As it turned out, tonight was not going to be one of those nights. Before I had even time to switch on the television, the telephone started to ring. Not a welcoming sound, believe me. In fact it was the last thing I needed at that moment in time. I didn't normally have many phone calls. I liked to keep myself to myself. Most of the calls I received were from people needing favours of one sort or another, and especially so at this time of evening. And to be quite honest, I'd done enough running about for one day. So, to say the least, I was more than a little hesitant in answering the damn thing. In fact I was determined not to answer it. But it kept ringing……..ringing, and ringing, and my determination grew weaker....weaker....and weaker. Conflicting thoughts passed through my mind, "Maybe it's something important No, it won't be, but then again, you never know, and you'll never find out if you don't answer it." The phone kept ringing…….ring…..ring……ring. Finally, curiosity got the better of me, and I reluctantly picked up the receiver. Before it had even reached my ear, I could hear a very distressed voice which I recognised immediately.

"Nicola, in trouble again. Nothing unusual," was my first reaction. "One big mistake. The end of my restful evening." Nicola was a girl of very little patience. She had a very impulsive personality. So I wasn't hearing anything surprisingly out of the ordinary when she screamed at me,

"Haydn! Must see you immediately." Such words I had heard so many times before, but they affected me every time I listened to her distraught voice. Basically she was a very close friend of mine, and I had promised her father long time past, just before he died, that I would keep a close eye on her for him. So....

"Go on then Nicola, tell me what's up with you tonight," I complacently enquired.

I shall never forget in a million years, the words she spluttered back to me.

"Yog's died on me Haydn!" she screamed, "What do I do?" She kept repeating the words over and over again. "What can I do, Haydn. Tell me, what do I do?" I didn't respond immediately. I must have been in a temporary state of shock, trying to take in what I had just heard.

"What are you on about Nicola, I don't understand what you're saying," was my stunned reply. My brain had temporarily frozen. Yog couldn't have died. With his unbelievable unique personality, I took it for granted that he and I would live forever. It just couldn't be true. I'd been informed he was fine, a few days ago. My mind was in total rejection mode. He was my best buddy. This couldn't be.

"If this is some sort of sick joke you're playing on me, it's not funny Nicola." was my initial response. She could pour out some exaggerated bullshit when she'd been on that vodka. Believe me.

"Oh, don't come that!" she cried out agonisingly. "As if I would joke about my brother dying, you Dick! Hello! I've just watched him die right in front of me."

Reality engulfed me. "Oh God!" I reacted, realising the terrible, awful truth of the situation. "You poor girl, I apologise profusely Nicola, I am so sorry".

"Must do something Haydn. My head's gone." she whimpered. "I'm coming up yours. I need to be with someone….NOW!…… it's alright i'n't it?"

"Don't be silly, 'course it is. Get your arse round here fast, I'll have a drink waiting. It might just help a little, Heeh."

With that, the line went dead, leaving me standing there, totally confused.

Yogurt and she were like two peas in a pod. They were so close to each other. Never been parted before. And now! It didn't bear thinking about. I was in pain, but I couldn't envisage the agony she was going through, trying to cope with her loving brother's tragic death.

It all hadn't sunk in yet. I needed a stiff drink. I paused for a while as various thoughts raced through my mind. We'd been through so much together, and now, I knew, I wouldn't ever see him again. That was impossible to imagine, life without him. "Things would never be the same again," I mumbled to myself. "An era in my life has abruptly ended." It was like coming to the end of an incredible book, and the wind blowing it away. Lost forever. So very, very sad.

I poured myself a drink, slumping down onto the sofa. "What is happening to the world around me," I thought sadly. "My life is beginning to crumble away again. All my friends are slowly disappearing, one by one, in tragic circumstances, leaving a black hole appearing in my life ".

I gulped down the drink and sat there, motionless and thoughtless…….timeless.

Suddenly the silence was broken by the front door flying open, banging onto the wall behind, as Nicola came bursting in, like a bull at a gate. She instinctively charged across the room towards me. We just collided. There wasn't time for words. We just hugged and cried on each other's shoulders for what seemed an eternity. Eventually I managed to pull away, placing the neat vodka I had already poured, into her hand as a gesture of consolement. In one massive gulp the glass was empty, automatically passing it back to me for a refill. Up to that moment, no words had been spoken. I looked into her face. She was in a right mess. Her makeup was smudged all over her face, due to her constantly crying and the wiping away of her tears with the back of her hands.

I hadn't a clue what to say to her. She was devastated. What can one say under such circumstances.

"How did he die?" was the obvious question. Throwing back her long brown hair that was straggled over her face, she replied, "They told me that possibly a blood vessel had burst in his neck. They won't really know till after the autopsy. That's all I know."

"Was he conscious at the end?" I asked her, striving to be as diplomatic as possible.

"No. He was under sedation at the time. It all happened so fast. They dragged me away, so I couldn't do anything for him. It was horrible. I fought my way back to him and gave him a right slap across his face, trying to get him to open his eyes. I wanted to believe he was playing one of his pranks on me, but obviously he wasn't this time."

"Well," I replied, "We should at least be thankful that he didn't suffer much at the very end."

"I suppose so," she muttered. "But it doesn't help the situation now, does it. He's still dead".

"Yeh, I know what you mean." I mumbled woefully. I was rather stuck for words, but kept the conversation rolling by enquiring, "How long had he been in hospital then?"

"About two days," she answered.

"It's a wonder they got him there in the first place," I remarked. "He must have felt really poorly 'cos ever since I've known him, Yog's avoided those places like the plague. didn't he just." Yog had this phobia about them. I think he sensed his own destiny. He always told me he would die tragically in hospital.

"It's ironic Haydn," she whimpered, tears rolling down her face again. "It was his birthday today. He actually died on his forty-second birthday would you believe. How sad is that. Life's shit in't it? That grim reaper must have been really rubbing his hands together tonight, finally catching up with him. Yog's been ducking and diving for years, hasn't he just"

"He sure has. But if I know Yog," I responded, "he'll be amusing 'em all up there at this moment, with his hilarious humour.”

Nicola became very quiet for a short while, then suddenly blurted out, ”Haydn I need you to promise me something. For me?”

“What Nicola?”

“Will you promise me that you'll never forget him,” she answered. “He must never be forgotten. Please promise me Haydn. For me.”

“Come on Nicola, I'll personally never forget him, I don't need to promise you that. I don't have to make that promise…….Yog has been a strong influence to me over the last few years. We've learned such a lot from each other about life in general. Him the slightly uneducated street minded character, and me the naive over educated businessman. It's as though we were thrown into some witches cauldron and seriously mixed together, both emerging much wiser people. My answer to your question Nicola is how could I ever forget him. He's a part of me, and a part of me has died with him. Can you understand what I am trying to say?”

She nodded respectfully. I noted the sadness in her eyes.

“But that doesn't mean everybody else is going to remember him. You know what it's like, three pints down and he'll be gone. You have to really know somebody to remember them. It's sad, but that's how it is.” She paused for a moment before adding, “So what can we do about it?”

I didn't answer straight away, but her words touched me, and stirred something in my imagination. “I know exactly what can be done Nicola, and it's something I've been thinking about doing for years, ever since I came to this town.”

“What's that?” she asked inquisitively.

“I'm going to write a book about all of the important characters that frequented the Padiham club. Yeah! And if everything turns out right I'll dedicate it to Yog. Him being one of the main characters anyway. That makes sense doesn't it? That will definitely slow down the forgetting process, won't it just. What do you think Nicola?".

"It sounds good to me, but are you capable of writing such a book?" Her countenance had changed a little and I noticed a profound sensitive feeling in her voice this time.

"I don't know Nicola, but I'm certainly gonna give it a try. The story needs telling anyway. It will definitely be a challenge, but that's alright Challenges are good for me. You never know, it might turn out to be a best seller. There's no harm in trying. You know what they say. Nothing ventured, nothing gained, that's what I think. Anyway, I'd be kicking myself for the rest of my life, wondering whether I could have pulled it off or not."

Once again, tears welled up in Nicola's eyes. She grabbed me and gave me a big hug.

"You're a good man Haydy babe. You always was and you always will be. I don't know what I'd do without you. You'll always be my bestest buddy, you know that."

At that, just like her entrance she left. That was Nicola. She couldn't stop in one place very long, at the best of times. It was like the room had been struck by a tornado. I went to the door, just in time to witness the waiting cab whisking her off round the corner. Where she was heading was anyone's guess.

The tidings she had brought me that night were very sad, but I was really touched by the fact that before anyone else, she had contacted me. It truly meant a lot to me….it really did.

With these thoughts in my mind, I returned back to the living room, pouring myself yet another drink. Slumping back on the sofa, I cried my eyes out. I was alone and it was my turn to grieve in privacy.

A sense of guilt engulfed me. It was not all that long ago that Yog, Nicola and I and a few others went for a swim in the forbidden area of Clowbridge reservoir near to where I live. We had a great afternoon, completely out of the blue. I distinctly remember Yogurt saying to me,

"It's just like old times when we were at the club, in't it

Haydy. We'll have to start doing things together again, more frequently. What do you think? I miss those times we spent together, don't you? Those were the good old days alright. Bloody great!"

I agreed with him. They certainly were good days, but nothing in life is straightforward. I had more important things to do on leaving the club. I was too busy doing other meaningless tasks, with thoughts of both of us getting together at some later date. Little did I know whilst speaking to him, that I would never ever see him again. The last thing I ever expected, was him dying on me.

His framed photograph was hanging on the wall in front of me. It seemed as though he was staring in judgement of me. I sat there, staring at him staring at me. His lifelike eyes were piercing my inner being.

"I didn't know you were going to die Yog, did I? I thought we'd both live for ever. I'm so sorry Yog, believe me."

He just looked straight at me, not uttering a word. Not altering his expression one iota. I half expected him to say something, but he never did. I'd learned a hard lesson that night. True friendship is very special, it comes before anything. Situations can never be reversed, so if a mistake is made, one has to live with it, and learn by it.

"Trust me Yog." 'Trust me' was his phrase to me. If I'd heard it once, I'd heard it a thousand times. "It might be late in the day, my big buddy, but I am still going to try to do my best for you. Goodbye my friend and sleep well, It's been a pleasure knowing you, and I promise you, I'm going to try my hardest to make sure you're never forgotten." And so, at the very end, it all begins again.

Myself

Nicola

Yogurt

Chapter 1 To blindly follow the light

It was Christmas morning 1995. It had been snowing overnight, covering the garden and road outside with an inevitable soft white blanket. Inside the sparkling trimmings were hanging randomly, totally covering the front lounge ceiling. A large bauble-covered Christmas tree stood majestically beside the imitation flame-effect fireplace. Presents of all colours and denominations surrounded its base. Each present had its own characteristic bow tied in silk ribbon. There were numerous Christmas cards covering a good percentage of the walls. What a beautiful comforting Christmas setting. To any outsider looking in, that was. From the inside looking out, nothing was as it seemed. A totally different picture altogether.

Carol, the girl I had been living with for quite a considerable while, and I, were not getting on very well at all., the relationship was becoming progressively worse, week by week. I was dreading facing this special day. I was receiving bad vibrations, and feeling very uneasy this morning.

She had four children, and we all used to live in a beautiful sixteenth century farmhouse called Longley Hall. I'd bought the place twenty years previously as a total ruin, and had spent at least two years renovating and transforming it into a total masterpiece. People used to come from miles away just to view, with my permission of course. I was very proud of the place, which I built authentically. On entering, it was like going through a time warp, back to the sixteenth century.

What a place that was. Original oak beams and trusses everywhere, jointed together by the same wooden pins they were originally constructed with.

A stone arched fireplace, you could walk into, sixteen feet long, twelve feet high, designed by my two five year old twin girls, Rachel and Georgina from a nursery rhyme book, copying Hansel and Gretel's cottage, with windows and stone roof to match, covered the total gable end wall of the main hall. The fireplace windows had oil lamps hanging in them, for effect. Logs burnt continuously, day and night for years, in the bulbous free-standing wrought iron dog grate. Six feet diameter wooden cartwheels hung from the oak beams on chains lit by numerous electric imitation candles.

The farm as I bought it

The farm as I was constructing it

My twin girls with their pet lambs on the farm

The forty feet long main hall was built on three levels. On the lowest level was a sixteenth century designed wrought iron bar, sixteen feet long, comprised of four arches, covered with forged grapes, vegetation and birds.

The highest level, which was the centre, had a medieval banquet table with ten high backed chairs to match, whilst the third lowest level, was designed as a cosy open plan lounge, comfortable but in context with the rest of the area, focused on two large patio windows, overlooking the immediate grounds and the picturesque hills and valley beyond. Unbelievably serene.

Besides this main hall, there was a smaller central lounge, kitchen to one side, toilets to the other. This lounge was surrounded by a winding open staircase, leading to the upstairs bedrooms and bathroom, and had large patio doors leading to an original enclosed swimming pool. Definitely a one off. The pool, including the platform steps into it, and the walkway round it, was completely constructed from stone paving slabs, and surrounding all this, was a conglomeration of large tropical plants, which crept across the ceiling, held up by fine, green netting. It was like an African jungle setting. It even had a six foot stuffed crocodile, crouching at the far end of the pool, whose scary jaws opened and closed electrically. It looked so alive, no one dare venture near it.

Large patio windows overlooking the grounds, gave the illusion of spaciousness. I used to spend hours by the side of that pool. It was definitely my favourite spot.

Besides all of this, we owned horses, farm animals, and a small lake full of fish and ducks. Then there were the cars, the power-boat, and the use of a Cessna light aircraft. I'm not bragging, I'm just trying to portray how things used to be.

The farm under construction

Carol had come into my life about eight years before. She was just a normal lass from the local village. On reflection, I don't think it was me, I think it was house she fell in love with. They say that money can't buy you happiness, but we did alright together considering she was twenty years younger than me. In fact I can't remember one argument between us throughout our first seven years together. We were both very happy. Not only the two of us, but also her four young children were proud to live there. We were all living in paradise.

The main hall semi-constructed fireplace in the newly-named Longley Hall

The bar area at Longley Hall

My twin girls at Longley Hall

But sadly, it wasn't to be, and unbeknown to me at that moment in time, I was heading for one big disaster. Carol was suffering from a mental disorder and was under the care of a psychiatrist. At the time, I was a successful forty six year old European building contractor, and had spent my final year at the farm contracting for the Russian Government in the Baltic. It was on my third weekly leave period, and I had come back home to discover she'd had a short standing affair with her shrink. So, after a week of arguments, I returned to Soviescque for my final three monthly visit and shagged virtually every woman in the village, just to get my own back. Needless to say, when I returned home, Carol and I were definitely not seeing eye to eye.

I continued to work with the Yorkshire Bank, purchasing land, developing and selling property, around the Northern England area. Business was great until one shocking weekend, Wall Street collapsed in America, and a freak hurricane hit London both in the same time spell, blocking most of the major roads into the centre of the city, resulting in total turmoil. Nobody could get to work at the London stock exchange in time to correct the computers which America had confused. The outcome caused Britain to go

My private aircraft

My twin girls at the pond at Longley Lane

E-Type Jag

into deep recession. And from that moment onwards, it was downhill all the way for me. It started a couple of days later, when our Prime Minister at the time, Mr. John Major, gave a flash broadcast to the British public, advising everybody to carry on normally, and not to panic because the crisis would be over in three weeks or so. What a load of bullshit. It took many years before we managed to crawl out of that mess. But I took his advice and invested all the money I could get hold of, to complete every contract I was involved in, ready for sale. The banks had promised to stick by me through the recession if I did just that. But after completion, some Australian conglomerate took over the Yorkshire Bank and one of the first things they did was to foreclose on me. So much for promises. I wasn't alone. half of Britain went down with me. And because nobody was buying property in such a financial climate, I eventually was paid less than half the value it was worth only months previously. Instead of coming out with the million I had planned on, I was penniless, homeless and jobless. I had just lost a lifetime's work.

But that's not where it ended. Carol was confined to hospital with serious mental problems and her children were temporarily put into care. Things were not good at all. I tried to keep my head together, but was losing control by the minute. I kept having anxiety attacks and suffering from acute depression. I couldn't work even if I had wanted to. My head had gone completely. My whole world as I knew it had fallen apart. The years I'd spent reaching this level, had been one massive waste of time. Even my so-called friends were slowly disappearing and I started to realise I'd been living an illusion. I honestly believed I was invincible. How wrong could a person be. Fortunately I knew some gypsy friends, willing to put a roof over my head, until I had sorted myself out. How my life had changed. It was all too sudden for me. Talk about riches to rags, the future scared the shit out of me. My only income now was forty two pounds on the dole, with no chance of me working for quite a while.

What a mess I was in. If the ground had opened, I'd have willingly jumped into the abyss. Looking back, I think I was on the verge of suicide. All this had happened due to no fault of my own. I was blameless. If I had made some blunder, I'd have expected a thump in the face, but for me, and half the country with me, to take the rap for other people's incompetence, was beyond comprehension.

The council had offered Carol some crap living accommodation, that wasn't fit for a dog to live in, when the doctors finally de-sectioned her. So I managed to sort her a decent rented house in Hebden Bridge, mainly for the children's sake, not hers. Carol could not understand politics, in fact, in my opinion she couldn't understand much of anything, and blamed me for everything that had happened. Her whole world had been lost, and I suspected that she wanted rid of me also. So when I introduced her and her children to her new landlord I wanted to walk away. But the children Jennifer, Amanda, Kathleen and Leon weren't having it, and all four threatened to leave with me if she didn't invite me back. She had no alternative really and so we started living together again, more as lodgers than lovers. Three years later and two houses down, we were still living under the same roof, barely tolerating each other. We'd gone from bad to worse. It wasn't totally her fault, as I was suffering from severe mental stress also. I used to think I could take anything that life threw at me, but this entire business had been far more than I could handle. I was definitely not the man I used to be. Gradually, she'd lost total respect for me. Once I was somebody and now, in her mind, I was nobody.

Time passed and the festive scene came around once more. This was that important Christmas morning when my whole life changed. I came downstairs about 8.30a.m, just to make sure all the presents were in place for my four stepchildren. I loved them, and needed them to be happy on this special day. They were good children who adored me but they were growing up now. The oldest was eighteen years old. I'd looked after them now for eleven years.

Ian, Jennifer's boyfriend, was already downstairs. He'd come in rather late Christmas Eve, and must have fallen asleep on the couch. Ian and I got on well together. He was a very likeable guy. Apart from him being an handsome 20yr old, although this morning he looked like he'd been dragged through the bushes and desperately in need of a shave, he was a very intelligent lad. A real trier. He ran his own small building firm, so we had something in common. It was comforting to witness a boy of his age trying to make good, not relying on anyone but himself. A complete contrast to most of the kids around his age.

I must have woken him up, sneaking down the creaky steps because he stretched, opened his eyes, trying to focus and forced a smile whilst yawning, all at the same time.

"Do you want a coffee?" I quietly asked him.

"Could murder one," was his enthusiastic reply. "I feel a bit rough this morning".

"Two coffees coming up."

Placing the drinks onto the coffee table, I plonked my body next to him on the sofa, in front of the fire.

"Happy Christmas Ian."

"Thanks Haydn," he replied. "I'd wish you the same, but we both know the shit you're going to be put through today, don't we." He understood the situation alright, he'd listened to it all for far too long.

You must understand, Carol had a problem with alcohol. Not the normal problem of drinking too much. She was a Jekyll and Hyde character. After around five halves of lager, she'd start twitching her head, which was a definite sign that she was changing from the happy, caring girl that everybody liked, into the evil monster to be avoided at all times. Whilst I lived with her, I closely monitored the amount she drank, and we never had this problem. But when I went to Russia, being by herself for long periods, she started to slide down the slippery slope. These last few years, she'd been hitting the town without me, and if she wasn't locked up for the night for causing a major disturbance after a drinking session, she'd come back home demoralising me. I tried to bring her back into line but she was having none of it. She shouted at me, not once but hundreds of hurtful insults. Things like:- "Aarrrgh.......you're nothing but a wanker, and a loser. I must be mad to be with an old man like you. You lost me my beautiful home because of your air-brained schemes. You thought you were the big, clever, high-flying businessman, and just look at you now. No woman in her right mind would entertain you! I hate you……..I hate you!" That sort of crap, I had to listen to, like it or not, every time she returned after a drinking session. And then the next morning she'd be back to her happy self again, as if nothing had happened. In her own mind she didn't believe anything was mentally wrong with her. But I knew alright. She was gradually destroying me.

I didn't want to talk about Carol to Ian that early in the morning, so I immediately changed the subject, enquiring where he'd been the previous night; what sort of night he'd had; what time they'd arrived back; were they pissed. You know, polite conversation in general. But the conversation changed again.

Out of the blue he enquired, "Why do you put up with all the shit Carol throws at you every day? I know I should be careful what I say. You know, me going out with Jennifer and all that, but if I were in your shoes, I'd have fucked off a long time ago. I know the kids will miss you, but it's not right what's happening around here. She's a heartless twat. Well that's my opinion if it means anything. She never lets up. And for what it's worth, you used to be the man. Just take a look at yourself now. But you can do it again Haydn. I know you can. You haven't run out of time yet. I'm telling you, you're wasting your time here, that's for sure, and you know that yourself don't you? You don't need telling. She doesn't deserve you. All you've done for her. I have to apologise for opening my mouth, but it had to be said. And another thing Jennifer, Amanda, Kathleen and Leon are with you all the way, believe me." Ian was the sort of guy who never minced his words. If he had something to say, he'd say it. That was Ian, and I respected him for it. At least I knew where I stood with him. That wasn't the first time he'd brought the subject up, but for some unknown reason, the words seemed to hit me from a different angle. Yes, they definitely hit the spot this special morning. It must have been the frame of mind I was in.

"Do you really think that's what I should do?" I cautiously asked him. "I've been thinking about it for a while Ian, but I needed reassurance. Just tell me I'll be making the correct move?"

"Come on Haydn, you know it's only a matter of time before it happens anyway."

I was not really convinced, but I felt the time had arrived. Now I'm not an irrational, impulsive person. I normally weigh the balance up first, and if the odds are against me I don't make a move. But this time was different. If I walked out of that door, I walked out with nothing. But I'd had enough. I couldn't take much more. All my time was spent trying to please her, whilst I should have been concentrating on building myself up. If that had carried on much longer, she would have been the death of me.

It was time. Not that afternoon. Not tomorrow. Not next week. NOW!

"Right Ian. I'll take your advice. Here goes. Wish me luck."

I stood up, tensing myself. Trying to build up enough courage to make the next move. Reaching for my coat, I held out my hand to him. He was noticeably shocked that I was about to follow his instructions. He didn't think I'd do it.

"Wish the kids a Merry Christmas from me, will you Ian, and tell them I love them and will be in touch with them soon."

"Don't worry Haydn, I'll see to things on this side, I promise you. You concentrate on looking after yourself and good luck, you're doing the right thing."

"Time will tell Ian. See you around. And make sure you

look after Jennifer. She's a diamond".

I don't know how I did it. I walked slowly out of the front door into the clean, thick snow. I have to admit, it took some guts in my unstable state of mind. All my confidence had disappeared years ago.

As I climbed into my clapped out yellow Merc', inspecting the snowy road ahead of me, I remember whispering to myself, "Haydn, you've just made a right dick of yourself, and even more so if you can't get the car out of this bloody cul-de-sac."

I started the car and took one last fleeting glance through the garden window, mentally comparing the warmth of the house to the cold, damp vehicle I was sitting in. Suddenly, through the window, appeared Carol. She was fast off the mark. She must have been listening all the time. I saw her drop to her knees, screaming at me to come back.

I waited for a moment, wondering whether she'd come outside to try and stop me, but she never did, so I endeavoured to set off up the cul-de-sac.

Still in two minds of turning back, I thought to myself, "Are you completely mad Haydn. It's Christmas day. What the hell are you playing at?" But it was too late for that. If I had returned I would have never been able to live it down, so, having no choice, the only thing to do was to head forward, wherever forward was. I'd made my choice, now I had to live with it. The question was, where was I heading? I had to think fast. It had started snowing again, and I didn't want to get bogged down. It just had to be Padiham.

I'd been renovating a workingmen's club there that had been closed for years, for a friend of mine, Eric. It had given me the chance to work again, in my own time, at my own pace. And, astonishingly, I had managed to complete it. The work had done me good, but he had only been using me. He was broke and owed me money.

The club was not yet occupied, waiting for new management to turn up. I was sure he wouldn't mind me stopping there for a few days, considering the circumstances, whilst I sorted myself out. There were living quarters above, so I knew I could manage for a little while. That's if I could get there. Luckily I'd just completed the contract and still had the keys to the place in my possession. So without further hesitation, I set off for Padiham, a Lancashire town about twenty miles away. It was quite a run. I was fighting snow storms, the car was damp and only running on three cylinders, the gears were acting up, and on top of all that, I was feeling totally depressed, cold and alone. My entire life had been a series of extreme highs and lows, and here I was, a lost soul, that had hit rock bottom once again. It was becoming a habit, and I wasn't impressed at all. I tried to obliterate all the negative thought waves from my mind and managed to buck myself up a little, just to force myself to keep going. Eventually, I actually did arrive outside the front door of the club.

Staring out, the contours of the building looked so forbidding, that harsh morning. All the downstairs windows had been blocked in permanently for security reasons. It looked more like a prison than a club. I kept trying to convince myself that eventually, everything was going to work out, and at the same time, I was checking the cobbled street above, looking for a certain 25yr old girl I knew, called Tracey, who lived nearby at the Starkey's Arms with her mother. I was half hoping she would appear, because she was the only person I knew in Padiham, and I needed some company right now. She used to pop into the club whilst I was working there, mainly to escape from her mother for a while, who was always on her case for one thing or another. Mind you, the kind of girl Tracey was, she probably deserved it. But her forward attitude amused me, and we had become good friends. But she was nowhere to be seen. Nobody's ever there when desperately needed.

I had to be careful getting out of the car. The cobbled street was dangerously icy, and it took a while for me to reach the main doors, slipping and sliding everywhere over the concrete parking strip. Rummaging in my pockets for the door key, suddenly directly above me, one of the upstairs windows flew open, and a round, weather beaten face of a 55yr old man appeared, giving me quite a turn. It was the last thing I expected. I had it in my mind the place was empty.

"Hiya Haydy. You're not working are you, not Christmas Day surely?"

It was Brian, a labourer who Eric had engaged to help me with the building.

He looked down at me, laughing haughtily. He was a rather jovial character at the worst of times.

"He shouldn't be here." were the perplexed thoughts passing through my mind. "Never mind me!" I shouted. "What are you doing here, for fuck's sake?"

"Had a bit of trouble with the Landlady. " he answered. "She threw me out a couple of days ago, so I came here for Christmas. Why not. Anyway, I'm pleased to see your face today, it's been a bit quiet round here. How long are you here for?"

"As long as Eric will let me. I'm hoping to be here for quite a while. I've just walked out on the missus myself, and haven't any plans on returning."

"Well.... not for a few days," Brian commented jokingly.

"Never ever again my friend if I have anything to do with it, believe me. Enough's enough. Anyway Brian, for fuck's sake let me in before I freeze to death." I'd realised the door had been bolted from the inside.

As he was making his way downstairs, a feeling of relief engulfed me. Brian wasn't my first choice in the world regarding companionship, but for me, it was better than being alone. I have some sort of phobia about loneliness. I needed company at all times. It was one of my many weaknesses. But nobody's perfect are they?

"Where's your suitcase, I'll help you up with it?" Brian kindly offered.

"I'm travelling light today Brian. I didn't get the privilege to pack, I'm afraid."

Brian with a Padiham friend

Tracey and I, at the club

"Oh. Well that saves a job don't it." he complacently remarked. "Come on in Haydy, and a merry Christmas to you my friend. At least you've done a great job on the heating. It's pretty warm in here. We're a bit lacking on bedding but we'll sort something out, I'm sure."

"Yes, 'course we will Brian. We'll get through one way or another. No sweat." I replied, appreciating his concerns. We trundled through the large, wooden entrance doors approaching the glass concert room doors, crossing the smallish lobby in the process. I followed Brian to the upstairs staircase directly in front of us. As I reached the ladies toilets at the top of the steps, a thought suddenly struck me. "Brian," I shouted, "How did you get in here initially?" Brian had already turned right and was walking past one of the two bedsitting rooms.

"The trapdoor in front of the bar downstairs, that they used to use to get to the obsolete beer cellar," he replied. "I knocked three or four large stones out of the blocked up entrance, where they unloaded the barrels in the back yard once upon a time. They were loose anyway. I just managed to squeeze through."

"Bloody hell, Brian," I exclaimed, "Surely you're not destroying the place already?"

"Don't worry Haydn. I found some sand and cement in one of those two adjoining storage rooms to the front side of the snooker room upstairs, so I gobbed them back in place again. It looks fine to me."

"Fair enough Brian. I suppose I'll have to let you off with that one then. My apologies," I jokingly remarked. "But tell me. If you go out, how do you lock up behind you? The only way out is either through the emergency fire door to the rear of the upstairs snooker room, or the one to the rear of the downstairs pool room next to the gent's toilets. If you use the push bars to open any of those two doors from the inside, you can't close them from the outside, can you?"

"I know." he replied. "But I've only been nipping down to the shop for a few minutes, that's all."

"Well that's no good Brian, is it? Don't use the emergency doors again will you? We don't want anyone sneaking in and robbing us, do we? If that happens, Eric's definitely going to be upset, in't he. He doesn't even know we're here."

"Right." agreed Brian. "So which door are we going to use?"

"Brian, there's only one external door left to pick from." He was a bit thick at times. "The door in the empty front side room. I'll get another key cut and we'll use that door only, OK. You can get into that room through the pool room, can't you?"

"Right," replied Brian.

"Oh, and Brian," I shouted, as he was sneaking off. "And another thing whilst we are at it. The beer cellar door in the front lobby and the wooden bar shutters, must remain locked at all times."

"But what about the small open kitchen at far end of the bar?" he constructively enquired for a pleasant change. "If we lock the bar, we won't be able to get to it?"

"I'll rip the electric cooker out, and reinstall it upstairs somewhere. That'll do the job wont it? Just take heed Brian, we need to get organised immediately."

"Right." I heard Brian repeat again for the fourth time as he finally disappeared round the corner at the top of the stairs. I think he was glad to escape from me, I'd been going on a bit, but these things have to be sorted out from the start.

The next few days passed uneventfully. We had everything we needed, thanks to Tracey inevitably turning up. Whatever we were short of, she managed to acquire. All the stuff came from the Starky's Arms when her mother's back was turned. She really was an angel in disguise. My room was definitely showing signs of improvement, and I could think much better in a pleasant environment. I didn't miss Carol at all, thank God, but I did miss the kids, although they kept in touch with me regularly, which gave me a boost. My mood had improved tremendously, due to all the positive moves I'd been making, but the question that really worried me was,

"How long would we be allowed to stop here?" Luckily the answer came to me quite naturally. There was a small snug downstairs situated between the front side room and the lobby, that housed a television, making it an ideal place for lounging about. Whilst I was in the process of cleaning it the following day, just in case Eric turned up unexpectedly, suddenly looking around, the potential of the place struck me in the face, and I realised that the obvious option to secure a roof over both of our heads, was to work on Eric's better nature and gain his permission to take over the business myself. Yes, that would definitely be the answer to our immediate problems. I knew I had to move fast, before the Christmas holiday ended because it was imperative that he didn't get the chance to employ a new manager. I hadn't been in touch with him since before Christmas, so he still didn't know we were living there. I sat down in the open plan concert room at the side of the central wooden dance floor to think the matter over in detail before approaching him because I needed to get my proposals in the correct order the first time round. I'd never run licensed premises before, but that did not bother me. The actual running of the club would be down to common sense and extensive research, like any other business. I couldn't envisage a problem there, as long as Eric agreed to the transaction, which in my mind he hadn't an option, due to the fact that he still owed me a considerable amount of money for renovating the place.

Eric and family

I'd known Eric for about two years. He was around 45yrs old. A tall, good-looking, very likeable con-merchant. He needed my professionalism in many trades to get through. He was always in a financial quandary, and never completed his promises of total payment. I could read him like a book and the only reason I was working for him, was for the chance to cope with working conditions again, given very little pressure. I was grateful because he had given me that chance, so I never expected full payment from him. I became accustomed to his bullshitting ways, but this time a plan was coming together in my head. If he agreed to my terms, after a settling in period, I could deduct what he owed me from the rent he'd be expecting every week, until we struck a balance. Sounded good to me. I needed money initially for stocks, and I couldn't ask Eric to finance me, but I was sure my mother who was living in Western Australia would help me out, if I asked her politely. The only thing I wasn't happy about, was the time I would have to spend running the club. I knew the licensing business was very time consuming, and I needed space to manoeuvre. So what was the solution? I thought for a moment. Brian had plonked himself opposite me on the freshly upholstered bench seating.

The notorious Padiham Sports & Social Club

"Brian, come over here a second." There was a slight delay whilst he dragged himself to where I was sitting. "What's your feelings if I put your name forward for the license to this place,?" I asked him hopefully. Brian was a simple minded person who had been pushed from pillar to post all his life. He was a very helpful, giving, trustworthy guy, but wasn't the most intelligent person in the world, and needed supervision at all times. "Could you help me to run this club Brian?" There was a silence. Repeating the question, "What do you think Brian?"

Brian answered this time. "What do you mean Haydn? I don't know if I will be able to handle the business myself," he replied. "I've never run a business before. All that paperwork and things. I'm not that educated you know. In fact I can hardly read at all."

"I know Brian. But don't worry about all that," I stressed, trying to reassure him. "All you have to do is serve the customers and I'll do the rest. Just serve the customers, have a drink yourself, get into the mood and chat to them. Make friends. Surely you can do that can't you?"

"Oh yes, I can do that, I've been behind bars before at one or two of Eric's pubs in Halifax, filling in for staff that let him down. I have operated tills before and I've never had any difficulties up to press. Yes, I can do that, as long as that's all it entails."

"Good!" I replied. "Then we've got a deal have we. Partners in crime, you might say. Yeah? That's assuming I can talk Eric around that is."

Brian stretched out his hand to me, with his usual beaming smile.

"Yeah, we'll shake on that." and the deal was done.

Lucky for me, Eric liked the idea, and was in full agreement. He decided to call it "The Padiham Sports and Social Club." I don't know where he got that name from. It sounded a bit boring to me. But, he owned the premises, so I had no choice but to agree with him.

Everything else went exactly to plan. A week or so passed, and we were ready to open. Brian had obtained a full on-licence, which meant the club could run as a normal pub, membership not required. I thought everything was sorted, and all I had to do was open the doors and earn money. Little did I know, in a town like this, you needed to be a Professor of physiology to survive, but it wasn't that long before I realised what I was up against. I couldn't possibly have foreseen what lay ahead of me in a million years.

,

Padiham on the brink of the year 2000: drinking spots near the club include The Bull, The King's and The Starkies

Chapter 2 Doubtful situations

Now Padiham, in the early days, was a totally isolated, close mining community, which did not welcome outsiders jeopardizing their employment opportunities, and as a result, much interbreeding was practised in the area, which is the reason why even now, many people are not quite sure who they are related to. A sort of Brigadoon, lost in time. Each family group having to exert a certain amount of strength of character to survive, creating friction between the families, and should any individual upset a family member, then that person would have to deal with the entire family's wrath, not just the member involved. (A sort of mini mafia.) It had to follow, that certain isolated people aimed to gain the reputation of being at the top of the fighting chain in town. Unfortunately amongst those, an odd one or two, took up the profession of town bully, extracting their needs from more vulnerable people than themselves. The shite of the town, one might say. And even now, to a much smaller degree, it is still happening, the people concerned being labelled "Padiham Thick Necks."

So understandably, this was not the easiest town for a Yorkshire man like myself to settle down and set up business in. But what choice did I have? Not a lot, in my eyes. So.........

My very first encounter with the Padiham public occurred about a couple of days prior to opening. A letter had been posted under the door, asking me to attend a meeting with "The Secret Order of the Buffalos," regarding the hire of the downstairs private room of the club once a week for their meetings. By all accounts, they had hired it years before when the club was called "The British Legion." The meeting took place at "The Railway Pub," in Padiham. It was important for me to attend, due to the fact that I was attempting to build up my customer list from zero, and this was as good a place to start as any.

Eric invited himself, and we turned up at the meeting place that Tuesday night, as arranged. I remember arriving early, in time for a couple of pints each in the main pub area. The place was virtually empty.

A guy walked in, under the influence, wearing a very heavy sheepskin jacket and we got talking. At first he was very hospitable towards us, but he kept downing the drinks. He had some sort of problem that night. I think his girlfriend had run out on him. He was not a happy man.

I remember him keep saying, "When the stallion bolts, always leave the stable door open," referring to his girlfriend I presumed. But the word stallion clicked up in my mind.

I bent forward to whisper to Eric, "Stallion. Seems a very odd word to describe his girlfriend. Is he gay?" It's funny how certain odd remarks stick in one's mind from long ago. I can't remember his name, but by all accounts, he had a big house in Cliviger, that he never stopped harping on about. Out of the blue, he invited the both of us back for the night and suggested we could stop a few days. Possibly he was a bit lonely and needed some innocent company, but Eric could be a bit snidey at times. He threw a few barbed comments at the guy in a joking fashion, regarding his masculinity, that definitely fell on barren territory. The guy took immediate offence, and I had to step in abruptly to stop Eric from getting his head kicked in. I was later informed that the guy used to be a street fighter, and not one to mess about with. He was dangerous and was going to have Eric. I was trying to ease the situation, when the committee room door opened and one of the Buff's gestured us both to enter, just in the nick of time. The guy tried to push his way in also but was stopped by a bunch of them. Those type of organisations really did uphold their vows of secrecy, with no uninvited personnel allowed to enter whatsoever.

"Thank God," I thought, "that was a close one. Here I am, trying to promote custom, and there's Eric, making enemies before I have even started. I definitely won't be bringing him to any future meetings in a hurry." Luckily that meeting turned out to be a success. We were dragging our heels a little in there, hoping that by the time the meeting was over, the guy would have disappeared. And fortunately for us, he had.

"Eric," I pointed out, as we were leaving. "We're Yorkshire men in a clicky Lancashire town. It's going to be an accomplishment, getting them on my side to start with, so please don't make it any harder than it is, for fuck's sake. You're going home tonight. I'm the one who has to face the music in the morning." He just looked at me, half sniggering, but said nothing. And that put an end to that, although I had already decided to keep Eric at a distance from then onwards.

Well, the time had arrived. It was 7pm, Thursday evening, and the club was about to open for its initial run. Just Brian manning the pumps and me feeling so tense, nervously overlooking. In my present mental state, I was fine at organising things from a distance, but when the time came to face the public, that was the moment when my lack of confidence cracked in. But Brian didn't seem bothered in the least, adopting the same happy carefree attitude as always. I don't think he was capable of thinking ahead of himself. He just lived for the moment, and I must admit, him being like that was a big advantage to me at times. He had enough confidence for the two of us, and it certainly helped to boost mine. All that was going through my mind was, "What if…. ……What if?"

Well, the club opened and people started drifting in, mainly noseying to see what was happening. Unknown, polite, enquiring faces. Some were very good at giving me advice, like who I should allow in and who not to, which didn't mean a thing to me because I didn't have a clue who they were talking about anyway. They kept mentioning different names, like Kenny for instance. Just a name to me.

But they did give me one good piece of advice, and that was to learn to know the people you were dealing with by employing someone you could rely on who could advise you well on the subject. They were all recommending the same person…… Jean. But first of all, I needed to take account of the turnover, to make sure there was enough money to cover her wages, before I approached her. It was early days, so I just listened and took notes.

"If tonight's got anything to do with it," I thought, "it's been uneventful, so there's no rush." But they did warn me to be careful because once the word was out that we were open, all the dickheads in town would be trying us out.

Eventually they all dwindled away, leaving just one person propping the bar and making conversation to me. He was drinking Bud's, and every time he had one, he bought me one. He was a tall, arrogant guy about thirty years old. I didn't particularly like him, he was too full of himself, but he was a customer and I had to appear friendly towards him.

Brian shouted over to me, "Can you handle the bar Haydn, by yourself. I'm tired and I'm going to bed?"

"No problem Brian," I replied. "See you in the morning." The guy and I carried on drinking for quite a while longer. He suddenly jumped off his stool to put his coat on, telling me at the same time, "Well I'm going now. See me out will you?" and as I walked out of the bar area to face him, he swung a friendly punch into my stomach, a hard man's way of saying, so long. It wasn't that much of a friendly punch, having quite an impact, but I had seen it coming and tensing my stomach muscles accordingly, his fist just bouncing off.

I threw a joking comment back at him, "You'll have to be faster than that mate to catch me on the hop," laughing at him. As we walked towards the door, he threw another one into my stomach just like before, but even harder this time. He thought he'd catch me off guard, but I was ready for him and his clenched fist bounced off my stomach once again.

I made a comment to him, realising later how stupid a thing to do. "You're just not fast enough, are you?" Now in this hard town, he must have took it as a total insult, because as I walked through the entrance doors, into the unlit street to see him off, I was suddenly bombarded with countless punches. I just didn't see them coming. It was too dark outside. Falling backward behind the entrance doors in agony but thinking quickly, I slammed the doors shut dropping the bottom bolt, barely in my reach from where I was lying.

He shouted through the letter box to me, "Are you alright in there mate?" not realising he'd badly hurt me. I never answered.

"The man's either on pills or he's a psycho." I silently mumbled to myself, "Just fuck off will you, and leave me alone!" Not hearing any reply, he must have thought I'd disappeared upstairs, and started to casually stroll away down the street.

I must have lain there for twenty minutes. The pain was not abating at all, but eventually managing to crawl to my feet, I had to abandon everything and retire to my bed, to obtain some relief. I was really tired, and even with the nagging pain in my stomach I managed to fall asleep.

The next morning I was awakened by Brian. By all accounts he'd been shaking me for a while with no response and was getting very concerned about the job. I felt terrible. I knew I was in serious trouble if I didn't get help fast. I felt like I was about to die, there and then. In fact I think I would have died if he hadn't disturbed me. I crawled out of bed in agony, stumbling to the top of the staircase where I lost my balance, falling down the full length of the steps. Brian, who hadn't a clue what was happening, picked me up and guided me to the nearest bench seat.

"What the fuck's up with you? Are you still pissed or something?"

"Get the phone and ring emergency 999. I need a ambulance fast."

"You what?" he enquired puzzled.

"Don't argue with me Brian. Just do as I say. I'm dying here!" I panicked. As he was making the call, I, under sufferance, explained to him what had happened, then we both waited for what seemed forever for the paramedics.

"Keep the club closed Brian 'till I get back from hospital will you?" I instructed him.

"By the look of you, you might not be coming back." he bluntly commented. Despite my agony and frustration, I forced a weary smile for him.

On the paramedics' arrival and initial examination, they decided it was an emergency, so without further ado the ambulance whisked me off to hospital with its siren blasting out and blue lights flashing, where a stretcher was waiting to rush me through many corridors to the emergency theatre. I kept staring at the ceiling watching the many fluorescent lights pass me by, whilst I was slowly getting weaker and weaker.

An examination revealed, that due to the fact that my bladder was full of urine at the time, it had been split pretty badly resulting in serious internal bleeding. I was in a critical state, and needed an emergency operation immediately. By this time I was writhing about in agony, with four nurses trying to hold me down whilst the anaesthetic was being administered. Within the count of three I had gone.

The next thing I remembered was opening my eyes, in a total daze, and trying to focus on someone staring down on me from above. It was the guy who had assaulted me the previous night, would you believe. Panic stricken, he stuck a thousand smackers into my hand. Just like that!

"Take this, and please don't grass me up, whatever you do," he stammered. "I'll get sent down for five years if I get charged with this one!" We silently glared at one another for a solitary moment then he turned and walked away without a further word spoken. It took me half an hour to come round and work out what had just happened.

I tucked the money away out of sight thinking, "If this is what I have to go through running a club in Padiham, you can stick it, before it even starts. I think I've bit off more than I can cope with."

Thankfully the operation was a success, but I had to stop in hospital a number of days wearing a catheter strapped to one of my legs, draining my bladder to aid the healing process. It was during this period I received a call from Brian, telling me the club had been broken into in my absence, would you credit.

"Fucking hell." I thought, "If it's not one thing it's another. That Brian's useless. I've no alternative. I'm going to have to pop out for an hour and see what's happening for myself." So I gathered my clothes from my locker, and waiting until there was no one around, I sneaked into a toilet, getting changed, ready to make my getaway. I thought, "If I'm fast off the mark, nobody's going to notice me missing. I can always bluff it out that I've been out for a smoke or something."

I had to catch the bus to Padiham, with the catheter still strapped to my leg feeling a right fool. But I eventually arrived at the club, to find the fire escape door damaged and the sound equipment that was installed on the corner stage to the rear of the concert room, missing.

"Where were you when all this was happening?" I asked Brian.

"Oh, I was at The King's having a drink." he replied nonchalantly.

"For fuck's sake Brian, I've only been away a few days and the job's gone to cock already. You are going to have to pull your finger out whilst I'm away, I'll be back in a few days. And nail that back door up before you do anything else, will you. I'm totally relying on you. I've no time. I have to get back to hospital before I'm missed."

Without further ado I jumped into my car and returned to hospital, sneaking through corridors heading for the toilets to change back again, and managing to return my clothes to the locker and retire to bed, before anyone had spotted me.

A short while afterwards, a nurse came running up to me, "We've been looking for you everywhere. Where have you been?"

"I've just been out for a smoke that's all........ it's alright in't it?"

"You're not supposed to go out of the ward without permission. You know that. Besides, your step-daughters have been to see you, but I think they've left now. Nobody could find you anywhere. Don't ever do that again." she instructed me, pausing momentarily. I could feel her mellowing by the second, to further remark, "Well I suppose I will have to go and check to see if they are still around for you."

"Got away with that one, thank God!" I thought, with a sigh of relief, as the situation rapidly returned to normality again.

About four days later I was discharged from hospital, badly scarred, still with the catheter strapped to my leg for another week. I was minus one sound system, and to compensate that I had a thousand smackers in my pocket which was not really a bonus because shortly afterwards I lost a three grand criminal compensation claim for refusing to disclose the bloke's name. As I quietly sat on the front step contemplating this present scenario, thinking to myself, "That's just been enough for one week," a guy called Ryan approached me enquiring whether I was interested in him stealing my sound equipment back for me for a fee of twenty pounds, knowing who had pinched it. It was all just getting too complicated for me.

" Oh yeah, and who might that be?" I asked nonchalantly.

"Never mind who it is. Do you want your sound equipment back or not?"

"Too damn true I want it back, twenty smackers did you say?"

"That's right," he smirked adding, "Oh there's just one snag. You're gonna have to help me. We'll have to use your car." So I had to run him close to the house in question, whilst he sneaked in the back door.

I thought, "What the heck have I got myself into now?" when, out he ran, and within two minutes my car was full of my stolen equipment and we were away. Although totally relieved on arriving back to the club with the incident behind me, my mind was in complete turmoil. I definitely needed to sit down to reconsider my position around here.

"This is one dangerous town. Only a madman would think o' taking on a place like this. Look at the state I'm in and I've only been open a day. What will I be like in a year's time?" My mentality had already taken three steps down the ladder in the past week. "It can't carry on like this," were the apprehensive thoughts passing through my mind.

Thankfully the following few days were slightly more reassuring, but I was very careful this time as to how I approached people, managing to relax a little in the process. Business was slowly building up. I had started helping Brian behind the bar a little, which passed the time whilst gaining experience, when a new punter arrived. He approached the bar and asked me to one side.

"Haydn. That's you isn't it. The gaffa here?"

"Yes. That's me," I cautiously replied. "Can I help you?"

"I'm Malcolm. You've a good place here. It'll do well," he commented enthusiastically. He sounded quite sincere to me.

"Anyway I'll see you later," he said, passing me some change for the beer I'd just served him. Without another word he went to sit down. Shortly afterwards he came back to the bar and ordered a full round of drinks. Whilst I was pulling them, he nipped over to the machine for some cigarettes, using coins I had given him, because he said he had no change, and on returning to the bar I informed him how much the round was.

He reached into his pocket for his wallet. "Shit!" he exclaimed. "My wallet must have slipped out of my pocket where I was sitting. I won't be a second," apologising profusely. After searching the area for a minute, he returned to the bar. "Put the drinks to one side of the bar for me will you. It's rough outside but never mind. I'm just going to nip down to the cash machine for some money. I can't find my wallet anywhere. I won't be long." It was snowing heavily, so, feeling sorry for him and trying to do the correct thing by telling him not to bother until it had stopped, he took his drinks back to his table. I was trying to be as hospitable as possible, for this initial period.

"Thanks Haydn," he shouted out. "I'll make sure you get the money within the hour."

"Cheers Malcolm. No sweat." I replied, and carried on serving someone else.

A short time after, on his way out, he shouted across to me, "I'll be back in a flash Haydn."

"OK Malc, I'll see you later," I replied as he disappeared out of the door.

The guy I was serving had been listening in. He turned to me and asked, "Malcolm doesn't owe you money does he?"

"Yes," I replied, "He's dropping it back to me shortly."

The guy laughed heartily. "You do realise, that 'shortly' could be up to a year. You've no chance of getting it back. He owes everybody in town. That's the last you'll see of him for a long while, believe me." I just looked at him, realising I had made a total cock-up. If he'd lost his wallet, he'd very likely lost his bank cards as well. I felt so stupid. It wasn't the money so much as the embarrassment, believing him. I must have appeared so gullible to the guy standing in front of me. Regardless of the money, I'd just possibly lost a year of his trade. He just smiled and walked away remarking, "Live and learn bud."

This carry on was definitely not good for business. I was already realising that this people business was more complicated than I had ever envisaged. What I needed to do for the next three months, was to observe and learn about the people I was dealing with, being as diplomatic as possible, and then would be the time to take some radical steps, not before. This was going to take quite a while.

The first night the buff's arrived for their weekly meeting, they locked themselves in the allocated room, with strictly no admittance to the general public. If they needed a drink they would ring the bar to place an order. Unbelievingly I had to take the trayfull of drinks, knock on the door, whilst being inspected through a surveillance hatch, before being allowed in to deliver and pick up the money due. What a carry on. It was on one of these occasions that I was talking to a bloke called Larry at the bar. He was a fully-fledged alcoholic. He blamed his dilemma on his brother dying on him not long back of leukaemia. He was a pleasant guy to talk to, always cracking jokes with a warm smile on his face at all times.

"Haydn, have I told you about the time I was at school in the same class as a mate of mine that you haven't met yet called Yogurt, whilst in the process of taking a maths exam?"

"Obviously not," I replied, "considering it's the first time I've ever spoken to you."

"Well, we weren't much good at maths you know, but my mate Yogurt had the edge on me. Which was handy 'cause he always let me copy off him."

"But did you always get away with it?" I enquired.

"Most times, but there was this one occasion they cottoned onto me. A silly mistake but it could have happened to anyone."

Why, what happened?" I enquired.

"They just approached me for what I thought, no reason at all and accused me to my face of cheating off Yogurt. I asked them what reason they had of accusing me. Nobody had caught me in the process."

After considerable bickering between us, one of the examiners chimed out, 'Look at question 15 on Yogurt's paper. What does it say? And read out loud what he's written.' The words, 'I don't fucking know,' were scribbled on the test paper. 'Now read out what you've written on your paper,' he asked me. I looked at my paper. The words I had written hit me in the face. How could I have possibly made such a stupid mistake like that. The words I had written were, 'I don't fucking know either!'"

Well, that started Larry off. He just couldn't stop laughing at his own silly joke, and was still laughing, the stupid sod, when the phone rang. It was time to deliver another round of drinks to the elite in the back room. I was away from the bar no longer than two minutes, returning to continue my interrupted conversation with Larry. Within minutes, a man named Shaun walked in, with a bottle of vodka in his hand.

"Is this yours Haydn. I just noticed it semi-hidden at the side of the steps as I was walking in." I looked up to check my spirits, and there was a bottle of vodka missing. Larry immediately chimed up, rather sheepishly,

"Well, time to fuck off home," and without further ado, he rushed out of the door. I was speechless. In the space of the two minutes I was absent from the bar, he had helped himself to the bottle of vodka and hid it outside, to pick up on his way home.

"There does seem to be one or two honest guys around here, thank God" I thought. "He'd have definitely got away with that one if it wasn't for Shaun."

"I'll tell you something about Larry" laughed Shaun. "If you go up to Ramsam's on a Monday morning, you know, the Post office on Vicy Road, I can guarantee you that when Larry's there he will always be at the front of the queue to collect his social."

"Why's that?" I asked, inquisitively.

"Because the second he spots Larry, Ramsam always shouts across to him, 'Larry my friend. Come to the front of the queue where I can keep an eye on you'. Every time something used to go missing, and it was a while before Ramsam cottoned on to him, but now he watches him like a hawk, believe me. He can't get away with anything any more, in there. So you make sure you always keep your eyes on him also, when he's around."

"Thanks Shaun for the advice and I appreciate your honesty. You just pissed Larry off big style that time."

"Glad to be of service," he answered, taking the glass out of my hand I had just poured for him.

Instances like these were happening frequently. Take Tracey for instance. I thought I knew her. She did me a great service when I first arrived in Padiham, but maybe it was her way of feathering her own nest. We had something in common from the past, which put her in a different category from other people, right or wrong. As it happened, Tracey came from Broadlea Terrace in Leeds. I had a girlfriend called Lorraine in the sixties, who also lived on Broadlea Terrace, just two doors away. Different times of course, in fact, thirty years spaced. I was a successful leader and rhythm guitarist in a very highly rated Leeds Rhythm group called "The Fabulous Young Ones." Anybody of any importance, we had played alongside on stage with. It was a scintillating ten years of my life, placing me in a world of my own. And through the whole of that period, Lorraine was by my side.

Larry

She was a beautiful girl in every way possible, who shared the same experiences that I did through that ten year period. She was only 13yrs old but looked much older when we started seeing each other, age not being an important issue in those days. I was18yrs old, and we had such a beautiful time together. But on our final year, so many tragic things occurred to Lorraine, her family and me. So much so that people in the terrace, who were around in the sixties, still talked about it whilst Tracey was living there. Tracey and I bumped into each other in Padiham, miles away from the big city, and although we'd never met before, she knew of me. What were the odds of that happening?

The Fabulous Young Ones

What actually occurred in that house doesn't bear thinking about - It was one Sunday teatime. Lorraine, her mum and dad, her elder brother Keith and I were having dinner. Roast beef, mashed potatoes, Yorkshire pudding, vegetables and gravy were on the menu. Suddenly Lorraine's eldest brother Raymond came barging in. He'd been out drinking all day and was mouthing quite a lot. Lorraine's mother couldn't tolerate him, whereas she used to spoil Keith rotten........a regular mummy's boy. Consequently, there was always friction between Keith and Raymond. On this occasion, the argument was over Keith's dinner and the leftovers his mother had offered Raymond to eat. A fight ensued, and Keith was badly injured. It could have been something to do with the wooden garden stake that Raymond smashed over his head. Anyway, it turned out that Keith had an exceptionally thin bone structure and he ended up with a fractured scull. Dragging himself up from the floor, he grabbed me by the arm, staring strangely into my face, "Please help me Haydn." were the only words he spoke, after which he staggered up to his bedroom, laid on the bed and died, Just like that! Raymond received a two year prison sentence in Armley for manslaughter, and although he had no intention of killing his brother, he suffered seriously from a guilt complex thereafter.

Lorraine, who was eight months pregnant at the time, had a baby boy called Dene, who died at the age of seven weeks in Lorraine's arms, causing her to suffer serious post-natal depression, whilst I had a bad period of grieving for my son causing us to slowly drift apart.

Lorraine

Lorraine and myself

Dancing with Lorraine

Six months later, her mother died of a broken heart, and shortly after that, her father died of cancer. What a tragic year that was. I finished up, running off with the next door neighbour, Gloria, just to try to get away from it all. Lorraine stayed around for a while trying to fight for me back, but gradually faded into the blue beyond, never to be seen again in twenty years.

Now that afternoon I was in my flat upstairs, counting my weekly take on the bed. There were twenty pound notes scattered everywhere, when suddenly Tracey came strolling in to see me. I saw the shocked expression on her face as she glanced quickly at all that lovely money. She was desperately short of money herself, and needed my consent to allow her to work that night, to help her out. I agreed and she retired downstairs to rejoin her boyfriend Craig.

My first impression of him was a little conniving, arrogant brat who endeavoured to make up his smallness in stature, by trying to convince himself and other people, that he was one of the Padiham mafia. It fell on stony ground because nobody was convinced. But as time passed we began to build a better understanding of each other. Maybe initially my judgement was swayed by the fact that I had a soft spot for Tracey, and he was in the way. I don't really know, but I did eventually learn to tolerate him.

After completing the finances I placed the money in a shoe box, entering Brian's room. I had a secret hiding place there above the suspended ceiling, that even Brian wasn't aware of. I preferred it that way, only me knowing, for peace of mind. Anyway, the lock on my door was faulty, so after securing his door with my spare key I retired downstairs, noticing Tracey and Craig sitting alone together, whispering to each other. This appeared rather strange to me, because normally she had a voice like a foghorn and generally liked to be heard. Not wanting to interrupt their conversation, I passed by without speaking, heading for the stage, where the DJ I'd employed for the evening was setting up his gear. I wasn't totally at ease with the situation, and kept spying on them through the corner of my eye. It was in my interest to observe everything that was going on around me. Another one of the things I instinctively learnt. She cautiously rose to her feet and made a beeline for the upstairs, thinking I hadn't noticed her. She could have been visiting the ladies, but not being too sure of myself I dropped everything to follow her. Craig had an unsettled facial expression as his beady eyes bore down on me. My suspicions were confirmed. She was in my room alright, snooping around.

"What are you doing here Tracey?" I asked her. In my mind, there was no reason for her to be there whatsoever.

"I left my purse up here." she answered and went straight to it, being stuck down the side of one of the chairs.

I thought, "She's put it there on purpose just to cover herself should she get nobbled. Tracey's not a stupid girl."

"Cheers Haydn," she blurted out as she picked it up and disappeared again out of the door. I definitely smelt a rat. She had been nowhere near that chair when she originally came in, and why would she be snooping around if she knew where her purse was. I knew exactly what she was up to. She was after skimming an odd twenty pounds or so, that could have been put down to miscounting on my part. But she hadn't pulled it off. I was well ahead, but very disillusioned with her. I felt she had let me down badly, and she had definitely gone down in my estimation. But I had to leave it at that for the moment, knowing what she'd been up to, but with no way of proving it. So I would just have to keep a closer eye out for her in the future. That's all I could do. At least I knew where I stood with her.

That evening I saw her nipping into the beer cellar to change a barrel. It was my ideal opportunity to have a word with her in private. My suspicions were festering in my brain.

I came straight out with it. "Tracey, you were trying to rob me this afternoon, weren't you. Give me some credit please. I'm not that stupid?"

She just looked at me, rather shamefaced. She was not the sort of person to brazenly lie. She was a wild bitch, but she would usually put her arms up if found out, and just laugh it off. Her silence told me everything. It put me on the spot, because I still thought a lot about her regardless of what had happened. Feelings don't change that fast. And since no harm had been done, I decided to let her off with a warning.

"Tracey," I informed her, "I don't know what was controlling your mind this afternoon, but please, don't ever think of trying that stunt again. I had you sussed from the very beginning. I was definitely one step ahead of you all the way..........Well, everybody makes mistakes and deserves a second chance, and I'm generously giving you that chance. Don't let it happen again. Please. I thought you were a friend of mine."

"I am a friend of yours, Haydn. I'm ashamed of myself. I'm really sorry. Please don't fall out with me. It was all that money. I'd never seen so much in one place before. I lost it for a moment. I told Craig, and it was him that pushed me into doing it. He can be a rather persuasive at times. Please forgive me. It will never happen again, on my mother's life. I promise you."

There was silence for a second. At least she'd been truthful. That's one consolation.

"OK, the matter's closed. Behave yourself Tracey. This sort of thing doesn't become you."

I walked out, leaving her alone to finish what she was doing, and to contemplate the situation, hoping she'd stand by her word from then on.

It was definitely a very bad period for me. Everybody was on the bandwagon. Especially the time I was serving behind the bar by myself one night with no one to turn to, and some dick dropped a couple of pills in my drink with the intention of spiking me. What an hour that was, I can tell you. I was doing everything in my power, under severe discomfort, to remain conscious. Trying to keep awake whilst my brain was telling me to sleep was definitely an ordeal. But I had to do it because if I went down it would have been a free house for everybody concerned, and I wasn't having that. I fought myself to the kitchen area and poured four pints of water, unceasingly forcing them down my throat until I was literally spewing up, and still having to keep drinking. It was close to being tortured, but I had to persevere, moving continuously.

I noticed one guy at the other side of the bar watching every move I made and thought, "I bet it's you that's done this, you pillock. If I ever find out for certain, I will get you back for this." I locked the till up and hid the key just to be safe. I also dropped a few shutters whilst people were puzzlingly enquiring what was happening.

"Just a temporary measure," I replied. "Everything will be back to normal in a short while," whilst urgently ringing Brian for help, who luckily arrived in the nick of time just before I was about to pass out.

"What's up with you Haydy?" Brian enquired.

"I've been spiked. You'd better guard your drinks round here in future, or else you'll be going down as well."

"Get your head down in the kitchen. I'm here now."

I just collapsed, having the most peaceful hours sleep in my life. What a relief.

The first thing I thought when I woke up was, "Don't worry Haydn. Patience rules the roost. I'll convert them to my way of thinking in the end believe it, if I have to die doing it." I was a little pissed off to say the least with what had just happened, so I decided to unfairly take it out on Eric by giving him a ring to inform him that I needed the money back that he owed me, so I'd be knocking it off the rent from now onwards. It was just the way I was feeling. He wasn't very happy either, but there wasn't anything he could do about it.

Steve came across to talk to me one evening, which was nothing unusual. I'd become quite friendly with him. He'd been frequenting the club since it opened and worked, part time, at Westgate House as a caretaker. I had taken him to work a couple of times, whilst out buying liquor, and had met the owner of the place. Steve's wife had died not long back of lung cancer, and he hadn't recovered from it yet. Instead he'd hit the bottle, drinking from dawn to dusk trying to drown his sorrow. But it wasn't working. He was a pleasant guy, even when drunk, who wouldn't harm a fly. But he didn't have the money to satisfy his habit.

"Haydn, I've had a bit of luck today, if you can call it that."

"And what might that be?" I enquired.

Steve

Steve with his wife

Tracey and Craig

"The guy I was working for at Westgate, you know, the guy you met, popped his clogs last week, and I've just had this letter from his solicitors."

"Oh yeah?" I replied, pricking my ears up. "He's left me a considerable amount of money, by all accounts, and I've to go to some meeting about it in a fortnight's time. Would you come with me. I'm useless at that sort of thing?" he enquired hopefully.

"Yes, I'll come, if you really want me to."

"Yes, I do. And I'll make sure you're adequately rewarded for your troubles, don't worry about that."

"Sounds good to me," I answered.

So, over the next fortnight I pulled him numerous pints on the house, to keep him sweet. He never asked for freebies, but I think he expected them from time to time. On the day of the meeting, he turned up telling me that he had received a letter from the solicitors, stating they'd given him another date in a week's time. He said he was going to bring the letter to show me which sounded half genuine to me, so a couple more days passed, and I treated him to a few more free pints. Up to press I hadn't seen any correspondence at all. Then whilst I was in town one morning, I nearly had an heart attack. About ten feet away, gesturing to acknowledge me, without a shadow of doubt, was the same guy who was supposed to have died. I couldn't believe it, I thought I'd seen a ghost. I looked again and again. It was definitely him.

Steve was in the club the next day, as normal. I mentioned it to Tracey what had happened. She just laughed. "That's Steve, that is. He's got a good heart, but he can be a bit of a dick at times. His life is ruled by alcohol. He'll do anything for a pint."

I thought for a minute, "Well, will you go across and pass a message on for me Tracey. Tell him I know the truth now, and although I am not very impressed with him, I'm not going to kick his head in this time. And also tell him that I will be very upset if he avoids the club 'cos he spends a lot of money around here in a week. That's the real reason why I treated him to a few free pints anyway. Tell him to approach me in a proper manner in the future if he's short of funds. And also mention to him that I'm going to pretend it never happened, this time." Tracey did as I asked and sure enough he kept coming in as if the incident had never occurred. But it was very noticeable that he made a special point of avoiding any conversation close to that subject for quite a while afterwards.

I had to watch a few of them closely because if they couldn't get to me personally, some of them would take it out on my property, namely my car. I had two cars burnt out, and a brick through my windscreen whilst parked outside the club in the first few weeks of being there. Pretty good, eh. One for kicking a person out, and another two for not letting them in. One of the cheeky bastards, Maki, I found out later, came the next morning, to help me clean a mess up from the previous night that he'd been responsible for. What about that then? On another occasion a fire engine and a cop car came to attend to my burning car outside the club whilst I was serving after time, and none of them even bothered knocking on the bolted door to inform me. I was watching the whole thing through the letter box. It was a shame about the old yellow Merc. that I first came to Padiham in. Although the car was worthless, by all accounts it originally belonged to Sir Cliff Richards, or so I was told. The name on the logbook was Harry Web and the reg. was H1 WEB, so quite possibly it did. I treated it as memorabilia considering my band was named after one of his hit songs.

For those reasons, I initially drove around in the oldest bangers I could find, but even so Padiham still was of the opinion that I was some eccentric millionaire that had hit the town from nowhere.

Jean behind the bar

Brian, Jean and myself

Jean and myself

All the things that were happening to me and many more, were giving me the feeling of total abandonment. I was getting to the point that I'd had enough. I needed help categorising these people, which brought Jean back into the picture. I decided to ring her to offer her employment without even seeing her. I felt I needed her help so desperately.

She arrived at the club the next day, mid-morning. I didn't really know what to expect. After weighing her up, first impressions were fine. She looked OK to me, being in her forties, slim, average height, with greyish brown, wavy hair and had a slightly weatherworn face. She was a very cheerful and talkative person, with a beaming smile displaying her beautiful white teeth. After talking for a while I was of the opinion she knew her job, and as people had already told me, she professed to know most of the people in town, so it didn't take much thinking about before I set her on as bar manager.

She had a few conditions that I also had to agree to, like joining the pub watch for added protection. And then there was something about a guy called Ernie, who I had never met. She was really adamant about keeping him out, for reasons she wouldn't disclose. I had to agree, so Jean started work the following week.

I joined the pub watch and she gave me a rundown on everybody who entered the place. It wasn't very long before I could recognise lots of people, not only by their appearance, but by their nature, which was a positive start I suppose. Padiham was full of these extreme characters.

One afternoon, I was visited by a guy who walked in, throwing a few polite words in my direction, and, after ordering a pint, sat down on a bench seat near the bar. Straight in front of me in fact. He'd had quite a lot to drink, but wasn't causing any trouble, so I just left him be. Eventually he fell asleep, his head tilted backwards, resting on the top of the bench seat. Jean rolled in to start her shift. She had her back to the bar, whilst she took her coat off and got organised with things in general. On turning around she immediately spotted this character, snoring his head off, totally out of it.

A startled expression appeared on her face. "Who let him in? Surely not you Haydn?"

I looked at her and then back at him, puzzled. "Why?" I enquired, "Is he making too much noise?"

"That's Ernie, the guy I was on about. He's not allowed in here. I'm sorry Haydn but that's how it is."

"No, it's me that's sorry Jean. I hadn't a clue who he was," I answered apologetically. "I didn't know. Just let it be this time," I implored her. "I won't let it happen again, now that I know who you're referring to."

She just looked at me, a stern look on her face. "Just keep a close eye on him. I don't want him anywhere near me. Do ya hear?" she replied. So to please her, I did keep a close eye on him. I didn't want to lose her services so soon. She hadn't been around that long, and had proven her worth, I must admit.

Ernie had his mouth wide open, periodically grunting and groaning in his sleep. Directly to the front of him on the table, was his full pint of beer. Suddenly he started coughing and spluttering, and his false teeth shot out of his mouth, and unfortunately landed in his beer. He settled back to sleep again. I thought I'd better not wake him up to tell him. It would be slightly embarrassing to say the least, so I let him be. A short while later, he began grunting again, reaching for his beer in a semi-conscious state, and taking a large drink, placed it down on the table again. Leaning back, he went to sleep again. Automatically his mouth fell wide open and unbelievably, there were his teeth, bang on in place within his mouth, as if they'd never been parted from him. I was astounded. I had to giggle. Very funny indeed. "Some magician if you ask me," I thought.

I turned to Jean. "Did you see that?" I shouted. She totally ignored me and walked to the other side of the bar. "Hey Jean, is he on the pub watch or something?" I asked her.

"No." was her simple reply.

"Then just what is the crack?"

"Don't even go there," was her threatening reply. "I'm going to the loo. Keep an eye on the bar will you?"

I wasn't happy. In my eyes, this wasn't right at all. Running a bar was a neutral thing. I had enough headaches of my own without bringing other people's personal problems into it, but I thought I'd better keep my mouth shut for a while longer, just to keep the peace.

I still had the nasty job of telling the man he was banned, for no apparent reason. "How can I do that?" I thought, just as he started to come round.

He stumbled to his feet, and tried to head for the exit, passing the side of the bar. He was a stockily-built person, about 55yrs old, with two bad hip joints, and needed a pair of sticks to get around. As he reached the concert room doors he signalled me to approach him, and, before I had a chance to speak, he said something that touched me.

"Thank you very much for your consideration towards me. I know I can be a pain in the arse at times, but I'm leaving now, anyway." He had a piece of paper in his hand, which he handed to me. "Take my address. It's only down the road. Call in anytime you're doing nothing and I'll make you a sandwich or something."

I was eager to accept. It got me off the hook for the moment, thank God and then he trundled out.

The second he disappeared Jean came running up to me. "Have you told him?" she demanded.

"No, not yet. I'm going to pop down to his house sometime and have words with him in private. Don't worry Jean, I'll do it. It's all part of the job I suppose," and nothing more was said about the subject that night.

The next morning I set off to see Ernie. I wasn't looking forward to the prospect of telling him he was barred. I needed a reason to do the deed, but maybe, just maybe, he could supply me with one, I didn't know. On the face of it, he seemed such a polite, helpful man. But as I had found out before, I could be wrong. Reluctantly arriving outside his house, I knocked on the open door, rather tickled to observe a sign displayed over it which read "Ernie's Fun Pub and Disco Bar"

"Come in! Sit yourself down Haydn and make yourself at home. I'm Ernie, can I get you anything?" was his initial comment.

"No thanks Ernie. I've come because I am a little confused, and in need of your help and advice." I thought I'd bull him up a little. It might ease the pain when the crunch came.

"Go on Haydn, spill it out. What's bothering ya? Or shall I tell you what's on ya mind?" He caught me on the hop. Not only was he a magician, he was possibly a mind reader as well. "It's that Jean isn't it Haydn. She doesn't want me in the club does she?"

Well that just floored me. He'd hit the nail right on the head, first time.

"You are one remarkable man, Ernie" I answered, as the pressure eased by the second.

"I know Haydn. You don't have to tell me that," he replied, bursting into laughter.

"So, go on Ernie, give me some answers why this situation exists and I'll decide what I'm going to do about it." I felt so comfortable and relaxed speaking to him, even though I didn't know him from Adam.

"Do you really want me to tell you?"

"Not really Ernie. It's not my business, your personal life and all. But Jean's really put me on the spot here. She's threatening to leave if I don't sort it out, and I totally rely on her to sort me out for a while longer. Catch 22 situation, you might say."

"You've got one thing to learn about some of the people of this town Haydn."

"One thing! I think I've got a hundred things to learn Ernie. The list gets longer every day."

"Well understand this, and understand well, because you're the person they are talking about at this moment in time. It only takes one slight insignificant step out of line on your part and within the hour, you'll have committed something on the level of a double murder. They can't half exaggerate to make their gossip sound interesting. And by the time it's gone round a handful of people, the sky's the limit, believe me."

"So what happened to you Ernie?"

"Well it goes back many years, and still they talk about it."

A while ago I was drinking with a few friends of mine in the Dutchman one dinnertime. You know, the pub on the main drag, near the traffic lights. Well there was a commotion outside on the central reservation. It seems Jean's daughter was having a stag party, and her mates had chained her to the railings on the central reservation, leaving her there alone for a while.

The guy I am, I decided an innocent kiss wouldn't be out of order on that special occasion, so I went outside and gave her one.......a kiss that is. I don't think she took kindly to it, but that didn't bother me, it was just for a laugh. Returning back to the pub for a giggle with my mates, I thought nothing more of it, but within twenty four hours that innocent act had blown into something gross, and since then I've never been able to live it down. They said I'd been playing with her tits in the middle of the busy road. What a load of rubbish. But that's what they are like, and I got branded. And that's what all this is about Haydn. Crappage from beginning to end."

I listened to him and was pretty relieved, to be quite honest. I was expecting something far more serious, the way she was going on.

"So Ernie, where do we go from here?"

"Simple," was his reply. "Do nothing."

"How do you mean?"

"I don't go out very often nowadays. And it's a bit of a struggle getting up there anyway. I only came in yesterday to nosey around. So we'll leave it for a few months shall we, till you've sorted yourself out, and then fuck Jean, I expect to be welcomed in with open arms. Is that alright with you?" he laughed.

"Good one Ernie," I replied. "I like your style. But you won't stop me coming down here to see you, will you?"

"You're welcome any time you want to show your face, day or night. Be my guest." It turned out to be one strange situation. I was a honoured guest in his home, yet he wasn't allowed to enter my club. Funny situation, to say the least, but I embraced his reasoning. He was definitely on the same wavelength as me.

Whilst we were talking I couldn't help but notice the vast amount of food he had stored in his front lounge.

"You like your food, don't you Ernie?" I joked.

Immediately turning to me he replied, "You know Haydn, I was brought up in the forties during the war, when wastage of food was totally unacceptable and in my eyes is still unacceptable. So if you've got some spare time on your hands you'd better pour yourself a drink, whilst I fill you in on all the sordid details. That's if you want to listen that is?"

"Yes. I'm free for an hour. Fire away." So I poured myself a vodka and snuggled into an easy chair to listen to what he had to say.

"This food. It involves the supermarket across the road," he said. "As you can see, my house overlooks the store's car park. Well, one morning whilst browsing out of my window I noticed a workman throwing lots of black bags into a skip that had recently appeared. Being of an inquisitive nature, I went across to investigate 'Alright mate!' I shouted cheerfully as I approached the skip, you're not throwing away anything that might be of use, are you?"

"No, I'm not pal," replied the shop assistant, "these bags are full of out of date food, that's all."

"Do you mind if I have a look," I asked.

"No, please yourself, I don't mind at all."

"I didn't need telling twice. I couldn't believe my luck when I started rummaging through the bags. There were tins of beans, tomatoes, fruit, soup, and loads of other stuff. Besides the tins, there were frozen chickens, bread butter and vegetables. Although very close, none of them had reached their sell by date, so turning to the bloke I asked, 'Is it alright to take some of these bags mate?'"

"Aye, you can take what you like as far as I am concerned. Mind you, I'm not speaking for the manager you understand?"

"And who's gonna tell him," I winked.

"Well, as long as you do it discreetly you should be alright."

A nod was as good as a wink to me and without further ado I started moving them across, a couple of bags at a time. Within half an hour I had ten full bags stored in my kitchen."

As I sat there listening to his story, a picture of a squirrel storing its nuts for the winter came into my mind.

"I discarded some of the perishables but kept everything else. There were occasions when I found cartons of cigarettes and bottles of beer also. So I made an habit of keeping a watchful eye for the disposal of food and was there in a flash to collect it. This routine has been going on for years. My house looks like a mini-market, as you've already noticed. But I'm not a greedy man and I share my proceeds amongst many of my friends immediately I receive them. I could make a fortune, but I'm too generous. Apart from what I need I just give the rest away". Ernie paused for a breath and then blurted out, "Oh, I have to tell you about this one. If I spot any strangers in the vicinity trying to pinch my food, I give them three quid to go buy a pizza for themselves, which is exactly what happened to me one day which tickled me no end. I was doing my daily rummaging routine when a rather official gentleman approached me. 'May I ask what you're up to sir?' he asked in an assertive manner.

"Thinking I'd been rumbled, I mumbled very convincingly, "I'm looking for som'et to eat. I'm starving. I haven't eaten for days."

The official looked at me sympathetically, pausing for a few seconds before reaching into his back pocket for his wallet. 'Here's a fiver mate. Go and treat yourself to a decent meal.' I, putting my full charm into action, very humbly thanked him as I took the money. The guy was nearly in tears and so was I, silently laughing at him for being so stupid. So Haydy, you understand now why I've so much food around here."

Grinning at him, I silently nodded.

The glass of vodka had gone down well, and because of it and the ones that followed, intense conversation carried on between us, lasting virtually all morning. I began piecing together a picture of him in my mind.

In his young days, he was a medic in the paratroopers. A strong handsome character that everybody liked, especially the women. When he came out of the army, he went into demolition. He could handle himself, and was a picture of health, being the north of England arm wrestling champion for quite a long period. He didn't need anyone to lean on, getting through life quite easily on his own intuition. Like the time in Margate, whilst contracted to remove the pier from the harbour. He was drinking at one of the local night clubs minding his own business, when trouble broke out behind him spoiling his peaceful domain, irritating him. Grabbing one of them by the scruff of his neck and the seat of his pants, he literally rushed him up a large flight of steps, and threw him out into the street, casually returning to finish his pint, as if nothing had happened. The owner, who happened to be one of The Kray Brothers' henchmen, having just quit the East End of London because of trouble brewing, approached him. Being so impressed with Ernie's actions, he offered him a permanent job, as his bouncer and bodyguard which Ernie refused, but even so the offer was noted.

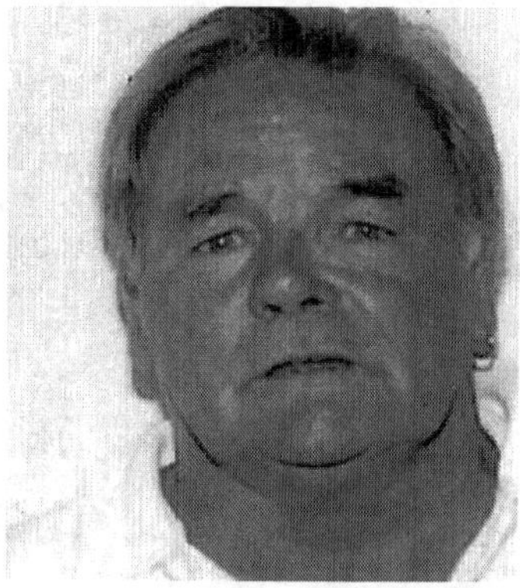

Ernie

He was a born control fiend, but had a heart of gold, and everybody relied on him to sort out their problems, which he did his utmost to help. He wouldn't see anyone on the streets.

At the age of 50 he'd had a serious accident on a children's roundabout would you believe, badly damaging both his hips, leaving him crippled. Even when his legs no longer functioned, at his young age, he was still in control. He couldn't get around easily anymore, but his positive attitude to life didn't change. His personality was so striking that everybody still came to see him. Not to keep him company, but so he could keep them company, young and old. So although he'd split up from his wife years previously, he was never short of male or female company, always having a full house. He was a remarkable guy, a one off. Nothing like the impression I had formed of him from Jean and her friends.

So on leaving his house that morning, I left on a special high because, I knew I had made a good friend that day, my first one in Padiham.

Dwarling and Ernie

Dwarling and myself

"What a welcoming morning," I thought. It had restored my faith in human nature. I'd only been around for a short while, but I had learned that the only person I could trust completely around the club was myself, and I didn't like that thought much. Ernie had gained everyone's respect down at his place, so why couldn't I do the same thing up here at the club? Respect to me was a very potent word. Respect was what I needed to survive in this town and respect was what I intended eventually to acquire, to become the man I used to be. Up to press, I wasn't having much luck. All that was going through most of my punters' minds, was how to get one up on me anyway they could, but circumstances had to change soon. They just had to.

I decided to call down at Ernie's again when I next had some free time and maybe meet some of his friends that hung around his place, just on a social basis you understand. It wouldn't do me any harm, in fact it might do me some good. By all accounts they were all roughly in their thirties, having stuck together through thick and thin since childhood. There was Yogurt, Hillis, John, Mervin, Dwarling, Keith, Alan and also Steve and Larry would you believe whom I'd already met. There were many others, but those were the main people. Ernie was twenty years older than the most of them, and in his environment, he was the gaffer of every one of them with the exception of Dwarling.

Dwarling, a gay lad, was similar to the character Dassyd Thomas, portrayed by "Matt Lucas," in the series Little Britain. (The only gay in town, and proud of it) He paid regular visits to Ernie's. But not for reassurance. Mainly to survey the landscape, investigating what potential conquests had arrived in town.

He was different from the rest, coming from rich parents, and going to a public boys' school, instead of the normal Padiham school, which may account for him being the way he was. He'd lived the good life ten years prior. His father died a while ago, leaving his mother and him a considerable amount of money. She sensibly invested her share, whilst he blew the lot within a year. Showing off, he did things like beating the time barrier in the Concorde so as to celebrate New Year's Eve in America and England on the same night, or buying Rolls Royces and hiring limousines to take Ernie and his mates out. I'd met him once or twice in the club. Don't get me wrong, when he had money he spent it freely, treated everyone around him, which was a definite advantage to the business. He just had to get rid of it fast. It was as if the money was burning a hole in his pocket. But when he was broke he was dangerous. He was a chronic alcoholic, a man to be watched, without any scruples whatsoever, being the biggest con-man in the north and proud of it. But wherever he was, he created an electric atmosphere and the room buzzed around him. He was very good company. That was the sort of guy he was.

He lived for a while, in his own villa, in Tunisia, with his solicitor boyfriend. But they had a fallout, sold up, and he returned home to Hapton, to live with his mother.

Now it passed through my mind that if I decided to build up enough courage to stop a while, it would be a sensible idea to buy the place, whilst it was going cheap. Deducting what Eric owed me, I might get away with about forty grand. But due to my previous experiences, I was very reluctant to borrow. I mentioned it to one or two people in the club, resulting in Dwarling approaching me over the matter.

Basically he had money in a Tunisian Bank, from the sale of his villa, and was willing to transfer £40,000 into my bank account for a 60% share in the property and club. I agreed, just to keep the climate friendly. He said he'd have the relevant documents rounded up by the following dinnertime, and would make the necessary telephone calls to his bank in Tunisia, arranging the money transfer whilst present at the club. So going along with him, humouring him, you might say, I gave him a few free whiskies at the end of the night, well worth the expense just to listen to the stuff he'd be coming out with.

There were quite a few people around the table, listening to him at the time, and when he came around the next day, the same people were there again, noseying. He dialled a number on his mobile, in front of them all, asking to be put through to a certain bank. Waiting a while, to everyone's amazement, he started a fluent conversation in French.

"Bonjour Pierre, je voudrais negocier le marche avec vous aussitot. Pouvez vous me envoyez le contrat avant la fin de la semaine sil vous plait?"

Babbling on for quite a few minutes, he astounded everybody listening. Nobody had ever heard him speak French before, and although nobody could understand a word of what he was saying, it sounded very convincing.

He definitely impressed everyone, apart from me that is. I didn't believe a word of it. Anyway, the account I had given him had nothing in it so I had nothing to lose. Thinking back I don't know who was conning who. He rang off, and turned to me. "Everything's sorted Haydn. It'll take about a week and a half. You'll have to keep checking your balance at the money machine," he said, placing the phone back in his pocket, so nobody could tamper with it. I supplied a few whiskies each night to keep him happy.

Nothing was ever deposited. Eventually losing patience, I instructed him to phone the bank again to verify what was happening, but on this occasion he slipped up using my mobile.........same old French shit.

I nudged Tracey "I'll bet there's nobody on the other end o' that phone."

So we both waited until he finally handed the phone back to me, instructing me at the same time that it was due in the next couple of days. I just couldn't wait to check who he had phoned, and would you believe, he hadn't phoned anybody, and what is more, he knew I knew. He just stood there, expecting me to show him up in front of everybody, but he was lucky that day because it wasn't my nature to do such a thing, so I just let it fizzle out naturally, much to his relief.

"What stunts are they going to pull on me next?" I thought to myself. I couldn't wait for the next episode.

I thought I'd weighed him up completely, silently congratulating myself, but as the weeks passed, and I began to get to know him better, I suddenly realised how wrong I had been. He wasn't interested, one iota, in bumming free beer out of me. He could do a con elsewhere, and make much more over the space of one night. Dwarling was like a cock bird on heat, displaying his multicoloured feathers, to attract a mate. There was someone in our company at that time, who he fancied and was trying to impress with his bravado act. I don't know who, and if he had made the conquest, nobody would have found out anyway. I remember him keep sending me down to the machine at 12.00pm odd nights to check the balance. Maybe to give him space to chat someone up in my absence, I don't know. But that was definitely his game, being nothing to do with conning me. I was just a pawn in his fantasy world. He did brag from time to time that he'd been with every straight guy in the town, and he knew more about them than their partners. Sometimes he did exaggerate a little, to say the least, but you could never be certain. But I did learn, that everybody is different and each one has to be weighed up as an individual before sentencing. Be that as it may, it goes without saying, I never did purchase the place.

I don't know to this day how I managed to get over the first three months at the club, the con tricks that people tried to play on me were mind-boggling. But with the exception of initially being hurt and the loss of two bangers, (which were covered on insurance anyway) I sailed through them all reasonably unblemished. One good thing that happened without realising it, was that dealing with all my punters, they had cured me of most of my mental disorders. My confidence was building up fast, and I was really grateful to them for that, even though they didn't know it. In the beginning it was a frightening experience facing the unknown. But now that I could read most of them like a book, it was turning into an enjoyable game of who can get the better of whom first. Banning them was not in the rules, being the very last resort, because taking that path would be the end to the game.

They were starting to realise that I wasn't as thick as they thought I was in the first place, and it wouldn't be long now before they'd give up acting the fool, and if that eventually did happen, it would be a feather in my cap.

I suppose you could say, that's Padiham.

Dwarling

Chapter 3 Glimmer of hope.

Roughly four months passed, when one night whilst I was sitting downstairs peacefully in conversation with a few customers, there was an almighty bang, shaking the place so much I thought an earthquake had occurred. Totally shocked I hurriedly checked around only to observe nothing whatsoever out of the ordinary, rushing upstairs, I found the same situation existed there also. Tracey and Craig were sitting in the corner together, and they seemed as shocked as I was. I returned downstairs to double check everywhere once more, nothing was amiss, leaving me in a totally confused state of mind. A few days later, I needed to access the false ceiling over the concert room, only to find that every fibrous plaster ceiling panel from the original ceiling had fallen onto it. It was a good job the false ceiling had been constructed well, otherwise the entire structure would have collapsed with the added weight. I remember the engineers who assembled the two ton snooker table informing me that it was touch and go whether the floor would take it. But they finally decided it was OK and for four months it was fine.

I just couldn't imagine what had tipped it over the edge. Then, about two days later, I overheard a conversation between Craig and his two brothers. Craig was bragging how Tracey and he had christened the snooker table the night in question and everything became very clear to me. It was them two that had brought the ceiling down, the randy twats. She must have thought she was having a right orgasm when the ceiling collapsed. They must have moved like lightning after the bang to where I spotted them sitting. "No wonder they looked so shook up," I thought, grinning to myself as a vivid picture flitted through my mind.

The snooker room was a blind spot when the bar was only operated by one person and should the bar be left unmanned to investigate the area involved, the till and the stock would be left vulnerable, which couldn't be tolerated at any cost. I thought of installing surveillance equipment up there, but they'd have only hung their coats on the camera, which was no solution to the problem.

Some of the snooker players were no better. Whoever won, had a niggling habit of sticking their snooker cues through the suspended ceiling exhibiting victorious gestures. They had no respect at all for other people's property, and the ceiling was beginning to resemble a pin cushion. It just had to stop.

One night whilst I was serving downstairs, some thoughtless person pinched a three-piece suite, would you believe, from one of the upstairs front store rooms, taking it out of the fire doors, which couldn't be bolted by law, down the fire escape, into the back yard, and away, without being noticed.

Another time Brian came running back down the stairs shouting over to me excitedly, “Come up here Haydn and take a gander at this for fuck's sake.” I followed him up to the ladies, and there was Mervin, with his pants round his ankles giving this girl what for. I had to laugh, witnessing the look on his face when he realised he had an audience. But that didn't seem to slow him down any. He just carried on until he'd finished. I was expecting him to take a bow at the finale, but he never bothered.

The position of the ladies toilets was a problem anyway, because the women had been complaining for quite a while that it was difficult for them to use the stairs when the need arose, especially when they were pissed. And you know how often ladies use the toilet in a night. There was a space for them downstairs next to the gents, so that problem could easily be solved. It was just a matter of getting the job done.

I had no alternative but to close that area down completely. Shame about the snooker table, but it wasn't the end of the world.

But a far more serious problem had occurred. I had received an “ASBO” for the noise we were causing. The neighbour down from us, whose dividing wall we both shared, had put some serious complaints forward to the council, resulting in the environmental health appearing with their decibel recording meters, warning me that if I didn't contain the noise immediately, they'd be taking steps to close me down. Which meant, I had to get rid of the small snug at the side of the bar, moving the pool table there from the large snug, and building a further well sound insulated room reaching from the front side room to the rear wall, leaving an access corridor to the toilets and fire escape doors. I would have to reinstall the seating I had lost, to the front of the bar, separating it from the concert room by an eight feet serving area.

Myself, sorting out the toilets

That was about the gist of it and all the work involved had to be completed whilst the place was still operating. So I had quite a lot on my plate to contend with and Brian wasn't helping much, due to the fact that because the place was running reasonably smooth for a change, he was spending less time behind the bar, and more time playing the big man role in the local pubs. But he was going to have to buck his ideas up dramatically, to help me complete this complex work, whether he liked it or not.

And there was also the question of music. It was costing far too much employing individual D.Js, rock groups and karaoke people, just for Saturday night, never mind the rest of the week. But fortunately this problem was immediately solved when a guy called Paul with his girlfriend Andrea walked in out of the blue needing work. By all accounts Paul could DJ well, and Andrea was an experienced barmaid, and without sounding too facetious, I could get a full week's work out of him, for the same price as what I had to pay somebody just for Saturday night. He was willing to buckle in, so giving it some serious thought I agreed to set him on as soon as I could acquire some karaoke equipment. As for Andrea, she was a good looker and wasn't stupid, so she started immediately.

Everything eventually sorted itself out with only one or two minor disasters, which turned out right in the end, like when Tracey and Craig offered to help me move some furnishings from the upstairs storeroom to the new room downstairs. There was a very heavy mahogany wardrobe. We had no problem resting it on its back at the top of the staircase, ready to slide it down to ground-floor level. I was about to position myself a few steps down to take the weight, when Craig jumped in.

"I'd better take the bottom," he volunteered. "This bloody thing weighs a ton!"

"Your alright Craig," I responded confidently, "there's no problem."

"No, I'm stronger than you. I'll take the bottom."

I thought to myself, "Stronger than me, my arse," but I let him have his way for fear of spoiling his self-image.

"Are you ready?" I asked, to prepare him for the sudden weight, when the balance swung his way.

"Yes, send it over," he replied.

The wardrobe was pivoted on the top step and as I lifted

the back of it slightly, it unexpectedly shot off down the staircase, taking Craig with it, squashing him with some force against the door frame at the bottom of the stairs. By the time I reached ground level he was rolling around the concert room floor in agony.

"Ring an ambulance fast. He's been badly hurt," I shouted to Tracey.

I was shitting bricks thinking he was going to die. But the paramedics examined him, reassuring me that he'd survive, and they whipped him off to hospital for x-rays. I classed it as retribution for trying to rob me, and as far as I was concerned we were even now. At least, him being away gave Tracey and I a chance to make friends again. He returned a couple of days later, a bit sore but still in one piece. So I reckoned he'd got off rather lightly that time, considering everything worked out right in the end. I still owed them a night out for their troubles, but I thought I'd leave it a while until he fully recovered. After that episode Craig and I got on much better together.

On another occasion, one night, a guy called Mick, pissed out of his brains, was sitting under a rather large television which Brian had repositioned a week or so before. I was behind the bar looking out, when I suddenly noticed the television slowly beginning to slide. It can't have been very stable because the impact of the bass music asserted on it must have been the culprit. I rushed into the concert room towards him but it was too late. The television came crashing down on to his head, finishing up on the floor in front of him, knocking his table over in the process. I noticed there wasn't any blood around but still panicking, I grabbed him and tried to revive him. He sort of half came round, rubbing his head, not aware in the slightest that the television had fallen on him. He just thought he had a bad hangover, that's all. How relieved I was. Stumbling to his feet he headed for the main door, with a half pint still in his hand, which Andrea relieved him of on leaving. As I was walking back towards her, she suddenly let out an almighty scream, dropping the glass in fright, which smashed to pieces on the floor. An eyeball rolled out of it. She was petrified for a second until she realised it was an artificial glass eye, which the guy must have deliberately placed in his beer to clean it or something. Initially, she thought one of his eyes had popped out when the television hit him. Well I suppose that was the logical way of thinking at the time. The next day he came in looking for it and enquired how he had acquired the extensive bruising on the top of his head. I didn't enlighten him, thinking it best to keep quiet.

I finally had everything just shipshape when one afternoon whilst completing my shopping ritual in Burnley, I returned back to the club only to find the bailiffs had broken in and removed every item of furniture, every machine in the beer cellar and bar, and all my beer stocks. I was told they'd filled two removal wagons before eventually leaving. I was livid.

A few weeks prior, the music royalties organisation in disguise had entered the club, ordering a couple of drinks, whilst listening to the karaoke. After about half a hour they approached Brian, being the license holder, informing him that because he wasn't in their organisation and was playing certain records that were on their itinerary, he would be expecting a summons for playing them, namely "I got you babe" and "Rock around the clock." Brian received it shortly afterwards demanding immediate payment of two grand, and that if he ignored it and decided to attended court in London to defend himself, be expecting a bill for around five grand. I wrote back telling them to stick the summons up their arse, which was the reason for the bailiffs' visitation.

Being rather put out for getting caught on the hop that day, I decided to ring Eric for advice, knowing he was excellent at squeezing out of nasty corners. So he immediately printed out some paperwork and the next morning after picking me up, we both headed for the bailiffs office in Preston. On arriving and knocking for a while on their office door, which was locked for some unknown reason, a guy eventually answered.

"Who might you be?" Eric asked.

"I'm the sheriff of Preston," he answered.

"Well, I'm Robin Hood and this is my associate Little John" Eric blurted out, pointing to me. "We need a confrontation with you." The guy just stared at us both in bewilderment but eventually invited us both in.

"What seems to be the problem?" he asked.

"Well I'm here on a mission. Your men have robbed my merry men of my belongings by accident and I want them back. Simple as that," Eric blurted out.

"I don't really know what you're on about," he replied. "Can I take some details?" With that Eric produced a list of items which he professed to be his, that Brian had supposedly hired and signed for. So not being his property the Sheriff's bailiffs had no right to remove them. After a detailed examination the Sheriff had to admit that they had made a slip up and would return and fix them immediately.

"The next time," the Sheriff commented, "please inform us before we arrive, will you? It's just cost this office about a grand."

"Tough. That's your problem mate, not ours." Eric replied. "We'd have informed you this time if you'd have given us the chance, but you broke in, jumping the gun. So hard cheese."

We received a silent response to that statement so on that note we decided to depart. Everything except the beer stock, which was Brian's property was returned. Spectators were totally confused. First they'd witnessed the place being emptied, and all sorts of stories were spreading round the town. Then seeing the whole of the gear being returned, they just didn't know what to think. They were goosed.

The following Monday I had to go to the local auctions to bid for the beer stocks back and to my surprise the auctioneer already knew me. I explained to him why I was present, and when my lot came up, he passed the explanation on to the rest of the bidders, asking them in decency not to bid against me, which is exactly what happened. Consequently, I retrieved my beer stocks for a song. "Good one!"

I'd just recovered from that incident when a guy from Halifax offered to sell me a massive fish-tank, housing a monster of a fish which was about fourteen inches long, and very vicious. Detecting any movement on the outside, it used to attack with such ferocity you'd have thought the glass would have shattered as the fish head-butted it. It had to be fed on tins of cat-food, which it instantaneously savagely shredded into small pieces. What a beast. I decided it would make a good focal point, situated at the far side of the serving area in an alcove. Being too heavy for me to handle myself, Paul volunteered to help me, and as we arrived back at the club with the fish-tank still in the car, panic erupted. Someone cried out, "Paul, your house has burnt down, and your two children have been burnt to death."

Paul and I froze. But more so Paul. The expression on his face, I couldn't describe, sheer panic and disbelief, he dragged me by the arm back to the car.

"Get me to my house now!" he frantically ordered.

"Fuck the tank," I thought, shooting off up the cobbled street at top speed, heading for the disaster zone as fast as I could. He didn't live far away, but on reaching his lane, what little hopes he had left were dashed. There were two fire engines, an ambulance, and two police cars blocking the entire thoroughfare. He opened his door and threw himself onto the pavement before the car had even stopped. Jumping up, he ran straight for the house, desperately fighting off anyone who tried to stop him. He was in a right state. I didn't want to get in the way so I remained in the car watching him at a distance though the windscreen. The police, grabbing him, took him to the open ambulance for a chat, where he stopped for quite a while. The fire had been extinguished by then. I kept waiting, expecting the worst when suddenly he appeared, still talking to the police, actually having a smile on his face, which was a hopeful sight. He came running back to me and climbed into the car.

"Thank God!" he exclaimed. "I've just lost my house, but everybody's OK, Fuuh! All my kids have been taken to hospital for check ups, but they're alright." He was hyperventilating. "I nearly had an heart attack then."

"Bloody hell Paul," I replied, "What a thing to be told by them bastards in the club. They hadn't got a fucking clue. You can't credit the mentality some people possess these days."

I ran him straight to hospital, leaving him there to sort his family out, so I could shoot back to the club, to give out some ear-ache. But fortunately for them, the mouthy twats had already left, which was just as well because I was hitching to smack somebody, I felt so concerned for Paul.

However, I still had to install the fish tank that night which had miraculously survived the ordeal turning out to be a job well worth doing. This fish definitely scared people. So whenever anyone approached the bar with the purpose of scrounging a free drink, and didn't qualify for one in my eyes, I used to throw a couple of pound coins into the fish-tank, telling them to roll up their sleeves, and retrieve the money if they wanted to buy themselves one, otherwise don't ask again. Not one person ever took up my offer. It was better for me that way, at least I had offered them the option. At the end of the night when no one was watching, I used my own personal net to retrieve the money. Good one!

Saturday night had arrived again and the place was swinging. Paul was doing an excellent job on karaoke, whilst Andrea and Jean were working well together behind the bar. Andrea was such a pleasant, relaxing person to talk to, who definitely knew her stuff and was a truly honest person. I think I could have trusted her with my life, but I'd think twice before putting it to the test. For the first time since I had arrived there, I felt I had someone I could really rely on, creating such a good feeling inside me, knowing I was not alone at work anymore. Brian was alright, but he needed leading all the way, not being able to stand on his own two feet. Jean had her own ideas about running the club, and her ideas were starting to conflict with what I had in mind. To be fair, I must add that she was a very honest, efficient and trustworthy person, but the problem was that she just wasn't on my wavelength. Where the subject of licensed premises arose, she came from the old school of thinking, always using her pet phrase, "Only deal with the real people." The real people she referred to were her friends, who weren't big drinkers, and reminded me of a herd of sheep that would scatter at the first sign of trouble. Boring people. But the way I saw it, whilst the others needed controlling, for a full night of laughs with a good profit to boot, everybody had to be in the equation. So I had to learn how to handle the full cross-section of people on their own level, not at pub-watch level, giving them freedom to breathe independently, which was a totally different approach to handling people, making it my vocation to gain total respect and control, so everybody could drink together in harmony. No landlord in Padiham had succeeded in achieving that status yet.

Suddenly Brian came running up to me. "There's a guy down there about to sing karaoke. He approached me this afternoon. He's on the pub-watch and wanted to come in. I told him to leave, but he's back again. Go down there and kick him out, Haydn, for me, will you?"

I got up and strolled down to his corner. There were about sixteen people who appeared to be his relations, all out on a do, totally behaving themselves. Paul had handed the bloke the microphone, and, stepping off the stage, he focused himself and began to sing. The song was "Suspicious Minds" by Elivis, and could he sing. He had a beautiful voice and he held everybody's attention to the very last note.

Pointing out that in complete contrast to this guy was Tracey's singing voice. Her song was Patsy Clyne's "Crazy," and because she couldn't sing too well, she deliberately rendered every note totally out of key, at the top of her voice, just to irritate everybody. It gave her a buzz. She was so bad, that 10yrs later, people could still tell you the name of the song she used to ruin. Once heard, never forgotten.

So comparing this guy, receiving a standing ovation from everybody, who I was supposed to kick out, to Tracey who wasn't banned, something just wasn't right.

He professionally passed the microphone back to Paul, giving everyone a polite nod in gratitude and walked across to me, holding his hand out for a handshake. "John's the name, but everybody calls me Elvis" were his initial words. "I'd like a word if I may."

I looked at him and his assumed relatives, and to be quite honest, I couldn't see any harm in any of them. "They tell me, you're on the pub-watch?"

"That's right," he answered. "You haven't come across here to kick me out have you? Not tonight of all nights. It's my sister's birthday."

"What did they put you on the pub-watch for?"

"For smoking cannabis," was his simple answer.

"And are you going to smoke cannabis here?"

"Not without your permission," he replied with a grin on his face.

"Well John," I answered, "you could get me into serious bother being here. But, I'll tell you what, you're going nowhere. You've a great voice and it's people like you I need to create a good atmosphere in this place. Carry on. I haven't seen you." I then turned around to walk back to Brian. I knew that if I had kicked him out, sixteen others would have left with him, and I would have been the biggest pillock in town, for no reason at all. There was no trouble, quite the reverse, and such action would have been totally defeating my object. Knowing I did the right thing, I realised that this Pub Watch business wasn't working for me. But I still had to face Brian and Jean, being in no doubt that they weren't impressed with me at all. They were even less impressed when Alan approached me, with the same problem, on the pub-watch for smoking cannabis. Obviously John had been talking about me to him. Good things I hoped. I'd let John through so I had no choice but to let Alan through also. He seemed a good lad anyway. Why not?

The next person to approach me that night was Yogurt.

John

John and Yog's Brother Paul

Andria and Paul

Andria

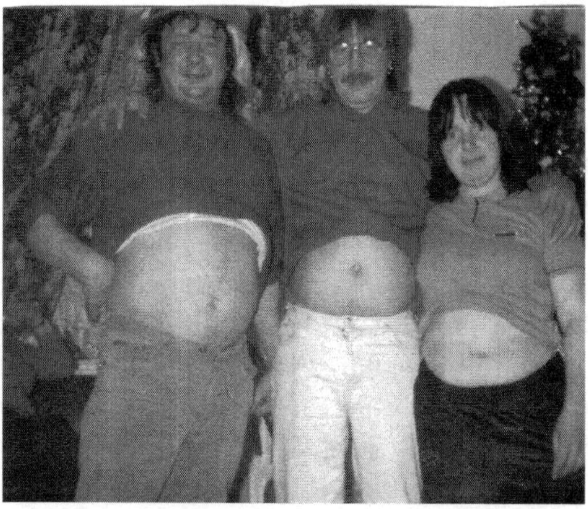

Yogurt, Keith and a friend

This was my very first encounter with him. He beckoned me over to his table.

"Don't tell me you're on the pub-watch too for smoking cannabis?" I joked.

"No," I'm not on the pub-watch. Don't insult me," he grinned, bobbing about as he was talking.

"Thank fuck for that. I'm Haydn. How can I help you?"

"Well I'm Yogurt, and John and Alan are my close buddies. And I've heard what you did for them tonight. I think you're alright, but I'd think of you as the greatest if I could strap a pint at the bar. I've run out of cash and I don't want to leave yet, it's buzzing in here."

"You can't go to the bar strapping beer" I told him point blank. "Everybody would be on the bandwagon. Here's a fiver, go and buy yourself one, for fuck's sake." He just looked at me astounded. I really shocked him. He wasn't expecting that. He jumped up, like he had a set of springs under his feet. A regular "Jack in the Box."

"Don't go anywhere 'til I get back," he growled. "We're going to talk for a while, me and you. I like your style Haydn.

Good one." On that note he went ducking, bobbing and joking around people all the way to the bar, coming back to the table carrying two pints, one for him and one for me, which was very kind of him, on my money. I'd noticed, in the small time I had been observing him, that he spoke to everybody, joking all the time, and it seemed to me that everyone was happy in his company. He sat down as if he'd known me for years, and that night nobody could get a word in edgeways. Yogurt and I never stopped talking, being such an interesting man having that special way with words, besides being full of charisma, rugged but good looking, a self-admitted honest rogue, well liked about town, and God knows what else. But he had a problem with the booze. It seemed that everybody had in this town, so I suppose in some weird way, you could call him 'normal'. Yogurt, John and Alan all frequented Ernie's place, and I was beginning to realise that Ernie had some interesting people visiting him, and I should make a special point this time, of visiting his place instead of just thinking about it. As the night drew to a close and Yogurt was departing, he promised me he'd never miss another day there. His duty, he said, was to keep an eye on me, at all times, would you believe. I would have thought the reverse should have applied. We just jelled. So not finding the words to explain it, I put it down to the chemistry. I also felt, in some strange way, that I had achieved something that night, not knowing exactly what, but the feeling was there.

The next day started quietly. There were not many people around, giving me time to think about the previous night, and whether I would have the privilege of Yog's company once again.

"It could have been all beer talk," I thought to myself, when suddenly Tracey burst in, grabbing me by the arm, and pulling me to one side.

"You're wanted next door at the Starkey's, Haydn. Can you spare a minute. I'll look after the bar for you whilst you're away."

"Why, what's up?" I enquired.

"It's Ernie's crowd. They want a word with you in private about something. I don't know what for, I'm just the messenger," she replied.

"Alright," I answered. "Hang about here, and don't take your eyes off the bar whatever you do. I won't be long," and on that note I left for the Starkey's, still rather puzzled. As I walked in, I saw a crowd in the corner all turn towards me. There was Steve, John, Yogurt, Mervin, Larry, Alan and another guy I hadn't had the pleasure of meeting yet, called Hillis. First impressions, I was a bit wary of him. He had no top on, and appeared to be an exhibitionist to me. He was stomping around like he was on duty guarding Buckingham Palace, an erect walking guy, sticking his chest out, showing off all his muscles, head upright, looking very arrogant. He spoke abruptly, striving to assert a sense of authority, with a snidy grin on his face most of the time. I thought I'd give him a wide berth until I found out more about him. Then out of the gents hobbled Ernie and I immediately sensed the object of the meeting.

"Don't tell me. Let me be the mind reader today," I commented, smiling at him.

"Go on then. I'll give you one spin of the wheel," grinned Ernie.

"Right. You're out for the afternoon with your buddies, doing a full round of the pubs in Padiham, and my place is next on the list, and you're not sure if I'm going to allow you in, with the rest of them. Am I close?"

"Bang on Haydn. So?"

"What can I say? I did promise you'd be back in within three months, and it's touching on four. And I can't go against my word, can I? That wouldn't go down well, would it?" I stopped for a second to think about the job.

"Go on then Haydn, spill it out. We're loosing precious drinking time," Ernie rapped.

"Well, just cooperate with me, will you for a little while longer. You don't have to remind me, I know I'm overdue sorting the matter out. Just give me a bit of breathing space will you, so it can be done in an amiable manner. alright?, and today and everyday until it's sorted, I'll allow you in the club until 7.00pm. That's just before Jean's shift starts. So make sure you're not there when she arrives, will you? And don't take offence. This is just business, nothing personal you understand. If I had my way, this situation wouldn't have arisen in the first place."

"Fair enough Haydy, I'll go along with that. Just get it sorted." was Ernie's calm reply. I was off the hook for another few days, but things were closing in on me rapidly, so something had to be done this time.

They all rose, walking out into the fresh air, following me down to the club, where Tracey was smiling and giving me the thumbs up as we all walked in.

Giving them a short while to settle down, I noticed Yog drinking with Hillis, and beckoned him over. He came bouncing across, throwing his arms in the air portraying a picture of energy whilst laughing and joking.

"Yeah! Yeah! Yeah!" he threw at me, ducking and diving as normal.

"I need to pick your brains for a second in private, Yog, if you don't mind?"

"Fire away."

"Tell me about Hillis, Yog. I need to know the man."

So, the obliging fellow that he was, he gave me the full lowdown.

It seemed, that years before, Hillis had been involved in a tragic road accident in a mini, on the topside of town. He, his brother and and three others had a head on collision with a bus. I don't know the finer details, but the outcome was devastating. Apart from Hillis, who had a miraculous escape, being thrown through the front passenger door window, everyone else was killed. By all accounts, it was a right mess with body parts scattered everywhere. After months of hospitalization, he returned home, not quite the person he used to be. His body had healed perfectly, but his brain had took a walloping. He had a serious guilt complex, causing a personality change, believing he should have died with the rest of them, not being fair to them that he was still alive. And since then, he couldn't care two shits about anything. I never heard him personally talking about what he'd been through to anybody, but the friends he had grown up with could read him like a book. He spent a lot of time by himself on his allotment, and a good percentage of his spare time talking to Ernie.

"Don't worry Haydy. Trust me. He's a bit of a bear at times, growling at people, but he's right, deep down. He won't cause any bother in here, believe me." Yog was his close friend, so nothing more needed to be said. I took his word for it.

Every afternoon, from then on, they all religiously turned up for a giggle. It was becoming their second home to Ernie's, making enjoyable company, so much so that I never stopped laughing. But the best of it was, they started to treat me like one of them, not just the landlord they had to comply with, which made me feel really privileged. A definite improvement.

There were still dickheads around, like Fart and his mate, trying to steal the one arm bandit out of the back fire escape doors, the only blind spot in the place, when my back was turned. But I eventually spotted them, having managed to get the machine stuck in the door frame, being too wide. As I approached them in awe, Fart just gave a shrug and a grin, as if to say, "Fair enough, been nobbled, you win, game over," calmly carrying the machine back to where it was, plugging it in, and walking away. I couldn't believe what I'd just witnessed. I went straight across to Yog, informing him what had just happened, and he in turn told Hillis, who immediately approached Fart, threatening to stick his head in the fish tank if it ever happened again, which I thought was a good enough deterrent, knowing he wouldn't have had much of a face left if that had happened. It passed through my mind that it could have been him who pinched the three-piece suite from upstairs.

Now whilst all this was happening, inevitably, news got around that I was letting certain people in that were on the pub-watch, and Jean got to know I was allowing Ernie in during the afternoons. I think it was my so-called partner Brian, who told her, due to the fact that they were as thick as thieves, recently discussing my affairs behind my back. Anyway I got summoned to attend the next pub-watch meeting and was given an ultimatum. "Either obey the rules, or get out of our organisation." I didn't need to think about it, telling them to stick the pub-watch up their arses, and leaving forthwith.

As for Jean, she approached me about Ernie, also giving me an ultimatum. "Either keep Ernie out or lose a bar manager." The club was my baby, and if I couldn't make my own rules stick, it was no good to me. So I had no alternative but to accept her week's notice. She had me over a barrel, but I couldn't succumb to her ways. By making this decision it did obviously solve the Ernie problem, so I made a special journey down to his place to break the news to him personally, first hand. There was quite a gathering of people down there as usual. Pouring me a celebratory drink, we had just began chatting when the front door flew open, and a guy with a shopping bag over his shoulder, came charging through the room, and disappeared out of the back door, without saying a word. Close behind him, two police officers came rushing in through the front door, fighting their way through us all. Ernie casually pointed to the back door. The officers politely nodded and rushed out in pursuit. No words were spoken at all. It was a bit like the Keystone Cops from the black and white silent movies.

I looked at Ernie, "What the fuck was all that about?" I enquired.

"Oh, they're just chasing shoplifters from the Coop across the road. No sweat, it's a regular occurrence. I'm getting used to it. They always pick my house to try and escape, but they get caught every time. One day the penny will drop." I was starting to convince myself, that I was dreaming this whole Padiham business, but obviously not. Too many things were happening to be a dream.

So getting back to reality, I was still not happy with Brian. He'd lost his buddy Jean to hide behind, being noticeably missing most of the time, and the times he was there he was an hindrance. Andrea ran the bar professionally, so when Brian went behind, he was only in the way. People began to take the piss out of him. I did feel a degree of sympathy towards him, but, because he was incapable of finding the correct words in a predicament, he'd flare up banning them on the spot, just to get out of an argument he shouldn't have been involved in anyway. Every morning, I had to check with him to find out who he'd banned the previous night, and then I had to seek them out for the sole purpose of reinstating them again with my sincere apologies. Obviously Brian didn't like it. I was undermining his authority, and it became a standing joke around town. So a few weeks later, he approached me, telling me that the town was getting too much for him and that he would be moving back to his sister's in Halifax in the following two weeks. This meant the club was going to be noticeably short on staff. Just Andrea, Paul and me.

Then one late afternoon, a charming young girl waltzed in. We'd just closed after the afternoon shift. She approached Brian, who was cleaning the bar down, having heard on the grapevine that possibly a job was coming available, and asked him if he was in charge. He pointed over to me, lying flat on my back, fast asleep on one of the bench seats. She made her way over, gently nudging me in the ribs, to wake me up. The club doors were wide open and the sun was glaring through, piercing the dark interior. She was stood directly between me and the door, and as I slowly opened my eyes, accustoming them to the dim surroundings, I could see this beautiful young girl in front of me, the sun was shining through her long, wavy hair, causing a brilliant aura to surround her, placing thoughts in my head for one isolated second, that she was an angel.

"Is there anything I can do for you?" I asked hopefully.

"I wondered if there was a job going behind the bar?" she enquired in an attractive Irish accent.

I just looked at her and thought, "What a beautiful sight to wake up to." So, without a further ado, I replied, "If you want it, the job's yours. Start at your convenience." I think everything was moving much faster than she'd expected, rendering her speechless. I thought, "Grab her while you can. Don't let her escape Haydn. No way!"

As she was dancing out of the club door, I shouted after her, "Hey! What's your name girl?"

"Gale," she replied, "See you tomorrow," were her only words as she disappeared round the corner. That was my staff problem sorted, without even trying. Life was moving fast. If I didn't stop and take time to look around once in a while, I'd miss it.

Gale

Gale and myself

Gale

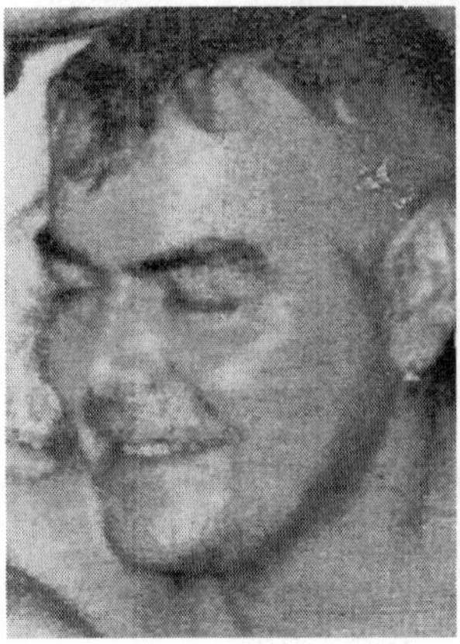 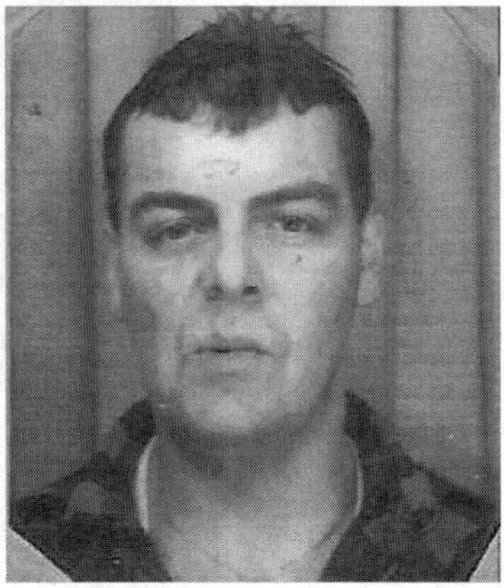

Hillis

Brian and Jean eventually departed, forcing me to change the license to my name, not that there were any problems there, from now onwards leaving me able to make my own decisions without surrounding criticism. It was like a breath of fresh air to me. A burden had been lifted from my shoulders. Now I could really organise myself.

I had booked a hypnotist for the following Saturday night, being a ticket do, which I didn't like, but the turn was rather expensive and his fees had to be covered. The night was unusual, to say the least, being very entertaining indeed. I personally couldn't understand how a person could be hypnotised. Was it all kidology? I hadn't a clue, but tonight I was going to find out, once and for all. The show eventually started, having a full house with everybody watching enthusiastically. Asking for twelve volunteers, one of whom being Andrea my bar maid, he sat them down in a line on the temporary stage I had erected across the rear of the concert room just for that special evening. I was talking to her earlier, and she volunteered for the sole purpose of proving to herself and Paul, that hypnotism was a load of rubbish. She was a quiet girl far from being an extrovert, who wouldn't say or do anything out of place, at any time.

The hypnotist switched on the strange, soothing music, emanating from two high pedestal speakers set at either side of the stage, immediately approaching everyone in turn. Spending no more than one minute on each person, he asked them all individually to do stupid things, like believing they were chickens laying eggs, or acting like pigs eating from troughs, you know, all silly stuff like that. Everybody did exactly what was asked of them. I'd have thought it would have taken much longer to induce hypnosis on a person, but I still think that one or two of them were pretending just for a giggle. But if they were he must have known. Anyway, he snapped them all out of it and immediately sent eight of them off the stage, leaving four. With these four, he repeated the exact process again sending another three packing, leaving only the one, who just happened to be Andrea. She was the chosen one, the most vulnerable, the easiest to be hypnotised. So with that in mind, he spent more effort on her, putting her well under his influence this time, making sure she knew what to listen for to snap out of it. He gave her definite instructions, the first being that her boyfriend Paul was standing in front of her, and he needed her to throw her arms round him, seductively embracing him whilst passionately kissing, which she did so realistically you'd have thought he was on stage with her. There were no out of place expressions on her face, she just accepted and believed everything. He then emphasised to her that Paul was on heat, and she had to give him a real going over. "That's what he needs you to do," which she started to attempt without hesitation. You could tell by the way she was acting that she really believed she was alone with Paul somewhere. It was so realistic that Paul, who was sat next to me in the audience, was getting embarrassed. The audience were crying with laughter, to see Andrea of all people, doing such things on stage.

Then stopping her before she went too far, he instructed her that Paul was hiding from her in the audience and he wanted her to go looking for him, and not stopping until she'd found him, to carry on making love to him where she'd left off. He told her she'd recognise him by his red and yellow striped underpants. She shot down off the stage into the audience, and any and every bloke she encountered, attempted to relieve them of their trousers, not messing around in any shape or form. She managed to succeed on about six blokes before panic set in, stampeding the male section of the audience away from her in every direction possible. She was causing a riot. Then Paul, on the hypnotist's instructions, was told to put on some red and yellow striped underpants, before feeding him to her. Grabbing him, not recognising him whatsoever, she began ripping his trousers off, suddenly stopping dead in her tracks. A contented look appeared on her face as she jumped him, right in the middle of the place. Paul was trying to fight her off. The hypnotist had to rush in and bring her out of it before she raped him on the spot, the poor lad. Andrea was once again her quiet self. She looked around puzzled, wondering why everyone was looking and laughing at her, whilst Paul tried to explain to her what she'd been up to. But she wasn't having any of it. There was no way she'd do anything like that, not in a million years.

Well, I was convinced. Hypnotism was something else. I could have done with him working behind the bar with me. He'd have quietened a few people down, for sure.

Eric had been visiting The Palatine Club which he owned, in Nelson, that night and had popped in to see the turn on his way home to Halifax. I introduced him to Yog. One big mistake. It seemed to me there was a real clash of personalities. He'd been talking to Yogurt for what must have been an hour, until it was time for him to leave for home, when he came strolling across to me to invite me to the Palatine Club the next evening needing advice of some description. I wasn't sure exactly what, but he did ask me, "Under no circumstances bring Yogurt," which seemed very strange to me considering he'd just spent so much time talking to him. As he disappeared out of the front entrance, Yogurt strolled over to me rubbing his hands and grinning.

"What happened there with Eric?" I asked him. "He seemed to be a bit wary of you."

"He thinks I'm going to run off with all his women. He might think he's good but I'm better," he grinned.

"I'm supposed to be going to the Palatine Club tomorrow teatime to see him and he's given me specific instructions not to bring you."

"I know," Yogurt replied. "He already told me to keep away. But I'm going to turn up regardless. You watch me Haydn. Just to guile him."

Eric's approach to women was identical to Dwarling's approach to men. They both tried to portray a sense of grandeur, tempting their prey into the trap, like, "Come into my parlour said the spider to the fly." But Yogurt didn't need this sort of approach. With his bursting personality, he was like a powerful magnet to women. As he strolled through life, they came out of the woodwork to be close to him. I've never experienced so many women running after one person before. I wasn't sure what he had, but he definitely had something special.

So the next evening, I espied the front street to make sure Yog wasn't around and then dashed out of the club into the car driving up to the main road junction. Suddenly Yog dashed out of the King's, opening my passenger door and jumped into the car, turning to me grinning extensively as usual.

"Thought you'd escape without me tonight did you? I've been watching out for you for the last hour. I told you I was coming."

There was nothing I could do. I'd done my best to avoid him, so I just smiled at him and set off.

As we entered the Palatine Club, there was a group of dolly birds, talking together in the foyer. Yog immediately approached them, bouncing about and laughing as normal. Throwing his arms up in the air he shouted, "Aba-Dada-

Duw!, I'm home babes!" They all turned and laughed at him. What an entrance. For the next half hour, he tried everything in his power to get into their knickers, (In a joking way, you understand) eventually giving it up as a bad job, and we went into the snooker room for a quiet pint each, making enquiries about the whereabouts of Eric.

By all accounts, he'd already been in with his prospective girlfriend, and had departed somewhere by himself, expected back soon.

So we had another pint.

Suddenly, one of the birds Yog had been chatting up, ran into the room, grabbed him by the arm and ordered him to dance with her. He had no alternative but to obey. They did two or three rounds on the dance floor, and then disappeared out of the main entrance, never to be seen again.

I instantaneously thought, "Well, if nothing else, that sorts out the Yog problem with Eric." I couldn't have been more mistaken. Eric eventually arrived back and came across to me, enquiring across the bar where Sandra was. I didn't recognise the name, so I assumed that was the girl Eric had palled up with that night.

"I last saw her dancing with Haydn's mate" the barmaid replied.

"Did you bring someone Haydn?" Eric asked me anxiously.

"That wasn't your bird was it?" I spluttered, in a somewhat exasperated manner nearly drowning in my own beer, "I might be wrong, but I think Yogurt's just fucked off with her."

"You what!" he exclaimed, "Yogurt!"

"Yes, I think so." But he didn't know, Eric. Of all the women in Nelson, he had to pick yours. This doesn't seem to be your night does it?" I laughed.

Eric angrily slapped the top of the bar, muttering, "The bastard! I told you not to bring him here," and stamped out of the door. "What a waste of time me coming here tonight," I thought. "Everybody has fucked off on me. But at least it gives me space away from Padiham to plan my next move."

I met up with Yog the following day, not having a clue that he'd run off with Eric's bird the previous night, but it definitely give him a buzz when I told him. It was like they were playing that strange game of, "who comes off best," and Yogurt had won the first round.

Chapter 4 The sun breaking through

Trinity Sunday, 15th May 1996, the first Sunday after Pentecost, known in Padiham as Walking Day, was the day when local families gathered together to watch the ritual procession pass through the town, concluding with a good excuse for a booze up, being the only day that children were unofficially allowed to be with their parents whilst drinking in the local pubs. And what an experience that turned out to be. I was pre-warned I was going to be busy, but I never envisaged how busy. I bought extra stock in readiness, but my entire stock was sold within the first hour and a half of trading. I spent most of the day emptying the local supermarkets, wine shops, and off-licenses of anything I could get my hands on. The afternoon was completely insane. I'd never experienced anything like it before. Everybody in town seemed to have landed at my place. You couldn't get another person in it was so packed, whilst all the other pubs were just ticking over. What an afternoon. The kitchen area, joining the far end of the bar, without exaggerating, was six foot deep, in empty bottles and cans, spilling over into the main bar area by the end of the afternoon. What an unbelievable amount of beer I turned over. I literally took thousands, without a hint of trouble. I must have been doing something right these last five months, because every Saturday night I could step outside to witness the police trying to contain the carnage outside the neighbouring two pubs, whilst I never had to call upon them once for any reason whatsoever. Minor incidents occurred that didn't warrant the police, but nothing I couldn't handle myself.

It was this particular day that Yog brought his sister,

Nicola, specially to see me, being the first time I had clapped eyes on her, but I didn't have time for conversation, I was far too busy. I remember her pleading for a job, and me replying that I'd put her onto the waiting list along with the other women who had applied, but that was the extent of our conversation, not giving it another thought that day. Eventually the crowds dwindled away, the place being in utter chaos, leaving me the formidable task of trying to clean up and restore some normality again.

"Wow!" I thought, as the night ended, "I could do with one of these days every week. I'd be a millionaire in no time."

That was one reassuring day and I thought that everything was falling into place and I was gaining control, when I experienced a major setback. My brother-in-law, who lived in Western Australia, rang me to tell me my mother had been taken ill, and that I needed to get over there urgently to visit her, possibly for the last time, given she was touching 90 years of age.

My mother

My relations in Australia

My sister Jean and Alan were married in the 60s and emigrated to Australia shortly afterward building a family of thirteen children. When my father died in the 80s my mother emigrated also to live with them in Perth on condition that I visited her on a yearly basis. I was not due in Australia for at least three months, but that wasn't allowing for emergencies.

Fortunately for me, Tracey and her boyfriend Craig had moved into my place for a short while, giving them breathing space to find somewhere permanent to live. Her mother was leaving the Starky's Arms and going back to Leeds. To be candid, it could have been because I was pinching all her trade. But besides that, Craig had been caught pulling beer, in the middle of the night, totally naked after just finishing a shagging session in the main lounge and that didn't go down well with mother at all. So Tracey and her mother were not seeing eye to eye at that moment. Being in a sticky situation I desperately needed their help, but I wasn't sure I was doing the correct thing. Knowing they could easily ruin me in a breath, and needing a club to come back to, could I take that chance and trust them? It was dodgy. But since they were living there, they might as well make themselves useful, so I eventually decided to chance it and ask them to look after it for me, whilst I was away. I was going to put it to them, that everything they earned would be theirs, and all they had to do was to keep it stocked up, making sure the wages were paid, then it wouldn't be in their interest to rob the business. I would have liked to have offered Andrea the opportunity, but there'd be a conflict with them living there, because in such a situation, Tracey and Craig would definitely have been pilfering beer aftertime, when Andrea had left on a night, having two young children to look after. So I explained to Andrea, why I had made that decision, not wanting her to think I was undermining her, being the only person I could trust and needing her on my side to report to me in Australia, how they were coping. Besides, Paul was not hard enough to run the place, whilst Tracey and Craig were. So approaching each of them in turn, thankfully they all individually agreed to cooperate. I really didn't need the pressure at this crucial point in time, it could knock me back months, but I had no option, I had to go, like it or not.

So I eventually left for Australia. Now for many years, there was one special person I looked forward to meeting every time I went visiting there and that was Bobby my nephew. Him and me were so alike in nearly every way, we could have been the same person, having the same independency like myself, or so I was led to think.

He was living with a beautiful girl called Christie. Every visit I made to Australia, I spent mainly with her, giving Bobby time for a few pints with his mates. Consequently Christie and I grew pretty close, hitting the nightlife together on very regular intervals. They were both always waiting for me when I landed in Australia, and she would cancel all arrangements to be with me during my visit. We had some really good times together, and frequently got into deep conversation about them coming to Padiham for a while to live and work at the club. I thought it would suit them down to the ground. They were waiting for me at Perth Airport with Alan my brother-in-law as usual, but this time I was going to have to spend much more time with my mother.

And what a tense time that was, having my fingers crossed for the entire month. My mother was really pleased to see me, which I think was the reason for her miraculous recovery. Andrea rang me a couple of times telling me that the stocks were slowly diminishing but otherwise everything was alright. So rather relieved I eventually landed back at Manchester Airport where Eric was waiting to run me back to the club. He was as anxious as I to know how things had transpired in Padiham, because I had told him not to interfere, not wanting him to put any pressure on them whilst I was away. It wouldn't have helped matters at all. So it was a tense moment, when we both walked back into the club to get a true perspective of things. Tracey and Craig were waiting for us at the open bar, with drawn, worried faces. Both of them were expecting a severe bollocking. Assessing the bar stocks, I realised they were on their last legs, but Andrea had already informed me of the situation, so I was ready for that one.

"So, what's the damage to the premises?" I reluctantly enquired.

"None. No damage at all," was their nervous reply. What a sheer relief those words were to me.

"What about the punters. Have they all disappeared in my absence?"

"You must be joking," Tracey replied. "You've gained loads o' respect round here, let me tell you. They've seriously missed you. Most of them have been genuinely concerned, not only about you but for your mother also, would you believe. Honestly, I mean that. They've been really helpful to us. No trouble at all."

"Possibly my away trip has done me a world of good around here, after all" I thought to myself. "Things seem to be right. Apart from the stock, and I assume, the float. But that was to be expected."

Eric pulled me to one side for a quiet whisper in my ear. He was never diplomatic, but I did sense he was trying a little harder this time. "Well Haydn, what do you think the damage is.?"

"Without looking into the till, about £500. Cheap at the price, to get my club back in one piece. I'm not upset with the outcome. In fact I'm rather pleased."

On turning I noticed a couple of blokes ear-wigging at the bar, but after glancing at them they scattered out of the place. I turned back to Tracey and Craig who were still expecting a bollocking, instead, grabbing them both together and throwing my arms around them, I gave them a big hug, thanking them profusely for holding the club together in my absence.

"Don't worry about things. Well all said and done, you're not what I'd class as the best business oriented couple in the world, are you? But you've done alright in my eyes. Good one!"

"Your not mad with us?" Tracey asked.

"No way." I laughed "I'll tell you what" I shouted as I began moving my luggage upstairs, "give me half an hour to unpack, and I'll take you both down to the White Horse for a meal, in gratitude for your services rendered. Alright?" That put a smile onto both of their faces.

So off we all trundled down to the White Horse, with the exception of Eric, who had left for Halifax a while before. We sat down, ordering a meal each, and casually looked around the place, just to check if there was anyone around I knew.

Tracey turned to me, "Do you get that feeling that everyone in here is looking and whispering about us this dinnertime?"

"It'll be me they're looking at." I replied. "I've just got back into town, haven't I" and we left it at that. I needed a piss, so I made my way to the gents.

I was propping up the piss stone, when the guy next to me commented, "Tell me something Haydn?"

"Go on," I answered, instinctively knowing a load of crap was about to come my way at any second.

"Why are you so friendly with that Tracey and her boyfriend. I don't know if you've realised it yet, but it's common knowledge round town, that she's just ripped you off for five grand, while you've been away," he commented sarcastically. He had been drinking heavily, which attributed for his tongue being looser than normal.

I turned to him. "So it's common knowledge is it around here." I sneered. "Then I don't need to explain anything to you, do I?" walking out disgusted with his snide comments. Sitting back down, I scanned the place a further time, only to discover that the two earwiggers from the club were now sitting directly across the room talking to a group of people there.

Ernie's words, when I first met him, came flowing back to me, regarding certain people in this town, who thrive on gossip. And now, as he had stated, it was my turn to get some shit thrown at me……. or was I?

The two earwiggers had heard a figure of £500 quoted, whilst propping my bar up, and had shot down to The White Horse for the sole purpose of spreading the word. Within the space of an hour, that £500 had increased to £5000. All I could think was. "I'm glad we didn't leave it until teatime, God knows what the figure would have been."

I turned to Tracey. I thought it best to put her in the picture, but I wasn't too sure I'd made the correct decision when she instantly flared up, sending her plate flying across the table, which I just managed to catch, by the skin of my teeth, in mid air.

"What a save." I laughed as I put it back where it belonged. But Tracey didn't find it funny at all, jumping up, looking for an empty table to clamber onto, leaving Craig and me totally perplexed. We hadn't a clue what her next intentions were going to be.

Screaming loudly to catch everyone's attention, she eventually won through. "So! The main topic of conversation this dinnertime seems to be me, Haydn and Craig." She was snarling like a tiger. "What's up!" she screamed. "Have all you wankers lost your tongues, all of a sudden. Well, you don't mind if I join in do you? Lets deal with the...aaah....

me knocking Haydn and Craig off at the same time bit first. Well, my answer to you is Yes! Yes! Yes! I am knocking both of them off together, and it's great. You want to try it sometime. You might not have the time to talk about other people then. Get real for once in your lives dickheads." There was silence throughout the place. "And then there's the question of me ripping Haydn off for five grand behind his back. Right! Again nobody uttered a sound. "Well my answer to you is very simple. Get your facts straight, dickheads, before you start slandering people off, will you? It makes life a lot simpler for everybody. For fuck's sake get real!"

She then climbed down from the table, calmly strolled to her seat and continued eating her dinner as if nothing had happened. Not one person in the whole place murmured a single word.

I turned to Tracey laughing. "God, I've missed Padiham this last month. It's good to be back home again." We weren't really having threesomes together, but they were most likely thinking it anyway. She just threw it in to make her speech sound a little more colourful. She could be quite a drama queen at times.

"Oh, by the way Haydn," Tracey calmly commented, "we've been offered an house in Ingham Street, so if it's alright with you, we'll be leaving next week. But if you need a hand at any time, I'm always available."

"Fair do Tracey, and a happy new home. Nothing's going to change anyway. You'll both be in every night as usual. And my thanks to you both for guarding my club. Much appreciated," I replied.

It had been a very tiresome couple of days having travelled around thirty five hours non-stop, and I was exhausted and badly in need of some sleep. But I still had things to do. So, parting company with them, crossing the road to Ernie's, I told him what had gone on, and he calmly replied, "I'm not surprised Haydn, I told you before what they're like in this town. There's a certain few of them that are nowt but wankers, and they're never happy unless they're dragging someone down to their level. Anyway, I wish I'd been there to see their faces when Tracey laid into 'em."

"Yeah, you missed something there. She's a wild 'ne alright. Anyway Ernie, I've come across to ask you to spread the news around that I'm back, and thank them for backing Tracey up at the club. Invite them all tomorrow night for free drinks celebrating my home coming. Let's have a ding-dong together. But tell 'em to keep it under their hats Ernie, will you? I'm not paying for the whole town. Oh!.....and don't forget to come yourself," I jokingly added. (As if Ernie would forget.)

I left to pick up some stocks and get to bed urgently, rising early the next morning with a work agenda which I'd been thinking about on the plane journey home, that needed completing before 7.p.m. that same evening.

I was having trouble with the expensive karaoke equipment, which was far too accessible on stage. People kept switching it on and helping themselves without permission, and consequently karaoke discs were disappearing. If anyone asked to sing karaoke when Paul wasn't around and there was only one person behind the bar, doing two jobs, leaving the bar to sort out the entertainment left the bar vulnerable. So to avoid these problems I decided to alter the installation. I could easily move the control unit with an additional microphone to the open kitchen area behind the bar, out of the way of everyone. Now I could pull a pint, put a disc on, and personally introduce the singers, all at the same time, giving me much more control. I was really pleased with the results. A total success. Although Paul wasn't that impressed, because he initially thought he would have to do his thing from the open hatch in the kitchen area, instead of being on stage where he loved exhibiting himself. But when I told him that the new installation was just for during the week and he could swing it back to the stage when he was working, it eased the situation no end.

That evening, I strolled downstairs to run the bar, only to

be flabbergasted by the sight of a guy sat on a bar-stool, dressed up in monks regalia, sandals and all. His face was covered with a long hairy beard, the top of his head being shaven, with a big wooden cross hanging round his neck on thongs.

I just stood there aghast, staring at him. "Who the fuck are you?" I inquired. I thought hearing the sound of his voice would be a give-away. But he never spoke a word. He just sat there motionless.

One of the punters shouted across, "That's Rasputin, the mad monk."

"Oh, is he," I replied smiling.

I kept asking him questions, but every time, someone else would answer for him, he remaining as silent and still as a statue. I kept trying to weigh him up, but he had me beat. I hadn't a clue who he was, the disguise was so good, and I was beginning to feel uneasy, him staring at me continuously with his expressionless face. It went on for about an hour.

In the end I had to hold my hands up. "All right, you win, disclose yourself, and there's a double whiskey waiting for you!"

He turned and looked at me. His expressionless face, what I could see of it for hairs, suddenly changed to a smile. "Got you there Haydy, well good and proper, didn't I just." It was Ernie. I'd have never believed it.

I studied him thinking, "He must have spent hours preparing himself. He even has padding in his cheeks, to alter the contours of his face." There were no walking sticks around, and he was sitting upright and still, which definitely threw me off the scent. "He's lost his way in life. He should have been an actor."

"Too true you did Ernie.......... I would never have guessed it was you in a month of Sundays you mad twat," I threw at him. "Where did you get all that bloody hair from?"

"I gave Yog an haircut this morning, and you know my philosophy. 'Waste not, want not', so I had to find a use for it."

"Well Ernie you certainly did that," I replied. "I should have guessed Yog had some't to do with it. You definitely deserve the whiskey I've poured you, although your timing's bad, because I'd promised you free beer tonight anyway, didn't I?" He didn't reply to that one.

That same night, in his fancy dress, getting pissed out of his brains, and trying to climb onto the stage to sing karaoke, he collapsed, totally out of it, face down with his monk's habit over his head. It wasn't a pretty sight. He wasn't wearing any underpants, revealing his bare backside to all and sundry, which was sticking up in the air like a homing beacon. We tried to get him off stage but he was too heavy, so we hurriedly dragged him to one side leaving him there whilst the person already on stage finished his song.

And then somebody shouted, "He needs to look more respectable, don't you think?"……….. me thinking to cover him up. But no. Somebody went on stage and stuck a bunch of imitation daffodils up his arsehole. And the karaoke carried on as normal. What an eye-opener, but nobody seemed offended by the spectacle, so fair do's.

But the laugh was yet to come. He'd formed himself a beard, and eyebrows and also a sprinkling of hair on the back of both his hands using super glue, would you believe. Well when it came to the time to remove it, it was impossible. It just wouldn't come off, having to cut it down bit by bit, walking around for a week with it coming off in patches, looking like he'd contacted some weird disease. What a sight. Everybody was laughing and taking the piss out of him for days, the mad head. But it didn't bother Ernie though……..What a character.

It was not long after, that Ernie paid a visit to the club, after hours, bringing Nicola with him. I always kept open till midnight for the regulars only, being a standard practice throughout the pubs in town. It was very quiet that night, with only six of Ernie's crowd in, which included Ernie and Nicola. The doors were bolted as a precaution. Ernie and Nicola were playing pool together, and I felt totally committed to watching her. Her presence attracted me like a magnet. She was dressed to kill, being the picture of fitness, and it was the first time I'd ever paid any attention to her. She was a slim, large bosomed 25 year old, with a beautiful arse, that she displayed pronouncedly as she bent over the pool table to take a shot. Nicola, by all accounts, was a very outgoing person, and when the game was over they sat down with the other four.

I was alone behind the bar secretly observing her activities when she suddenly shouted across to me, "Get some decent music on, for fuck's sake." Not very ladylike I must admit, but that's how they all spoke in Padiham. She'd never spoken to me up to this outbreak which had shocked me a little to say the least, so to be polite, I made a calculated guess as to what would appeal to her and she began sexily dancing by herself on the stage. They were all cheering her, urging her to strip off, which she did without a second thought. She didn't take much persuading.

Eventually, down to her knickers and bra, flaunting herself all around the dance floor, she suddenly beckoned me to approach her to read the motif embroidered on the top of her briefs. I don't know why but I began to tremble from head to foot. No girl had ever affected me this way before, scaring the shit out of me, but I still felt compelled to approach her. She was seductively holding her briefs away from the front of her body, making it easier for me to read. I remember to this day. It read, "Brief Encounters." The moment I was in reach she made a grab at me, whisking me around the dance floor, whispering quietly in my ear, "This is your brief encounter with me for the night." It was all so overpowering. I felt really unsure of myself in her presence. In fact, I was speechless, but I definitely wouldn't have had it any other way. I liked the feel of her. In fact I was loving the moment. After half an hour of sheer madness, the night eventually reverted back to normal, the outcome being that Nicola and I became good friends.

Nicola

It was about this time, that Libby, Tracey's sister showed up in town, with some of her mates. It seemed, unbeknown to anyone, Tracey had two small children in Leeds, that some relation of hers were looking after. Up to press, she had been secretly visiting them on a regular basis, but now she had a house of her own, Tracey needed them with her permanently.

After bringing the children over, Libby fell in love with Padiham, or it could have been the guys, deciding to stop for a few weeks, to cause sheer havoc around town. She was a good looker, a slightly younger version of Tracey, but she was as mad as an hatter, always instigating parties everywhere in town at everyone's expense.

Hillis and Craig fell head over heels for the girls. Libby's crowd were from the big city and acted accordingly, (if you know what what I mean) manipulating in their eyes the country yokels.

One morning, having no spondulis for beer to gate crash one of their parties, Hillis and Craig frantically broke into my beer cellar for a few cans and bottles, whilst I was out shopping for supplies. On returning I noticed immediately, shooting down to see Ernie to enquire as to whether he'd heard anything on the grapevine. He said he hadn't. There was an unwritten law in Padiham not to grass, even on your worst enemy, that must be complied with at all times, so whether Ernie had heard any whispers or not, I wasn't quite sure. Ernie usually knew everything, but I wasn't going to push him, although I did notice a couple of empty bottles on his table, which just happened to be the same unusual Newcastle brand that I sold, so I asked him, "Who's been drinking these beers?"

At that moment, Tracey came stampeding in, demanding to know where Craig was. Ernie answered for both of us. "Hillis and Craig have both gone to a party down the road, with Libby's lot."

I grabbed Tracey by the arm. "Craig's just broken into my place and stole some beer."

"And Libby's shagging my boyfriend," was her reply.

"Then we'd better go down and sort it out. OK?

"You're doing nothing Haydn," was her reply. You leave it to me. I'm going down there and I'm going to smash them and that fucking house to bits. Trust me!"……..and off she stormed. She'd obviously caught him doing something close, because she did exactly what she threatened to do. What a state they were all in when she'd finished with them. She certainly wasn't one to mess about with, the mad cow.

Shortly after that incident she left Padiham, returning back to Leeds, never to set foot in Padiham again. She did ask me to look her up, which eventually happened, but that's another story. I have to admit, I really missed her She left a gaping hole in the energy surrounding me.

But life carried on.

To occupy my mind I had the idea of creating seven flats for rent, covering the general upstairs area, with the thought of eventually establishing a sizeable income. So I ordered a load of building materials, and in my spare time erected a few partitions.

"This will take months," I thought, "but I'll get it done eventually. I'll just plodded along in my own time. Downstairs was the area I had to concentrate on, and things were still happening around me. But not all bad. All the cons had stopped. There were a few fights, but even those were insignificant and easily handled. There was no more malicious damage to my cars. Things were improving fast. However there were still one or two existing problems.

Namely, certain people were pilfering bottles or cans from behind the bar when my back was turned, but in an honest sort of way. They used to admit to me how many they had got away with at the end of the night, and that it was my fault for letting them. It resembled a course on pilfering, that I had to pay to learn. And believe me, I eventually did learn to be that one step ahead of them at all times. There was no damage done. If they hadn't have taken a bottle, I'd have most likely treated them to one anyway.

The other problem was more serious. Unbeknown to me,

from the word go, people kept sneaking their own drinks in which was not to be tolerated at any cost. I tried to stop it, but at the end of each night, whilst cleaning up, there was still the alien cans and bottles appearing. So what should I do to combat this problem? I didn't want to ban anyone, as that was against my better nature, but I did spread it around that henceforth freebies would stop if the situation didn't alter. My little speech had amazing results. For a crowd that never grassed on anyone, they can't have classed this situation as being in that category, because they were all fast off the mark at playing the informant, with the intentions of being personally exonerated. It surprised me what the threat of no more freebies would do. Eventually it became an unwritten law, made by them, not to tolerate it either. Anyone attempting to do so, did it against the welfare of the club and were sorted out accordingly, by them not me. A total success on my part. I had to give myself a few stripes and a pat on the back over that one.

Now despite dealing with some tough people, I never had need to call in the police for assistance, and the police were aware of this. They didn't miss much at all. And although I didn't realise it at the time, this was going to change everything in the near future. So taking everything into account, I was definitely on the winning side.

One night, appearing from nowhere, Nicola emerged on the scene, bursting with energy just like her brother Yogurt, shouting "Get that karaoke set up immediately, you're singing with me!" Now this was a new experience for me. Over the past ten months, I've lost count of the amount of people who had tried to get me onto that stage. One night, three lads were dragging me by my legs, whilst I was anchoring myself to one of the bench seats. I could do most things, but singing in public was not one of them. However, on this occasion, I shouted back to her, 'O.K!' following her like a lamb to the slaughter onto the stage. I couldn't believe what I'd done, being so meek and mild. We sang, "Where Eagles Fly" a karaoke duo, and do you know, we received a standing ovation, sounding great, even to me. I didn't think I was capable of singing so well to an audience. I was bubbling so we picked another tune. This time, "That's What Friends Are For," another duo, and the same thing happened again. It was unreal. I thought, "I must be in love or something. This is definitely not me." But it was, and ever since that time I became totally hooked. They couldn't tear me off the bloody machine.

Now Yogurt had never sang in his life before. Amongst all his attributes, a good voice was not one of them, but he wanted to be in on the act. That was Yogurt. So I volunteered to give him a few singing lessons, (me would you believe), when we were alone together in the place, and sorted out a few songs within his limited range which sounded half right to me. One was, "New York, New York," and another was "Moon River," waiting for one Saturday night when the atmosphere felt right for him to pluck up some courage and try it out. Nobody had a clue he'd been practising. He strolled onto the stage, having a quiet word with Paul, whilst arranging the microphone. Everybody stopped in their tracks, staring at him. He was a well-known figure around town and this was an unusual sight. He'd never been known to sing before, so when he cracked up all their faces dropped in awe. He was trying his utmost and sounded professional. Yogurt's vibrant personality made up for all his small deficiencies, and the crowd loved him. An original sighting. And when he eventually finished, he too brought the house down, shouting their heads off for more. He was so pleased with himself that he never stopped prancing about all night. In his mind, he was thinking about me and Nicola, and how, through perseverance, he hadn't been left behind. That's how it was. That was Yog to a tee.

Paul DJ

It was Paul's 26th birthday, the following Saturday night and the place was full. He was doing his bit on stage. I'd been somewhere, and was just passing through the front side room from the outside. The buff's had left months ago because I hadn't the time to be running about for them like some servant. Andrea and Gale were on the bar. Nicola was hanging about with two of Andrea's friends. They spotted me leaving the room, and all rushed towards me, except for Gale who remained serving. Ushering me back into the front room, they locked the door behind them. I hadn't a clue what was happening. Without a single word spoken, they all pounced on me, pinning me onto the double bed that was situated there.

"Hey!" I screamed. "What's happening".

"Shut up and comply," grinned Andrea, starting to rip my clothes off.

"Blimey!" I thought, "They must be raping me. Who am I to complain...........Carry on." They started taking their knickers, bras and skirts off in front of me. I was sweating slightly at this stage. All I could think was, "What the hell is happening? This is not normal?"

Then, still holding me down, they began dressing me up in all their discarded clothing. I don't remember if I was relieved, disappointed or totally confused, but I think the latter applied. Placing a wig on my head they performed a full makeup job on me, not completed until they were all satisfied with the results. Then Andrea disappeared, locking the door behind her. Still nobody was giving anything away, leaving me totally in the dark. Finally, Andrea returned, giving me specific instructions. "Right Haydn, in about one minute, the lights are going down, and you have to head for the stage. I'll be there introducing you. There will be a spot light on me which will fade away the instant you get close. Get up there and give Paul a passionate kiss……..You're his kissagram tonight."

I looked at her startled. "I can't do that Andrea!"

"You've no choice. When I get to the stage they're going to throw you out into the packed concert room," and as she left, I was pushed out also.

"The twats," I muttered. I didn't know what to do. At first I thought of doing a runner out the front door, but that would be worse than complying. I was so nervous. Yogurt was stood in front of me with his back to me. I don't know why I did it, but I run straight to him tapping him on the shoulder, maybe for reassurance, I don't know. As he turned I put my arms around his neck, just as the lights were going down but not before he'd seen me.

Startled, he threw me off him, shouting, "Get away you ugly bitch!" which didn't help my self-esteem a lot, I can tell you. Then the spotlight went on Andrea as she began introducing me. So I had no option but to make my way to the stage. What else could I do? What a predicament to be in. As I was approaching, the stage spotlight faded into darkness. Jumping onto the stage I immediately grabbed hold of Paul before he had a chance to think and started passionately kissing him. He could only see my outline, and joined in fervently kissing me back, bemused and stunned. A few seconds passed and then suddenly all the lights came back on again. Well, he nearly had an heart attack! Taking one quick look at me, he threw me off screaming, dashing off the stage about a hundred miles an hour. I pissed myself laughing, his reaction was so funny. At first, nobody in the audience had a clue who I was, the last person they'd suspect, until Andrea stepped back onto the stage, carrying my neatly folded clothes and placing them on a buffet behind me, reaching for the microphone to introduce me as their landlord.

"Thank fuck that's over!" I thought as sweat trickled down my brow. Or was it? As everybody clapped and laughed, seeing the funny side to it all, and I was relaxing again, she walked to the D.J. Console and the music started. I didn't need telling what she'd put on. Only "The Full Monty," the stripper song.

"Go for it Haydn!" she shouted as she disappeared as fast as she could off stage out of my way.

"You fucking bitch!" I shouted back. But I had no option but to humour them all before the music ended. I clumsily tried to portray a sexy female dancer moving round the stage, whilst throwing clothes off in all directions and must have looked a real pillock. I was trying to smile, but kept cursing her, under my breath. The audience loved it though, thank God, because I wasn't, I can tell you. I got to the knickers and thought, "Fuck it, I might as well do the Full Monty, considering I've come this far." So, turning my back to the audience, I whipped them off, hiding my bits and pieces with them, and turned back to face them. I received a good response, which was the only thing that really mattered, so fair do's, but I had the last laugh. One of the girls was not wearing her knickers, because I had them in my hand, so, after first slipping my trousers on, I put them on the end of a pool cue, displaying them to all and sundry, asking the person who was not wearing her knickers to own up. I kept rapping over the microphone, "Would the real slim, shady bitch who owns these knickers, please stand up. Please stand up" (Emenem, with a difference.) Eventually, red faced and bare arsed, Andrea came running onto the stage and snatched them away, amusing the punters no end.

I laughed haughtily, "You embarrass me, I'll embarrass you, you bitch!" In fun of course. But weighing everything up, it was all executed rather well, because if they hadn't have done it the way they did, it would have never got done, not by me anyway. So fair does to them all.

Time was passing quickly, and I hadn't realised I'd been at the club for a year. I'd had more laughs in that year than in all the twenty years prior. What a place I'd accidentally discovered. It was brilliant, and I just hoped the fun would continue for ever. Tuesday afternoon arrived and Nicola rolled in for an hour, her visits becoming more frequent now. She was living next door to her boyfriend Stephen in Gannow Lane, and not getting on with him very well. She'd acquired a house in Russell Terrace, but needed her furniture moving. So I eagerly jumped in to volunteer, like you do. I hired a box van, loading it with all her belongings, as arranged. As we were leaving, she commented. "Oh Haydn, I threw Stephen's clothes into the back garden a couple of days ago. He won't be coming back for them. Take them, if you want. There might be something amongst them that suits you." They were in a couple of suitcases, so I threw them into the van with the rest of the furniture, and took off to Russell Terrace to unload, not thinking anymore about them. We were now approaching the Christmas period and we both had lots to do to organise ourselves, so after unloading, she promised to call into the club without fail at the stroke of midnight New Year's Eve. Christmas passed and the special evening arrived, the place being packed as usual as midnight approached rapidly. There was no sign of Nicola. I'd left the upstairs fire escape doors open, for chance nobody heard her at the front due to the noise. Big Ben chimed and still there was no Nicola. Another hour passed and she still hadn't arrived. I was so disappointed because I was really looking forward to seeing her again. I'd missed her over Christmas........I really had. I was just about to give her up when I heard fast moving footsteps above me. Continuing to listen, I heard them descending the steps to the locked staircase door, opposite me. Someone started thumping on the door, whilst Kenny went running across to open it, and out rolled Nicola, half pissed. She instantly spotted me eyeing her from the end of the bar, and came running across, apologising for being late, whilst throwing her arms around me to drown me with one passionate kiss.

From out of nowhere, a guy jumped up at the end of the concert room, and ran across to grab her whilst screeching at me at the same time, "What the fuck are you playing about at with my woman!" and immediately dragged her out of the club. Gone! She'd only been in about one minute.

"He must have been lurking around, waiting for her to show up for hours," I thought to myself. "That was short and sweet. They obviously must have got back together again since I last saw her. Just my luck." The next evening, because I had no clean clothes to wear, I was going through the garments that Nicola had given me, selecting a full rig-out of designer gear for the night. I felt well and people commented on how smart I looked. The uneventful evening passed by, until I was serving aftertime that was, when someone started banging on the front door. I asked Alan to open it, whilst I was finishing pouring a pint, and in runs Nicola.

"Lock the doors behind me, and don't let anyone in!" she shouted.

"What happened to you last night?" I enquired.

"Did a runner from him, and was keeping a low profile, till I thought he'd pissed off. I didn't think he'd be waiting for me in the club. He caught me right on the hop, didn't he just?"

"And what's happening tonight?"

I've done another runner. If anybody knocks, leave it be, for fuck's sake" she answered, gliding to the table where John and his girlfriend Julie were seated, just right of the bar. Within a few minutes, someone started banging again on the front door. I was pulling a round of drinks at the time as Alan jumped up to open it. I had my hands full, so I shouted, "Don't open it Alan, leave it!"

"I can handle it," he replied, totally ignoring my instructions, and pulled the bolts down. Well, the doors flew open, knocking Alan backwards to the floor, and Stephen came running in, like a bull elephant, virtually trampling him into the ground. This was becoming a habit.

"Thank fuck I don't employ Alan as my bodyguard," I thought, "I'd be dead within the hour."

Stephen ran straight to where Nicola was sitting, shouting at her, "What are you doing drinking with this low life for?"

I immediately butted in, "Who the fuck are you calling low life, they're my punters you're talking about, dick!"

Interrupting his verbal attack on Nicola, he shot across to me shouting, "And who the fuck are you talking to?" staring me full in the face. Suddenly his face dropped in shock. "They're my clothes you're wearing, ya prat!" he shouted, immediately starting to climb over the bar pumps to get at me. At this precise moment his brother-in-law bounded in through the open doors, pulling him back to the ground being a stronger man than Stephen fortunately. Whilst apologising to us all, he managed with a scuffle to drag him back outside. Forthwith, I ran to the door, slamming the bolts in place again.

"That was a bit too close for comfort." I thought to myself. "Better get these clothes off fast, and thank you Nicola for nearly getting me killed."

All Nicola said was, "He just won't accept that I've finished with him, but he's going to have to sooner or later."

I never saw Stephen again after that incident, so he must have taken the hint. There were no repercussions regarding the clothes, but the night wasn't over yet. Nicola stopped for quite a while, which was just long enough to witness the next state of affairs.

Once again there was a banging on the door. I cautiously peered through the letter box, this time to find it was only Marilyn standing there. She was a pleasant lady, about forty five years old, who'd had a rough life due to her husband always knocking her around. Rumour had it she used to be the prettiest girl in town, but she looked far from it now, poor lass. I was told by half the town that years ago she held up one of the Padiham banks with a banana, would you believe, and got away with around five grand. The police arrested her within the hour, and the money was returned immediately. They knew who they were looking for because she never bothered disguising herself. I never did get to the bottom of that story.

Now there was an order against her husband seeing her at the time, which was the reason she was living at a women's hostel in Burnley. But being bored and missing Padiham, she had approached me and asked if she could come to the club aftertimes for a drink in secret. She didn't want her husband to find out she was there. I agreed. She was no trouble at all usually, but tonight was different. I let her in, and supplied her with a drink. She knew everybody there so there were no problems, or so I thought. Somebody left, and as the doors were opened her husband charged in. She must have been bubbled that night because she had been coming for weeks.

I thought, "Not another one in the same night, surely." He sat down in front of her, making friendly, rather personal conversation, so my customers discreetly moved away, so they could speak in private to one another. Half an hour passed, and then suddenly he flared up, punching her continuously in the face, spraying blood all over the wall behind her. She just sat there motionless, letting it all happen. But it wasn't going to occur in front of me, so I promptly jumped in to stop it, pulling him off her. A tussling match began around the dance floor, ending up with me finally thumping him to quieten him down. There was no love lost between us. Astonishingly, the moment I hit him, Marilyn bounced up, giving me abuse, would you believe, for hitting her husband.

Heading for the bar to a line of empty glasses, she started grabbing them one by one, and launching them at me. I was ducking and diving everywhere.

"Don't you hit my husband!" she shouted, continuously throwing empty glasses at me. So, after a minute's dodging about the place, I was so relieved when grabbing his arm, she hurriedly dragged him out outside in a real huff. I thought I was protecting her, but it seemed to me she enjoyed being beaten, I didn't know. I turned to Nicola, John and Julie, silently shrugging with a puzzled expression on my face. They just laughed at me. But I did learn one thing that night, and that was to never poke my nose into anyone else's personal business again. I heard later that her husband, a total piss artist, had fallen asleep in-between the rear wheels of an articulator down Padiham centre, on his way home, which had set off without knowing he was there and virtually flattened him. The wagon didn't kill him, but it did cause him some damage, which definitely slowed him down, so he couldn't do much Marilyn bashing after that.

When it came to knowing about people, I never stopped learning.

That same night, Julie asked me to set up a birthday spread for John. She'd help me, but she specified that nobody must have an inkling about it, except the two of us. She wanted to give him the surprise of his life. It was on the 7th of February.

The special day came and she and I spent all morning, setting the buffet, and all the *Happy Birthday, John* streamers up. We'd barely finished when Nicola ambled in absorbing the scene around her. The expression on her face changed abruptly, not being very amused at all.

"What's up Nicola?" I enquired.

"Do you know whose birthday it is today?" she asked me.

"What do you mean? Of course I do. It's John's obviously," I replied.

"It's mine also," she bitterly commented. "So where's my birthday party?"

I just looked at her. "I didn't know. How was I to know, I'm not a mind reader?"

I went across to give her a big kiss, and after a nice cuddle I wished her Happy Birthday and promised to take her to "The Cellar Bar Restaurant" that evening, to personally celebrate her birthday. She accepted. The second she left, I had to rush to the restaurant, hoping to catch somebody of authority to sort me out with an impressive spread at such short notice. Fortunately I knew the manager well, due to the fact that over the last few weeks Hetty Wainthrop's film crew had been around, and either my place or "The Cellar Bar," not both, were going to be offered a contract to film some of the scenes there. The film crew had already been in, panning out, and measuring the camera positions, whatever, and unfortunately for me "The Cellar Bar" won. So naturally they owed me a favour, and giving them their due, they kept to their word by really looking after me.

We were booked for 9 p.m. that night, so I went round to Nicola's place to inform her of the arrangements. She was to meet me at the club, no later than 7 p.m. for a few drinks, turning up sober. Then I went and bought her the largest birthday card I could find, delivering it personally to "The Cellar Bar."

Watch out Hetty's about

THE Burnley area looks certain to again feature in the next series of the BBC hit "Hetty Wainthropp Investigates" - when filming starts in April.

"Location searching will begin soon — and it is almost certain that some of the stories will need the beautiful scenery and impressive features of your part of the world," said a programme spokesman this week.

Despite its Northern tag, the series starring Patricia Routledge is made by a team based in London.

Sabden was the location for one early story and Padiham, Burnley, Newton, Slaidburn and Clitheroe are among other places which have hosted the star, supporting actors and camera crews.

Darwen is the main base for the townscapes used in the programme, but scenes have been shot over a wide area, including the Ribble Valley and Burnley.

"We are always very grateful for the helpfulness and friendliness of everyone we encounter during filming," said the spokesman.

"Where we can use local people, we do."

In a few weeks the BBC's advance team is likely to be approaching owners of any property it wants to feature.

Everything was set in place, and I needed to successfully pull this one off, because over the last couple of weeks, I had been approached by quite a few girls in the club, warning me to be wary of Nicola.

"She'll suck you in, and spit you out, in a breath." they commented. "She's done it so many times, with so many men."

This began to piss me off a little listening to them, when one night Nicola showed her face with some bloke, and I shouted across to her, something to the effect of what I'd been informed, which didn't go down well at all. But then again, my words didn't come out quite like I had wanted them to, (That's what you get for drinking). I immediately regretted opening my mouth. She came charging across at me, like a streak of lightning, jumping in the air as she approached me. One arm was bent backwards. Fists clenched. She was going to knock my head off. I'll never forget the angry, hurtful expression on her face as I just stood there, motionless, not even trying to protect myself, waiting with clenched teeth for the impact. I deserved it. Her fist must have reached within an inch of my cheek bone, when it stopped dead.

Looking at me straight in the eyes she commented, "I don't deserve that sort of talk Haydn," turning and walking away again. She made me feel so low, I could have slid underneath a stone, vowing to myself at the time that nothing like this would ever happen again. For one second in time I had slipped, and it had to be over a woman I had many feelings for. Yes she was dangerous, one wild bitch, but that's the way I liked them, not being able to tolerate boring people. Anyway I was not planning for her to be my girlfriend, establishing myself on her rejected list with the others, but I did realise she could cast spells on me, so I had to assert much self control in the future if I was to get on with her. I needed her as a true soul compadre. That's what I wanted, and I would have to keep my head together in her company, better than I did that night, to achieve such a status. Her and her brother were definitely good company, and worth fighting for.

Anyway, given a second chance, Nicola turned up on time for her birthday do, looking like a million dollars, and sober. We had a few drinks together, making our way to "The Cellar Bar," where they'd made a beautiful job of it, on the house. They really must have had a guilty conscience about the contract they'd won from me. Birthday cake, gorgeous food, candles, violinists serenading us, the lot. The service being second to none. Even the best wine, that went down very well. Quite a night, especially at such short a notice. I was chuffed, not only for myself but also for Nicola, who I could see was highly delighted. This was the first time I had taken her out and it was a total success. Good one. We returned to the club for a few hours, sang a few songs together and then she ordered a taxi home. But we came to a solid agreement to go out together every Friday on my night off, to somewhere completely different, just for the laugh. So everything worked out fine that night, and I couldn't wait for the outcome of further events together.

Chapter 5. Fun and laughter

The next three monthly period was something else altogether, with Nicola and I hitting the Yorkshire and Lancashire scene big style. In fact, big style was not the word for it. It could only be described as a mind-boggling experience starting off at a very respectable, well established karaoke club going by the title of "Upstairs, Downstairs," in Leeds, close to where I used to live so long ago. It was a massive establishment with all the up to date stage equipment, such as spotlights, faders, footlights, colour changers, steam generators and fancy curtains which opened for each singer independently, being personally introduced before starting their vocal, where only the best singers dared to venture. Except for us, that was. The crowd didn't know what had hit them when we arrived. We'd arranged to meet up with Tracey and all her friends just as I promised her I would some while before, all feeling like superstars entertaining audiences of around five hundred people.

The second we initially walked into the place Nicola was determined to assert control, turning to me and commenting, "We're going to show this Leeds crowd what Padiham's made of, you watch me." I think she was retaliating against the way Libby's crowd had tried to handle Padiham when they'd stopped for that hectic fortnight. And she did just that, their heads were spinning before she decided to ease off. The laughs we had together were beyond comprehension. Tracey and Nicola were as mad as each other……..what a team. And as a bonus, the management weren't offended, seeming to take it all in fun, thank God. Well we weren't kicked out, or given instructions not to turn up again, so they must have found us amusing to some degree. What a brilliant time we all had.

Originally arranging to stop at Tracey's friends for the

nights when visiting Leeds being so far from home, at the last minute we decided to attempt to travel back to Padiham for last aftertime orders at the club. This suited me fine, because it meant I was in control of the money and security at the close of every late shift, concluding the night with another three or four drinks together when everybody had departed, before ringing for a taxi for her home.

It was not only Leeds we visited. We did a full round of Halifax, which was a little easier to return from, some Fridays spending the whole afternoon and night there drinking. We always started off at a small Irish pub, owned by Eric called "The Orange Tree," a real cosy, quiet place, well until we arrived, that is. Within a couple of hours of our first visit, Nicola had persuaded everyone, some being in their fifties, to dance with her to the jukebox, on top of the round, copper-plated tables.

They'd never experienced a girl quite like her before, asking me regularly, "Are they all like Nicola in Padiham? She's fucking possessed." She definitely made their day alright.

On one occasion we stumbled out of a pub, in the middle of the afternoon, espying a young man, guitar in hand, with his dog beside him. Both were sat on a blanket against one of the walls in the main precinct, whilst he was trying to sing for his supper. But consequently, not having a good voice he was not making very much at all. Nicola spotted the dog first and sat down beside it pampering it, immediately gesturing to me to sit down on the other side of the young man. After enticing him under her spell, she took an itinerary of what tunes he could play from the song sheets he possessed, and we all began singing together, creating a much better atmosphere, whilst he strummed his guitar. It sounded great, harmonising and all, and the money started rolling in as the watching crowd slowly increased in volume. Nicola made sure of that, by continuously jumping up and accosting anyone and everyone that were either listening or passing. Nobody escaped. Suddenly a girl showed up whom nobody was paying any attention to at all. She stopped in her tracks and doubled back, staring down at me.

"Haydn!" she shouted, "What the fuck are you playing about at, begging in the streets?" I looked up at her, half pissed, and focusing on her face whilst thinking about a thousand other things, I received such a shock. Well I don't know if it was a shock or a surprise. It was Amanda, my step-daughter who I had left behind in Halifax, to live in Padiham. She was the last person I thought I'd bump into, I hadn't seen her for yonks. Being a proud teenager, who didn't like being shown up in any shape or form, which was how I had brought her up to be, she really thought things weren't working out for me, and I was genuinely begging. I jumped up and introduced her to Nicola, trying to explain the situation to her, which took a while to sink in, but I think we finally got through to her in the end.

Anyway when she eventually continued on her way down the road, she looked back smiling, "You set of mad twats! Just don't forget to keep in touch Haydn will you, it's been too long?" Eventually handing all the lovely money over to the budding musician, we headed for the next place. He was well excited.

Another time, hitting the main centre of Halifax, I think it was the Yates Wine Lodge, the place being packed to capacity, the first thing Nicola did without even asking, was to book me and her in separately for a song. Not knowing my name was on the list, when they called me up to sing, I hadn't a clue what song she'd booked me in for. Jumping onto the stage, the DJ handed me the microphone and the music began, not giving me a chance to speak as Robby Williams "Angels" cracked up.

You might say, "So?" Well, that number had only been out a week or so, and I hadn't a clue how to sing it. Fighting through the first few lines, Nicola immediately knew I was in trouble and without hesitation, she jumped straight onto the stage to help me through it. Was I relieved? The audience never bothered though, I suppose they'd heard it all so many times before. We just had a giggle together. End of.

There were two other occasions, one at a pole-dancing club, where on strolling in she immediately shouted, "Clear the stage, I've arrived. I'll show you all how it's done!" and although they were very hesitant at first, it didn't take her long to persuade them to leave, and she was stripping and dancing before the manager could stop her, totally in control of the stage. He kept crying on my shoulder about having to have insurance to dance up there, of all things. If that was the only problem he had, there wasn't a problem.

The other instance was at the Coiner's Arms where she cleared a bird cage that was high in the air, having an elevated access gantry joining it, suspended over the main lounge with a dancer in it, to do her thing. I thought we'd get kicked out that time, but she managed to get away with it. The manager was quite amused in fact, offering Nicola a job when she eventually climbed down. She could get away with murder, and they'd still laugh at her. Whenever the crack was over she'd grab my arm and drag me outside.

"Come on Haydn" she mused, "Let's go and liven another place up," never hanging about for one second. And if anyone was fancying her, and tried to chat her up, she would tell them, "If you want to buy me a drink, you can, but Haydn's part of the deal, so you must buy him one as well." That really threw them off balance, but all the same, lots of them did actually buy me one.

She had a good heart, no matter what people said about her, and would flit around from table to table where old people were seated, chatting with them all in her own special way, having a natural born way of brightening their lives, nobody having spoken to them in such a manner for a very long time.

She used to work at Calderstones Hospital caring for the elderly and mentally handicapped, and I think a piece of them had rubbed off on her.

Nicola loved to dance. At first I shied away whenever a dance was mentioned but Nicola wasn't having that at all, dragging me onto the dance floor, whether I liked it or not, and giving me a few precise instructions on how to do the job.

"Come on Haydn, relax and let your hair down. Just pretend you're shagging me on the dance floor, and it will come to you automatically." Simple instructions, but it worked. My dancing ability increased ten fold.

There was one weekend in Burnley "The Blues Festival," when we arrived outside the Mechanic's Theatre. It was a full house and nobody else was allowed in, except for Nicola who immediately won the bouncers over, talking us both in as normal. The place was so chocker I could hardly breathe, taking half an hour to get a drink, but did that bother her, no way.

Turning to me, she shouted, "Keep a tight hold of your drink, and follow me Haydn!" as she headed for the elevated stage where a very high profile blues band, straight from America, were playing a classic number. Climbing the steps onto the private observation platform, just to the side of the stage on the same level where all the band's girlfriends were standing together drinking away from the main crowd, without a care in the world she began chatting to them in such a way that it felt we were meant to be up there. Within no time at all, the ladies persuaded someone in the audience to pass a small table and two buffets up to us, positioning them about eight foot away from the group, and invited us to sit down. Nicola and I were the last ones in, but there we were, sat on the stage with the performing group, whilst below us countless bodies were packed in like sardines. It's hard to envisage but it's true, that's exactly what happened. I couldn't go wrong, being with Nicola, that's how she affected people, being another one of those special times. But to top that, when the group had finished playing, having to pack up to move to their next venue, they invited Nicola and me to hop into their vehicles, and join them as their special guests. Needless to say, we accepted without even thinking. How good was that.

We both worshipped "The Blues." It was great music that

pierced the depths of our souls, both definitely being on the same wavelength.

We had a full day in Blackpool not long afterwards, and between us created total havoc. It started off normal, depending on what level you class normality, by visiting a quaint workingmen's club which was full of elderly people. She was in her element there, which proved to me as an observer that it was possible to have a good laugh at any level in life if you were in the right company. After which, hitting another few pubs, we eventually found a karaoke bar on the front close to the north pier. The DJ, wouldn't tolerate us, because we'd been drinking, which was a bit farcical considering they were licensed premises, in fact slightly hypocritical in my eyes. So we hung about until the DJ went for a piss, leaving the high stage unguarded, giving us both the opportunity to clamber onto it. She passed me the microphone whilst taking charge of the karaoke and video recording equipment, being excellent at that sort of thing, managing to set it up correctly in no time at all, whilst I kept everybody from climbing up onto the stage. We managed under sufferance, to sing and record one decent song each, before the management eventually waylaid us, kicking us out into the street. But we felt it was worth it, just to get one up on them.

"Serves them right, the twats. They got what was coming to them" laughed Nicola. "Did you see the look on the DJ's face. I was splitting my sides in there."

"Too right Nicola, we really wiped the smile off their faces that time, didn't we."

"Yeah, but we're not finished yet Haydn. We're going back to that club we started from…….OK!"

"Right Nicola, lead the way." and off we staggered back along the promenade, getting away with the videos, as a bonus.

On reaching our destination, I had to take my belt off and strap her to a lamp post, due to the fact that she kept falling on her face. I climbed the stairs only to find it was shut. I had a feeling it would be, time was knocking on.

"Good move tying her down there, she'd have broken her neck for nothing coming up here." I thought to myself.

Heading down to unbuckle her, I noticed many passers by were staring at her from all angles. I wondered why. But it didn't bother us. It was time to depart anyway, so homeward bound we headed, and another successful day was had by all.

Besides Leeds, Halifax and Burnley, we covered many other places, like the gay village that Dwarling had pointed out to us, situated around Canal Street, Manchester. We were part of the furniture there, and had a really good laugh with some of those gays. They certainly had a sense of humour.

And then there was always Padiham to fall back on, as a last resort. We got around alright and drank gallons of ale in the process. Those were the best three months of my life, and whatever confidence I had lost during my failed business venture now had now grown to astronomical levels, making me complete again for the first time in years, all due to my soul companion Nicola. I felt like the Devil's advocate, where I supplied Nicola the place and the means of her letting her hair down in return for her supplying me with my youth back again. It was as if I had returned back to the days when I was a professional guitarist in my Rock-n-Roll band, in Leeds, full of laughs, with places to go, and people to meet, the world at my feet. Nicola was definitely good for me, and highly promoted the club during our escapades, because wherever we were, she used to talk about it to everyone, and after experiencing an hour with Nicola, people were so intrigued with her that they couldn't help but investigate. Consequently many people turned up from far and wide on different occasions to share some time with us there.

One particular night, I heard a banging on the door, opening it to witness Jamane, a punter of mine, standing there.

"Alright Haydy" he grinned "I've brought a few people from Burnley with me. Nicola bumped into one or two of them the other night, and they wanted to come along. It's

OK if they come in in't it?" Without looking out I could see about eight people.

"Course it is," I replied, "you're all welcome".

He turned, cupping his hands around his mouth and shouted up the road, "It's OK you can all come in!" Curiously I poked my head out to see who he was talking to. WELL! I just couldn't believe what I was seeing. There must have been sixty people lining the street. As they all made their way in, Jamane pulled me to one side,

"I take it that's free drinks for me for the rest of the night?"

"You assume correct," I replied. "Keep the job rolling," and the beer started to flow to all and sundry. Another excellent night.

I didn't actually offer Nicola a job behind the bar, she just grew into it naturally, by being about and mucking around in general. I finished up paying her to work beside me, because it seemed the common sense thing to do, because if she wasn't working at the club, she was either drinking there or out with me. We made a formidable team. Any hint of trouble whatsoever, she was always first to get involved. Being able to handle men was her speciality, a definite advantage to me. I had no problems handling the women, so the job was a good'ne. Even the local police force knew her on a friendly basis, being a "special" there, once upon a time.

She still had occasional boyfriends, when they could find her that was, due to the fact that she was always with me, so they soon got pissed off with her, not bothering her in the least because none of them could understand or handle her, anyway. I felt very lucky and honoured to have her in my company. All I had to do was to keep my head, while everybody around me was losing theirs, and I'd be the man. Her friend (John Kipperling, with a difference).

It was time to develop other habits like, "Tequila night." So every Thursday we'd open a bottle of tequila. Whilst behind the bar together, we dabbed some salt into our mouths, downing a glass of Tequila in one almighty gulp, and then squeezed a lemon segment into it to quell the taste, leaving only enough time to pour another two drinks. This process was repeated continuously, until one of us couldn't possibly drink any more for fear of spewing up, putting us both in the right mood to get through the evening shift, as happy as Larry. We usually got through about half a litre of the stuff in the first five minutes, before having to give up, with the full crew watching from the other side of the bar, with their tongues hanging out in envy. If there was anything left, we used to share it out evenly between them. If not, then hard cheese.

Following that was the "Tom Cruise, Cocktail Hour" which meant that if anyone wanted a short, we had to pour it from the bottle that had completed a couple of back flips in the air, before catching it in the pouring position. (just like in the film.) At first we used to spill the liquor everywhere, so I had to fit special pouring caps onto the bottles to prevent liquor escaping whilst in flight. It was all rather technical, but it worked a treat. But Nicola and I had to practice for hours on end to get on top of those moves without calamities. She did well but I couldn't totally master it so I brought Yogurt in to replace me, him being a natural and looking more the part anyway. Customers came from everywhere to watch him and Nicola perform. They definitely mastered the art. Talk about juggling, circus performers had nothing on them. The punters were intrigued, hoping for a few breakages, but they usually disappointed them, turning a few heads in the process, keeping Yogurt happy by giving him the feeling of well-being as a team member. The competitiveness generated between Nicola and Yogurt was electrifying. But we had to let him join the Tequila club to keep him in a happy frame of mind and that was when he started occasionally helping me behind the bar. He loved it and felt that he'd found his purpose in life, being a lot happier now than he had ever been.

It was during the time that Nicola and I were on the rampage, that he had a slight confrontation with me. He felt as if he was getting pushed out and was becoming slightly jealous of Nicola for taking all the limelight, so he organised salmon poaching trips, every other week, to show me how good he was at it. At first, I was very apprehensive, knowing full well that it wasn't totally above board, not needing the embarrassment of getting locked up just yet. Things were going well for me and I didn't want to spoil it. But eventually he persuaded me to go along with his air-brained scheme, our first visit, being just Yogurt, Ernie and me. God knows where he was taking us.

We drove miles, finishing up in deep countryside, crossing open fields, finally parking at the side of a narrowish river behind a clump of bushes, so we couldn't be spotted by the estate river wardens. I felt very uneasy, but Yogurt was lapping it up. He was buzzing and raring to go.

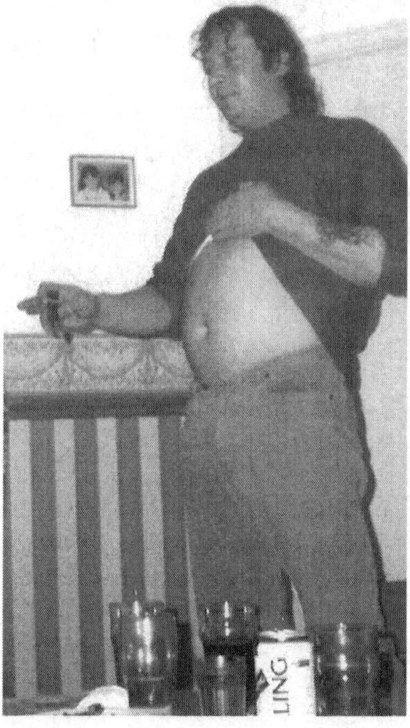

Yogurt

His father, Bob, had been a well known poacher throughout his life, being the master of the profession in Padiham, and Yog had followed in the family tradition. He was now the master. Tickling salmon was one thing he could do really well, although I was told much later that his brother Paul had caught the largest fish.

Ernie decided to stop in the car, having been there many times before, and was only out for the ride, but Yogurt was determined to involve me.

"You have to keep watch Haydn, there's cameras everywhere" Yogurt insisted. "We're alright here, but don't wander off past this stretch of the river or you'll get nobbled. Just hang around the bank and I'll show you how it's done." Without further ado he stripped off to his underpants. It was only a smallish river, about thirty foot wide and four foot deep in the deepest place. Testing the water it was freezing, not summer yet, but although it was pretty chilly out there, it didn't seem to affect Yogurt one little bit.

I thought, "Better you than me Yog."

He instructed me, "Now what I do is this. You see those overhanging rocks on the opposite bank?"

"Yes," I replied, intrigued.

"Well, I'll start at the far end, upstream, and slowly work downstream."

"And what do you do?" I enquired. I'd never experienced anything like this before.

"Well, first off, I'm gonna tell you what YOU do." I looked at him puzzled.

"You're going to keep your eyes open for the wardens. And I'm going in. What I'll do, is gently feel with both hands, under the submerged overhanging rocks. All the scared salmon shoot under them in lines, their heads facing the bank, to hide. They will not move if I gently touch them, having no place to go. So I'll carefully slide my hands up either side of their body till I reach their gills. And then the fight starts."

"What do you mean?"

"You'll see," he laughed. "Once I get a good hold of the

inside of their gills, I have to hang on for dear life."

It passed through my mind. "What sort of fish is he dealing with?" I'd pictured one about a foot long. Was I mistaken? He tiptoed, sort of, into the freezing water, which didn't seem to bother him, making his way to the rocks where he started groping under, being virtually underwater himself. He kept bobbing up for air and trying again in different places, shouting across to me, "Trust me, I'll find one soon. Don't you worry," bobbing under again. Suddenly the water came alive. That's the only way I can explain it. That whole area looked like it was erupting. I stepped back in shock. There was Yogurt rolling about in the water, with a monster fish, which must have been four foot long. He was trying his utmost to keep it pinned to his chest, whilst the fish was doing everything in its power to escape. Yogurt was hanging on for dear life, knowing he wouldn't have been able to hold his face up in public if he lost this one. So the fight went on.

I was astounded at what I was witnessing. "Crocodile Dundee" were the only words passing through my mind. "I thought we were out here fishing."

I nervously kept checking the banks for wardens whilst watching the struggle continue. It took quite a while before the fish eventually gave up the ghost, and out came Yogurt, proudly pulling his prey behind him. What a beautiful specimen he'd caught. With his bare hands. I couldn't believe it.

"That's how you catch fish," he boasted. "Fuck the fishing rod."

There was silence for a spell whilst he got his breath back. He was exhausted.

"Well, the river's knackered now, so we'd better blow fast, before someone spots us," he laughed, hitting the fish on the head with a stone, and then loading it into the boot. Grabbing his clothes he jumped into the back of the car. "Do one, fast," he rapped, whilst we're on the winning side," and away we sped.

"Did you see that Ernie?" I enquired.

"Oh, I've seen him do it loads 'o times afore," he answered, "Impressive in't it."

"You're not kidding mate. Impressive is not the word."

Yogurt just sat there beaming. He was definitely the hero of the day, and he knew it. And he'd make a bit of money to boot, always having someone in the town ready to buy his catch, especially salmon.

There was another time I took him on a similar excursion under very similar circumstances but stood on the opposite bank watching him again, when suddenly he shot out from under the water, throwing a smaller fish into the air which came flying across the river, actually landing in my outstretched arms, flapping about furiously. I rushed to the car, dumping it on Ernie's lap for a joke, who was seriously restricted for movement in such a confined space, due to his legs. You'd better believe the ripe language he fired at me, whilst the fish was flapping about all over him.

But I'll never forget the day that Yogurt, Larry, Hillis and myself went on one of these poaching trips. Yogurt didn't catch anything that day, which was unusual, but maybe it was because Hillis was pissing about all afternoon. Anyway as we were driving over the moors on our way home, a herd of sheep appeared in front of us.

"Stop the car!" Hillis shouted, " I'm not going home with nothing. I'm going to get myself a sheep." Hillis always spelt trouble. I reluctantly pulled in, not being happy with the situation at all, smelling trouble a mile off. But not wanting to be the odd man out, I had no option but to go along with them, like it or not. They all rushed out of the car, half cut, attempting to chase the sheep in all directions. But the sheep were too nippy for them, so, much to my relief, they didn't catch any. Whilst this was happening, a four-wheel drive that was passing on the road, stopped for a second and then took off again. They all got back into the car disgusted with each other, passing Special Brew cans around as a consolation prize, which I was offered and fortunately refused because as we were leaving the moors, approaching the main road near

Clitheroe, we were confronted by a convoy of police cars, pulling me across to have words with me. They took one look at them all drinking, and escorted me to a police van for breathalising and questioning. Whilst the others searched my car, I was politely asked where I'd been and where I was heading for.

"We've been on The Padiham Sports and Social Club trip to Morecambe and we're on our way back home," I replied.

The breathaliser read negative, and there was nothing illegal inside the car, so reluctantly they had to let us go. They were sure they were going to have us for rustling. The guy in the four-wheel drive must have reported us. It was a close one and a warning to me, but it was a big giggle to the lads. Fortunately it worked out well for me in the end, because the story spread throughout the club, and everyone came to the opinion that I was alright and could be trusted. I was one of the lads now. Customers were starting to approach me with their personal troubles, wanting advice, or help, and I was beginning to find out everything that was happening in town. Things were looking up.

Yet another poaching trip was organised by Hillis. He just didn't want to be left out of the picture, but I pretended I was busy, giving him a wide birth. I definitely was not going with Hillis again. So they persuaded Paul, Yog's brother to run them instead, and do you know what? They all got arrested and heavily fined, just as I had expected. So that was the end of the salmon run for a while. There was the odd occasion when Yogurt would knock me up at five in the morning, in a restless state of mind, dragging me up to Pendle village to tickle some brown trout. We'd only get a slap on the wrist if we were caught up there. Nothing serious. I used to wade in the stream with him, actually catching one or two myself, slowly learning the art. But they were tiddlers compared to the salmon and sea trout, which Yogurt specialised in catching.

Yogurt, at scarce intervals, used to get so pissed off with himself for one reason or another that he had to get away, dragging me to the top of Pendle Hill for a session. We could see for miles in any direction. He used to love it up there feeling so close to nature, his whole being melting into the scenery, far removed from reality. We used to take a few cans with us and just sit there talking for hours on end until the sun went down. On one of these occasions, about the same period as him and Nicola's "Tom Cruise Cocktail" escapades, we both fell asleep on the moor. Dawn approached and the temperature dropped, the chill in the air waking me up. I was lying on my back, facing the sky. When I opened my eyes, eventually focusing on a ring of gorgonlike heads with horns looking down on me, whilst completely surrounding me. I thought I had woke up in hell. Honestly, what a terrifying sight. I jumped up in shock, only to find that I had been surrounded by a herd of nosey sheep. Was I relieved. When I woke Yog up and told him, he just couldn't stop laughing. It really touched his funny spot. Every time we went up there together, we'd come off that mountain new, refreshed people, ready to face another day.

In general, things were going well, but there was always the unexpected, that I could have done without. This time it was Nicola's father, Bob, who'd got it all wrong, but didn't think so. He blamed me for the amount of alcohol Nicola was drinking, and that I was too old for her, and was definitely a bad influence on her. I couldn't believe what he was saying, but I'd heard it all before from different people in my past, and I suppose I would hear it many times again in the future. I was determined to fight life to the bitter end and the only thing that was certain was that I was not getting any younger. I tried to explain but he was having none of it. It was Nicola, that was leading me astray, and I was enjoying it thoroughly. Nicola and Yogurt remained Nicola and Yogurt. It was me who was becoming a new person. Bob's intentions were honourable. He loved his daughter and wanted to look after her at all times, but he had definitely got it wrong. He forbade us to see each other, and threatened that if he ever spotted us together he'd have me. But we weren't going anywhere. The club was my home, and her life at that moment in time also, so what could any of us do about it. We just carried on as normal, as if nothing had been said. Bob never came into the club so we were pretty safe there. He couldn't stop her working, surely. But outside in Padiham, for a while, we had to be careful not to be seen together. He was a builder in the town, and was everywhere. It was like the secret service. If we needed to meet each other, we'd select a designated place, but on one occasion somebody must have bubbled us.

Nicola was on the main road, six large trees up from me, outside Gawthorpe Hall Estate, and I was walking towards her, maybe a hundred yards apart.

Bob was driving up the main road, on my side, in his car. He spotted me and slammed on the brakes, skidding to a halt. Abandoning his car on the main thoroughfare, he made a mad dash for me, seizing me by the throat and pinning me against a tree. Traffic was piling up on the main road, all papping at his abandoned car. Nicola, seeing everything, ran for cover behind a large tree close by, cautiously peeping out watching.

"I've been told you're still seeing my daughter. I've warned you once, I won't be warning you again. End of, next time, Haydn. Just take heed will you. It could get very messy."

I never spoke. He put me down. Jumped into his car and sped off up the road, passing Nicola who was still hiding.

When he'd disappeared, she came running up to me. "What the fuck happened there?"

"Oh, nothing. Your dad's on one, that's all."

Bob was going about it all wrong. I wouldn't allow myself ever to buckle down to anybody's threats. It was against my principles, and I had to live up to them in this town, otherwise everything would have been for nothing. I was in a bit of a predicament. I couldn't fight back. It was Nicola's father. I just had to take whatever he gave me and laugh whilst he was doing it.

"We'll have to be a little more careful for a few days

Haydn," she remarked. "I'll keep away from the club for a short while. Meet me on the derelict railway lines tomorrow morning at ten. You know, on the stone bridge above me. Nobody will see us there." I agreed and left fast.

The next morning we met as arranged. I took a drink up for us both, and we chatted for about an hour, then decided to go our separate ways. She went down one side of the embankment, and I went down the other. I had to pass under the bridge to head in the correct direction. As I reached the other side thinking she'd be well away by then, I spotted her father pointing the gable end of a house close by, who had collared Nicola. I was walking straight for him with two empty glasses in my hand. On seeing me, he cottoned on immediately. Making a hasty U-turn, I scurried away back under the bridge like a hunted rabbit retreating to its warren.

Although the incident put me on edge for the rest of the day, the afternoon passed uneventfully, until I was serving behind the bar around tea time and Yogurt came rushing in. He came straight behind the bar taking an order, without acknowledging me whatsoever and I knew something was wrong just by the way he was acting.

Eventually turning to me, he shouted, "You're in trouble Haydn."

"What do you mean Yog?"

"They're coming down for you."

"Who?" I enquired, as if I didn't know.

"My dad and Paul." Paul was Yog's elder brother, not a man to reckon with, who didn't normally frequent the club, except when he was selling meat on a Saturday, after working at the local slaughter house. " Take off Haydn, now, and I'll take over."

"I'm going nowhere Yog, but you'd better make yourself scarce. It's your family so don't get involved."

"I'm going nowhere, Haydn. If it comes to it we'll go down together, heah, so don't argue." I looked at him respectfully, thinking what a good companion I had next to me. So nothing more was said. We just hung about waiting for the crunch, occasionally glancing at each other from time to time, both being very tensed up. But nothing happened. Nobody came. I was reprieved yet again. Even so, Yog had gone well up the ladder in my estimation.

However, the next day, as I sat on the stone steps outside the front side door, who should be coming down the street but Paul. He spotted me in a breath, heading straight for me. Crouching in front of me, an evil smile appeared the full width of his face.

"I know that look. Here we go. Expect trouble," I thought. "Be ready for him."

He didn't mince his words. He just let go with a powerful flying punch to my face, with his left hand. I instinctively lifted my right arm up level with it, and by some miracle, deflected the blow, resulting in him hitting the stone wall to the right side of my head with such a force, that it made me cringe. Saying nothing, not displaying any pain whatsoever, he just rose to his feet and walked off. Later, I was told he'd gone to Ernie's to be bandaged up due to the fact that he had broken his knuckles on the wall (Better than my face).

"That fucking old bastard up there's as fast as lightning, the old cunt," he'd said to Ernie, "I'm not trying 'owt on him again in a hurry."

When Ernie eventually told me, it made me feel, "Oh so good!"

It might have been his brother, but Yog was chuffed to death as well, when he heard what had happened.

I never did have trouble from any of them again and they gave Nicola up as a bad job also, so she started coming in again as normal. And it was because of all this that I began to get a reputation for being tough, would you credit. It must have gone to my head because not long after, a bloke called Meci, who was normally OK but on this particular night started throwing buffets about and knocking tables over in the club. But he was pushing his luck too far when he picked up a further buffet, heading for the karaoke monitor, with the intention of smashing it to pieces. Yogurt was propping up the end of the bar whilst I was keeping ahead of the pathetic situation. I could see exactly what was going to happen, and shooting out onto the dance floor, I launched myself into the air toward him, landing on top of him, knocking him flat on his back, with my hands gripping his throat, giving him a severe punch to the face. The second that happened, over a dozen people jumped on top of me. Fortunately for me, my feet must have been sticking out from under the bottom of the pile, because Yog came running up, grabbing them and pulled me out from under them.

"You fucking mad twat!" he roared laughing at me. "What are you playing at?" The pile of blokes on the floor didn't even know I was missing, just carrying on punching blindly at each other. Luckily, when everything settled down there were no repercussions, all fading away gracefully.

I'd caught the side of my face on the buffet leg he was brandishing above his head when I dived at him, giving me a right pearler, which gave me something to brag about for the next couple of days. Even an ex-military policeman called Tony, who had frequented the club day and night since being retired from his lifetime duties to the army, complimented me on my fast reaction in a difficult situation.

He was another lost soul, who couldn't adjust to civilian life, not being able to come to terms with the mundane life he was living now. In his final year in the army, he'd been a bodyguard to the high and mighty, working under the Official Secrets Act, a sort of modern day 007, with a licence to kill if necessary, working alongside the SAS many times. He didn't normally share many conversations with anyone, but over the period I had known him, for some unknown reason, he had grown to trust and confide in me, and the stories he told me would rattle my brains.

He lived in a flat nearby, but didn't spend much time there. I think he was a very lonely man, which was the reason he was always the last person to leave my place. I felt very sympathetic towards him, having been there myself on occasions. It wasn't a nice place to be. Eventually he got around to asking me if he could get his head down on the bench seats at the end of the night, rather than going home, and in return he promised to help out around the bar, which I immediately agreed to. It was no skin of my nose. He was as trustworthy as they come, and as I was due for my annual visit to Australia very soon, it crossed my mind that he could keep his eye on the place in the background during my absence, seeing as how he'd handled that sort of shit all his life. I'd already discussed the matter with Andrea and Paul, and they'd agreed to look after it for me, knowing Andrea would not let me down, but I thought some of the punters might pick on Paul a little. But I concluded that if Tony was around to back him up, everything should be fine. Nicola was a bit upset that I didn't offer her the job, but I didn't think that was a good move at all, because if anything went wrong, it was on her head, and would affect our relationship. Anyway, I knew she couldn't run the whole business single handed without transport, not having a driving licence. Besides, there was a guy nicknamed 'Scarface' sniffing around her, who I didn't trust in my absence. I may have been wrong, I'll never know, but I did install a fax machine in the club, for her to keep in touch with me on a daily basis. So everything seemed to be sorted.

As it happened Hillis was determined to have a last go at me, before I left, walking into the club one night as stroppy as they come. He'd been drinking, and wobbling straight to the pool table, he slapped a twenty pound note on it, hard.

He turned to me shouting. "You're playing with me. End of! Get your money down on the table now!" That's how Hillis talked, in a series of orders. Noticing the glass of my special concoction in my hand, he commented, "And I'm drinking what you're drinking on the house……..Right! "

He was a cheeky rat, but that's how he was. He looked on me as a threat, forever determined to get one up on me, which I took as a compliment. He was a far better player than me, thinking he could wipe me clean, sort of rubbing my nose in it, but I could see he was pissed, and thought I stood a good chance of winning. So after placing twenty pounds on the table which Yog rounded up, acting as referee, I immediately mixed him a drink, comprised of half a pint Baileys, whiskey, vodka and Tia Maria. This he swallowed down in one gulp and we started playing. Half an hour into the game and I was holding my own but struggling badly, I have to admit. I went to the bar to mix myself another cocktail, being under severe pressure, only to witness Hillis cheekily following me, holding his empty glass out for another drink, which I courteously replenished. Just like before it went straight down the hatch, without touching the sides. Whilst following me back to continue our game, he suddenly stumbled, falling flat on his face in front of the bar, totally gone to the world, or so I thought. Asking Yog to prop him up on one of the bench seats, not looking right leaving him on the floor with everybody having to walk round him, we picked up his lifeless body. With closed eyes, he miraculously stretched out one of his arms and grabbed me by the bollocks, squeezing them aggressively. I was in agony, but even in the circumstances, we managed to get him on the bench seating, where I forced his grip free from me.

I thought, "The pillock. Even in an unconscious state, he's still attacking me." I turned to Yogurt. "Come on Yog, cough it up looks like I win."

From that night onwards Hillis was even more determined to get one over on me.

There had been a similar incident just a week before, when Nicola and I were playing Yogurt and Drabble at pool. Nicola and I didn't stand a chance. God knows how I managed to be involved with the game in the first place. There was money on the table, being half way through the game, when suddenly the police came strolling in. Drabble immediately made a beeline for the gents, but eventually returned to the table when he realised it was Yog they wanted, carting him away.

The police commented to me as they were leaving, "Its pretty good, is this place. When we want anybody, we automatically know where to find them," disappearing back to the van with Yogurt.

Drabble jumps in, "Hey, the game's not over yet mate. In this situation, I 'm entitled to play for both of us." So not wanting to lose the prize money, we continued to play again. We weren't much further into the game when the police reappeared again, this time waltzing Drabble off. They'd obviously spotted him, and checking, must have found a warrant against him, which unbelievably left me and Nicola as the winners. The second the police left, Nicola immediately insisted on someone's help to lift the pool table onto its side, which was a strange request, I thought. Feeling round all the pockets, she shrugged to herself and rushed into the gents toilet causing havoc.

"What is the matter with her?" I thought, not having a clue what was happening. The next I saw of her was her rushing out from the gents toilets frantically searching everywhere.

"He's hid it somewhere when the cops came in for sure, the crafty bastard," she muttered, " but I'll find it!"

"Find what?" I curiously asked.

"His gange. He always carries some on him".

She was right, but she never found it. I discovered later that he had dumped it in the guttering on his way out, so nobody acquired it.

Well, a fortnight passed and once again the time had come for me to leave for Australia. I was setting off early the following morning, having arranged for Paul to run me close to London and pick me up in a month's time, just in time for Walking day, whilst in-between times having the full use of my car. Nicola rolled in with Scarface to see me off, eventually disappearing with him, which was actually a good thing for me, but really upset me at the time. Unfortunately, I was beginning to slip again feeling I'd fallen in love with her, which was one road to disaster, believe me. So not wanting that to happen, I had to try to get in line fast, pulling myself together before I lost a soul mate for good. I wouldn't be seeing her for a month, which would help considerably, giving time to build my resistance up again. Women definitely can be a problem at times.

Paul ran me down to a Holiday Inn on the outskirts of north London, and leaving me there, returned home to run the club. I was flying the following afternoon from Heathrow, which gave me ample time, or so I thought, to get there. But the next morning, would you believe, there was an underground strike, everybody taking to the roads, which consequently brought London to a standstill. I asked a taxi driver if he could get me to the airport on time, being quite a distance.

He said, "Possibly, but it will cost you. I will have to use every back street in London to get there." I had to agree, and fortunately he did manage to drop me at Heathrow Airport within one hour of my flight. It was a close call, but I did see London in the process, costing me fifty pounds for the privilege, which wasn't a good start to the excursion at all.

But what a flight. I was plonked in the third section of a Boeing 747, when one of the three Asian hostesses who were looking after that section of the plane, approached me asking if I wanted a drink, ordering a coke because I had been drinking heavy the previous night and still had a hangover. The guy sitting next to me turned to introduce himself, explaining to me that he was a photographer for a bungy jumping crew in Dubai, and that he wasn't much of a drinker himself. He always took a large bottle of Jack Daniels with him, that would last him his six week stay, returning back to England again for his next break to buy another one.

He politely offered, "I've also got a bottle of coke in my bag, so would you fancy a few drinks with me. Just to be friendly, you understand. It's going to be a long journey?"

"A long journey for me." I thought, "Not that long a journey for you," but I agreed and he poured some Jack Daniels into my coke. Well the hours went by, and the Jack Daniels went down, and we became rather merry, becoming very friendly with the air hostesses looking after our section, not causing any trouble you understand apart from them warning us to hide the bottle, as it was against regulations. They were going along with us for the laugh and we were all doing fine together. They were from Royal Brunei, which was where I was supposed to be taking my stopover, so we had lots to talk about.

As the flight was within one hour of Dubai, I actually remember struggling to the front of the third section of the aircraft singing wartime songs to the passengers there, managing to get through a couple of numbers as I recall, before being escorted back to my seat. We had drank the full bottle, would you believe.

We landed in Dubai, and, shaking my hand, he told me it was the best flight he had ever experienced in his life, whilst trying to get up from his seat, mentioning there was someone waiting for him at the checkout. I wasn't allowed off the plane as I had another eight hours to do, but he was having trouble standing, and when he eventually managed to do so, he definitely couldn't walk unescorted. Feeling half right myself, or so I thought, I asked one of the hostesses, if they'd allow me off the plane to help him on his way. They had little choice but to agree, so as we exited the plane together. I asked them to keep a check on me, for chance I got lost. They were preparing to leave themselves, so I don't suppose it was out of their way to keep an eye on me in the process, so they kindly agreed to do just that. I had to dump him in a luggage trolley to make things easier for me. There was a guy in the distance trying to gain my attention, pointing to his mate, so I gave him his passport, and launched him through passport control while he was still slouching in the trolley, not being allowed to cross myself. Having managed to get rid of him, I returned to the international lounge, plonking myself in front of one of the monitors to try to recall what gate I had just come from. And that's the last I remember

I woke up in a hotel room that looked as if a bomb had hit it, clothes and belongings thrown everywhere. There was a woman naked in the shower, and I vaguely recall someone had just left the room. I struggled to the balcony to try to establish my whereabouts in total confusion. All that registered were lots of Arabs strolling around.

"This definitely is not Australia," I thought. "Where the fuck am I?"

Just then somebody entered the room. It was one of the air hostesses from the plane. I just looked at her bemused.

"Don't worry Haydn. Calm down, everything is in order."

"Where am I?" I asked in desperation.

"Don't you remember last night?"

"I don't remember anything," I replied. That Jack Daniels must have given me a complete mental block.

"It was our stopover. We rounded you up as promised, but they wouldn't let you back on the plane in the state you were in at that moment, so we've rearranged your flights, to join the original plane you booked in Brunei. You'll be flying with us this morning. And this time behave yourself will you?" As she was speaking to me, my mind was in turmoil trying to remember anything at all. It did come back to me, booking a stopover in Brunei.

"So I'm in Dubai now am I?"

"That's right. Surely you remember what happened last night?" she asked.

"No, honestly. I don't remember anything. I don't even know your names."

"Well you're not going to find out anything from us," she answered, rather amused with herself. "We're taking you to the airport when we're ready, but you'll have to find your own way onto the plane. We've got things to do. You can handle that can't you? We rounded up your hand luggage. All your documents are in order. So I can't foresee a problem, can you?"

"No," I answered, still a little dazed with what was happening. "Well, I suppose I should thank you for all you've done for me, whatever that was," I added smiling at her.

"Think nothing of it," she cheekily answered.

I did give myself enough time to send a postcard to Nicola at the airport, just to confuse her as much as I was confused myself, successfully boarding. As the flight progressed, they were again approaching me one at a time for a quiet giggle, but not one of them would disclose anything about what had happened the previous night. All I got was that I'd come round fast and was on top form. I begged them to fill me in on the missing evening, but no joy, their mouths were sealed. I did get to know the names of those three beautiful girls, but it was only because it was pinned to their uniform. And to this day I have tried to remember the details of that particular night, but I never have. But I will tell you this though, I have never drank Jack Daniels since.

So after all those occurrences, I actually arrived at Perth Airport on time, which was just as well because Bobby and my brother-in-law Alan were waiting for me there as arranged, although he nearly left me behind because I had to go through a full body search for drugs, treating me like a criminal, because of my regular visits to Australia whilst running a club in Padiham. But we eventually embarked on our travels, lacking one Christie to my disappointment.

“Where's Christie?” I enquired, “she's usually around to greet me.”

“Oh, we've split up Haydn. She's with someone else now. But don't worry, she asked me to tell you she'd be contacting you soon.”

“So you’re still speaking then?” I enquired, slightly stunned with what I was hearing, but relieved she was still in the picture.

“Oh yeah. I still look after Shauna on a fifty-fifty basis. It could be worse.” I thought it wise not to push the conversation any further, so silence prevailed for a while.

It was about fifty miles north of Perth to my mother and brother-in-law's house, a coastal suburb called Two Rocks (Yanshep in aboriginie), surrounded by endless bushland, and what a laborious trek that was after such a long flight, but we eventually arrived. I was ready for some shut eye and as I was undressing for bed, to my utter shock, a lump of gange that had been wedged in my top pocket lining, dropped onto the top of the dressing table, finding out later that Nicola had stuck it there, to help me on my journey. That gesture of friendship nearly had me arrested at the airport. Luckily for me they hadn't spotted it, but it was definitely a close call.

As I snuggled up in my cosy bed totally exhausted, I got to thinking about the effect that bottle of Jack Daniels had on me causing the mental blank I had experienced. It had all been very scary. It happened once before whilst I was in Russia, but I'd wiped it out of my mind as being a freak of nature, but it seemed I was wrong. And this phenomenon didn't just personally affect me because I remember Larry rolling into the club with a litre bottle of the Jack Daniels in his hand one evening, having already drunk most of it. It seems he'd been arguing with his girlfriend Jackie all day and she must have disappeared on him. I hid him away in a corner all by himself, so he wouldn't be a nuisance to anybody, whilst everybody else were littering the bar. Drinking the rest of the bottle, he became very quiet, which was very unusual for Larry. I suppose the Jack Daniels was kicking in. We were all watching him as he suddenly tried to struggle to his feet, wobbling to one end of the concert room, where he gradually groped his way round the entire room walls. He kept muttering something to himself continuously, which was annoying Yogurt. So sneaking up to him to try to decipher what he was harping on about, Yog returned to the bar with a puzzled look on his face, telling us that he seemed to be looking for someone. Larry finished stroking the whole of the concert room walls, bringing him close to the bar, and sort of steadying himself, he attempted to walk towards us. Suddenly he glanced at a tall bar stool nearby, a beaming smile appearing on his face as he stumbled towards it, and dropping to his knees, he threw both his arms round it, uttering a total sigh of relief.

“Found you my little darling, where the fuck have you been hiding!” we all heard him exclaim, looking at each other in bewilderment.

“What the fuck are you playing at Larry?” Yogurt queried.

" Jackie!" he shouted. "She's been hiding from me," Larry then proceeded to give the buffet a passionate kiss, as we all looked at each other, bursting out laughing.

Yogurt had seen enough, pushing everybody to one side, opening the trapdoor in the floor in front of the bar, and grabbing Larry he shoved him down the hole, which was only about four feet deep, passing the buffet down to him also, whilst shouting, "You and Jackie need a bit of privacy to make up, so we'll leave you both to it for a hour, to cool off." He then closed the trap on him, on the top of which he placed a buffet and sat on it. There was silence once more until we eventually decided to release him. When he came round he couldn't remember one solitary thing that he'd said or done. I bet I was not the only one that never touched Jack Daniels again. It was definitely potent stuff and had a lot to account for.

I must have dozed off after those thoughts, waking up the next morning with Nicola on my mind. "Would I hear from her?" I thought to myself, being very dubious whether she'd fax me or not, but delightfully, Nicola did as promised, receiving regular messages, like "Get your arse back here pronto, we're missing you," and all sorts of rubbish like that, which gave me a good feeling inside because I was really missing her as well. Fortunately Christie did contact me, so I spent quite a few nights out with her regardless of her new boyfriend which eased the pain considerably. But this meant I was seeing Christie and Bobby at separate intervals, both separately confiding in me their own personal problems, being sworn to secrecy. I was sort of delicately stuck in the middle because I thought a lot about Bob and Christie and didn't want to upset any either of them. Christie and her boyfriend had arranged to do a runner with her child. I wasn't happy about being told about it by Christie because it wasn't my problem and was determined not to get involved. But now she'd put me in a compromising position. If I opened my mouth to Bobby I lost Christie's friendship and if I didn't and Bobby found out, he'd be pretty upset with me.

Luckily Bob cottoned on in time, catching them exactly as they were about to leave, completely foiling the plot. But it did come to his notice that I already knew what was about to happen, so he lost face with me. It was what one would call a no win situation.

The fax machine at the club broke down next, and Nicola began ringing me on the bar land line. Every time she rang, I could hear Scarface harping on in the background, and it was starting to annoy me. I know I shouldn't have let it, but I felt helpless, being so far away, even though I was spending much time with Christie. This special night, I slipped again starting an argument with her, concerning Scarface. Sometimes I can be my own worst enemy, but as I have said before, nobody is perfect.

I was really upset. It was about two in the morning in Perth and the previous day my Lada car had broken down on me. Trust a Lada!

Erratically stamping out of the house, I trudged along the beach into the bush in a right huff, but sticking to the sea front so I couldn't get lost. Inland there's 3000 miles of bushland and getting lost in there could result in inevitable death. I walked for miles and miles, trying to clear my head in the fresh, morning air. A couple of hours or more must have passed, continuously walking. Eventually needing to rest, I sat on a rock, dangling my bare feet in the cool water to sooth them. The sun hadn't come up yet and all I could see were silhouettes around me in the moonlight. Suddenly the surface of the water exploded directly in front of me, and out of the ocean appeared a long dark shape, viciously biting a half inch diameter chunk out of the side of my left leg. The creature disappeared as fast as it appeared. I reeled back in total shock. There was blood everywhere. I never felt any pain but it frightened me to death, which was an appropriate phrase because I actually thought I was going to die. I'd done a very stupid thing which I'd been warned about so many times, not to walk bare legged in the bush, especially at night.

(Stand on a snake and it would definitely attack. I even got a book out, so I could recognise any nasties that had bitten me, to save precious time determining the antidote, considering there were hundreds of different types of nasties in Australia, and depending what had bitten, the time span ranged from one to ten hours to obtain the appropriate antidote, or die.)

And there was I, bare footed and bare legged, just asking for trouble. But funnily enough I didn't panic at all. I just made a couple of joints from the gange Nicola had given me, and, smoking them, became totally calm, not caring two shits about anything. I could have tried to get home, but I still had no car to get me to hospital, which was fifty miles away from my empty house. If it was poisonous, I wouldn't have made it in time, especially not knowing what exactly had bitten me so I just had to face the consequences. And that was what I decided to do. I thought within the hour, if I'd run out of luck I would be in agony, so I had to move fast. I made a comfortable bed out of dried seaweed, and got kipped down for the night. Maybe forever. I smoked my last remaining joint, and tried to sleep before the pain came. I could feel something spreading up my leg, but it could have been my imagination.

I complacently thought, "I could think of worst ways to die. Everybody has to die sometime. Why not like this. It's a pity about Padiham, but whatever. It won't be my concern in the morning. Within a day, the dingos will have disposed of me, and I will be talked about for years, as a mysterious disappearance. They won't forget me in a hurry."

I was calm and relaxed and definitely not scared, considering that I was actually staring into the face of my maker. When I think back it was all so very strange. Quite the opposite to how I'd thought I'd react. Cannabis can be a good thing at times, settling me down to the point of actually going to sleep, no trouble at all.

When my eyes eventually opened it was morning again, with coloured parrots trudging all around me squawking at each other, and the sea in front of me being a brilliant light blue in colour with waves of pearly white. The smooth, undisturbed beach stretching out endlessly on either side of me looking so serene. Even the rugged bush behind me seemed to be bursting full of life. I was in Paradise again. I looked down at my dried bloodstained, ant ridden leg, realising, "Yes I am in Paradise but still alive alright." The feeling that came over me was indescribable. I am not a religious guy, but I felt I was being protected by something unknown, and that it had purposely given me more time to finish the job I was doing.

I was not quite the same guy from that day onwards, utterly grateful, and humble, for being allowed to live. So I managed to return home on schedule to London after all, having mixed feelings due to Bobby being so upset with me. Thank God Paul was waiting to pick me up to whisk me safely back to the club.

Yanshep

Chapter 6 In unison with the law

Andrea and Paul did a brilliant job running the club whilst I was away. There wasn't one item I could fault them on. I definitely knew who I could rely on should I ever have to depart for a while again in the near future.

So it goes without saying, very little out of the ordinary had happened at the club whilst I was away, apart for the day when a crew were filming a few sets from the drama, "On the Preston Front," on the street outside.

The television crew were preparing to film "The Dream Scene." constructing tracks down the entire length of Mill Street for the cameras to gently run on. Mill Street was a steep cobbled hill, and the setting was a dolly bird adorned in scanty underwear riding a double bed down the bumpy cobblestones, being totally out of control. Well, that's what I was told. By all accounts, anybody and everybody was there to observe. There was a generator situated at the bottom of the street, well away from the set, so that the noise from it wouldn't affect the take, and everybody was asked to be quiet whilst filming. The film crew had set up office in the main concert room area of the club, whilst Paul was behind the bar acting as host.

This was an ideal excuse for a full day's piss up, and Ernie's team were taking full advantage of it.

The scene was set. Everything was ready for the go ahead. All the cameras were in position. But a serious problem came to light. Wherever shooting started Ernie and the others were in the take. Take after take this occurred, wasting valuable time. The director, becoming really fed up with them to say the least, ultimately led them all into the club to offer them an open tab at the bar, on condition that they kept clear of the filming. Back in position again, and ready to go, when Andrea rolled up to work on her horse. They asked her to keep the horse well clear, but she had other ideas and tethered it to the main club doors, close to where she was about to start working behind the bar.

Now the horse, like everyone else in Padiham, was an addict, adoring Guinness, it could sense its presence around, somewhere close.

The shoot started once again, and the dollybird came rolling down the street on her double bed. The sudden movement frightened the horse to the extent that it broke from its tether to complete a few circles of the filming area, rearing up on its hind legs and snorting in the process, scattering people in all directions, before dashing into the club to find that drink of Guinness it so badly needed (where else would an horse go for a drink?).

Rubbing his hands together excitedly, this was Yogurt's opportunity to dash onto the set and jump into the bed, which took off down the hill at top speed. I am not sure whether the bird was still in bed or not, because nobody could quite remember when I enquired, they were all too pissed, but knowing Yogurt she possibly was. Anyway the bed finished up smashing into the pavement below, and one severe bollocking was received by all. The television crew really had their work cut out that day. But I think, through sheer perseverance, they eventually completed their task, no thanks to Ernie's crowd. I just wish I'd have been there to witness everything that happened, but at least I was thankful for getting back in time for my second "Walking Day," followed by my birthday. There were new arrangements to make at the club, but I had to get these two occasions over with first before I put my mind to anything else.

Walking Day arrived. The bar was fully staffed, which included Yog and Nicola. I thought there was a vast amount of punters last year, but this year topped it, hands down. I thought I was well stocked up this time, but I still finished running up and down the town for supplies. Last year all the other pubs were reasonably quiet. This year they were empty. I'd acquired the whole town this session, and didn't I know it.

Padiham's streets of television fame

By Victoria Eglington

FAMILIAR Padiham streets can be seen on television from Monday when the new series of "On the Preston Front" starts on BBC1 at 10 p.m.

Back in April the town was taken over by camera crews, limousines, catering trailers and, more importantly, television stars for the filming of the Lancashire-based show.

Look out for Padiham's Mill Street, where a large part of the filming took place, and the Starkie Arms Hotel, in Church Street, under its television name "The Roker Arms".

The programme is about three friends who are in the Territorial Army together and was filmed in locations across the county including Blackpool.

Familiar faces of pupils from Padiham County Primary School can also be seen when one of the characters, "Hodge", remembers his schooldays.

PICTURE: Stars Stephen Churchett (left) and Colin Buchanan took a break from filming with the extras from Padiham County Primary School. (BX8066)

THE crowds turned out in the sunshine to enjoy Padiham's traditional walking day - don't miss Friday's Padiham Express for lots more photos. (BX9495)

The police made three attempts, trying to persuade me to close down because there were too many under eighteen year olds there, and three times Yogurt told them to fuck off and stop bothering us. Eventually getting the message they left, which was just as well because if they had entered asserting their authority, they would have instigated a national riot. On top of all this, people were trying to sell me various items for beer money, acquiring some real bargains and making a noticeable killing that day. And the laugh of it was in my spare time, when I occasionally frequented other pubs in town, people still advised me where I was going wrong, which mainly referred to the clientele I was letting in. They hadn't a clue what they were talking about. I was turning over a lot of money at the club without having to hire bouncers or body guards for protection, because should any trouble arise, my own customers sorted it out themselves. Each one of many families standing up and stating to the instigators in question, "This is MY personal club and nobody abuses it, under any circumstances," guarding my interests, like I'd become someone very special. I was definitely gaining respect in this town.

There were still two or three knobheads, that I couldn't let in who didn't possess enough brain cells to reason with, especially under the influence of drink or drugs. I was very wary of those types being very dangerous people capable of anything. And then there was the town hardman, Kenny, who treated me like a gentleman, but mainly because I was under his father's protection, Buffalo, a good man and a very close friend of mine. His sister Angela was also a dear friend of mine.

If Kenny was around everybody would leave, just to be safe, being a natural born killer. I used to be one of the very few people that stood up to him. I think he respected me for that, although I got a beating for it once, but it was well worth it due to the fact that when the others heard about it, they treated me like I was some kind of martyr. It happened one morning when I was upstairs with friends of mine, Sharon and Darren. Suddenly we heard Kenny shouting and bawling outside. His voice couldn't be mistaken.

"Darren, I know you're in there. Come out now, I'm not leaving until I've collared you. You're in for a beating my friend!" continuously banging and banging on the entrance doors, never letting up. Darren was trembling like a leaf in the wind, and hid himself in one of the storage rooms. But the banging continued, and in the end, I lost it completely and rushed downstairs to stop him making such a terrible racket in the street below. It was an unwritten rule that all trouble had to be contained inside the club at all times, to avoid complaints from the neighbours, that could result in my clean police record getting tarnished. Dashing out of the place, I was confronted by Kenny with Yogurt standing slightly to the rear of him.

"What the fuck is all the noise about, you dick. Darren's

not here, so will you please fuck off now!" I shouted at him aggressively. Yogurt was in the background silently ushering me to shut up before Kenny knocked my head off.

"You talking to me, you gobshite! Nobody talks to me like that in this town!"

"I do, you dick!" I growled, totally ignoring Yogurt's advice. "Fuck off, away from here!"

On that note, he just totally lost it and flew at me, giving me one tremendous punch in the mouth, lifting me off my feet. As I hit the ground, realising what he'd done, I witnessed him fleeing round the side of the building, and away. Wobbling to my feet with blood pouring from the side of my mouth, but otherwise surviving, with Yog's help I made my way inside.

Darren and Sharon approached, shouting, "You mad bastard Haydn. We were peeping from the upstairs window. What did you shout at him like that for? You know what he's like, he could have killed you"

"I did it to stop him killing you, you prat," was my answer to Darren. "He's gone now, so be thankful."

Yogurt grabbed me and rushed me to the nearest sink to clean the blood from my face. "Are you alright mate?"

"Fine Yog. Just a scratch. Forget about it. Matter closed."

The next Monday morning there was a quiet knock on the door, and Kenny was standing there. "I heard you had a bit of trouble in the club last weekend," he stated.

"Did I?" I answered. I thought to myself, "If I did, it was so minute, I can't remember."

"Well, no sweat. It won't happen again. I've sorted it," He answered and walked off.

"He must have clobbered somebody," I mumbled as I was going back up the stairs. "Poor bleeders. I wonder who it was?" I never found out, but I do know this, he did it because he had a guilty conscience regarding thumping me, and that made me feel good, because I knew he wouldn't ever try it again.

In-between all of these happenings, on regular intervals,

because Eric was getting slightly perturbed due to the fact that he still wasn't getting any rent, he'd send potential buyers to look the place over, to try to render me obsolete. But I always organised total chaos throughout the club when they arrived, telling them that they had to be out of their mind thinking of taking over a place like this. Nobody ever came back. I definitely frightened the shit out of them, good for a few freebies. These things had to be done to survive, giving me that needed breathing space.

And then, out of the blue, something very unpredictable happened that completely changed everything. In fact it was the most significant happening of the club's life.

The police came to visit me. Not for anything bad. They needed to talk with me in private. It seemed very unusual, what could they possibly want? It couldn't be for any annoyance I had caused in town, because I hadn't caused any. In fact, during my eighteen months reign I hadn't called the police in once.

Earlier, around the end of the previous year, there had been a campaign going on, wanting ideas on how to tackle crime in Padiham. The local press were bringing out headlines like, "JOIN OUR FIGHT FOR A SAFER PLACE TO LIVE." Padiham Express, 4th Dec 1996. Views and options were invited. Every other week similar headlines were being printed, putting pressure on the local police force.

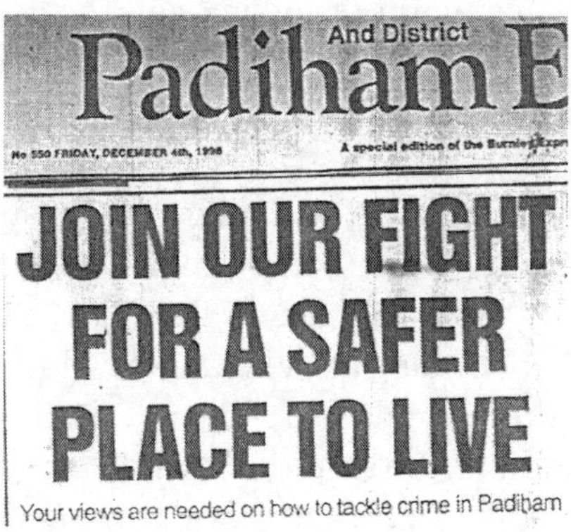
Padiham E And District

JOIN OUR FIGHT FOR A SAFER PLACE TO LIVE

Your views are needed on how to tackle crime in Padiham

“Can we come in?” one of them asked.

“Sure, why not,” I replied, a little puzzled, thinking, “What possibly do they want?” The club wasn't open yet but Steve was present helping me clean the place up. I beckoned to him to keep a low profile and positioned myself behind the bar in my place of authority. Two police officers followed me and grabbing a bar stool each sat down in front of me.

“We need your cooperation on a few matters,” one of them blurted out.

I immediately thought they wanted me to grass on somebody. If that was the case, they had no chance. That was completely against the rules.

“Like what?” I cautiously enquired.

“We've been monitoring your activities since you appeared in this town,” the other officer replied, “ and to be quite honest, we think you’re doing an excellent job. You're quite the topic of conversation down at the station.”

I was chuffed with myself, listening to that initial statement.

“So we have come up here with a proposition for you.”

“Like what?”

“Well as you must already know, Padiham is having trouble with mainly drink orientated vandalism and fighting late on at night when the pubs close, and it's causing us shit. We want it stopping, or at least reducing to a minimum. It's giving us a bad name.

Steve became very curious and reduced the gap between us, so he could earwig without the police officers spotting him. I listened, and immediately assumed that they were going to tell me that I had to close down on time. But were they?...... I don't think so.

One of the officers put me out of my suspense, “Well, it's like this, we want you to keep your customers in until our night shift ends, early morning. That doesn't mean refusing them exit, that would be kidnapping, but it does mean anybody you don't think fit to hit the road, make sure they don't start wandering around the town. Can you do that?”

I was flabbergasted at what I was listening to. I thought for a moment before replying, "Yes, it can be done, but you'll have to give me a week or so to organise a different routine. Just let me get this right. You're telling me I am unofficially exempt from the licensing laws here if I do a good job keeping drunkards off the streets for you people, late at night?"

"That's about it," one of them answered. "What do you think?"

"Right, I'll give it a go," I answered, "there's nothing lost in trying."

An astonished grin appeared on Steve's face as he slunk back to where he was originally cleaning.

"Just take heed, this conversation never happened, if you know what I mean. Mum's the word." I was thinking that surely they were not taking it on their heads to organise this saga themselves. It's more than their jobs worth. The orders must be coming from higher authority.

"But what about Mcneal's night club at the top of town?" I asked, "Won't they start complaining when they get to know the crack?"

"They won't get to know, will they? Anyway, any complaint is our business, not yours. OK?" they replied, as they got up to leave.

As they were leaving the premises, I shouted after them, "I'll keep you in touch." They nodded in response and left.

I turned to Steve absolutely stunned, "Did you hear that? They've given me diplomatic immunity in Padiham."

"Unbelievable!" he replied. "The mind boggles. It just shows how they can twist the law to their own benefit."

"Well, I don't see it that way Steve. My philosophy is, if the law isn't working around here, something extreme needs to be done to control the issues involved. And if the extreme approach eventually works, then it's time to rethink the law."

"When you put it that way, well yes, I suppose you're right," Steve answered.

"Anyway, I'm going to do my utmost to help them. It's not a question of turnover. This town has only so much money to spend on alcohol every week, and when that's gone, that's it. The only extra revenue would possibly come from outside the town limits. Anyway, getting back to the point, you haven't heard this conversation. You heard the man Steve, didn't you?"

"Don't worry. Trust me." was his final remark as he reorganised himself again.

I did get waylaid a couple of days later, whilst celebrating my birthday. Everybody who meant anything to me was there, including three of my step-children, Jennifer, Amanda and Kathleen. Out of the blue, a male and female police officer walked in, who I didn't recognise. The male stood guarding the door and the female approached me. I was stood in front of the bar talking to my step-children. Nicola spotted them and ran behind the bar. I assumed she was getting out of the way. Because of their stern faces, it seemed obvious that this was not a friendly visit.

The female police officer blurted out, "We have reason to believe you are involved in certain unlawful activities in the town and are taking you down to the station for questioning. She read me my rights, turned me round and handcuffed me. Everybody, especially me, was in a state of shock. I hadn't a clue what was going on. It was only a couple of days before, they were my best buddies. Why the sudden change?

"What's going on?" I asked in panic. My mind was in a complete whirl.

"You'll find out shortly." was her answer. "Just bide your time."

Suddenly Nicola dashes into the disco area, behind the bar and switched everything on, blasting out the popped up version of, "*Happy birthday to you*," whilst doing a moonie to me at the same time. The police woman turned me round to face her, her stern look changing to a sexy smirk, and started disrobing herself in front of me, her clothes flying in every direction. The penny dropped. She was my kissagram. She grabbed my head and sunk my face deep into her large pair of tits. "Get a lick of these," she giggled. The punters cheered and egged me on. "Go for it Haydn, get stuck in there!"

I was too embarrassed to do anything, especially with my three step-children being present, who didn't look very amused with the situation at all. She was not what you would class as one of the sexiest people in the world, a bit bulbous and looked like she could handle herself, like you'd imagine a female police officer to look (No disrespect meant.)

The other guy must have been her bodyguard, not that her body needed guarding. It amused everybody and that was the main objective, so I had to pretend to be amused also. When they had departed, Nicola confessed to being responsible for hiring and paying for her. Nobody else knew, but they definitely were convincing, believe me. She apologised for the ugly bitch they had sent, and said she would be claiming a discount in the morning.

Now that I had got my birthday over with, it was time to make some fast alterations to the club, before I altered my serving times. Mainly I needed to do away with the staircase that was in the way of the very slow installation of the upstairs bedsits. It would create more floor space to the concert room area, which meant I had to change the upstairs fire exit door for a conventional outside door, being the only access to the upstairs from then on.

Besides that I needed to stop serving draught beer which was very costly, and replace it with cans, which had a much greater profit margin.

I had my own converted eleven gallon keg, which I could access for cleaning and refilling with draught cider only. By filling it myself and gassing it up, I could save a considerable amount of money, compared to buying the sealed kegs from the brewery. I was not committed to any brewery so I was not breaking any agreements by doing this. Eric wouldn't be pleased, due to the fact that he personally received bonuses from the brewery that supplied my beers. But I never received any of these financial credits, so it was not my concern. My new scheme did have its setbacks. Some of my older end customers were not very happy about the beer conversion. They had been used to draught all their lives, and told me it wouldn't work and would drive people away. But I bought reputable makes of canned beer that had widgets in them, so that when poured into a pint glass, the beer and the head was always at a constant high standard. The cans didn't quite fill a pint glass, but I just modified the price accordingly. Nobody could tell the difference, and I won the older end over almost immediately they started drinking it. And if anyone came in complaining, who hadn't been around before, the older end would convince them that everything was OK. So there were no problem created whatsoever in that field.

Having completed all the changeover, I altered the opening hours, much to the delight of the majority of customers, especially an elderly couple called Harold and Marleen. There was many a night when they never moved. They had no intention of leaving. It was too much like hard work for them. In the end I just used to leave them to it and go to bed. The next morning they'd still be in the same place propping the bar up, drinking their heads off. There was always a pile of money at the side of them and a list of drinks they had consumed, which always tallied. In the end I stopped checking it, it wasn't in their nature to do me out of a penny.

Steve was another very late person. But the only thing I had to do with him to send him on his way was to pour him a triple Pernod and orange and it was guaranteed that he'd be heading for the door within the following twenty minutes.

Tony was there constantly day and night now. He helped me out on the night shift, and if I had to go anywhere I left him in charge. Being an ex-military policeman, he could really handle the job, which was a bonus, and he followed my rules explicitly.

I had to organise transportation for customers to their homes, at a few minutes notice, which I successfully did with a local minicab company. If they couldn't pay for the lift themselves, the onus was on me. But that was the agreement.

Only pissed ones got this service, which tempted the others to drink more.

There was also the question of punters nipping out for takeaways. To get round this, I had to organise my own incoming delivery service, but received commission for bringing them custom, and as a bonus, the local bakers supplied me with trays of hot pies straight from the oven at three in the morning, which was a godsend.

My scheme was working well, and the police commented, "Well done. There's been a definite improvement. Keep it up, you're becoming a legend in this town."

Nicola was part of the establishment now, but as prophesied, we both had trouble with McNeal's. The management banned her from drinking there for no apparent reason, and I was out on the town one night with a very good customer of mine, called Billy. He was adamant that he had met me before, whilst locked up on the Isle of Sheppey, which wasn't true but I wanted to keep him in suspense for the laugh. I invited him to accompany me for a drink at McNeal's.

He answered, "It's no good me going up there, they ain't gonna let me in. They never do."

"You'll be alright Billy," I laughed. "You're with me. I'm looking after you tonight." So we both made our way to the nightclub and, knocking on the door to gain access, the inspection shutter lifted, and the door opened.

"Hello Billy," I heard a voice say. I was positioned to the side of the door where I couldn't be seen. "How are you tonight? Come in." As he made his way inside, I moved into position outside.

The owner looked at me and blurted, "As for you Haydn, you've no chance. You're banned for life." I couldn't believe it. Billy had gained access but I hadn't. Again no reason given. I just walked away disgusted and made my way back to the club. Somebody told me later that the reason he'd banned Nicola and me was because we were pinching all his trade. How childish is that? But I got my own back, like I normally do, because he'd been a regular visitor to my club with his friends. I got the impression he only came to spy on me, to see how many customers were there at the time. Even after banning both Nicola and me from his place, he had the audacity to come into my club one night to treat his friends to a drink. Well what could I do?

I had no option but to approach him, "Sorry mate but you'll have to leave. I've got you down as banned for life." He just gave me a nasty stare, and stamped out with his friends scurrying after him. He was one of the very few people I banned from my place, and it was ironical that I banned him for being childish, and not for tearing the place apart. I didn't need people like that anyway. I was not short of punters and new faces were showing up every week. Like a pretty 25 year old girl called Suzey, who originally came from Padiham which was why everybody knew her except me of-course. She had been away for quite a long time at a rehabilitation centre in Sheffield, being treated for an heroin addiction, and was cured by all accounts, having just arrived back into town looking for a place to live. We were chatting for quite a while and she seemed alright to me. I offered her the empty downstairs back room for a day or so, until she got sorted if she could stand the noise of the place at night, which she accepted. Next day somebody told me that Kenny had put her up the previous night at his caravan, which was parked on some minor road, at the top of town and whilst she'd been sitting on its step, she had suddenly keeled over in a deep mong. There was a puddle in front of her, about an inch deep, which she would have actually drowned in, if Kenny hadn't come to her aid. If that was true, it didn't sound to me like she was off the heroin, and I wondered if I had made a big mistake letting her stop there. But it turned out that she was no trouble at all and stopped for quite a while seriously enjoying herself there. I suppose it was due to the fact that she was a new face in town, and everyone was chatting her up. I did notice though that she always made a point of covering her arms up, but I did once get a glimpse of them, only to find out what a horrible mess they were in, full of self inflicted slash marks, done by a knife or a razor blade, which put me off her slightly.

"Surely not another Psycho," I thought to myself. "But don't jump the gun Haydn. Just keep a close eye on her."

Myself

She used to sing karaoke with me all the time, her favourite vocal being "*But I Won't do That*," by Meatloaf, which I thought we did well together. In fact, thinking back, my whole attitude to music had changed. There were many songs that I would never have given a second thought to prior, which I had begun to enjoy listening and singing to. I was classing albums played by "The Verve" and "Oasis" as excellent music to be appreciated, and paying attention to the lyrics I began to understand how the young generation thought. It was different music to what I had been brought up with, but the new scores got the whole place in the mood and I loved to be part of it all. I began to realise that as times change and people gradually adapt to the changes without realising, if a situation arises where the past is brought into the present, with the assumption that everything will carry on as normal, the finality of the situation will be that it just will not work anymore. Take for instance the next situation that occurred. Mentioning the words "Déjà vu," was nothing to what happened next.

Gloria, my ex-wife, the girl who stepped into Lorraine's shoes that fated year long ago, was one of the most gorgeous women that ever walked this planet. She was five years younger than me and was doing a runner from her mundane boyfriend who was living with her at the time. He was at that moment spending the weekend in police cells for non-payment of fines. I moved her belongings to her new abode and never left. She was a seductive temptress, who could entice any normal man to obey her wishes at any instant in time, living a totally sexually orientated life, and wallowing in it. We created Photographic studios, model agencies, even a Leeds brothel together. She was the Mecca Locarno beauty queen one year and Miss January girl for the Yorkshire Evening Post another. She had a spell as a high-class prostitute, operating at Leeds biggest hotel and casino at the time, talking her way into small Yorkshire Television Parts in the process. She was a very intelligent person who made public performances singing Scottish folk songs and wrote love poetry in her spare time. And on top of all this she was bi-sexual and used to bring her girlfriends back to our marital home for threesomes every week. A man's dream come true. I had twin girls to her, Rachel and Georgina and was with her 10yrs, married for one year, divorcing me on the grounds of adultery for sleeping with other women. The women concerned were the ones she kept bringing back to our marital home, would you believe. She and I purchased the farm previously described, but I bought her share out and she finally did a runner from me taking the children with her.

Retribution you might say. And up to this moment in time, I had never seen any of them in thirteen years, apart from one isolated incident when I received an anonymous published book of verse in 1988, covering my full relationship with her. Reading the poems really did convince me that she did love me in her own way once upon a time.

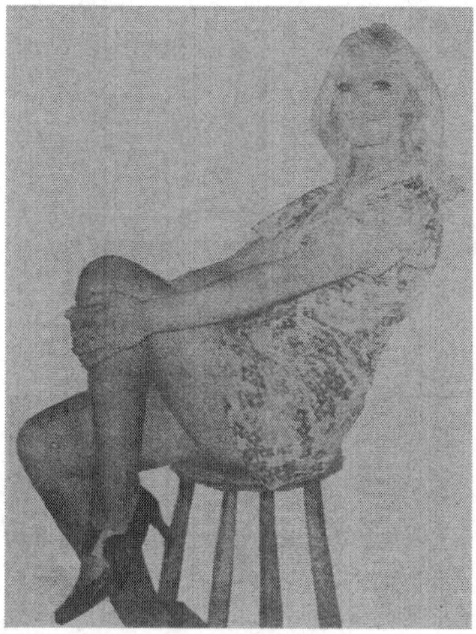

Gloria

My marriage day

Well, this certain morning at the club, I received a very unexpected postcard that had actually been written by Gloria, asking me to visit her and the children, at a certain address in Morecambe. I felt like someone had fired a taser gun at me, not being able to work my feelings out. I did love her once, but she'd caused me so much grief when she went into hiding, years ago. She had been a dangerous woman in the past, and here was I, in the present, trying to achieve my goal in Padiham, needing as little aggravation as possible.

"Would it be wise to see her after all this time," I pondered. "She could cause one hell of a lot of trouble around here, destroying everything I had worked for?" That was my cautious side thinking, but then my reckless side took over. "But I would be over the moon to see my children again, after all this time. Just what should I do? Decision time?"

After much pondering, the decision was inevitable, and I decided to visit her in Morecambe, still very wary of her. I was inquisitive to find out how she'd worn over the past years, whether she was still the most beautiful looking girl she used to be, and this was the only way to find out. So off I set to Morecambe. Shit or bust!

My original family *My twin girls*
at Longley Hall

My twin girls in living caravan during construction

My twin girls and a friend during construction at Longley Hall

My daughter Rachel the last time I saw her

On arriving at the house, my children were there to welcome me at the door. I was so pleased to be in their presence after all the time spent without them, but they looked apprehensive towards me. They courteously invited me inside, remarking, "Mum's in the kitchen preparing a meal. Go in and see her." Before I'd reached the door, she popped her head out smiling.

"So you made it then?" she asked as if nothing at all had happened between us in our past years. I looked at her. Her voice and mannerisms hadn't changed one iota, but her beauty was fading. She looked slightly weathered and she'd put some weight on since I last saw her, but at least she made me feel very welcome. We all sat down together at the meal table and exchanged stories of what had happened over the last thirteen years, not seeing each other. My kids had grown up now. I could hardly recognise them.

"How did you find me?" I asked.

"We were planning to go to Australia for a while, so I contacted your mother, and she told me where you were." she answered. "She said she would put us all up at her place. That's if we wanted?"

"And are you still thinking of going?" I asked.

"I don't know yet. We'll see how things work out."

I thought to myself, "We'll see how things work out with who?" The thought temporarily frightened me, not wanting to get too close to her at this stage of the game. Besides, I now had Nicola to consider. But taking all this into account, I still finished up sleeping with her that night. She hadn't lost her persuasive attributes, but I was very apprehensive making love to her, being so scared of becoming involved again so soon, and she, realising this, was rather put out with the job.

My children were very distant with me during the whole of the period that I was there, not being the same people that I remembered so long ago, which upset me considerably. I tried making conversation with them, mainly about the time when they were only five years old, and lived with me for a year on the farm, when Gloria abandoned them to live with an Arab hotel owner in Tunisia. As one can imagine, in such circumstances they were extremely insecure, and used to cling to me like glue, for fear of losing me also.

"Do you remember concocting that letter between the two of you, giving that eighteen year old nanny that was living with us one week's notice because you thought she was a threat to you both, regarding me?" They both smiled at each other and nodded. "And I had to sack her to gain your reassurance." They smiled again and nodded. "And do you remember both standing on the lawn together, shouting at me to get down whilst I was working on the stone roof, because if I fell and killed myself, who would look after you both?" They both looked at each other and smiled again. I tried, but I just couldn't get a decent conversation started. It was hard work. I thought to myself, "Haydn, you're not getting through to them at all are you. They don't want to know me anymore."

Thinking back, they were very unsettled children without their mother, and although I loved and did my utmost for them, there were times that I must have scared them to death with the things I got up to. One such occasion was the time my co-partner in a Cessna light aircraft which I had an interest in, had just passed his pilot's licence but still needed his navigation certificate. This meant we could only fly up to one thousand feet with a clear visibility at all times. I was the temporary navigator with my Bartholomew's road atlas in my hands. This arrangement turned out to be rather embarrassing one day when we accidentally entered Manchester airspace, being ordered to clear the area immediately, which was nigh impossible, not knowing which way to turn, due to the fact that there were no roads around to compare. After three wrong guesses and the same amount of severe warnings, I managed by some fluke to make the right choice. We were always getting into dilemmas for one thing or another, but this special day I decided to take the children up with us, the purpose of the flight being to take aerial photographs of the farm. Rachel and Georgina who were only very young at the time, were harnessed into the back seating area whilst my mate piloted the plane. I was in the front passenger seat, unharnessed with the passenger window wide open so I could stretch out to obtain a clear view of my land and property below to get a good shot. There must have been an 80mph wind blowing in my face and the propellers frighteningly whirling in my left ear didn't help whatsoever.

"Have you got a clear view?" he shouted to me, trying to be heard over the noise of the engine.

"No!" I awkwardly shouted back, "the wheels are inhibiting the view!"

"I'll just gently tilt the plane your way a little. That should cure the problem. Alright?"

Rachel butted in, "Be careful dad!"

"Don't worry you two, everything's in order," I replied trying to reassure them both. "Go on then, gently tilt the plane and let's see if it improve things. Well, not being fully conversant with the aircrafts manoeuvrability, instead of a gentle tilt, the plane gave such a jerk that I shot a distance of about three feet out of the window. I instinctively let go of the camera and grabbed the vacant seat belt in the process, whilst my mate made a mad lunge for the end of one of my trousers, trying to stop me from being completely blown out of the window. And whilst all this was happening, my children were screaming their heads off in the back. Turmoil was everywhere. Thank God I managed to grab the seat belt otherwise I'd have come a right cropper, but even so it was a terrifying position to be in. The propeller in my lug hole, the wind trying to blow me away, dangling upside down outside of the aircraft, facing the ground a thousand feet below me, James Bond had nothing on me that day. I had to keep focused, quite aware that one wrong move could end everything, whilst at the same time ridiculously trying to console my screaming children. It must have taken me at least five minutes to slowly and methodically juggle my way back into the passenger seat with my mate trying to pilot the plane whilst at the same time pulling his guts out endeavouring to drag me in by the trouser bottoms.

Fortunately I was a very strong, agile person bursting with confidence in those days, but even so, when I eventually survived the ordeal, I was trembling from head to foot. I have often wondered what my scared children were thinking about me at that moment in time, having a right knobhead of a father. They definitely weren't impressed with me at all. I just couldn't wait to get them out off the plane that afternoon. On the way back home it came to my notice that the pilot had it in his mind to try to fly us back to our private airstrip near Leeds forty air miles away with me stuck outside. I don't think for one second I'd have made it, hung on there for my dear life, and if we had, what a sight we would have been whilst landing. I think he would have had his licence revoked on the spot. A few days later I was searching for the camera in the field in front of the farm, when believe it or not, there it was all smashed up, embedded in some soft soil directly in front of me. Miraculously the film cassette survived, preserving that final picture to forever remind me of that terrifying moment.

Luckily for my children our flying experiences didn't last that long anyway because one afternoon whilst watching television together, the national news came on showing a private aircraft that had crashed, finishing up nose down in the ground with broken propellers, in the middle of a French potato field, and a bride in all her wedding regalia being helped out of the field by numerous farm workers, holding her dress slightly in the air to prevent it from getting mudded up. At a closer look I suddenly realised it was our plane and the girl was my mate's girlfriend, who now appeared to be his wife. For two days I was left in the darkness, not knowing what the heck had happened, but my children were over the moon in relief, knowing I wouldn't be flying in that plane ever again the state it was in. It turned out that they were secretly married and had decided to fly to the South of France not telling anyone at all, for their honeymoon. Running dangerously short of fuel they tried to land at a couple of French military bases and were refused access, so in total desperation attempted to land in that special potato field, actually pulling it off with no injuries, which I'll give him full marks for in his madness. Mind you she told me later that she would never fly again for the rest of her life, she was so scared. It's a wonder they weren't married and divorced in the same day.

So preparing to vacate Gloria's abode that morning, I thought I'd been totally outcasted, but on leaving, even though I had mentioned Nicola to her, she invited herself to the club if only to be nosey. I didn't know what to think about the situation.

On the journey back to the club, this whole flying business brought back a recent memory of an happening I'd had with Dwarling whilst having a laugh about these flying experiences to a group of my punters over a few beers at my place one dinnertime.

Dwarling unexpectedly and arrogantly chimed up, "I passed my pilot's licence last week. I used my mate's Cessna, it's a piece of piss this flying business. Well that's when he can make time to take me that is. Actually I'm going this afternoon, and I'd love you to come along Haydn but he'd never allow it. I'm sorry about that Haydn. Some other time eh?"

Turning to him I thought to myself, "Can't he just flannel. He always has to be in the limelight with some fictitious story."

But prior to leaving he made a last minute phone call, out of the blue shouting across to me, "He says you can come along for the ride if you want to. Hows about it Haydn?"

Well I just didn't know what to think.

"What is he up to now?" I queried. "Only time will tell." was the thought passing through my mind as we embarked on this mysterious journey, which finished up at a private flying club's airport drinking lounge at Blackpool Airport for a few rounds of lagers.

His mate, who had been deathly quiet for the full length of the journey, not giving me that chance to pick his brains, suddenly stood up beckoning Dwarling to follow. Dwarling commented to me, "Won't be long Haydn. We just have to report for our flight programme before taking off that's all."

Still totally disbelieving, I thought to myself, "There's no way he can fly a plane, not in a thousand years," but on returning they beckoned me to follow them to the secure area where all the private aircraft were hangered up. "U..um," I pondered. "He's just a passenger with me, out for the ride. He'll make some excuse any second now." But wasn't I just wrong. Approaching a Cessna that had been dragged into place by some member of the club, Dwarling took immediate and complete control of the aircraft from the word go, portraying the illusion that he had been flying for years.

Tuning his head phones in, whilst automatically switching and checking instruments in a very methodical manner, he began taxiing to the main runway at entrance 3, instructing the control tower in extremely impressive flying lingo, "Oskar, Delta, Tango, Foxtrot, entrance3, ready for takeoff, awaiting instructions."

"Runway clear. Ok to proceed. Maintain altitude of 1000 feet on exit," was the immediate response from the control tower, and with a final acknowledgement Dwarling taxied onto the runway for takeoff.

"Wish me luck," he shouted to us all and off he set at full throttle to execute a perfect manoeuvre. Funnily enough, full faith in him began to engulf me as total disbelief crumbled away, just by witnessing the smooth and efficient way he had pulled it off, even though he was a novice. I was astounded with everything I had witnessed being quite conversant with Cessnas, knowing he was definitely in control of the situation.

"Good one Dwarling!" I shouted to him through the noise, "If I hadn't witnessed it with my own eyes I'd have never believed it in a month of Sundays." He just turned and smiled at me, taking me for a very comfortable flight over Morecambe Bay across the Lake District and finally performed a perfect landing in a cross wind, back to where we started. A serious apology was in order for all the wrong things I had thought about him. He'd seriously shot me down this time and knew it. He must have purposely spent around three grand in secret flying lessons for the privilege of doing just that.

Gloria arrived the next afternoon by herself, with her overnight travelling bag, planning to stop a couple of days. Nicola was there, putting me really on the spot.

"What should I do to get out of this situation?" I thought to myself. I had definitely lost interest in Gloria over the years, and besides that my children had been brainwashed by her in my absence. She immediately made the club her own, brazenly seducing a small percentage of my punters just for the laugh, being a joke to her, but they were taking it seriously. I didn't like what I was witnessing, but was relieved that she wasn't closing in on me. At the end of her night she retired to bed in the downstairs front side room, where I thought I could keep an eye on her whilst I was still serving. But a group of four guys, who's names I shall not mention but were not part of Ernie's team, sneaked into her room which she'd forgot to lock, to shag her as jokingly promised, without me noticing them. Consequently she came running out for my protection, closely followed by the same four guys, resulting in a bad scuffle occurring, with Yog and Hillis running up to forcefully calm the situation down. I didn't need this at all, it was just as I had envisaged would happen. So placing Tony on the bar, I marched her to my room upstairs, keeping her well out of the way until she sobered up next morning returning to the bar to explain and try to make friends with everyone. Fortunately Nicola had left early and never witnessed all the carry on, but Yogurt really fancied Gloria. She was not due back in Morecambe until Monday morning, which meant I had to put up with her for another day.

I waited until everyone was leaving for the night and called Yogurt over. "Tomorrow Yog, will you make sure you're around all day to keep Gloria company. Don't worry about money, I'll sort your beer out."

"Too right, Haydn, trust me," he replied energetically rubbing his hands together.

"Right then. Don't let me down, for fuck's sake."

"Oh, don't worry about it, I'm going to love it!" he shouted back at me, his final words for the night.

The next afternoon everyone was laughing and drinking together. I was behind the bar pulling a short, when I felt a tap on my shoulder, and Yogurt's there, whispering bluntly into my ear, "Can I have your permission to shag your missus in the back room, Haydn?"

I turned and looked at him in surprise "He's actually asked permission," I thought. "How novel!"

"Yog, she's not my missus, and you can do what the fuck you like with her, as long as you keep her happy."

"Oh, I'll do that all right," he answered, rubbing his hands together as he walked off. An hour later he approached me again. "Haydn, I'm being a bit cheeky here but I need your permission again?"

I just looked at him and laughed. You're definitely looking after her today, aren't you?" I commented.

"Trust me!" he grinned as he was walking away.

But Gloria had to be Gloria. Nicola entered the club, and the three of them got chatting together. Now Nicola was a wild bitch, but she totally underestimated Gloria, who was even wilder. As Time passed, getting rather late, with the music playing and me being busy behind the bar, suddenly Steve comes running over to me.

"Have you seen that bitch of yours? She's all over Nicola!" he pouted excitedly. He couldn't take in what he was seeing. I looked across and there was Gloria and Nicola kissing and canoodling in the corner, bringing back memories of my past, pissing me off to say the least. I wasn't on my own because Yogurt wasn't too happy with the situation either. They were always in competition with each other, but never over the same girl. This was ludicrous, a one off for him. Time had gone by and I was a bit out of practice with this sort of thing also, but it was still not my business to comment, and there was no reoccurrences that night so I just turned a blind eye.

The next morning, when she was leaving, she turned to me, and laughing her head off, blurted out, "I got you last night didn't I?"

"About what?" I enquired.

"About me persuading Nicola to kiss me, for the sole reason of pissing Yog and you off. Just for the crack you understand. But I got you, didn't I?"

"Some sick joke Gloria. But that's about your mentality isn't it," I replied.

"You're so right. Anything for the crack. I love it when a plan pays off."

Both Yog and Nicola were there to see her off. Nicola had a guilty look on her face for being talked into Gloria's nasty scheme and sincerely apologised to me, putting it down to being over merry at the time. I let it ride over my head knowing how persuasive Gloria could be when she wanted to, and was very relieved to see her depart.

I got lumbered though into taking Yog for regular visits over the Trough of Bowland, to see Gloria, having totally lost his head for her. It was during one of the trips that the three of us went for a meal in a Chinese restaurant on the sea front, inevitably getting involved in an heated discussion related to our past, concluding in her tipping a full plate of king prawn chop suey over my head. Then, later on that night, she apologised by proposing a remarriage to me, not Yog, would you believe, one strange bitch. It goes without saying I never gave her an answer.

Then one weekend, on her instructions, I took Nicola to see her. She wanted the both of us to stop for the weekend at her place, but I had to get back to run the club, thank God, so I finished up leaving Nicola there alone with her. I could foresee trouble, but Nicola was confident she could handle the situation accordingly. So it got to about four in the morning, and I was still serving behind the bar, when I received a telephone call from Nicola.

"Get me out of here, now!" She screamed.

Yogurt turned to me. "Who's that?" he enquired.

"It's Nicola. Sounds like she's in trouble again."

"Give me that phone here," he growled, having harsh words with her before he passed the phone back to me, commenting "She's rang off. Looks like me and you are going to Morecambe, to pick her up."

"Is that so?" I replied, adamantly. "If you think I'm gonna"..........he stopped me in my tracks,

"Yes you are. Get organised!" He was looking forward to the run, missing the Trough of Bowland, but I knew he wanted to see Gloria again.......... who was he trying to kid?

I left Tony in charge, and we headed for the hills. I had recently acquired a white BMW from Eric that could really handle the road, being our own person when driving over that isolated moor, and we could flog that car, knowing every inch of the road. As we were approaching Gloria's house, Nicola came running down the road towards us. Throwing herself into the back, she gave the order, "Do a fast one, before she spots me. Now!" She looked really disturbed but Yogurt wasn't showing her any sympathy at all, because he'd missed his chance that night of confronting Gloria.

"What's the problem around here?" I asked her.

"You won't believe me if I tell you."

"Go on then, try me".

"Well get a load of this. Gloria picked up two guys and took them to her place."

"You what!" I replied, rather upset and angry for a moment.

"Don't get upset Haydn. I was planning of doing a runner anyway. But these two guys turned out to be undertakers, wanting to shag us both in empty coffins surrounded by stiffs, in their garden of rest, and Gloria was all for it! Well, I made an excuse to go to the loo, and was out of the door in a flash. There was no chance o' me hanging around there, the weird bitch."

"What a story," I disbelievingly remarked, and just stared at her, wondering whether she was flannelling or not. But later, it did come to my attention that for once it was pretty close to the truth. I eased off her slightly, but Yogurt remained well pissed off with her. So on our way back over the Trough, spotting a dead rabbit on the road he shouted to me to stop. On retrieving it, he ordered Nicola to sit in the front seat, whilst he jumped into the back. I drove off again, nothing being said, due to none of us being in a good mood. Then Yogurt began skinning the rabbit with his teeth and bare hands. Neither Nicola nor I commented knowing Yogurt was still wearing his angry head, although I was very inquisitive as to what he was up to. Suddenly he leaned forward, gripping her firmly from the rear, and began slowly smearing the bloody carcass all over Nicola's face, screaming at her, "That'll teach you, you fat bitch." There was blood everywhere. It was even running down the windows. It looked like the chainsaw massacre.

Nicola still didn't say anything, knowing to keep as quiet as a mouse until he had calmed down. But after a while, grins slowly began to spread over all our faces, which eventually turned to laughter. There was a funny side to it, looking at her covered in rabbit's blood. Anyway she always professed to be a vampire.

We stopped at the River Brun in Whalley to get cleaned up, but there was still blood all over the car windows. I had to drive through Whalley and Padiham like that, knowing that if any police spotted us we would all be taken down the station for questioning without a shadow of a doubt. Fortunately we managed to get back safely, without any further complications. So bringing the past into the present didn't work too well, and it was not over yet. In fact, far from it.

Straight after that incident, I received a letter from Lorraine after all this time, with a cheque for £600, reading to the effect that she had been investigating my whereabouts, and once again, my mother who was the only link between Gloria, Lorraine and myself had informed her where I was residing. It thanked me for all the beautiful times she had spent with me in the sixties, the money being a small token of her appreciation. She asked me to meet up with her again, because she would like to take us both on the Oriana, a luxurious cruise ship, for a North Atlantic cruise all expenses paid. Well what could I answer to an offer like that. She didn't leave her telephone number, but I had her forwarding address, so I wrote back to her, stating how humble and guilty she made me feel for the actions I had taken so long ago, and told her I would be privileged to join her for a couple of weeks cruise to get to know each other again on a friendly basis. I made it clear I was very busy and would appreciate her visiting me in Padiham in the near future to discuss our options, using the excuse that Leeds was too far away, having a club to keep my eye on. But she didn't write back.

Then in the middle of the night I received a phone call, expecting Lorraine, I got Carol instead, would you believe. "I'm ringing up Haydn, to say goodbye to you." She spluttered. She hadn't rang me in the last twenty months, so I couldn't weigh up why she was ringing now.

"The world is going berserk these last few weeks. What the fuck is happening to me with all these ex-women of mine?" was my initial reaction.

Being the kind of man I was I politely asked, "Why, where are you going?"

"I'm going to kill myself tonight. Goodbye!" she screamed and slammed the phone down on me. I tried ringing her back but she'd left the receiver of the hook.

I thought for a moment, "Is she bluffing or does she mean it." I knew she was mentally unstable at times, so there was a possibility that she meant it. "What shall I do?" I thought. "Can't take the chance. I'd better get there fast." I rushed to my car, but realising I hadn't much fuel left, it seemed I wasn't going anywhere, considering there were no petrol stations open around Padiham at that time of night. My mind engaged into overload mode. "What should I do? I don't need Carol's death on my hands?" I knew she could be a bitch at times, but in a strange way, I still had feelings for her.

I decided to ring the Halifax police. After going through all the channels, and determining my identity, address, and telephone number, I heard a female voice.

"How can we help you sir?"

"I think a girl I once knew is committing suicide tonight, can you please check it out for me, because there's no means of me doing it myself?"

I supplied her with Carol's name and address, and she transmitted the instructions to another department to investigate the matter. I was informed they'd be in contact with me.

Half an hour passed by before the phone rang and a police officer answered. "It's just as you instructed us sir. The front door is wide open, and the telephone is off the hook. There are empty pill containers everywhere, but there is no sign of her. Have you any idea which way she'd be heading sir?"

I racked my mind searching for an answer. "I reckon she's taken the pills and panicked. It's my guess she's heading for her mate Moira, who lives at the other side of the main road, past the fire station."

"Well we're giving you an open line," he answered, "Stick with us while we check it out." There was silence for a while, but then the officer came back to me. " We've found her sir, unconscious in the base of a telephone cubicle. We previously passed her twice without spotting her. She's just been taken to Halifax General. She'll be alright I think, we found her in time." Wasn't I relieved, thanking him profusely and putting the telephone down.

"Thank God for that!" I thought. "In the morning, I'd better buy a bunch of flowers and make a special point of visiting her." Which was exactly what I did, walking into the ward and placing the flowers beside her locker. She had come round, but was rather docile, due to all the pills and medication that had entered her system, in the last twelve hours. Taking one look at me, she grabbed the flowers, throwing them with all her strength into my face.

"Why the fuck didn't you leave me to die?" she growled.

"Always poking your nose into other people's affairs, ain't you?"

"She hasn't changed," I thought. "Still the same old Carol I knew two years ago."

The nurse collared me, taking me to one side. "The doctor is coming round to assess her now, and if I can assure him she will be under constant supervision for the next couple of days, he will release her into your care. I take it that's correct isn't it?"

"Oh no, I'm lumbered again!" I groaned to myself. Seeing the stunned look on my face she repeated the question.

"Yes," I answered. "That is correct."

So Carol was released into my custody, and I had no option but to take her back to Padiham with me, whether she liked it or not. I had a fight on my hands, but by the time we reached the club she was her happy self again, and for the first two or three hours everybody loved her. She even had a go behind the bar, to make herself the focal point of the room. But then she started twitching her neck again, and I knew instinctively I was in trouble. She started shouting at me from behind the bar. "This fanny down here is mine, not yours. So you can fuck off!" I was so embarrassed. I didn't need this palaver. She was degrading me in front of my punters.

"I'm not going anywhere Carol. But you are.!" I growled.

"You bet I am!" she screeched, grabbing her coat and charging out of the door, not having a clue where she was going, because she hadn't a clue where she was to start with. There was one of my punters called Jimmy, who'd been fancying her and getting on great with her earlier, when she was in her right mind, who suddenly went rushing after her out of the door. Grabbing him on the way out, I advised him that he was making one big mistake, but he ignored me completely thinking I was jealous or something. That was the last I saw of them that night.

I hadn't seen Nicola all week, whilst all this was happening, me being slightly upset over the Morecambe business.

Anyway I had too much on my mind to take it on board.

Getting rid of my Punters about five in the morning, I went to bed downstairs feeling totally exhausted. Ten o'clock arrived and there was a loud banging on the club door, waking me up with a start. Just having woken up after an arduous night shift, I was completely disorientated. I cautiously opened the door and squinted out, shielding my eyes from the blinding sunlight, only to eventually focus on Gloria, Carol, Lorraine and Nicola. I couldn't believe my eyes. There they were, all together in a straight line, smiling sheepishly back at me. Well my heart missed a few beats and giving an almighty gasp, I took two steps backwards in shock, not for one moment believing what I was witnessing. Slamming the door shut in their faces in panic, I ran to the bar for a whiskey, downing it in one gulp, giving me time to contemplate the situation, before returning back to the door for another look, thinking to myself, "I must have been fucking mistaken," but sure enough, they were all still there. My whole life, past and present, was in front of me, staring at me from the outside pavement. Oh, what a very peculiar feeling I was experiencing at that moment.

It turned out that Jimmy had taken Carol to his flat, which he rented off his sister. Carol had turned nasty, and smashed the place to pieces, resulting in Jimmy being thrown out never being able to return again. So they had gone down to Ernie's for a while. By this time, I suppose Carol had sobered up. Nicola was already there, and the two were introduced to each other for the first time. Now all that Carol wanted to do was to apologise to me for the aggravation she'd given me the previous night and to thank me belatedly for saving her life. All that Nicola wanted to do was make friends with me, so she offered to take Carol up to the club as an excuse to see me again, which Carol accepted. As they set off together heading for my place, they reached the traffic lights, just as a driver's side window descended, and a woman asked, "Do you know someone called Haydn, who runs a club somewhere local?"

They were both gobsmacked and curious, and told her, "We're heading there ourselves. Do you want us to show you?"

"Yeah, if you don't mind. Hop in the back," she replied. Consequently they all landed together outside the club. The lady was Lorraine and when she told them who she was, total confusion set in. To complicate things further, while they were talking, Gloria pulled up enquiring where Nicola had disappeared to the other night. Poor Lorraine was wondering what the heck she had let herself in for.

I beckoned them all in, and poured them a drink, giving Carol an orange juice, just to be safe. I was in control because I wasn't going out with any of them at the time, so how could I possibly be doing anything underhanded. The closest was Nicola, who I felt a lot for, and she was the first person I give a bollocking to Immediately I started on her, the rest of them rallied around to back her up. Astonishingly they were all together for one fleeting moment.. Carol was right with me, so I offered her a lift home, whilst Nicola agreed to watch the bar for me whilst I was away. I apologised profusely to Lorraine, and told her how pleased I was to see her, and could she possibly hang on for two hours until I returned. She agreed. And as for Gloria, I told her I would have words with her when I got back. But Lorraine and Gloria hated each other from way back, and Nicola was not too impressed with Gloria either, so after a heated argument, Gloria, being outnumbered, drove off in a right huff, never to be seen again. After much explaining, Nicola, Lorraine and I had a brilliant day together down at Ernie's place where Lorraine invited him to visit her in Leeds one night in the near future for a booze up, with me of course, so she could make arrangements to take me on a possible cruise, to boot.

The only thing I felt really sad about was the absence of my two children, Rachel and Georgina, who I have always missed, and because of my visits to Morecambe, I was missing them even more.

But all I can say is, "That's Life," by Frank Sinatra, a song which I made my signature tune on karaoke, portraying, as it did, the story of my life.

Chapter 7 Anxious Moments

The annual Padiham Pit Trip, a long standing tradition from the old days when coal mines flourished in Padiham, was imminent. It was a one day a year ritual, when complete family members, would all visit Morecambe for their bank holiday, virtually taking the town over completely for one massive booze up. Although it is not practised to the extent it used to be, it still continues on a smaller scale to this day. And this was the day.

I had arranged to take a full carload myself, but couldn't stop there due to the fact I had the club to run. But whilst I was there, it would be a good opportunity to look my children up again, to try for a second time to communicate with them on a better level, which was important to me.

Steve, John, and another guy called Robert filled the rear seats of the car, whilst Yogurt invited himself to keep me company, sitting in the privileged passenger seat, possibly with Gloria in mind, but definitely because we had to cross the Trough of Bowland. We were just about to leave when Suzey came running out towards the car.

"Is there any room for me Haydn? I'll be bored around here without you two."

"Sorry Suzey," Yogurt butted in, "there's no room, we're a bit squashed as it is."

She wasn't to be put off. "I'll get in, don't you worry. I'll sit between you and Haydy on the centre consul, in the front. I won't get in your way, I promise."

Yog and I just looked at each other and silently shrugged as she crawled in, over me, making herself as comfortable as she could, astride the centre consul, fully opening the sun roof for extra breathing space. This was rather embarrassing because every time I changed gear, I had to grope around for the gear stick, between her legs, but regardless of all these inconveniences we managed to set off. We had just reached the Trough, when Robert, who had been drinking black cans continuously for the last hour, tried to stand up and, squashing past Suzey, forced his head and shoulders out of the sunroof to shout abuse at passing motorists. This went on for a short while, rather annoying us to say the least, especially Yogurt in the front.

He nudged me and whispered, "You know every inch of this road don't you? Well put your foot down Haydy. That'll shut the twat up." So down went my foot, and off spun the car at top speed, throwing Rob back into his seat, causing all three backseat passengers to panic. But Yog and Suzey were definitely lapping it up. We carried on for a mile or so at breakneck speed, experiencing total silence in the back. They were shitting bricks, but Yog and Suzey were buzzing. The road in front was completely clear, being visible for miles. There was a humpback bridge with an acute left hand bend directly following, which Yog and I had ridden many times before. Knowing my capabilities, I hit the top of the bridge with the car shooting into the air. Unexpectedly, Suzey almost disappeared out of the sunroof. Instinctively, Yogurt grabbed her left ankle whilst I grabbed her right one, miraculously forcing her back down into the car. I hit the road at the other side of the bridge having to manoeuvre the tricky bend using only my right arm, the car taking it perfectly without one small skid. Pulling over to catch my breath and to check the back seat at the same time, I noticed all three of their faces had a greenish haze about them, rendering them speechless.

Laughing his cock off, Yog reached over and patted me on the shoulder, "A bit of good driving, that, brilliant Haydn!"

I glared at Suzey, mentally checking on her, who didn't seem scared at all, but then again she hadn't a clue whether she was in this world or Fuller's world. I was quite confident of the manoeuvre over the bridge, but I have to admit I hadn't expected Suzey to be leaving us so abruptly. John gave me direct instructions to take it more steady from then on, otherwise he was getting out and walking, whilst Robert never spoke another word until we got to Morecambe.

On reaching our destination and eventually getting shut of them, leaving just Yog, Suzey and myself, we decided to visit Gloria whilst we were in the vicinity. But would you believe, the house was up for sale. They had all departed, and I have never set eyes on any of them to this day.

Shortly after that incident Suzey met a guy in Padiham called Saul and they began seeing each other on a regular basis. But this special night having had a bad argument, she was heading back to the club alone. It was on the same night that a new female had shown her face there, and she and I were getting on great together, drinking, singing karaoke and talking in general.

Hillis had to appear at the entrance first, half pissed as usual. Spotting us sitting there, he ambled towards us, plonking his body at our table, and flexing his chest muscles in front of us both, stated in his authoritative way, "I'll be taking her off you before the night's over."

"Just fuck off, and shut up," I rapped, having no time for him at all. Getting up smirking, he casually wandered off to talk to someone else.

Then Suzey appeared, in a very distraught state, ranting and raving about Saul, walking straight to the bar and helping herself to a very large whiskey. Down the hatch it went, whilst I was thinking, "That's a bit much Suzey, helping yourself without even asking. People don't do things like that around here." But she did. And after she'd done it she erratically picked up a knife and rushed for the ladies, locking herself in. It was not long afterwards that I heard a bang coming from inside the toilets, as if someone had fallen, and rushing to the scene I shouted through the door, "Are you alright in there?" There was some moaning and groaning, but no definite answer, so I struggled to force the door, only being able to open it about a foot, because she was laid on the floor blocking it, but I could see there was blood around.

Shouting to Hillis, who had now changed tables and was

sitting with the girl I had been chatting up, "Hillis, for fuck's sake, come across here and help me open this door. Suzey's inside and she's done something bad to herself. There's blood everywhere," to which he answered with his arrogant attitude,

"Fuck Suzey! She's most likely riddled with Hep C anyway. I'm not going near her, the smackhead she is. Sort her out yourself, whilst I entertain your woman." Hillis was definitely thinking that he had got one up on me for the first time, and he was determined to hang on to her in spite of everything. But regardless of this, I managed to get the door open myself only to find that she had some self-inflicted wounds on one of her arms with an abundance of blood. But although there were many, they were not as serious as I imagined them to be. She was just needing attention that was all. Thankfully at that moment Saul walked in, always putting me in mind of someone who was not quite with it.

"Hey you," I called out to him, "sort your girlfriend out over here, she's not my responsibility. She's been slashing herself again. There's a first aid kit behind the bar," and I stamped off. Saul bandaged her arms and rushed her to hospital in a taxi. As I made my way back to the girl, Hillis started to laugh, "You've lost her now, so fuck off and sit somewhere else." He was imitating what I'd said to him earlier, being really chuffed with himself.

The night went on and on, until there was only the three of us left, and Tony, of course, in the background, asleep on one of the benches.

I shouted across to Hillis, "Well Hillis, it's time I was closing. Take your bird and do one." He tried to get up but being too pissed he just couldn't make it, struggling for about ten minutes trying to get the lady and himself to the door. But it wasn't happening, she was as pissed as he was.

After watching them perform for a while, gradually losing patience, I shouted over, "There's a taxi waiting outside and he's getting impatient. If you don't make it there in the next minute, I'm taking you there." They still couldn't make it to the door, so grabbing hold of Hillis by the scruff of the neck, I dragged him outside and plonked him inside the taxi whilst he was calling for his bird.

I told him very smugly, “You're going, she's stopping,” closing the taxi door on him, giving the driver instructions, and payment, and sending him on his way.

“I just took the girl back to the bench seats, laid her down and covered her up with a blanket for the rest of the night, and left her to it.

“Hillis, you mucked my night up completely, but YOU didn't get anywhere yourself did you?” was the consoling thought passing through my mind as I made my way to bed.

The following Sunday dinnertime, being slightly bored with ourselves, Nicola, Yogurt, Suzey, Saul and I were drinking vodka, wondering what to do with the day, when Nicola came out with a new proposal.

“Let's all go skiing! She stood up and shouted out with her arms above head, clenching her fists. Everybody was half cut and thought it was a brilliant idea, even though, not one of us had ever been skiing in our lives before. There was a dry ski slope near the nick of Pendle, at a place called Well's Springs. We had been itching to try it out, so off we went. We sat on the hillside outside the complex trying to gain more courage with another bottle of vodka. In the distance we spotted a farmer driving a four-wheel buggy, rounding up sheep, very slowly working his way towards us. Suzey, unbeknown to Saul, fancying a ride, just for the laugh, had moved stealthily forward from us to hide behind a bush. Saul, as dumb as a brush, hadn't registered yet what was happening. Waiting until the farmer was passing by, she suddenly shot out, performing an almighty leap onto the back of the buggy, completely startling him. He eventually calmed down and could be seen chatting to her in an amiable manner. We couldn't hear what they were saying, but obviously she was asking him to run her around for a while, and he must have accepted because they both took off together across the fields, disappearing over a distant hill.

By this time the penny had dropped and Saul was doing his

head in, jumping up raving, "I'm going skiing!" Being rather annoyed with what had just happened, he was looking for a release, so we all followed him into the complex.

As we approached the top of the steepest slope, all geared up, the attendant asked, "Are you all capable of skiing?"

"You what mate?" Saul blankly replied, "I'm a national contender, I'll have you know?" so studying us for a while he eventually let us through. I had just finished putting my skies on, when Saul was about to take off. I butted in to give him some advice, not that I had a clue either, he just took off, half way through my first sentence, not listening to one word. As he shot down the slope at top speed in a straight line, not capable of weaving from side to side, approaching a small rise and fall towards the bottom of the slope, he was thrown off balance completely, flying into the air, losing both his skies in the process. An instructor came running up to him to severely reprimand him, when I set off doing exactly the same thing, except I was heading straight for them. When I got to the rise, somehow both my skis' tips stuck in the matting, causing me to catapult into the air, doing a double somersault right over their heads, as they stood there petrified. Hitting the matting with some force, experiencing terrible pain, I had to bluff it out that I wasn't hurt, because there were a few skiers sat nearby, who all stood up purposely to give me a standing ovation for the best jump they'd seen that season. The instructor abandoned Saul and came running over to me, with the sole intention of banning me also from the large slope, pointing out that there were other smaller ones for learners.

Yogurt was still at the top of the slope waiting his turn, but after witnessing our spectacle, he shouted, "Fuck this for a game of soldiers!" throwing his skies to one side and disappearing into nowhere. I was struggling and decided to make my way back to the car, needing to return to the club as soon as possible for medication, later being informed that I had broken three ribs. But to my dismay, the car, and everybody else, was missing. Thoughts passed through my mind, “It's three miles to the village, I'll never make it on foot. That Yog, he's done it on me again.” Yogurt was always pinching my car, but this time I blamed myself because I must have accidentally left the keys in the ignition. Fortunately for me, he always brought it back in one piece, well, up to press that is, but that wasn't the point, I needed it now. I struggled on for a short distance looking for any one of them, bumping into Saul who in turn was wandering around, still looking for Suzey. Nicola, who hadn't participated that day, was spotted sunbathing on the grass nearby, oblivious to everything. So rounding her up, we all endeavoured to begin our long arduous trek back to Padiham. We'd walked no more than an hundred yards down the hill when who should be coming towards us, but Yogurt and Suzey in my car. They had been to Padiham for a burger.

He just laughed, “Ha, ha, ha! I've had a great day watching you lot make pillocks of yourselves. I borrowed your car. You don't mind do you?”

Well I was livid, and even though I had three broken ribs, I grabbed him by the scruff of the neck, dragging him out of the car whilst I ordered the rest of them to get in, and drove off, leaving him stranded on a rock. I hadn't travelled more than a hundred yards down the road when my conscience forced me to stop.

“I can't leave him behind,” I blurted guiltily. “Let's round him up again,” so, reversing, I offered him a lift home.

Taking the car was a sore point with me. Yogurt who was an excellent driver, but didn't possess a driving licence, had this thing about being behind the wheel of a car. He was always trying to persuade me to let him have a spin in it, for a short while by himself, which I always refused on legal grounds. It wasn't too long ago that Hillis had been goading him to obtain my car keys which I used to leave at the end of the bar, and off they went without my knowledge or consent.

Some time later they both came rushing in, and Yogurt shouted to me as he sneaked the keys back to the end of the bar, “You haven't seen us Haydn,” and both disappeared out of the fire escape door.

I thought, "What's he been up to now?" but found out a few seconds later when the police came running in.

That car outside is still yours isn't it?" they enquired.

"Yes," I answered, rather puzzled. "Why?"

"Have you the car keys?" they enquired

"Yes, of course I have," I answered, picking the keys up from the end of the bar, and dangling them in front of them.

"Well you'll have to come down to the station with us for breathalizing," they replied.

"I haven't been anywhere," I exclaimed.

"That's not our opinion," they commented. "You've been driving rather erratically up and down the main road five minutes ago. The engine's still hot."

"There's eighty witnesses here to say I haven't moved from this bar," I replied.

"Well you must have lent the car to somebody. Most likely Yogurt."

"I've lent the car to nobody," I replied not telling any lies.

"Well how come the keys are here then." One of the officers had taken them to the car to make sure they belonged.

"Your guess is as good as mine," I replied. "I haven't a clue."

Giving me the keys back, they had a secret conversation between themselves and started on their way.

"We know it was Yogurt." one of them stated, "Tell him we'll have him next time," and they both left.

I thought, "I'll kill the twat when I see him." But you don't get any change out of Yog. He just laughs at you.

Due to the skiing saga, I was having trouble serving for long spells behind the bar. For a week, I couldn't do more than about twenty minutes at a time, and then couldn't get comfortable sitting around watching over the place. So I made a very unusual move that was talked about for years afterwards. I moved my double bed onto the stage, and when the bar was getting too much for me, I retired, fully clothed for a lie down, so I could still be in contact with my punters from the comfort of my bed. After resting for a while, I'd attempt another small session behind the bar again. At first it was a novelty, but people got used to it, so long after I was well again, the bed stopped. It was so convenient for me, and I felt safer watching over the place at all times. I had a stroke of bad luck mind you, when initially moving the bed down from the upstairs. I had left the upstairs back door wide open and a council official walked in to see me about some matter, and couldn't fail to notice that I was in the middle of a building project, converting the upstairs to seven bedsitters.

"Oh shit!" I thought. "He's bound to report me 'cos I haven't notified building control yet." I was right. In a flash, the building inspector and the local fire officer were around to inspect the upstairs premises. They served a prohibition order on me, stating that until such time that the project was completed to safety requirements, nobody was allowed to sleep upstairs. I was rather annoyed but it didn't put me out too much, because there would be nobody sleeping upstairs for a while anyway, still having a vacant front room downstairs which I could use if necessary. It shouldn't have happened, but it was just one of those things.

Now not long afterwards, I started to get bad vibrations about Suzey, suspecting that she was possibly back on the heroin again. I fired loads of questions at her trying to find the truth out for myself, but she simply lied through her teeth, pleading her innocence. I knew from my past experiences of addicts just what they were capable of when craving for a fix. In such circumstances she'd rob me without thinking twice about it to get her hands on some smack, which was exactly what happened. Suzey was helping me behind the bar one late afternoon, after just changing some money for the till. Placing my briefcase down in the kitchen area behind the bar for a second, I shot off to the gents for no more than a minute being desperate for a piss, returning only to find Suzey had disappeared, leaving the bar unattended. On investigating I found my briefcase had disappeared with her. I shouted desperately to Yogurt to get after her fast, to retrieve it for me, my hands being tied running the bar. Without hesitation he shot out of the club, returning within twenty minutes with my briefcase in his hand and not one penny missing.

"I caught her in the Gardeners" he sneered, "she'd just ordered a load of drinks, and was waiting for someone to turn up to supply her with some smack, I suppose. I snatched the briefcase off her, gave her some abuse and came straight back here. Is everything in order Haydy?"

"Bang on" I replied. "Thank you very much Yog, you're a gentleman. You just saved my life."

But it meant that Suzey had given me the nasty job of kicking her and her boyfriend out, without a minute's notice, not to be trusted around the club any more, Heroin, amphetamines, Es, cocaine, and their associated addicts being a "No-go" from the start. But these rules didn't apply to cannabis, which was a totally different story. I know the media make it look all so bad, but frig the media, it's been around forever and a day and I have never experienced trouble related to people smoking it, so there was nothing out of the ordinary seeing odd people using the stuff around me. In fact it helped me considerably, because after a few joints, they were too relaxed to cause any sort of trouble whatsoever. Cannabis through the ages has always been associated with peace - the red Indians smoking their pipes of peace, while the American government were sending its troops in to slaughter them; the hippies smoking it, whilst trying to portray to the world an image of world peace. Remember Flower Power, the strength of the cannabis plant, make love not war and Ban the Bomb. Then there were great people emerging like "Bob Dylan," writing and singing their music, trying to stop the carnage that was going on around them in Vietnam with songs like, "Blowing in the wind," smoking a joint at the same time whilst he was writing, it being common knowledge that he was partial to the stuff. Also one of our greatest personalities "Mr. John Lennon," who spent much time smoking cannabis whilst trying to bring peace to the world, with songs like "Give peace a chance." Now, regarding my club in Padiham, which was insignificant to the rest of the world, but definitely wasn't to the people who surrounded me, people who had spent a lifetime bickering between themselves, were starting to come together in harmony, to smoke and pass a joint around to each other in the name of Peace. A totally neutral area in the sordid world we lived in, making me think, "Surely it was time to get real. Whatever."

Which brings me to a strange situation which occurred about a fortnight after I'd sacked Suzey and Saul, which I'm not saying was related but is definitely open for opinions.

It was the early hours of Saturday morning, the club was closed with only Tony and me left, and the time was approaching for us to catch some shuteye. I had formed the front downstairs room into a very comfortable bedroom, which I was planning to start using in the near future.

For some unknown reason I decided that early morning to use it for the first time, informing Tony that if he so desired, he could kip down in my bed on the stage, which seemed common sense to me at the time, which he agreed to, so we both got our heads down for the night.

Every Friday night, I religiously carried my full week's takings, in a money pouch on my person. My routine was in readiness to cash in my takings at the Post Office the first thing Saturday morning. This morning was no different. I fell asleep immediately, only to be awakened about three hours later by the bedroom door forcefully flying open and Tony rolling in. Not being able to see him too good at first, I needed a few seconds to focus my eyes to the dark surroundings. When I did I was mortified to find he was literally tied up from head to foot, lying there on the floor besides me. Well, you can imagine my reactions.

Shocked as they come, I spluttered, "What the hell, has happened to you?"

I heard him trying to mumble something and I realised he

was also gagged. Jumping out of bed I untied the cloth that was biting into his bloodstained mouth.

"We've just had an armed robbery!" he screamed out. Now Tony was a calm character at the worst of situations, but on this occasion he was rather put out, and was trembling badly.

"Calm down Tony whilst I untie you."

Whilst I was doing this, he blurted out, "There were some bloody armed robbers with loaded shotguns. They held them to my head, threatening to kill me. I've been in some sticky situations, but I thought I was a gonner just then. They scared the shit out of me!"

I was gobsmacked. All I could think was, "What the fuck are you talking about, nobody has disturbed me?"

"There's no way in Tony."

"Oh, there is. No mistake. They came in through the trapdoor in the ceiling with a ladder, and left the same way," he replied.

"What happened?" I asked nervously, as by now I too was in a state of uneasiness.

"I only knew of their presence when they started nudging me in the ribs with the barrel of a sawn off shotgun. I woke up to two of 'em pointing guns at me and demanding money that I was carrying. I gave them my last forty quid dole money, only to get hit in the face with the butt of a gun, and him telling me to stop taking the piss, and to hand over the weekly take. It was only then that I realised that they thought I was you, but they didn't get any sense out of me. They searched me, and tied me up. I think they were a bit pissed off if you ask me. They searched the bed and the stage, and then went over to the till but couldn't get into that either. They were starting to lose their rag. Finally they spotted that wall safe in the kitchen. You know, the one you were going to install and never got round to it. Luckily it was locked, so they struggled up the ladder with it, pulling the ladder up behind them and disappeared, thank God."

"Bloody hell Tony. Did you recognise any of them?"

"Not a chance. They were both hooded."

By this time I'd completely untied him, his wrists were in a real state from rope burns caused by trying to free himself.

"Well it's going to take 'em days to break into that safe," I replied, "and there's nothing in it anyway. They will be pleased."

"You did a good job with that till, enclosing it and bolting it down. They struggled for ages before eventually giving up the ghost."

I ran across to the till to inspect it, confirming that it hadn't been opened, which was just as well as there was still about three hundred pounds float left in it.

"What a set of dickheads, they haven't done one thing correct," I thought to myself as I cautiously surveyed the street outside, rushing round the back to check the damage upstairs. The door frame was broken but everything else was in order, so I decided I'd got off very lightly, returning downstairs to pour us both a strong drink to calm us down, before discussing what had actually happened.

"Well they can't have been from Padiham, if they thought you were me, can they Tony?"

"No, but they knew how to get in, for sure. They must have brought their own ladder because we haven't one, have we? And they knew you were very likely carrying a decent sum of money, didn't they?"

"Weren't you scared Tony?" I asked.

"I was shitting bricks, but if it's time to go, it's time to go. It's as easy as that," he joked. "He mustn't have wanted me upstairs yet."

"Anyway Tony, I have to thank you for keeping your trap shut about me."

"Give me more credit than that. I don't grass on people. You should know that by now," was his sincere answer.

"All the same, thanks again Tony, you're a star."

"You'd better report it to the police in the morning, they robbed me of forty quid remember." Tony replied. I reached into my money bag pulling out forty pounds. "You'd better take this," I insisted, passing him the money. He didn't refuse.

The next day, after reporting the incident to the main Burney police, two CID detectives came round to question us, and even though Tony's wrists were burnt to hell, I don't think any of them believed one word we were saying. They thought we were into some sort of insurance scam or something. They kept giving it to me that we were wasting their time, and that I had an answer for everything.

"That's because it really happened," I kept telling them.

All they kept saying was, "We are in the middle of a murder investigation, and we don't need this."

"Murder investigation!" I muttered sarcastically. "You're not fit to serve hamburgers in the Burnley Precinct." And even more so when they took off with all the money out of the unopened till for fingerprint examination. That was a total waste of time, even a five year old would have known better. I think they did it for the sole purpose of inconveniencing me, because it took me six weeks to persuade them to give it back. So after mending the back door, making it much more secure this time, I gave it all up has a bad job, coming to the conclusion that it was done by some out-of-towners, instructed by someone who had a grudge against me, and knew my routines backwards. I could only think of one person that fitted the bill?????? But I couldn't name anyone, because I couldn't prove a thing.

Then, about six weeks later, I had another very trying incident which happened in the early hours of the morning in October 1997. There were about ten regulars including Yogurt in the bar area, Yogurt being slightly pissed.

"Can I get my head down for an hour, in your downstairs front room?" he wearily asked.

"Why not," I replied. I'll wake you up in about an hour's time," and off he trundled. An hour passed, and I went to wake him up having just put a new barrel on, so having a few pints going spare, I gave him one...... a pint that is.

Another half an hour passed by, and then Harold, one of the older end, commented, "Can you see that thin, still layer of smoke above us?"

We all glanced up, and sure enough there was some smoke, eight feet in length, hovering above our heads. So totally puzzled, I went to investigate. I opened the front bedroom door where Yogurt had been kipping, AND!!!!!!!!!!!! EMERGENCY! There were flames everywhere. The entire room was engulfed. My first reaction was to grab a fire extinguisher and I rushed in to douse the flames, but it was too hot and smoky. Within three seconds I was out again like a shot.

"Ring the fire brigade!" I panicked, as I rushed outside to the other door, trying to tackle it from another angle. But it was useless, the flames had really taken hold. Within minutes a fire officer appeared, commanding all my punters who were still at the bar drinking to evacuate the place.

"What about our beer?" one of them shouted.

"Fuck the beer. Get out fast. Now! This is an emergency," one of the fire officers shouted. More firemen were outside, fitting their hoses into position, and whilst all this was happening, I couldn't believe what my customers were up to. They were carrying tables and buffets to the outside opposite pavement with all their beer, so they could sit down in comfort and not have their drinking interrupted by the fire, whilst they watched the spectacle. It was 2.00am in the morning and in-between time my club was burning down. The fire was too intense for one engine, and even after calling upon a further high-pressure unit to help, it took a while to get the fire under control. And whilst all this was happening, my customers were complaining to the police and fire officers, because nobody would let them inside to obtain another round of drinks. It was just pure madness.

Unbelievingly one of the police officers came to me asking, "What scam are you up to this time Haydn?" Assuming he was referring to the armed robbery, I just sternly turned and stared at him in stony silence. The only thought passing through MY mind was, "While everybody is having an excellent night out and making jokes of it, my whole existence here is being destroyed in front of me."

Harold

Harold & Friend

Yog sympathetically approached me, "What are you going to do now Haydy?"

"Let's wait till the fire brigade has gone, and I can assess the situation. I'll tell you better then," I replied.

"Well, I'm telling you this Haydn. No matter what the damage, this club is carrying on, and you're going nowhere, even if I have to round up every last person in town to voluntarily help us do the job. Trust me Haydn. This town would never be the same again if you left."

Those words brought a tear of consolation to my eyes, even though the situation was critical. Nobody had said meaningful things like that to me for one hell of a while, and it touched me deeply. It's strange, the circumstances that one finds their best friends in life. It must have been Yogurt in his intoxicated state who had started the fire by dropping a cigarette or something. I knew he was suffering from a severe guilt complex, and was trying to rectify it in his own way, but to be honest, the fire was a pure accident, and nobody was to blame. At least nobody was hurt, and that was a blessing. If I hadn't woken him up when I did, he would have most likely died in the flames.

The fire brigade and police left me to it, the club being rendered safe, and my punters left, leaving Yog and I to move the tables, buffets and empty glasses inside on our own.

"Very thoughtful of them," I thought. But I didn't pay much heed to it, because I had more important things on my mind.........what was left of the club. I was dreading that moment.

My first job was to switch the power back on, which the fire brigade had automatically de-energised to avoid electrocution by water. There were a few bangs and flashes as the fuses blew, but would you credit it, every light came on, in the main club area. There was abundant smoke, dirt and water damage but that was all. I couldn't believe the outcome.

I walked to the vicinity of the fire and realised the two side rooms were totally gutted, the ceilings being completely knackered, but floor joists above the ceiling had survived. I was very relieved with what I saw. It seemed the alterations I had completed, over and above regulation standards, concerning soundproofing and fire protection, had paid dividends, and although the two side rooms needed a lot of work, the fire had been contained and restricted long enough for the fire brigade to do their job. I was so relieved, feeling that someone was watching over me. Dropping everything and grabbing Yogurt, I took him for a rant round the dance floor being so tensed up with relief. I just locked the main doors, and we both ran down to Ernie's to wake him up to break the bad news to him, hoping for a drink in the comfort of his home to calm us down.

Early that next day, leaving Ernie's place, Yogurt disappeared round the corner without a word, whilst I made my way to the club to start cleaning up the debris. There was a skip due to be dropped outside, and whilst I was waiting for it to be delivered, some Lancashire Telegraph reporters turned up to take photographs of me in the middle of the street, with a fire extinguisher in my hand. I eventually made the headlines "Padiham Landlord Tackles Burning Club Single-Handed." I didn't waste precious time. There I was, loading rubble into the skip, when Yogurt turned up with a full gang of helpers.

"We're all spending the day, putting this place back on the map" he shouted excitedly. "All right with you Haydn?"

"All right with me Yog. Thanks everybody. Very much appreciated." On that note we all got stuck into the job. Even Ernie turned up later, balancing on tables with his two bad legs, plastering away. What a team. It wasn't just Ernie's crew, other people I had never seen before arrived. What a turn out it was. One was a young girl, about fifteen years old, very pretty, who acted and spoke far older than her age and insisted on ripping the ceilings down in the two side rooms, and filling the skip up with the rubbish. Her name was Leanne.

"You can't attempt that," I told her." Have you ever seen the soot and filth that drops from these ceilings when you start hacking into the plaster lats that haven't been touched for a hundred years? It's not a young girl's job, I can assure you"

"It doesn't matter what you say," she insisted, "That's what I've come here to do, and that's exactly what I am going to do, so just button up will you?"

"I give up," I answered. "But don't say you haven't been warned," giving her a pair of overhauls that were six sizes too big, and asking her to watch me.

"Get on these steps and using this garden spade only, slot it between the lats and the upstairs floorboards and pull down with all your might. And shut your eyes and don't breathe while the shit's falling. Alright?"

"Alright", she answered. And DID she tear into it.

"Bloody hell!" I thought, "She couldn't half work for a young 'ne." I was astonished watching her.

The place was washed down, cleaned up and painted in no time at all. The back rooms were stripped, cleaned up and made safe. I couldn't credit it. By seven that evening the skip had gone, showing no signs of a fire, the club being open again for business, minus two side rooms of course. And do you know what happened? A customer of mine came in complaining of a slight smell of smoke, immediately causing a well known saying to flash through my mind - "You can please some of the people all the time, and all the people some of the time, but you can't please all the people all of the time, believe me."

Subsequently, for all the people participating that day, it was party time on the house, with my full gratitude. Especially Leanne. The girl looked like one of the chimney sweeps from a "Charles Dickens" novel.

"Ah, ah, ah!" I laughed heartily as I approached her, "Look in the mirror. Have you seen the state of yourself?" She'd been working like a trooper all day, refusing any sort of help, and not only had she stripped the two ceilings completely and cleaned up after herself, but she'd also removed every single protruding nail, ready for reinstalling. There was a four inch sewer drain running over the fire damaged section of the ceiling that was badly burnt, causing it to sag, accumulating raw sewage inside of it. As she was ripping it down, the contents poured onto her head soaking her from head to foot in black soot and shit. Didn't she stink. But that didn't put her off, she carried on regardless. What a lass!

"Yeh," she uttered, smiling at me. "I am in a state aren't I, but it feels great doesn't it!"

Yog was buzzing that night. The mission he had organised, was completed successfully, really making up for his pecadillo.

The main reason for the rush to get the club back on its feet fast, was because I didn't want Eric to find out until it reopened. It could have been a good excuse to get me out. Consequently there was no insurance claimed.

A couple of police officers came that evening, I imagine to survey the damage. They nearly dropped down dead, when they witnessed me up and running again. They couldn't believe it. I personally visited the local fire station to thank them for services rendered, and offered them a freebie if they were ever passing.

Now let me take time to tell you about Leanne. She was another of those wild women with a problem. She was a very forward and intelligent girl, which I sensed immediately listening to her. However she suffered from dyslexia, and was illiterate, not being able to read nor write. She'd worked hard on the ceiling at the club that day to prove to me she was not stupid like many people assumed, and also that she was willing to work. I got to know her well. She had been expelled from school because she was a rebel, and she was a rebel, because people kept ridiculing her because she couldn't read. Because of her past experience she refused point blank to attend any other future school, so her mother Gale was ordered to teach her. But she wasn't cut out for the job so consequently Leanne's education suffered further, getting nowhere fast. But now I was in her life, we both made a pact. She truly wanted to be part of my team and promised she would help me in all the work she was legally allowed to do for a pittance, and in return I would teach her to read. I knew I had a job on my hands but we both agreed to give it a try, so she became my labourer you might say, and a pretty one at that. There were many envious comments, believe me.

"Leanne," I told her, "First of all, never be ashamed that you cannot read. Are you listening to me?"

"Yes", she answered. "I'm listening."

"Good," I replied. "Because the guy who owns this place, Eric, is dyslexic also, and it doesn't seem to have held him back does it?"

"Is that right?" she surprisingly exclaimed.

"That's right, so take heed." He still relies on me to read him all his important documents. "You'll get on well together, you two. A beaming smile appeared on her face, and I knew I'd said the correct words to her.

Leanne

Nicola, Dwarling, Ernie & Leanne

Sonya, Kirsty, Gurney & myself

I began teaching her by mixing work and her lessons together. Whatever we were dealing with, I used to tell her its name, spelling it out, pronouncing, and then told her to try it herself, and try it again and again until she mastered it. We went through thousands of different objects, and in the evening, over a drink together, I'd teach her how to recognise and pronounce the alphabet, slowly progressing, until the moment came when she was able to rumble through an infant book. But then she shot forward, stumbling over difficult words, but, determined to succeed, she eventually got there. It took about six months to complete the course, but she came out of it a much better person.

She beamed with confidence always being very grateful to me for spending so much time on her. Her mother and father, Gale and Gary, became good friends of mine also, because of it. Everything worked out well, and our friendship survived over the years. She has never forgotten what I did for her, but I always tell her I enjoyed every second of doing it.

What I did for her must have sparked something off deep down inside of me, because I started thinking of the children around Padiham who were so bored and frustrated, having nothing to do and nowhere to spend their time. I called in at the local police station to enquire if I was in order opening a children's disco one day a week for them all. They had no objections, as long as there was no alcohol displayed behind the bar whatsoever. I got to thinking that I was working too many hours and was in the process of closing down on two of the quietest days of the week to reopen again at seven on those evenings. One of those afternoons would be ideal for my new project, although it didn't help my rest period at all. But I thought it would be worth it to see those little kids enjoying themselves. I was going to charge one pound per head, and supply them with as much free pop and crisps as they wanted. I spread flyers round all the local school information boards and waited for the result, thinking the club would be an ideal place for them to congregate after school, and intended to open from 2-30pm until 6-30pm, leaving me ample time to re-open at seven for the evening shift. I couldn't employ anyone on that shift, because there was no profit to be made, doing it purely for kindness because I thought something like this was desperately needed in Padiham.

Wednesday afternoon arrived and I expected only one or two people on the first day. Wasn't I wrong, again, they arrived in droves and all dressed up to kill, ten to sixteen year olds from all walks of life. Acting all so polite, they immediately melted my heart, so much so that I could have cried. There were quite a few that didn't have any money, but looking at them standing there so cute, I didn't have the heart to turn them away. So, to be fair, I immediately stopped the entrance fee for all of them, which meant that this day was costing me for the privilege of their company. But that didn't bother me at all, I enjoyed every second of it, but it was very hard work keeping up with them. Kids will be kids, but I have to give them their due, I became a friend to them all, and they respected my premises likewise, every child having fun. They used to come to the bar, and politely order a round of drinks, just as if they were grown-ups having a beer at the pub, tickling me no end, and always bringing their empty glasses back. I was in complete control, for some unknown reason. I suppose they didn't want to be kicked out for being out of hand. The fifteen and sixteen year olds loved the place too. I remember a lovely girl called Sonya, whose family I knew, being my customers, who used to religiously help me during the day with the disco, keeping everyone happy, becoming one big asset to me at the time. In fact I don't know what I'd have done without her. I thought she would be more qualified to sort out what music those kids wanted than me, but I soon learnt that it boiled down to a choice between "The Spice Girls" and "The Spice Girls." Pretty simple really. They'd put on "The Spice Girls," jump onto the stage, all in a line, and everyone sang their little heads off, with all the actions thrown in, as if they'd rehearsed it for weeks. They were great to watch. But when it got to finishing time I had one hell of a job to get them to leave. And immediately on the stroke of seven, my regulars would appear, pushing me to serve them, which I couldn't do until the very last child had left, still having to transfer alcohol back to the bar from the beer cellar, But I was never short of volunteers when it came to that, my punters having no patience at all.

After one of those rewarding sessions, I felt like I'd just completed an hundred hour shift with no sleep, totally exhausted, really taking it out of me. But I wouldn't have missed it for the world. More and more fourteen to sixteen year old girls kept appearing every week, starting to arrive earlier and earlier, telling me they were on their free time. This crowd used to come in about one and leave at three normally. Three or four of the cheeky ones would beg me for a lift, so they didn't miss the school bus.

Then out of the blue, I got an official complaint from the headmistress of Ivy Bank school, stating that certain pupils were never in school Wednesday afternoons and I was responsible for their absence. I told her I was not responsible for anyone but myself, and that they all had minds of their own, but even so, I had to make sure that I didn't open till three-thirty in future, which was the time the younger ones came in. The children's club ran for a long time, becoming a legend in the children's eyes. Even years after it had gone teenagers unknown to me, would pull me up on the street, on first name terms, to thank me for those special times I devoted to them. It was just one of those times that made me feel that life really was worth living.

Chapter 8 A kind of magic

Christmas was approaching, so Ernie and I decided it was a ideal time to give Lorraine a visit in Leeds. She was expecting us. Ernie took a bottle of sherry to be hospitable, but when we arrived she wasn't having any of that.

"When you're with me," she stated, "you drink my spirits only, and no argument about it……OK." So we had to put ourselves out and spent a couple of hours drinking her supplies gratis.

Our initial conversation just had to be Gloria.

"I couldn't believe my eyes when I saw that bitch in Padiham, Haydn," she remarked.

"Yes," I replied. "That was a bit of bad timing, wasn't it."

"Has she been back since?"

"No, I don't think I'll be seeing her again for a long while."

"Really?" she quizzed.

"Really!" I emphasised.

"You were a fool Haydn, packing the group up for her," she remarked.

"I didn't pack it up for her. We'd had an argument over some woman I'd picked up at "The Talk of the Town" in London, just after you and I had fallen out. She was sat in the front privileged passenger seat of our van, whilst they were all squashed like sardines in the back amongst all the equipment. They were all very annoyed about the situation, and rightfully so, being totally exhausted after playing all night, and still having to travel 200 miles to return home, resulting in them pissing off in all directions in Nottingham around five in the morning. That's what it all started over. A woman. They can cause complications at times."

"But they all came back, didn't they?" she added.

I waited a few days for them to contact me, but they never did. So finally I had no choice but to cancel our two years bookings in advance, otherwise I would have been the one getting sued for not turning up. We'd already let one or two venues down."

Lorraine butted in again. "Right. But you didn't lose much time jumping into kip with Gloria, did you?" I got the feeling I was been interrogated.

"I have to admit, that was not on. But she was a temptress in those days and offered me everything I needed."

"And what was that?" she asked. "As if I don't know."

"After constantly being on the road for ten years, day and night, she offered me total comfort and rest," "Okay, and loads 'o nookie too"

"And did you make the right decision?"

"At the time, yes. But after my well-needed rest period, I started desperately to miss the glamour. When the other members of the group eventually came back to try to convince me to reform, I had already cancelled everything, so I told them it couldn't be. That was one of the biggest mistakes in my life, and I have made a few, I can tell you. When I think back, that decision was influenced by Gloria. She put me through some shit. And, believe it or not, she was having another go at me, the other week when you turned up. It never ends does it?" There was silence for a short while.

"I miss those days," she reminisced. "Do you remember when you were playing at the Darwen Cooperative Hall, with Gerry and the Pacemakers. He'd just brought out *"How do you do what you do to me?."* and a group of women were trying to get into your joint dressing room to rape him. You grabbed the door trying to shut them out and got your nose broken with a flying punch from one of the mad teenagers in the process?"

"Remember it! How can I forget a thing like that?"

"Well it didn't knock any sense into you did it?" she laughed. How could I answer that, she'd rendered me speechless.

The fabulous Young Ones

Ernie was getting a little irritated because he was not part of the conversation so we all decided it was time to hit the town at Lorraine's expense, and what a brilliant time we had finishing up at "The Star" about 500yds from her house.

Ernie was desperately fancying her. He was putting on all his airs and graces in an attempt to impress her. I'd given him the go ahead if he could pull it off, but she still, after thirty years, had a thing for me. The three of us were propping the bar up, with Lorraine in the middle, and Ernie persistently chatted her up.

After humouring him for a little while, she blurted out, "I don't want to sound ignorant, but I have got my man here," nodding my way.

"Oh, fucking hell," I thought, "here we go again!" and instinctively backed off. Ernie instantly took the huff and went to sit in the corner by himself, like a little boy who couldn't get his own way. We were all very pissed at the time, so none of us were paying undue attention to each other. Eventually, on checking the room, Lorraine realised Ernie's absence. She commented, "Ernie's missing Haydn. I hope I didn't upset him too much and he's pissed off?"

"He hasn't gone anywhere. He hasn't a clue where he is, apart from being somewhere in the middle of Leeds," I replied.

"Well we'd better look for him," she insisted. We made our way into the music room, only to witness him without his sticks, on stage teaching a line of twenty dolly birds how to dance his special way, using slow body movements to the music.

"Good old Ernie," I chuckled. He was the focal point of the whole room, and the women were loving it. I don't think they had ever met anyone quite like him, by the expressions on their faces.

"The man is definitely not dead yet," I thought to myself as I joined in with the crack, amongst all the talent. We were all buzzing.

Lorraine was the next to take the huff for being neglected and disappeared outside, leaving just Ernie and me to struggle back to her place at the end of the night.

"Don't lose me," he begged, "I haven't a clue where I am."

"Don't worry Ernie, we'll get there. Trust me," I answered

as we trudged up the road together under sufferance, eventually reaching her house. Lorraine was still not speaking to us, and rounded her two Yorkshire terriers up on leads to take them out for a walk, to distance herself from us. Moments passed by and she didn't return, so I decided, not before time, to look for her, which didn't take long because there she was, face down on the front lawn, totally out of this world, still holding the dogs. I took them in first and with a real struggle on my hands, I managed to drag Lorraine to bed. Then I had to attempt getting Ernie tucked in. He was a dead weight but I eventually managed it. After locking up, it was time to get my head down also for a well-deserved rest.

The next morning we all woke up and came down for breakfast around the same time. I was expecting trouble.

To my surprise Lorraine chimed up, "What a brilliant night we had last night Ernie, did you enjoy it?"

Ernie piped up, "Thoroughly. A great night, wasn't it. No trouble at all. We'll have to do it again sometime soon."

I was listening to it all totally astounded, thinking, "None of them can remember Jack shit about the end of last night, the flannelling twats. Maybe it's just as well. It brings the situation back to normal again, thank God." So unbelievably, we all had an amiable breakfast together and Ernie and I returned home with the same bottle he came with.

As for Yogurt, he wasn't around to witness the Christmas period. It all started when he bought a sandwich, and innocently brought it into the club to consume in the peace of the morning, giving him time to recover from the previous evening. Meanwhile Hillis had taken it on himself to go joyriding in my car again, seeing as he had got away with it the last time. Once again he had somehow managed to obtain the keys. My guard was down thinking he wouldn't attempt it again because of his previous close call, but I was wrong. As he was leaving the club, he made some comment to Yogurt, and Yog must have immediately cottoned on to what he was up to. Yog didn't say anything to me for chance I went berserk, and rushed out after Hillis to stop him. But it was too late, Hillis was attempting to drive off with difficulty. He was pissed and couldn't drive at the best of times. Yog just managed to dive through the open, front passenger window to try to reason with him, but Hillis, being his arrogant self, wasn't listening, and they sped off up the road, smashing into three parked vehicles. In no time at all, the police were in pursuit. Hillis parked in Ingham Street and Yog told him to do a runner fast, down an adjacent alley, knowing that if they both ran, they would have eventually been picked up and done together. So he just sat there, on top of the hood of the car, finishing his sandwich waiting for the police to catch up with him to arrest him. He had it in his mind to take the all the blame. Yog always felt it was his duty to look after Hillis in his unstable mental state having both grown up together, and remembering him as he was before the accident. Nobody could dislike Hillis. He was one of those characters that made Padiham. So for trying to retrieve my car, Yogurt spent the next three months in Preston prison, poor lad. He was a rogue, but he was a very honourable person. The police towed my car back to the club, in a badly dented state but not having the heart to part with it being such a brilliant car to drive, I was determined to put it back on the road again. But during my next visit to Australia, Ernie rang me to inform me that he had spotted Eric, given the opportunity whilst I was out of commission, towing it away for badly needed spares, the twat. Annoyed was definitely not the word that I was feeling at the time.

The police were really chuffed for collaring Yog, not knowing they'd arrested the wrong person. I took Hillis at a later date to Preston to visit him, and he even got thrown out of there for acting the fool. You couldn't take him anywhere.

So that Christmas was destined to be an uneventful one, which was exactly how it turned out, apart from one solitary night when I was just preparing to close down. The club was empty, when two latecomers suddenly arrived, pleading to be served. So courteously I let them inside for a last hour.

There was a Scottish guy that I knew well, and a beautiful

25 year-old Scottish maiden that I had never seen before. She and I engaged in deep, personal conversation, whilst he slowly slipped into unconsciousness. He told me earlier that the girl was his daughter and I believed him.

The guy was now totally out of this world, and I had turned the main lighting down and was just about to try to bring him round again to finally close down for the night, when she went to the ladies opposite, shouting across at me, "Don't move a muscle till I get back!" To my total shock, she emerged totally naked, running towards me, jumping on my lap, legs apart. Well she definitely caught me on the hop there, without a shadow of a doubt.

"Shag me Haydn!" she screamed. "Give me what for!" The guy she had come in with never moved one iota.

"What!" I replied, "Next to your father?"

"Who said he was my father?" she impatiently enquired.

"He did."

"Not in a month of Sundays. Just get on with it before he wakes up." Well I won't go into details but for the next half an hour we both made mad passionate love over virtually every table in the place, breaking one in the process. What a well-needed session I had, doing me a world of good. I have to give her her due, she was an excellent performer. In time, we got dressed and sat down to relax and finish our drinks, when the guy woke up.

Looking around the room, whilst fighting to return to the land of the living, he turned to me and commented, "Well thank you for such an excellent night, well appreciated. We'd better get going now whilst I'm still standing."

And I thought, "And thank you for such an excellent night. Come again soon."

Early the next evening they appeared again and I thought, "Is this going to be another of those unexpected evenings?" when who should roll through the door but Steve. He just stood there and immediately focused on the new bird in town.

Turning to him, I could read his mind like a book, shouting

across to him, "Don't even think about it Steve!"

"Think about what?" he enquired, with a grin all over his face.

"You know what I'm talking about. Make one move toward her and you're banned for life." I jokingly replied. Just mentioning anything related to beer, and he would obey immediately.

But things didn't work out for me that night and I never did get a second piece of the pie. I was rather disappointed with the outcome.

But just after Steve had shown his face in the club that evening, a guy called Chris appeared. He'd been coming in on a frequent basis lately, and the first thing he'd do on entering was to throw his arms up into the air and shout at the top of his voice, "I'm Jesus Christ and I can walk on water." If he'd said it once, he'd said it a dozen times within the last couple of days, and he was starting to get on my tits. That evening was no exception. He chimed up again with all the same old crap.

I went over to him and tapped him on the shoulder. "So you're Jesus Christ are you?" I politely enquired, at the same time retrieving a plastic bag from behind him that I'd plonked there earlier at the side of the bar.

"Too right I am," was his immediate reply.

"So do me a favour mate, will you?" I calmly asked him. "Jump onto those bench seats at the bottom of the concert room and face me, back to the wall, holding your arms up in the air. If you can do that I'd appreciate it."

"Why?" was his puzzled reply as I emptied the contents of the bag onto the bar top.

"Because Chris," picking up a hammer and four six inch nails from where I'd emptied them, "If you don't button up once and for all, I'm gonna nail you to that wall. You'll never, for the rest of your life, forget the meaning of the word crucifixion." He must have taken the hint because I never heard him come out with that expression again.

It was times like these that I missed Yog during that festive period, so I decided to fly to Australia a little earlier than usual for my monthly visit. Eric, who I thought was being helpful, offered to supply two of his best bar staff to run the club whilst I was away which I reluctantly agreed to, mainly because Paul was not getting on too well with Andrea at the time. There had to be a certain amount of diplomacy between us, well, all said and done, he was my landlord. So off I embarked on my travels to Australia again, leaving them in charge.

It was my intention of convincing Bobby to spend a sizeable working holiday at the club to patch things up, but when I jumped into my brother-in-law's car at Perth Airport, he greeted me with, "You're not planning on seeing Christie this session are you Haydn? because if you're thinking of doing so forget it."

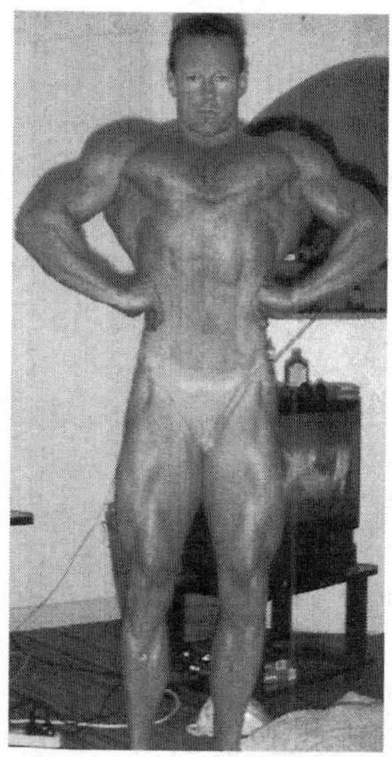

Bobby

Christie

I stared at him rather shocked for a few seconds, not expecting such an abrupt welcome. "What are you trying to say?" I asked.

"I'd better explain the present situation to you, so you don't cock up," he replied.

"After you left from your last visit, a legal battle transpired over access of their child. Bobby was having to pay a one hundred dollars supervision order every time he saw her, on the family court's instructions, which pissed him off big style. So he decided to abduct her on the next supervised visit, passing her through a toilet window into a waiting car which his sister was driving and they all headed for a friend's house in Adelaide, out of state boundaries."

"Bloody hell, things have been happening in my absence," I let out.

"Dave was drawing Bobby's social out of the cash machines in Perth, and secretly sending it to him, to throw Christie off track, but he asked me to ask you if you'd do it instead? He's scared of being spotted by the cameras. They don't know your face, do they?"

"Yes, I don't mind," I answered, thinking it would help repair our relationship.

Christie

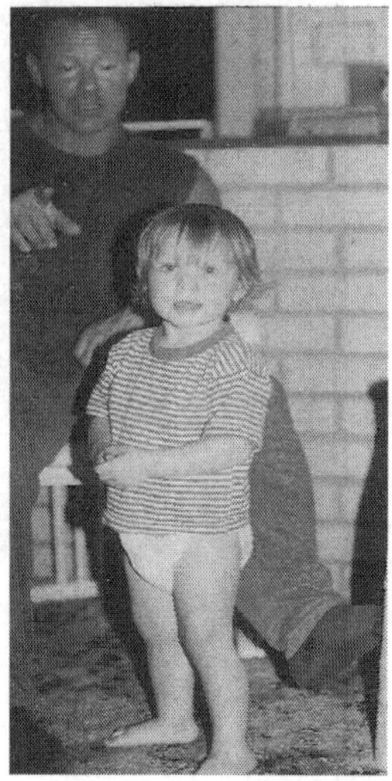

Bobby & daughter

For a week or so I complied with the family's instructions, but with Christie in the fore of my mind, not being wise to go looking for her with such a situation surrounding me. Now the next thing I witnessed took my breath away. It was Christie on national television, crying her eyes out, begging Bobby to return her daughter, and make sure no harm would come to her.

I realised then, that this was getting serious, and trying to help Bobby I sent an up to date West Australian newspaper across to him with his money and told him to have a photograph taken with it and the child and send it back to me so I could post it in Perth to the police for verification that the child was OK. His daughter was far closer to Bobby than to her mother at that time, so the child was happy being with him anyway. This he did, which hit the media once again.

"This family is beginning to become celebrities," I thought

to myself, "which I reluctantly seem to be playing a focal point in." But it wasn't right seeing Christie so upset. I was bang in the middle of the two of them, and not a happy chappy, trapped from the start.

I must have been spotted drawing his money out because Christie unexpectedly approached me in Yanshep outside my brother-in-law's house begging me to tell her where they both were. This was the last thing I needed. Up to press I was just in the background, but now, not being capable of grassing on Bobby, I was going to have to lie to her. This was going to be the end of our long friendship, I could feel it coming. It was all getting totally out of hand, not having a clue which way to turn and knowing one of them was going to be upset in the process. This was the second time the same situation had cropped up, me covering for Christie the first time and now covering for Bobby. I finished up hinting to her that they were in Melbourne, out of state, at one of my nieces' homes. What I didn't know was that Christie happened to be wired, and undercover police were standing by taking a full recording of the conversation. The next day my niece in Melbourne had a police raid on her home, coming up with nothing obviously. So the police came back to me wanting information, warning me that if I didn't comply, they would be waiting for me at the airport to serve an injunction on me, stopping me leaving Western Australia. But even with these threats resting on my head, I just couldn't grass on Bobby.

I wasn't approached again, but when the departure date arrived I was expecting to be arrested at the airport. I was in a worried state because I needed to get back to the club, I'd been away too long. But the C.I.B. must have been bluffing because nobody stopped me boarding. So much for a quiet holiday with my mother. Instead of them all coming to Padiham for a while, it had all backfired, and I had lost the trust of two dear friends.

That's what you get for being stupid enough to be persuaded to get indirectly involved in other people's affairs. I should have given them both the thumbs down from the word go. I was told a week later that Bobby had given himself up and they were back together again, unbelievably all doing fine. The mind boggles.

Anyway, when I eventually reached Padiham, as I dismounted the bus at the town hall, Yogurt was there waiting for me. God knows how he knew I was on that bus. I reckon he'd been waiting there most of the day. We were both delighted to see each other again, three months being quite a while, both missing each other immensely. After the hugging ritual, he took my suitcase from me, escorting me straight to Ernie's where Nicola and the others were waiting to welcome me home, all really pleased to see me again. Nicola gave me a big hug and a kiss just as if we were all family together, giving me that wanted feeling. But when that moment had passed, and they had given me an update on the club, I immediately took a downer, needing to get up there fast to find out what the hell was happening.

It seemed that Eric, always in financial trouble for one thing or another, had planned a takeover bid in my absence. He still owed me money but didn't have the patience to wait for his rental income from the place. I should have rejected his help from the start. But what he didn't take into account was that the people of Padiham, my loyal friends now, would stick with me through thick and thin.

The middle aged couple who had moved in during my absence, were running the place like any other pub, at conventional pub hours, totally displeasing everyone around them, cancelling the children's disco with no freebies and banning everyone in sight for virtually nothing. They weren't liked at all in the town and consequently were a police hindrance. Padiham couldn't cope with the change, praying for the day when I returned home, which was what Padiham was now, my home. Most of the punters went elsewhere, whilst the others made this couple's lives a misery. When I entered the club, they made it quite clear to me that they were stopping a while on Eric's instructions and I was no longer in charge. I tried to ring Eric but each time there was no answer. I could have gone across to Halifax, but if he didn't want to be found, he wouldn't be. They informed me I was still allowed to live upstairs but I would eventually be bubbled to the council for breaking the prohibition order. So sadly I thought I had come to the end of the line, without totally fulfilling my dream. But was I mistaken. It only took one small conversation to Yog, Nicola and the others at Ernie's, and my situation spread round Padiham like a flash. Yog and Steve were the main instigators, not only boycotting the place themselves, but they also formed petitions stopping anyone else entering, resembling olden day strikers stopping black legs from entering their place of work. They even had large hand-written banners telling the new proprietors to get out, because they weren't welcome in town. On top of this they were working on my license, which I threatened to notify the licensing authority that I hadn't given them permission, which would have caused a small inconvenience to them reapplying on their own behalf. Within four days they gave up the fight and I reinstated myself much to the joy of all my punters and the police. Within the week everything was back to normal, everybody being their happy selves again. Realising how much I had been missed was the best homecoming ever. The couple that had run the club then worked for a very short spell at the top club, but she ran off with a Padiham guy forcing him to do a runner out of town. One big mistake him visiting Padiham in the first place.

Eric pleaded ignorance to the whole matter, as usual, but I knew what was going through his mind at the time. Not being able to fall out with him because he was my landlord, I just had to let the matter fade away into oblivion.

But for Eric to keep face, he offered me a small well-paid job at his home in Halifax, on condition that I had Leanne labouring for me. He really fancied her, but I knew he didn't stand a chance in a million.

I had only one day a week available so we had to move fast. The contract was to create two door openings out of two three feet thick stone walls, in the loft space and making the existing stone clad roof safe. Leanne's job was to move about ten ton of surplus stone down two stories to the back yard, which, for one sixteen year old girl, was a fete in itself. Everybody who visited Eric that day poked their noses in to say hello to Leanne, being such a beautiful looking creature, even when covered in muck, having something about her that glowed radiantly. She used to smoke spliffs continuously all day long without any effect on her at all. The amount she smoked would put any normal person out for a week. In the beginning of our friendship she used to offer me half of every joint she lit up, but I soon learned to refuse, point-blank because of previous experiences with her. I remember having my head down a toilet for an hour once, trying to get some sense out of myself after a smoking session with her. Nobody had a hope of keeping up with her, although some people thought they could, but lived to regret it.

The evening came round and we had completed the job. Some of Eric's friends invited us both out on the town at their expense, Leanne having mesmerized them. And after preparing herself for the evening, they definitely didn't know what had hit them. Each one of them was praying to be the prize winner at the end of the night and I wasn't happy about it, because I was supposed to be the person who was looking after her at all times, on her parents' instructions. I don't know about me looking after her, I should have said the reverse was true. I warned her about them, but all she replied was, "Don't worry Haydn, I can handle myself quite well, with or without you," so I left her to it. After quite a few pubs around Halifax, we finished up at a karaoke bar in King's Cross called "The Junction." They were slacking now but Leanne kept onto them to supply the next rounds of drinks, and insisted that everyone had to drink with her, to be polite. It didn't take long before they were all totally intoxicated, except for Eric that is, who was cunningly keeping out of the limelight whilst I was trying to remain sober to keep a close eye on her. Leanne didn't seem like she'd had a drink. Another hour passed by. Leanne, urging them to buy round after round as they'd promised they would, was pushing them to the limit. Not being able to stand the pace, they were collapsing all over the place and eventually shown the door. I was well oiled, but not to that extent, whilst Leanne unbelievably was still going strong. Eric was the only one standing amongst his crew, having weighed the job up, and hoping for a conquest. It was time to leave, and the three of us finished up back at his place, him thinking we weren't carrying any money due to the fact that he had purposely held back payment that day thinking we couldn't get back to Burnley that night. After emptying another bottle of wine into us, feeling very confident, I quite unexpectedly reached into my back pocket, pulling out a £20 note, politely asking Eric to order us a taxi whilst complimenting him on a brilliant night. His face nearly hit the deck. He definitely wasn't expecting that one, forcing his plans up the spout, and we left laughing little apples all the way home. As if I'd jeopardise her without a backup plan......... No way!

Not only could Leanne smoke people's heads off, she could drink anyone under the table at any time. I'd never seen her drink like that before. Anyway, they never tried that on her again. Us Padihamers are not that stupid.

That summer, Nicola got the bug for swimming. We used to go down to the fat pipe regularly, lounging in the middle of the weir together, laughing and joking for hours whilst drinking vodka. We must have looked a right spectacle, her with hardly anything on, and me the mad professor. Families taking their children for a walk down the riverbanks, used to take one look at us, and give us a wide berth. A guy called Tommy, always came with us acting as our waiter for free drinks, but having to serve it to us in the middle of the weir, which was not easy to do without spilling the drinks. He managed most of the time, up to getting pissed himself that was, but sometimes we had to make do with a mixture of vodka and river water.

We fancied a change one day, and went to Pendle reservoir swimming, the sun blazing down on us, whilst standing on a high concrete platform above the deep water. I was the first to jump. Nicola was tuning herself in to follow me. Now usually I was always prepared for the unexpected and up to press had always pulled it off. But this time after submerging about ten feet into the unbearably cold water, and my heated body cooling down much faster than it should have done, the vodka not helping either, I started to experience palpitations, a feeling I'd never been through before. I barely managed to fight to the surface, knowing I was in serious trouble.

"Nicola! For fuck's sake help me! I'm drowning!!!" I shouted as I went under again, my body going numb with the cold, just managing to struggle back to the surface again. Nicola had resumed a lower level, for convenience, not rushing, because she thought I was having the crack with her.

"Nicola if you don't come in and help me now, I'm dead. I can hardly move. I'm drowning!" She was studying me for what seemed an eternity, as I began to submerge yet again. Then the penny dropped, and realising I really was in trouble, she made a shallow dive, very professionally rescuing me, no sweat at all.

I remember thinking at the time, "With tits that size, there's no chance of her sinking." Wasn't I relieved when she finally dragged me out of that forbidding water. The experience had frightened me to death, really believing I was a gonner.

That was the second time she'd saved my life in the same year, the first time being when I took her on a small electrical job I was involved in.

She asked me, "I've always wanted to know about electrics, will you teach me Haydn?"

"Yeah, if you want, get into the car," I replied, and sped off down the road.

Now I was a qualified, highly rated, time served electrician who had been working on electrical installations for forty years, and although I have had some nasty belts in my time, I wouldn't have classed any of them as life threatening. It was just one of those upheavals that came with the trade. But this special time I was showing Nicola the ins and outs of electrics, bulling her up thinking that she was really getting into the swing of the job, whilst I was stood on a metal buffet in a damp cellar messing about with some lighting cables that I thought were dead. Nicola was in front of me watching every move. But the wires were still live for some unknown reason. Now normally a belt would have hurt a little. End of. I was aware that an electric current could paralyse a person, but in the forty years I had dealt with it, I had never personally experienced it and thought it to be a fallacy. But this time proved me wrong. Grabbing a wire with each hand, I received an almighty belt, the current travelling down one arm, across my chest and up the other, totally paralysing me. I just stood there taking it, not even being able to speak, with a strange buzzing noise vibrating from me, knowing I was in serious trouble. Another twenty seconds more and I'd have been dead. Nicola, who was watching me closely, knew immediately I was in trouble, and without any hesitation at all, ran at me, kicking the stool from under me. As I fell onto a pile of concrete blocks, the wires pulled free of my grip, and consequently the current stopped flowing. Was I relieved, knowing her sudden impulsive move had saved my life.

"Fucking hell Nicola, that was a close one. I nearly had it then. That was fast thinking on your part, I definitely owe you one there. God knows was would have happened if you hadn't have been around."

"Are you all right?" she enquired.

"Better than I was a minute ago."

"Well I'll tell you what," she blurted out, "you can fuck electrics for me. I'll never touch them again as long as I live!"

"Don't blame you Nicola, I spluttered. "I think it's put me off for a lifetime as well. I wonder if it's all the vodka I've been drinking these last couple or so years, that's thinned my blood out. That's never happened to me before?"

All these escapades were discussed and laughed about by everybody at the club, and it was mentioned that because of all the high living experienced by me over the last two and a half years, bets were being taken in Padiham on how long I'd survive. Just typical of them. But I hadn't died yet, still having lots of things to experience before that time eventually arrives.

"So where were we? Oh yes……..swimming." The lads had arranged a trip to "Devil's Bridge," at Kirby Lonsdale, being a beautiful August bank holiday, taking two cars of which I was driving one with Nicola, Yogurt and Ernie as my passengers, whilst Keith, who was one of Ernie's team but hadn't been around for a couple of years, was driving the other, with John and his girlfriend Julie as his passengers. We were attempting the trough, when Nicola shouted out, "Stop the car, I need a piss. Now!" The car stopped and as she crawled out from the back seat a bottle of vodka fell out smashing on the roadside. Nobody was amused, all giving her some stick, being an unforgivable sin to waste liquor around Padihamers. Her only way out was to promise to buy another one in Caister, so hearing this they temporarily let her be. But on reaching the off-license, she hadn't enough money, so Yogurt, having to bail her out, did a runner with one so his sister could save face. That's how it worked, enabling us to carry on, on our way, to eventually arrive at our destination.

Keith

Finding ourselves a cosy spot half way up the bank, looking across to the bridge, which was on a level with us, we began organising ourselves, preparing for a Bar-B-Q. It was the first time I'd been there and what a beautiful setting, the river meandering well below us, so narrow and very deep where it flowed under the bridge. People jumped off it just for the crack, but I wasn't too happy about it, looking at the unbelievable drop. But as the vodka went down, my mood changed and I decided I'd be the first one of us to have a go for some strange reason. The hills were full of spectators, all relaxing for the afternoon. I sneaked to my feet trying not to be noticed, and taking my shoes and trousers off I ambled to the apex of the bridge.

"Where you going?" Yog shouted, accidentally spotting me. "You're not going to jump are you?"

"No," I replied. "I'm just going to survey the scenery, that's all. I won't be long." Looking down at the river far below me, I could feel chills running down my spine as I forced myself to give it a try. None of the lads were watching so I couldn't make a fool of myself, but it never passed through my mind that I might kill myself. To jump I had to be accurate because there was only a ten feet gap from bank to bank in the dropping area, and the banks were solid rock, but I was popped up with vodka and couldn't care a shit. So, without hesitating, I just launched myself into the air. It was one hell of a drop, which I remember thinking to myself half way down, "Surely I should have hit the water by now?" and then BANG!!! I did hit it, feeling like I'd landed on a block of concrete. Fortunately I had completed a perfect jump, but what I didn't account for was the underside of my bare feet, which felt like someone had been hitting them with a cricket bat. I couldn't walk for an hour, they were so tender. I just managed to tiptoe back to Ernie's lot to receive a pat on the back from Yogurt who'd spotted me.

About an hour later Nicola jumped up, grabbing me by the arm "Come on Haydy babe, we're both going to have a go at this jumping business."

Ernie also hobbled to his feet shouting, "You're not leaving me behind, I'm coming with you."

I turned to him, "You're going nowhere Ernie. Believe me, you'll lose both your legs if you jump." So after much persuasion it finished up that only Nicola and I were up for it, but this time with my shoes on, thinking to cure the last hiccup. I climbed onto the bridge wall, surrounded by quite a few people this time. A rumour started spreading, "That old bastard's going to jump!"

"Too right I am!" I shouted, immediately taking off into the air. I must have been leaning slightly backwards, because when I hit the water, my whole back jarred to such an extent that I was convinced that I had broken it, finishing up about twenty feet below. I could see the bubbling brightness well above me, but made no attempt to surface, because being so worried, I was too concerned about testing whether everything was working correctly on my body, finally deciding I was OK but in terrific pain. As I eventually surfaced, to add to it all, I could see the obituaries of about a dozen people who had died jumping, etched into the rock, which really cheered me up no end. Suddenly Nicola's face appeared over the bridge well above me.

"Alright Haydn?"

"No problems Nicola!" I shouted back thinking, "I've jumped so it's your turn now. Jump you bitch." She spontaneously launched herself into the air as I was trying to get out of the water in agony, but she was leaning slightly forward and hit the water with such a crack that it could be heard for miles, disappearing into the depths. I sat there waiting for her to surface, but she never did. Almost a minute passed and still she hadn't surfaced.

I was starting to panic. Thoughts passed through my mind like, "With this back of mine, I haven't a chance of diving down twenty feet to look for her, what do I do?" I was feeling so vulnerable, when out of the blue, an aqualung diver, who must have been down there all the time, shot out of the water, holding Nicola, in a semi-conscious state, in his arms. What a relief. The water had completely knocked her out for a moment, and she was receiving a proper bollocking from the diver for jumping whilst under the influence. But even so, we were all very grateful to him for saving her life. Within an hour she had developed one massive bruise which started from her neck and finished at her waist. All her front, including her tits, had turned black. What a mess.

But this didn't put Yogurt off, who dashed straight to the bridge, executing a spectacular dive, so spectacular that every picnicker in the area who witnessed it, stood up to clap. He didn't do just one, he had to do another five to follow. Now that was what you call rubbing it in. He was buzzing.

I have visited the bridge many times since, and not once have I ever seen anyone dive from it, Yog being the only one.

Nicola and I both took it very steady from then onwards, but decided to attend hospital immediately we returned home, giving us one wheelchair to share, which caused a right argument as to who was pushing who, me finishing up losing of course. Fortunately we were both very lucky not to have any permanent injuries, but even so, that ended our swimming escapades for the year, finishing up with her mother giving me a good telling off, for leading her astray again, as normal.

Back at the club, Yogurt was completely confusing me for a short while, He was truly a character in his own right, definitely one on his own. He would come to the club, early every morning with his mother's vacuum cleaner, to clean the concert room carpet and bench seats, making a thorough job of it every time, without even asking for a drink. What he was doing was a godsend to me. "Thanks very much Yog," I'd say, "Keep the job rolling."

"It's right enough, that's what friends are for aren't they?" Yog smiled

"Yeah, I know. But this is not you Yog, is it? What are you getting out of it?"

"Nothing, you're right Haydn. I don't want anything."

"Maybe not now, but you can have a couple of drinks later.

"All right then, if you insist. But only a couple."

I'd always liked Yogurt but now I was completely intrigued by his sudden kindness. I just couldn't weigh up his change of character. This was definitely not Yog. It went on for quite some time before somebody accidentally let it slip out. The reason he was doing it was his way of recovering all the cannabis which finished up on the carpet the previous night because of pissed punters dropping their supply and unable to find it, or not even realising they had dropped it. Every morning Yog used to vacuum up enough to supply a few of his friends for the whole day. When I eventually found the nature of his project, I had to laugh. I was usually one step in front of everybody. But in this instance, Yogurt was definitely one step ahead of me from the very start.

Now Yog had one or two friends that had been hooked on heroin. I didn't agree with him mixing with them, but it was not my business to comment.

He approached me early one morning asking, "Haydn, will you do me a big favour?"

"And what would that be?" I replied.

"I have two friends who are on the smack, that want to do cold turkey." (Cold turkey was the terrible first week one experiences when trying to come off heroin.)

"So. What's it to do with me? You know I can't do with smackheads. They're a waste of time?"

"Come on Haydn. They're friends of mine. On their instructions, they want blindfolding and running to some desolate spot in the country, miles away from anywhere, with camping equipment and enough food to last them a week, but no money at all to get back with, and they want us to pick them up in seven days time. Do it for me, will you?"

"Sounds mad to me. But if that's what you want, go on then, I'll do it."

"Good," he replied, "we'll pick them up in an hour, so be ready. I know just the spot." With that he made a quick call and disappeared.

On picking the two guys up from their house, I loaded the

equipment into the boot, whilst Yog thoroughly searched each one of them for money and drugs, before blindfolding them. He guided them into the back seat and placed a further paper bag on both their heads to make sure they hadn't a chance of peeping. They looked so conspicuous sat there in the back of the car that I had to politely tell them to lie down out of sight. Deep into the Lake District we travelled. Over cart tracks and everywhere, in order to find the ideal spot, which was more difficult than it seemed, because there was always that isolated farmhouse cropping up. But eventually we managed it, and unloaded them and the equipment into a large wooded gully, next to a clear water stream, with a small flat area just big enough to pitch a tent. Perfect. It was up to them now. I'd done my bit. So Yog and I left them to it, after making arrangements to pick them up. We called in at one or two pubs on the way home, making it quite late that evening when we eventually arrived back at the club.

"I'll just nip round, to tell their mates that we've done the job!" he shouted, as he headed for the door, and disappeared into the street.

It wasn't long before he returned, looking rather irritated. "The bastards!" he shouted, bouncing all over the place. "Do you know what? They've beat us back home, would you believe."

It didn't surprise me. "That's a smackhead," I thought. "They're capable of anything for a bag." All that time and effort we'd spent on them that day was for nothing. I should have followed my instincts and let them wallow in their own misery. They're just a total waste of space.

On returning to town that night from that wasted journey, I noticed a nightclub, called "The La Grande" was about to start up, in Station Rd, next to the police station. It used to be an old cinema and this new venture was going to be a big threat to my existence. Keeping a close eye on the situation, it began taking in customers the following November, but thankfully for me, within three weeks of opening the doors, had to shut down, due to noise and trouble on the road outside. Initially they hadn't a clue what they had committed themselves to until it was too late, not having a chance in a million of coping with the town.

"Thank God!" I thought, "My fears have been laid to rest with the problem immediately solving itself. I wish every problem was so simple."

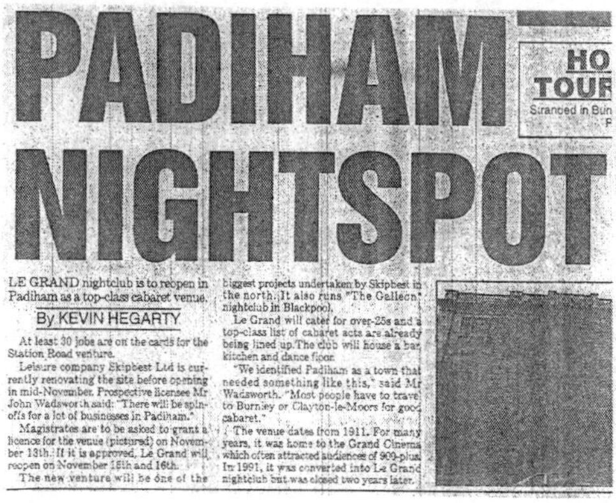

PADIHAM NIGHTSPOT

HO
TOUR
Stranded in Bur

LE GRAND nightclub is to reopen in Padiham as a top-class cabaret venue.

By KEVIN HEGARTY

At least 30 jobs are on the cards for the Station Road venture.

Leisure company Skipbest Ltd is currently renovating the site before opening in mid-November. Prospective licensee Mr John Wadsworth said: "There will be spin-offs for a lot of businesses in Padiham."

Magistrates are to be asked to grant a licence for the venue (pictured) on November 13th. If it is approved, Le Grand will reopen on November 15th and 16th.

The new venture will be one of the biggest projects undertaken by Skipbest in the north. It also runs "The Galleon" nightclub in Blackpool.

Le Grand will cater for over-25s and a top-class list of cabaret acts are already being lined up. The club will house a bar, kitchen and dance floor.

"We identified Padiham as a town that needed something like this," said Mr Wadsworth. "Most people have to travel to Burnley or Clayton-le-Moors for good cabaret."

The venue dates from 1911. For many years, it was home to the Grand Cinema which often attracted audiences of 900-plus. In 1991, it was converted into Le Grand nightclub but was closed two years later.

It was the same month, early November, when out of the blue I received a telephone call at the club from the couple who had purchased my farm at Norland years past, asking me if I would spend a couple of months on the property, putting it back together again for an agreed sum of money. They were arranging a large celebration party on New Year's Eve and needed the place up to scratch by then.

My mind was forced back to the period when I was about to lose Longley Hall. The banks were moving in fast to repossess the property, but I had two so-called friends at the time called Big Ian and Sue who had fallen in love with the place, and hoped that one day it could possibly be theirs. Big Ian represented me in court, regarding all my collapsed business affairs. They only had a certain amount of capital they could get their hands on, which was not enough to cover the valuation of the property. Without any offer reaching that level, a sale would not be considered by the authorities involved. I didn't want the banks to take over. To them, repossessed property was abundant and valueless in the present economic climate and they would sell it for a pittance. But the chances of Ian or Sue obtaining it were remote.

So Ian, Sue and I came up with a plan, to make sure it was them who finally obtained the property, making no odds to me because I was going to lose it anyway. Between us, we each picked up a sledgehammer and went to town on it, seriously smashing the place up. It still belonged to me so I could do anything I wanted with it. The demolition process seriously brought the property valuation down, so after officially evaluating it again, it just managed to come within their maximum budget. Moving very fast, a private purchase was completed between us. The timing was so crucial that within two hours of the completion, the bailiffs were moving in to repossess the property, in vain of course, having to leave empty-handed. The property was fully charged up to the hilt, so any proceeds of the sale went to the bank automatically. So Ian and Sue took over and I left. The final arrangement between us was that should they ever sell the property, a considerable amount of money would come my way. That was the agreement, but up to press nothing had transpired.

So with my future interests in mind, I agreed to survey the property, and in doing so, all my memories came flooding back to the time when I lived there and all the things I had previously done to it, to make it what it was. It was a very nostalgic moment. I could have cried, there and then, but I thought to myself, "Shape yourself up Haydn, that was my past life. I'm living a better one now so fuck all the material assets you lost, they're worth nothing, compared to all the friends I have made in the last three years."

So with these thoughts in mind I agreed to do the job. So pairing Alan up, who was Ernie's mate, an excellent tradesman, with Yogurt labouring for him, both acting on my instructions whilst I ran the club, the contract started. I used to take them every morning and bring them back at teatime, and for a month everything went exactly to plan. Then one late afternoon, about the time I arrived there to pick them up,

Yogurt was rushing up the stairs with a small electric cooker in his arms to complete a job so he could leave for a well needed pint. Consequently his legs accidentally became tangled in the trailing wire causing him to lose his balance and tumble backwards down the steps with the cooker on top of him. The iron griddle landed on the back of his left hand inflicting one hell of an injury. There was blood everywhere. We were in the centre snug watching, but it happened so fast, we couldn't do a thing about it.

He just lay there dazed and silent. I ran up to him and upon inspecting his hand, my conclusion was that he was going to lose it.

"Get him to the table whilst I find something to stop the bleeding!" I shouted. I rummaged around the kitchen cupboards for some first-aid bits and bats. But the only things I could find were some dish cloths and a roll of insulation tape. However, I managed to nip the wound up into position and taped it, padded and secure.

"Better get him to hospital fast! I shouted to Alan.

"I'm with you," he replied as we helped him outside into the car, and away at top speed, heading for Burnley.

"I'm not going to hospital. You've no chance of getting me there," he kept insisting. But I completely ignored his remarks.

"You are going to hospital, as far as I'm concerned. And that's that," I eventually muttered. But he was still adamant that he was not going.

We were passing through Todmorden when he suddenly shouted, "Pull up at that shop, I need a can!" He didn't seem bothered about his hand as long as he had a can in it. So we obliged him. As we entered the hospital grounds he started again, "You won't get me in there. Trust me."

"You're going in whether you like it or not. That hand's a mess. It needs looking at urgently," I blurted out. And I just dragged him out of the car pushing him into the reception.

As I was booking him in, the receptionist turned to me and asked, "Who's the patient?"

"Yog, the guy next to me."

She looked at me with a puzzled expression on her face, "There's no one next to you," she replied. I looked sideways and sure enough, he'd done a runner. There was no chance of catching him, so we had to give it up as a bad job. We found out later that he had only gone to Ernie's to have it stitched up and dressed. Ernie was good at First-Aid, as he was an ex-medic in the Royal Army Medical Corps, and Paratroopers. His experience came in very handy at times. But on this occasion the wound was so contaminated, anything could happen.

When I eventually caught up with Yogurt, I told him, "Take a few days off and for fuck's sake look after that hand of yours."

He just grinned at me and walked off. I'd replaced him for a while with Leanne, who could do the job just as efficiently, so the job carried on regardless. But Yog's hand wasn't getting any better. I was sure gangrene was setting in, because the stink that was being emitted from it was unbearable. In fact, it became so bad that people were moving away from him, whenever he sat down in the club. Eventually I had to drag him down to the Padiham medical centre to see the district nurse. Explaining the situation in detail, she was good enough to treat him, and supply him antibiotics. Fortunately for him, the infection abated and his hand began to heal up, returning to work a fortnight later as if nothing had happened. Nothing ever bothered him at all.

The contract was completed with only two days to spare. Everyone was sweating slightly, but very relieved with the outcome, resulting in Leanne, Yog, Alan and myself all receiving invitations as their honoured guests to the party, in appreciation.

It was New Year's Eve and prior to the event I went to pick them up at Keith's place. I walked up the garden drive into the house, and looked around inquisitively. "What the fuck's been happening here?" I thought. "Have they been having their own private party without inviting me?" The house and garden were full of people from the club.

"It's alright if we all come as well?" one them shouted.

I just looked at them all flabbergasted, "How the hell can I take you lot? It's pushing my luck a little bit to say the least." But they kept on at me until in the end I had to reply, "It's on your heads. I can't guarantee they'll let us all in, but if you want to give it a go, let's do it! But no trouble if they refuse, mind you. That's the condition."

"OK, let's go. We'll follow you. But don't lose us." So off we set in one large procession, heading for the hills of Sowerby Bridge.

The party was already in full swing when we pulled into the car-parking area. As we all walked into the main hall together the music stopped and there was silence as everyone turned towards us, strangely staring, wondering who the hell we all were. It was like "The War of the Roses," between Lancashire and Yorkshire had started again. My crowd all stood there not even murmuring, whilst I walked up to Ian, sitting him down to explained the situation.

"If it's unacceptable to you Ian, nobody will cause any trouble, they've all agreed to leave as they entered…….in silence."

He thought for a second, and then shouted over to his friends, "What do you think lads, are Haydy's friends welcome here?"

No problems with us," replied Justine, one of Ian's sons, who had organised the party.

"Then Happy New Year everybody. Please come in and enjoy yourselves. If you're friends of Haydn's, you're friends of mine." And every Padihamer shook hands with him in gratitude. We were in a different world now compared to Padiham and everything was overwhelming. The authenticity of the building, the lavish bar full of every drink possible, all for free, and the massive log-lit open fire which gave warmth to everything, was difficult to absorb in one initial glance. It was a medieval castle not a house, and the atmosphere was electric. There were beautiful Yorkshire maidens darting around everywhere, one couldn't help but have a good time. Most of the Padihamers knew about the farm that I once owned, but none of them envisaged anything of this standard. They were astounded at the magnificent place, which gave me a good feeling even though I didn't own it anymore. At least it was me who built it, and nobody could take that away from me.

I had a further surprise for all the members of Ernie's crew, when I personally gave each of them their new year's present in private, so as not to upset the others. They were one inch cubes wrapped in Christmas paper, decorated with a bow. One for each of them. A lump of gange to help them get through the night. All the Yorkshire lads smoked it so there wasn't a problem. In fact there would be more of a problem if our lads hadn't any. Everybody was ecstatic, not knowing what had hit them. What a New Year's Eve it turned out to be. They'd be talking about it for years.

Everybody got on great with each other, especially Yogurt, Nicola, Leanne and Ernie, who really made an impression on them all. But there was always one dickhead, this time a guy that had invited himself from Padiham, who was nothing to do with our crowd. Instead of going to the bar to ask for a drink like every other normal person, he decided to take some cans from a piled up stock in the corner, clumsily breaking the packaging, causing them to tumble to the floor rolling everywhere. I think he had it in his mind that he was pilfering drinks, which was stupid because all the drinks were free anyway. He always was a dickhead. Anyway, he received numerous bollockings unbeknown to us, and stamped off into the kitchen, where there was every kind of food imaginable on display for consumption, angrily picking up plates and throwing the food at the kitchen walls. He was off his trolley. Justine spotted him and came running in to inform Yogurt, who by this time had won them all over.

"Yogurt!" he shouted, "There's one of your crew going berserk in there. Step in and do something fast, or we'll do it for you. He'll finish up being dumped on the moor." So without a word of a lie, Yogurt went running into the kitchen, laying him out with one almighty punch. He then dumped him in the boot of Keith's car, whereas poor Keith and his girlfriend got the sorry task of running him home that minute so as to avoid further upset. This spoilt Keith's night completely, he wasn't a happy chappy. Prior to the incident, he was just about to settling down for a good night. I think the guy was a relative of his girlfriend and he felt obliged to get rid of him. Anyway, Yogurt went bouncing back into the main hall, greeted by pats on the back and handshakes all round from the Yorkshire crew. Yogurt was in his element once again, needing people to respond like that to survive.

The next morning Big Ian took us all down to the "Stirk Bridge" pub for an egg and bacon sandwich each before sending us on our way. But it didn't end there. We all finished up at the top club in Padiham that was open early every morning. As Nicola and I walked in together the first person to spot us was Nicola's father Bob playing snooker on the full size table there. Nicola shot off in one direction whilst Bob approached me. I was seriously expecting to get my face kicked in.

"Haydn!" he shouted, "I need a quiet word with you."

"Here we go," I thought, "Wait for it." He took my arm and forced me to sit beside him on a bench seat, reaching out his hand out to me. "Happy New Year Haydn. That's for you not for me." I looked at him very puzzled. I didn't understand quite what he was saying and couldn't believe he was wishing me of all people the best, having just seen me with Nicola. What was up with him?

"Haydn, I know I've been oining you for the last two years for seeing my daughter, but I know now your heart's in the right place and I also know you'll never let any harm come to her or her future children. So I want you to promise me that you will carry on the good work when I've gone?"

"Why. Where are you going?" I asked.

"I've just been diagnosed with cancer of the liver. They've

given me no longer than eighteen months to live." I just looked at him speechless. Words weren't coming easy. Death wasn't an easy thing to talk about.

"Nicola and Yogurt don't know yet. Don't tell her anything. I will eventually find the right time, I suppose. Until then, there's only you who knows so please keep your mouth shut, will you Haydn?"

"You have my promise, if it comes to what you've just told me, which I sincerely hope it doesn't, I shall always be watching over her at a distance."

"Thanks Haydn. That's all I wanted to hear. I can die in peace now," and he walked away.

Nicola approached me, "What did he want, Haydn?"

"He just wished me all the best and asked if we could be friends for the New Year," I replied.

"God!" she answered, things are looking up this year. I can't believe that."

I thought, "If you only knew what you're heading for, you poor lass." What a bad end to such an excellent experience.

But I had a real surprise coming my way to take my mind off things. That same night, the club was more crowded at opening than normal. In fact I thought New Year's Night would be very quiet indeed. Everybody was especially friendly to me at the start of the evening, insisting on buying me drinks all the time.

I thought, "There's something funny going on tonight, that I don't know about." I asked one or two punters but didn't get any answers. Then right in the middle of the night when everything had warmed up nicely, Paul asked me to step onto the stage next to him. As I made my way, I was astonished to experience everyone clapping and cheering at me.

I was totally bemused. "What is about to happen?" I queried. "What is going on, that I don't know of?" Paul had a large sealed envelope in his right hand. He ushered me to the centre of the stage beside him and everybody suddenly paused. There was a deathly silence about the place.

Turning to me, Paul broke the silence, "Well Haydn my

friend, on behalf of everybody here, and also our absent friends, I have been asked to present you with this small token of appreciation for your services rendered to this community." He passed the envelope to me. There was this elaborate certificate with a load of small print that I couldn't read at the time because I hadn't my glasses with me, but I could read the big print.

I read it and gasped. It said, "The Godfather of Padiham." I'd done it!!! Just think of it – me, *The Godfather of Padiham!* Yes!!!! I'd done it!!!!! I held my arms straight in the air with clenched fists giving it what for to my audience, whilst they were all cheering me. Both Yogurt and Nicola dived onto the stage, either side of me, each holding my arms up and shaking them.

"What a moment!" I shouted. "What a brilliant moment! It has taken me three years to reach my goal but I have enjoyed every second of it. I came into this town without a friend in the world and now I have hundreds. Life has been really good to me in Padiham. I feel very humble and thank you all for cooperating with me to bring this most unusual club together.........God bless you all." I had reached my goal. The challenge I had set myself was complete. From now on everything was a bonus.

Chapter 9 Accepting the inevitable.

For eight months everything ticked along in a relaxed, uneventful, clockwork manner. One or two of the local hardmen would even give Dwarling a peck on the cheek in polite acknowledgement as they entered, which if I hadn't seen it with my own eyes, I wouldn't have believed it.

"What a peaceful place this has turned out to be." I thought to myself. "I just couldn't have envisaged anything like this four years ago when I first arrived in Padiham. What a remarkable change. It just proves what can be achieved by being focused and an abundance of hard work." And as for Yogurt, he was in his element bobbing about, having just that bit more authority regarding the running of the establishment, mainly due to the fact that he was a close friend of mine.

Myself in the club

Nicola & friends

But regarding the club, I had reached my peak, so I had to try to hold tight at this level, preparing myself for the unexpected that could be waiting for me round the corner to bring me down. My life has been a series of extreme highs and lows, so considering that I had been riding high for quite a while, it goes without saying that a low was imminent. I had reached my goal, proving to myself that I was a Mr. Somebody once again, which initially was the main object of the exercise. But now the path I had been strolling along these last few years had come to an end, and I was not the sort of person to remain stagnant. My main concern was for the people around me that relied on me, and I didn't want to let them down in any way. They were all my friends. But if that wasn't possible, at the very end I was prepared for the unexpected because that would be the only way I could find a new path to stroll up facing new challenges. And that was exactly what happened. The story of my life.

It came in the form of the existing police chief inspector and the Padiham Inspector, perfect gentlemen, for whom I had total respect. Both of them were about to retire within three months of each other, and I knew that life as I had known it for the last four years was about to end, without a shadow of a doubt. As soon as the new Inspector of Padiham took over, all the pubs, with me at the top of his hit list, started to experience police raids trying to stop aftertime drinking completely. They say a new brush sweeps clean. Well maybe so in some cases, but definitely not in this case. His actions couldn't possibly work. He had, by pressurising my club, destroyed a fully proven, successful, unique way of handling people, in a happy, close-knit, thriving community.

In one week, my club was raided twice. The police were not particularly to blame, because they all personally approached me to apologise for what they unwillingly had to do. They had to obey higher orders, even though they knew the new inspector hadn't a clue what he was dealing with and the repercussions it could cause. The constant raids uprooted my whole plan of existence in Padiham and I knew that if it carried on, the club would have to close. One night for some unknown reason I unlocked the doors and walked outside for a breath of fresh air, something I had never done before. I must have felt the negative wavelengths around me. The club was absolutely packed, and mine was the only place defying police instructions because I had no option at the time, being the only way I could work. A series of police cars and vans turned into the bottom of the street from the main road, and I knew instantly they were heading for me. With lightning speed I relocked the doors, ran to the bar, switching off the music. I picked the microphone up, and standing on a table, announced to all my punters,

"This is an Emergency!!! There is a police raid due in three minutes, and the welfare of this club is a stake. If you want to safeguard it, do exactly as I say, no messing around. Now!" It was about three in the morning and everyone was well oiled, and if I pulled this one off it would be a miracle.

"Form a line, and everyone of you get out of the rear fire escape doors. Fast! Take your drinks with you and return the glasses in the morning. And for fuck's sake don't piss about!"

To my amazement, within two minutes the place was empty, except for one man called Melvin who politely asked me, "I don't have to go as well do I, Haydn?"

"Pick a brush up and start sweeping," I replied, "you can

be my witness to all of this." Suddenly there was a loud banging on the front door. I checked the place out and made sure the fire escape doors were closed, then I wandered casually towards it to let them in. A number of police entered, led by the new inspector.

He looked around and seeing no one, he grudgingly shouted to one of his officers, "Check the place out, he's hid them somewhere!"

Eventually after a thorough search the officer shouted back to him, "There's no one in here Sir." Melvin was leaning on his brush, absorbing everything that was happening around him in total amusement. The inspector approached me. I was stood in the middle of the dance floor knee deep in used streamers littering the floor from an earlier celebration.

The other police officers were stood in a line behind the inspector, observing.

He tapped me on the shoulder and blurted out, "Haydn. There's taking the piss and taking the piss. But you're TAKING the PISS!!!!" As he spoke, all the police officers were silently laughing and a couple of them held their thumbs up to me. Melvin by this time was on the floor roaring with laughter.

The police inspector wasn't amused, roaring at me for demeaning his authority, "You're going to regret this Haydn. In the next few weeks I'm going to have you strung up by the bollocks." He then stamped out angrily followed by his band of merry men. A little while later a police lady reappeared by herself wearing a big grin the width of her face.

She approached me chiming, "Do you know there's about two hundred people around here, all with drinks in their hands. They're everywhere, and not one of them will admit to being here. What a guy you are Haydn. This town is never going to stop talking about you after you've gone." With that she got hold of me and gave me a quick peck on the cheek, perplexingly shaking her head in bemusement, as she made her way out again into the dark exterior.

"Got the real thing this time." I thought, "No kissagrams

for me."

Melvin couldn't wait to spread it around town the next day what had happened.

Just as the inspector had promised, a few days later I had another raid, which I was expecting and had unbolted the till for easy removal. Except this time I knew the police would have had instructions to guard the back doors, so I had to grin and bear it. They scoured the place and took statements from about a dozen people asking who had served them, what had been served to them and at what times they were served. Steve was helping me that night and everyone had their fingers pointing at him. But when it came to taking till statements, the till was not present. With foresight I had hidden it upstairs, which really annoyed the police who told me to close down for the night immediately, and expect a summons. Under sufferance I had to obey.

Steve and I appeared in court unrepresented, a few days later. We were allowed to read the prosecution evidence against us. The police officer in charge was laughing as he showed them to us. "Well I've read some statements in my time, but none like these. Every statement is a non-incriminating load of bullshit, telling us what dickheads we all are, nothing against you at all. And every last one of them has retracted their statements and will not be turning up today in court, due to the fact that not one solitary person wants to hurt you in any possible way. So basically, because the till was missing and we have no proof of purchase, it boils down to the magistrates' decision."

Steve and I took up our courtroom positions and the three magistrates listened to what the police inspector had to say.

Turning to me, one of them commented, "Have you anything to say on this matter?"

I pondered a moment before answering. "Well your Honour, it's like this"............I realised that I couldn't operate as I needed to, due to recent complications arising and was planning to wind up the business forthwith. So I had decided, in all fairness, to give all my punters the treat of a lifetime, by using up the full extent of my stock, free gratis, for nothing, in appreciation for all the great times I had spent with them over the past three and half years. This was a private do, where no money changed hands, which was the reason there was no till.

So regarding the charges placed on me today, in fairness I plead innocent."

We played questions and answers for a short while, and then the Magistrates retired for a considerable period to discuss the verdict. The door opened and they all resumed their sitting positions.

"Well Mr. Woollard," one of them chimed up, "we unanimously have come to the decision that we can't find you guilty, but a problem occurs if we find you innocent. This case could be used in future cases as a precedent, and we do not want that responsibility on our heads, so, in very polite court language, they really told us in our language, "Fuck of out of here the both of you! We haven't seen you!"

Steve and I trundled off, both of us thinking, "And up your arse, Mr. Inspector!"

One of the Padiham police officers approached me, "Do you need a lift back to the club Haydn?"

"Yes if you don't mind. It would be much appreciated."

"You're not really leaving are you?" he asked. "A legend like you can't just give up and disappear. You've done a great job in this town, you can't leave."

"I'm sorry but the time is approaching to call it a draw. That's if I can live with all the disappointed people in Padiham. They're going to be lost without me, but your dickhead inspector has caused this, not me. I know he has to uphold the law, but this is all over a personal vendetta he has against me for his lack of a sense of humour," was my reply.

On reaching the club, as I climbed out of the car he sincerely wished me good luck for the future. What a pleasant police officer.

But the crowning blow was when I was informed by Nicola that she was pregnant, and the guy involved had instructed her to give her drinking habits a total miss for the next nine months in consideration of her future child's welfare, and must hand in her notice at the club. That really was the final straw. She was my right-hand girl, and everybody enjoyed her company so much, working alongside me. I had to admit that she was irreplaceable.

The club never opened again, but it was not quite the end. The building had its own ideas. It was like a living person that could think for itself, and it wasn't letting any other person but me run it, for sure.

I was in Halifax a while later. It was a Saturday afternoon, when I received a urgent telephone call from Drabble.

"Haydn. Get back here fast, the club's burning down! Can you hear me?"

"Yes I can hear you. Is it bad?"

"Believe me, it's bad. Get your arse into gear now," he stammered.

"I'm on my way,." I answered, and he rang off.

I rang Eric, "Pick me up at the farm and get me to Padiham fast. The club's burning down." He didn't seem too bothered about the situation. I wonder why? We eventually reached the bottom of the street. Yogurt was the first person to confront us. He came running up to us, taking deep breaths and smiling, whilst throwing his arms about in all directions.

"Can you smell it?" he shouted.

"Can I smell what?" I asked curiously, but more concerned about the state of the club that I hadn't reached yet.

"My stash of cannabis I've been collecting, that I've been hiding away in the club without you knowing. It's burnt away and there's a smell of cannabis everywhere. Doesn't it smell great?" He took another deep breath and let us by.

"The mad fool," I thought, "he never changes."

The fire had been extinguished and there was a semi-circular ring of masked firefighters and police inside facing the door discussing matters in general. Eric and I walked in to meet them surveying the damage at the same time. The place was gutted completely. What a mess. All the false ceilings had collapsed under the intensity of the fire. There was burnt rubble six feet deep everywhere. I could have cried.

Yogurt appeared at the door to the side of me. He drew my attention secretly by pointing to a circular section of the floor in front of us. I looked down to try to work out what he was harping on about, and would you believe, there was his stash of cannabis burning merrily away right in front of us.

The fumes from it were enough to knock out a bull elephant. But because everybody except Yogurt, Eric and myself was wearing breathing equipment, nobody could smell it but us. Yogurt was itching to retrieve the remainder of his booty but I silently ordered him, with my fists, to stop where he was until everybody had left the vicinity. He would have had me locked up that day for his stash.

It was at that moment, one of the masked firefighters nudged me on the arm and asked, "Have you seen her around lately then?"

"I looked at him totally confused. I had just arrived to utter devastation and this guy's asking about some woman.

"Who are we talking about?" I asked, not recognising him because of the breathing equipment.

"Nicola, have you seen her lately?"

Then I knew immediately who he was. Whilst there was a lull in the action at the club, he had left his wife of twenty years and run off with Nicola to live in Rishton. The stupid idiot. Within a fortnight she'd done a runner, leaving him up the creek without a paddle.

"Sorry mate, I've been out of town. I can't help you." I thought, "This is the last thing I need at this moment in time," and walked off.

As soon as the place was deemed safe, everyone packed up and departed, leaving just the three of us. Yogurt immediately gathered up what little cannabis remained. On inspection the only things that had not been touched were the main doors that still locked, and my close friend the fish.

Suddenly Dwarling turned up from nowhere. I hadn't seen him for a short while. He must have been on one of his long standing escapades. He got talking to Eric about a static caravan which Eric was selling, parked on a residential sight at Harden, near Keighley not too far away.

"Hang on Eric," I butted in. "Are you planning to put this place in order again? Because if you are, this static would be an ideal place for us to live for a short while, 'till we get things sorted out around here."

But Eric didn't give two shits what my proposals were. The only thing on his mind was the insurance claim, and possibly a caravan sale as well. One lucky day for him. After a short negotiation, Dwarling bought it, there and then, without even seeing it, and Eric passed him the keys, stating,

"You're the proud owner of a static caravan. It's all yours now. But the water boiler has been disconnected at the moment. It's in one of the wardrobes. It works, but I didn't want the frost to damage it this coming winter," then he walked away.

I looked at the fire damage, and something struck me. The main reason that there was a prohibition order on the upstairs, was because the downstairs ceiling didn't pass fire regulations. The entire downstairs ceiling needed double lining with half-inch asbestolux. In the club's previous condition, it was an impossible job to do without ripping the club out completely. But now, the state it was in, there wasn't a problem. So I got to thinking that maybe it would be possible to release the flats upstairs.

Anyway, it was time to called it a day and I went down to Ernie's to give him an update. I stayed the night, and the next day Steve and I got stuck into cleaning the fire damaged rubble out of the ground floor area once again. It was becoming a habit.

I was later informed by the police, that two young children had got into the empty club and lit a fire in front of the hundred year old alcohol soaked bar. One of the children was the fireman's son who I was talking to at the scene of the fire the previous day.

INFERNO GUTS POPULAR CLUB

By PETER DEWHURST

ONE of Pendle's best-known clubs – the Palatine in Norfolk Street, Nelson – was extensively damaged in a spectacular fire in the early hours of Saturday morning.

Around half the roof of the building was destroyed in the blaze. Six fire crews from Nelson, Colne, Burnley and Accrington were called in, along with a turntable ladder and an incident support unit.

It was around 2-46 a.m. when crews were called to the scene. The large building was already well alight and within minutes of the first fire-fighters arriving it broke through the roof.

Crews in breathing apparatus went inside to tackle the blaze but were withdrawn when it became clear the fire was too dangerous to fight from inside.

Fire-fighters were at the scene for several hours. Neighbours of the club, including flats which are attached to it, were awakened by sounds like rifle-shots coming from the exploding asbestos on the roof.

Occupants of the flats were evacuated with the help of the fire and rescue service, but their homes were not, in the end, affected by the fire.

Maurice Kay(51) said: "I was just making a brew. I heard the bangs and thought it was someone letting off fireworks. Then a neighbour came knocking on the door to tell us the club was on fire."

Fire-fighters arrived and help rouse other residents. Along with neighbours Peter Mulligan (46) and Stephen Kirby (29), Mr Kay got out of the house safely.

Divisional Officer Stuart Tracey, who led the fire-fighting operation, said: "The first floor was worst affected, although it is possible the fire started on the ground floor. The worst damage is to the main clubroom area, although there is smoke, heat and water damage to the ballroom."

The Palatine was for years one of Nelson's premier working men's clubs, but it was bought privately last year.

It provides a home to the Harlequin Dance Centre and has also been the venue for reunions from that other great Nelson club to burn down – the Imperial Ballroom.

"If that's true," I thought, "there's nothing like keeping the fire business in the family, one lights it, the other puts it out."

Anyway, it took about ten skips to clear all the rubble and clean the club out completely. But we finally did it. Fortunately the ceiling structure had survived so it was just a matter of relining the joists and renewing the electrics. Surprisingly, the guy who helped me do the job was Malcolm. He was the guy who had run off with my money years ago, and still hadn't paid me back yet, so I deducted it off his wages with interest. Swings and roundabouts, one might say. So fair do's.

I was rather accident-prone at times and this was no exception to the rule.

I was working on some mobile scaffolding in the main concert room area, which was now just an empty room space. There was one part of the ceiling where I had previously removed the staircase and hurriedly repaired the open space and appropriate upstairs floor area. I'd done a makeshift job and it was annoying me because it was noticeably out of level, so I attempted to prise it into place with a six foot crowbar, using all the strength I could muster. In the process of doing this, the scaffolding toppled over sideways under the pressure and I went down with it about nine feet. If that wasn't bad enough, the crowbar landed on the top of my head, splitting my scalp wide open. I just laid there straggling the fallen scaffolding, face down. All I could see were stars and a continuous stream of blood that was running down my face, dripping from my nose, causing a puddle on the floor below me. For a few seconds I didn't move, trying to mentally assess the damage I'd just inflicted on myself. I honestly thought I'd fatally injured myself and was waiting for the end. But I'd been reprieved once again, and realising I needed immediate emergency treatment to stop the bleeding, I ripped off my white shirt and tied it in a make shift bandage round my head, soaking the blood up, immediately making it look ten times worse than it was. I then made a mad rush down the crowded street with everybody staring at me, to the Padiham Medical Centre to see the district nurse for urgent help.

She took one look at me and panicked, "You'd better get yourself to the hospital, it's too big a job for me!" she screeched showing me the door.

"Good one," I disgustingly thought, "so much for medical help. And thank you very much for your consideration."

It was too far to the hospital, which left me with only one alternative, and that was to get to Ernie's fast for assistance. I was confident he could do something for me, he'd seen a lot worse than this. I crossed the road, running straight into his house, losing blood fast and was panicking somewhat.

"What the hell's happened to you?" he uttered, all cool, calm and collected.

"I need your help Ernie. A six foot crowbar's just attacked me. I need something doing fast." He hobbled towards me and inspected the wound.

"Nasty," he commented. "You'd better sit down and don't stain my settee. I can do soma't for you Haydn, but it's going to hurt you, be warned. I don't carry anaesthetics, but take a swig 'o this, it might help a bit," he calmly replied handing me a glass of whiskey.

"Just get on with it Ernie," I answered. "I'll have to grin and bear it." He hobbled into the kitchen to prepare his surgical tools in boiling hot water. His implements comprised of a pair of pliers, a bradall for making holes in wood, a large rugging needle and a small ball of fine string, the only things he could muster up at the time. Arranging all these sterilised tools on a coffee tray close to me he started to work on my scalp.

"It's bloody thick," he complained. "It's like a chunk of thick leather," lifting part of my scalp up with the pliers whilst piercing a hole through it with the bradawl. "Am I hurting you?"

"That's a silly question Ernie," I replied, "Just keep going and don't mind me." He threaded the needle and carefully started to stitch the wound back into place, pulling the string through the holes with the pliers. It was a struggle. At one stage he had to prop his knee on the top of my head to obtain enough leverage to pull the thread through, but after about ten minutes he'd completed it. Standing back to admire his handiwork, he blurted out, "I think that'll hold it Haydn. We'll give it a day or so to find out. If any infection sets in, don't delay in visiting the hospital." After cleaning all the coagulated blood from my head, he passed me a small hand mirror so I could inspect his work. There was a neat row of bows all in line across the top of my head. I was just relieved that the bleeding had stopped.

Three days later, there was a foreign body still badly irritating my eye, so I had to visit the hospital to have it removed and whilst I was there the nurse asked me if there was anything else she needed to look at. My head was covered by a woolly hat at the time for protection.

"I hurt my head about three days ago," I replied, "but it feels OK to me."

"We'd better have a ganders at it, just in case. Better safe than sorry," was the nurse's reply. Removing my hat, she took a deep gulp, stepping back in shock.

"Hang on here," she instructed me and went rushing off for the doctor, who arrived to examine the wound.

The nurse turned to the medical officer, "Shall I make arrangements for re-stitching? she asked.

He turned to her and replied, "In such a basic situation,

could you have done as good a job as this, given no surgical instruments whatsoever?"

She answered, "Well.........No."

He turned to me, "Tell your friend that if he ever wants a part-time job around here, he has my full recommendation. He's done a perfect job. Come back in ten days time to have them removed. Make an appointment at the reception." There was a slight lull before adding, "Forget it. Ask your mate to remove them, he's quite capable of doing the job." On that note he walked away.

As I was waiting in the curtained cubicle to be discharged, it seemed the circumstances of my injury had already spread round the neighbouring sections, because a nurse came running in shouting across the department,

"Which cubicle's Rambo in?" Her comments tickled me at the time, and made my day. Ernie reacted in a similar manner when I told him what they thought of his work. It made his day also. But I don't know to this day what the Padiham nurse was supposed to be trained to do.

It was about this time that Sharon appeared on the scene. A latecomer. I was missing Nicola so I was glad of her company. Sharon was in her late twenties, small in stature, very pretty when she wanted to be, and could pass as a teenager. In fact she was always being asked for identification when buying cigarettes and alcohol, which gave her a buzz, being a woman and all. She was a highly intelligent person who could always come up with the right answer when problems arose. If anyone needed help for anything whatsoever, she would always be the first on the spot. She had a heart of gold. Her problem was, she had a habit of listening to the wrong people, and was always getting herself into bad situations she couldn't escape from without help. That was where I came in. She deserved a lot better than some people treated her, and I used to feel responsible for her. I didn't know why but that's how it was.

Sharon

The Isle of Madeira

Cruise ship Oriana

We got on really well together as very close friends, although her bad minded family didn't want her anywhere near me. They thought they knew me better than I did. How stubbornly wrong can people be. She was wandering up the street, feeling very sorry for herself having just fallen out with her boyfriend Darren and was looking for some temporary place to stay, so I offered her accommodation at my place. Yog was always around, but I thought the extra company wouldn't go amiss. She moved in without hesitation. The downstairs ceiling now complied with fire regulations so we both could have separate flats upstairs. I couldn't foresee a problem, and besides that, I had arranged to go on that North Atlantic Cruise with Lorraine for the Millennium so she could caretake for me whilst I was away.

Everything worked to plan, and I spent a unbelievable New Year, anchored with five other cruise ships off the Isle of Madeira, six feet deep in steamers and firework displays everywhere. What a New Year's Eve!

Lorraine proposed to me on board, but I felt guilty of living the high life, whilst leaving Sharon all by herself at the club, so I delayed my answer in the most diplomatic fashion, and managed to get away with it once again. It was a compliment, all these proposals I was getting over those last few years, but I had acclimatised myself to being totally independent and to be honest I didn't want it any other way. Nothing's perfect but I loved being responsible for myself only. At the time it suited me down to the ground.

On returning, Dwarling, who had been showing his face regularly at the club whilst I was away, keeping Sharon company for some underlying reason, decided it would be a good idea for the three of us to stop at his static caravan in Harden, for a complete well needed change of environment, for a short while, which we all agreed to.

It was the middle of the night when we first arrived at the caravan site. None of us had been there before and hadn't a clue what the caravan looked like or where it was positioned.

Dwarling turned to Sharon, "The static's somewhere in this vicinity but I'm not sure exactly where."

"No sweat. Give me the key. I'll find it in a jiffy," Sharon eagerly replied, itching to help, and curious to know what state the caravan was in. Dwarling passed her the key and off she trotted trying every vacant static in the vicinity.

Suddenly she shouted, "I've got it Dwarling, It's across here!" and we all piled into it. Switching the light on, we were astonished to find such quality state of art décor.

"Bloody Hell!" exclaimed Dwarling, "This is a turn up for the book. Not like Eric at all. He's really done us proud this time. I wonder what was in his mind when he sold me this?" He reached out, picking a red wine from the vacant selection on one of the adjacent shelves in front of him, and poured three drinks into crystal glasses. "Might as well get into the flavour of the night," he commented, passing Sharon and me a glass each and holding his glass out to be toasted. And we started drinking. About three bottles later, Sharon, who couldn't resist mooching, pulled out an extremely oversize woman's dress from a fitted wardrobe, laughing as she did it, "What size woman did Eric last have here?" she commented as she displayed the dress to Dwarling.

He stared at it with a puzzled look on his face, then glanced over to the kitchen area. "Did he mention that he'd disconnected the boiler?" he asked. "because that one's still on the wall. I've a funny feeling we're in the wrong trailer." I too glanced over to the kitchen area, only to verify that Dwarling's observations were correct.

"You'd better see if you can get hold of Eric," I blurted, which miraculously at that time of night Dwarling managed to do.

"Eric. Describe the interior of the caravan you sold me. I think we are in the wrong one?"

"What colour are the curtains?" Eric enquired.

"Blue." was Dwarling's reply.

Eric could be heard laughing through the phone, "Well Dwarling, you're not wrong. You are definitely in the wrong trailer."

Dwarling, rather irritated, threw the key for Sharon to catch, instructing her, "You'd better have another go at finding the correct caravan," and off she toggled again into the darkness. It just happened that the caravan Dwarling purchased was directly to the side of the one we were already in, so we tidied up the best we could, and moved next door to a much lesser quality model as originally expected, taking our drinks and glasses with us. We were just settling down for the night when we noticed Sharon had gone missing, and managed to find her in the original trailer, scribbling an apology letter to the unknown owners. She liked scribbling things on pieces of paper, it kept her occupied for hours. But not this time. It was definitely not a wise decision to make.

A family eventually turned up one weekend, but I didn't hear anybody complain about intrusions. "Thank goodness for that," I thought, "we could have been batting on a sticky wicket."

It was a beautiful setting where wild deer tapped on the windows early in the morning to be fed. There was a crystal clear rock pool just above us that had a picturesque waterfall flowing into it, with no swimming or fishing signs displayed everywhere, which we used to bathe in early mornings. It resembled a bubble bath when we'd finished with it, but cleared rapidly.

During the next few weeks we visited the site nightly. But nobody told us we couldn't use the TV after midnight, and music was banned after 11 pm. We always arrived late at night and departed early in the morning so we never got much chance to talk to anyone. During our stay, we played music and had the TV on all night, over a few beers. Then out of the blue Eric approached us, telling Dwarling that he had received instructions from the owners of the site, informing him that he was banned from taking up residence there and must tow his trailer off the site immediately. Refusal to comply would result in the site owners doing it for him and destroying the trailer in the process. So Dwarling, really perturbed about losing two thousand pounds of his money, abandoned it, and Sharon and I went back to live at the club. But it came over the grapevine weeks later, that the trailer was still there and Eric was selling it again to another prospective buyer, would you believe. I couldn't wait to tell Dwarling. Dwarling the conman had been conned by Eric. Not good for his morale at all. So Dwarling put Eric top of his hit list to be ripped off at the very first opportunity. Once he got a bee in his bonnet, he'd dig his heels in and stick at it until he received satisfaction. And it wasn't long before he got his money back and more, from a slip up which Eric accidentally made, concerning a pub in Hebden Bridge. Let's call it swings and roundabouts again.

It wasn't long afterwards that Dwarling, Sharon, and I pulled into "The Marriot Hotel" in Glasgow, on our way to the Mull of Kintyre, to visit a guy I had met on my North Atlantic Cruise. Dwarling was carrying about two grand and had volunteered to finance a three-day break for us all. He virtually abandoned the car in front of the main hotel entrance, marching into the reception and throwing the car keys onto the main counter.

"Park my car!" were his plain instructions.

"Yes Sir," was the simple reply as one of the hotel porters rushed to obey his command.

"What can I do for you sir?" asked the receptionist.

"I want two of your best rooms in the hotel for the night," Dwarling insisted.

"We only have the two penthouse Bridal suites," she answered.

"Well, we'll take them," Dwarling replied.

"Can I have your card Sir?" she insisted.

"I don't deal in cards," he answered, "How much are the rooms?"

"Five hundred pounds sir," was her reply.

"Well here's a thousand in cash. Hold onto the rest to cover any incidental expenses will you. I'll collect the difference in the morning."

"Very good sir" was her reply as she handed him the room keys and his car key which the porter had returned, and we all toggled off to the bar, ordering round after round of drinks, booking them to his room. Then we hit the dining room, ordering the most expensive meals in the place, again booking them to the room. Dwarling ordered monkfish delivered personally to the table by the head chef. And what an ugly fish it was. Its wide gaping mouth full of teeth, looked like it was about to bite his hand off. Dwarling reeled backwards in shock. "What the bloody hell's that?" he exclaimed.

"The speciality of the house sir," was the reply.

"Well you know what to do with your speciality of the house. Get it out of my sight immediately. It looks evil." Instantaneously two other chefs approached the table. There was a difference of opinion expressed and the fish was eventually taken away, charged to Dwarling's room. He didn't bother with another meal, but while Sharon and I were eating ours, Dwarling called for the wine waiter.

"What would you like to drink sir?" he asked.

"Better give us every bottle of wine on the menu," Dwarling replied, "Just to be safe." Dwarling could be real bombastic at times. The wine waiter looked at him aghast and walked away to collect the wine, which was also booked to his room, about eight bottles in total, of which we drank about four and then retired to our rooms taking the rest with us. By this time everybody in the hotel had noticed Dwarling. That was his intention. He had to be noticed when lashing money out wastefully. Immediately we reached the rooms he rang the manager for permission to have a swim in the internal swimming pool.

"Sorry sir," was his first answer, "There's no lifeguard on duty at this time of night, so we can't allow you in."

"Well go and find one and book it to my room." he insisted. So it wasn't long before we were able to go for a swim, booking our swimming attire to his room. Later, back in the hotel room, Dwarling ordered an exclusive breakfast for us all. Then it all happened. He must have decided he'd caused a big enough impression for one night and started ringing up all the waiters, trying to persuade one to visit his room for a paid shag. This was what it was all about. I should have cottoned on when he initially ordered two rooms. He'd gone through this procedure many times before. At first it used to totally embarrass me, but it opened my eyes to realise how many so called straight people bit when money was involved.

But this time his luck was out, and the manager rang him instead, "I'm warning you that if you don't stop telephoning, you will be thrown out immediately."

Dwarling was annoyed, "Nobody speaks to me like that, I shall have to teach him a lesson in life." Gay Dwarling was a strange person at times. His portrayal of an executive businessman could change in a click of the fingers to that of a spoilt child who couldn't get his own way. He paused for a minute to do some calculations, and worked out that besides the money he had left in the reception, he still owed the hotel about three hundred pounds. "I think they've had enough off me for one night, so it's time to go. Now! Fuck the breakfast, we'll go somewhere else." And since he was holding all the money we didn't have a choice in the matter.

He sent Sharon out first carrying all the surplus wine and room drinks which were in the two rooms coolers in two large hold-alls, and instructed her to sit beside the dual carriageway waiting for him to pick her up. We could see her crossing the parking lot from the fifth floor window, which was our cue to make a move. Crossing the reception, teaming with newly arrived American tourists, nobody was paying any attention to us at all. We entered the secure parking area, not having a clue where the car was, but eventually found it. There was a notice near by, stating that to exit the parking area a token was needed from the main reception, to operate the exit barriers.

"Get in Haydn!" he shouted. He was getting really annoyed by this time. There was a Rolls in front of us, in the process of exiting. As the barrier lifted, Dwarling virtually pushed the Rolls out, so we could get through the barrier as well before it dropped. The driver in front was cursing him but we managed to exit in the nick of time. Dwarling turned into the busy morning Glasgow traffic and stopped the car, giving Sharon just enough time to load the back seat, literally throwing herself in head first. The dual carriageway had come to a halt. People watching on must have thought we were in the process of a bank raid or something. Dwarling just casually drove off as if nothing had happened. He was a happy man again. But the cheek of it all was, he asked me a couple of months later, if I fancied going back again for another do, ringing the hotel and booking us both in at the same time, would you believe. Of course I gave him a wide berth that time. Everything was just a game to him. A leopard can't change its spots.

Dwarling only appeared on the scene occasionally when he was bored and needed a hectic couple of days blowout, which gave me ample time to concentrate on the club.

The fire brigade was certainly kept busy in Padiham around that period because McNeal's, which was operating under another name, had recently burnt down. This was good news for me, leaving an open spot for a nightclub in Padiham.

Besides that, Nicola was back on the scene again, complaining she was totally bored after having the child, and needed to come back to work, if I could get the club together again. So I decided to give it a go. Not just for her but for Yog as well, who was definitely suffering from the closedown. In fact the whole town was lost and were continuously on my back pushing me to open again. I didn't think I would have any trouble with the licence, since my records were impeccably clean. So keeping my fingers crossed for the future, I started work, and continued to work on the club, trying to keep as low a profile as possible. It was shaping up well and I was becoming excited to experience the finished results. A very small scattering of people in town who thought they were above the likes of me, nicknamed my former club "The Rat Trap," so just to rub their noses into the mud, I decided to go along with them. All my future renovations were going to be based on "The Theme from the Pied Piper," and of course the hundreds of rats he attracted. I had it all planned down to the last rat, and believed the final results would be rather novel to say the least. What could they possibly call my club then? The entire thing was just a game of win or lose, and I always have been a bad loser.

One miserable morning Yog came in and told me that he'd had bad words with Bob, his father, and although he was seriously ill in hospital he wasn't going to visit him again. He wasn't aware that his dad was about to die, but I'd been having words with Nicola and knew it was possibly on the cards. So I eventually persuaded him to change his mind as it could be the last time.

"If you don't go and he dies," I implored him, "you'll never forgive yourself Yog. So for once in your life do a bit of crawling, and let him come out on top for the last time." He took my advice and shortly afterwards his dad died, leaving me with the legacy of keeping an eye on Nicola and her children for him, as promised.

So there we were, Yogart, Steve, Sharon and me trying our utmost to reopen the club again for the third time, with the whole town on our backs, bored stupid, eagerly waiting in anticipation. Then out of the blue, I had to confront my worst fear. The dark angel appeared at the open doors, silhouetted against the bright background. It was the bulky uniformed figure of the new Police Inspector of Padiham. Not a reassuring sight at all. His presence filled the air with unpleasantness.

"I hear you are thinking of starting up again," he cynically remarked as he scanned the area in front of him with his beady eyes. "Well I am here to inform you that the licensing committee go on my recommendations, and I am putting it to them that in my opinion you are not an appropriate person to run a club of this nature. Also your license is due for renewal in six weeks time and I will be asking them to revoke it completely, just like I personally promised I'd do the first time we met." With my impeccably clean record that definitely sounded to me like a personal vendetta, not police policy. Not a very nice person at all.

As he walked away smirking to himself down the cobble stones, I thought to myself, "What a pathetic specimen of a human being." He was letting the whole town down besides myself. I felt like a hundred buffalos had just trampled me down.

But there was one last chance. I gave Andrea a ring asking her to take the license over on my behalf, which she agreed to straight away without even thinking. But then what happened?.......the arsehole of an inspector stepped in again and banned her from taking the license, on the grounds that I was lurking in the background. It was time to admit to myself that this was the end, and I had to give up, because I hadn't the power to fight the twat any more. And in doing so, he personally, not the police he represented, destroyed a way of life in Padiham that was a definite deterrent against drink-related crime and vandalism in the town. I had no alternative but to let the town go back to how it originally was before I arrived, many moons ago. Virtually all the local police approached me in sympathy, to shake my hand on a job well done, and to apologise to me about the decisions taken by their superior, whose orders they had no alternative but to follow, no matter how rank they were.

I continued living at the club with my friend Sharon until Christmas 2002. Similar to the rest of Padiham I was a lost soul again for a while, so I decided to rip a few partitions out from the upstairs to accommodate a spacious lounge for an endless succession of private parties. I was not catering anymore for the whole town but at least Ernie's crew were reasonable happy. It wasn't the same but it was better than nothing. I still had the karaoke equipment so I built a small pole-dancing stage, and I was never short of volunteers to do a bit of exotic dancing, especially two new faces that arrived from nowhere, Kelly and Kirsty, "The dynamic Duo." So life kept ticking over, but on a much smaller scale this time.

Yogurt wasn't the king anymore, which was against his nature, but he tolerated it for quite a while. He still had his moments from time to time, although he was starting noticeably to lose his rag more often. He walked in one night and for no apparent reason started smacking Steve in the face. Now Steve in his youth had been a black belt in ju-jitsu and had learned how to take a punch correctly. Well that's what he told everybody but nobody believed him. But unbelievably, he absorbed the punch as if he had never been touched, no marks showing at all. He just picked up his beer, took a drink and put it down as if nothing had happened. Yogurt stared at him annoyingly and give him another one. The same happened again. Steve just took the punch in his stride. I tried to step in, but Steve told me to let him be, so all I could do was watch. Believe it or not this happened about ten times. All Steve was doing was having a drink and smiling back at him every time he struck him. Now Yogurt was supposed to be able to handle himself when the occasion arose, but he was making a total fool of himself, creating no impression on Steve at all. Eventually, totally frustrated, Yogurt threw his arms up in the air giving up the ghost completely and ran out of the place. I approached Steve to evaluate the damage, and inspecting his face I was astonished to find that there wasn't one mark on him whatsoever. I just couldn't believe it. Maybe he wasn't flannelling about all that ju-jitsu business after all. I don't know. Anyway Yogurt came back a short while later, when he'd cooled down to apologise, but it seemed there was nothing to apologise about because there was no damage done.

Whilst all this was happening Nicola wasn't around. Her time was taken up looking after her young baby Brandon. I used to go round to her place on a regular basis babysitting for her, to give her a needed break, which, without realising, was bringing me closer to him. Sharon had left the club not long back and had taken up residence in a block of apartments off Manchester Rd, Burnley, and it was because of these circumstances that I started to grow closer to Kelly and Kirsty.

Since that New Year's Eve celebration, Ian and Sue were in constant contact with me and informed me that I could have total control of the main hall at Longley Hall if I so required, considering they still owed me a considerable amount of money regarding the agreement we made on purchase. So planning for the future, realising that I wouldn't be at the club indefinitely, I agreed. I installed some karaoke equipment and Yogurt, Kelly, Kirsty and I spent many a day laughing, acting about, drinking and singing there. The girls used to come to the club and sit on the doorstep waiting for me to arrive to pick them up, and the second I came into view, they would both run out into the middle of the road in front of me doing mooneys as I approached them. What a laugh they were. It gave Yogurt something different to occupy his mind and he did enjoy the times we were at Longley Hall together. He knew everybody there, which helped considerably.

Kelly was about eighteen years old, and she was the most beautiful specimen in town at that moment in time, her long blond hair rippling in the breeze, giving her that special look. What a stunner she was. And what is more, she knew it and flaunted it. She was another Leanne who swore by her cannabis. In fact that was why she initially showed her face at my place, just to get away from the main stream for a needed joint. Kirsty was about the same age, not having quite the attributes as Kelly but she had a vibrant personality to make up for it. They were both great to be with and that's all that mattered.

Kelly

I was travelling across the moors above Clivinger one evening with them, heading for Longley Hall, in a XR2 which was rated highly on performance and I assumed the car would be just as good as my previous BMW. on manoeuvring. I'd had a few joints and a few beers, but I didn't think I was over the limit. I could see for miles in every direction and was alone on the road. Besides that I had never seen a police car up there in years. It was no-man's territory, the border line between Yorkshire and Lancashire. The stretch we were travelling was dead straight, but it had a forever continuing tight bend at the end of it. I remember thinking to myself,

"Slow down a little Haydn, you're going too fast." and I remember answering myself, "Fuck it Haydn, you've been along this stretch faster than this before." That was the cannabis talking. I couldn't care a shit about anything after smoking a few joints. What I didn't think and should have, was "You're in a different car Haydn, aren't you. Be careful." But it was too late. I drove into the bend and immediately realised I was in trouble. The car wouldn't manoeuvre at all and we finished up in the middle of an adjacent field with a smashed up front. No injuries though. Luckily.

There was a lesson to be learned even though it was late in the day, and that was never drive and smoke cannabis. The two things don't mix.

Kirsty

Temporary panic set in, but immediately realising nobody was hurt, Kelly chimed up, “I think you took the wrong turning Haydn,” a smile engulfing her face. Instances like these amused her no end. She had a weird sense of humour.

Kirsty also, giggling her head off in a deep throated tone, casually commented, “I thought you could drive Haydn? I just looked at them both bewildered.

The car was knackered, but that didn't bother me because I was disgusted with it anyway. If it wouldn't stop on the road, it was no good to me. So I reached for my mobile and tried to dial for help, but there was no signal up on the hills. We had a choice of walking down the valley to the main road far below us, or hitching a lift on the top road which we had just took off from. I decided on the latter. It was getting dark now, but luckily a pair of headlights were approaching, so I flagged them down. It only turned out to be a police car. How lucky was that.

“I take it you want a lift,” shouted out one of them whilst getting out of their car to breathalise me. There was a pause whilst they observed the reading on the meter after testing me. “Well we're going to give you a lift alright, to Halifax nick for the night.”

I hope you’re going to give us two a lift back to Padiham first?” Kelly demanded of them, “You can't leave us up here on this isolated moor, it's more than your job's worth.”

“We'll drop you both off at a Burnley bus stop on the main road below, and you can make your own way from there,” one of the police officers answered. And reluctantly they both had to agree.

“As I departed company from them, Kelly shouted after me, “Good luck Haydn. Don't let the bastards grind you down. See you tomorrow,” and off I was taken.

I remember the police commenting to me, “You were very unlucky tonight Haydn. We never go up there normally, but there was a report of rustling over the last few nights and we were sent up to observe. And when we spotted you in the middle of that field with your headlights on, it looked a bit suspicious to say the least." They were pretty good guys, all taken into account, because one of them remarked, "We're going to give you a chance Haydn. We're going the long way round so start doing some heavy breathing and by the time we reach Halifax and put you on the official machine, there's a chance you might get away with it." But it didn't happen. They all placed a bet nearest to the reading that would come up on the machine and asked me if I wanted to join in, which I agreed to just to be sociable. I registered 42, two points over, winning the bet. But after collecting my winnings, I was locked up for the night to appear in court within the following two months. I was pissed off but in between times I just had to carry on as normal.

There was a day that we decided to visit "The Stirk Bridge" pub which was in the valley below Longley Hall, just for a refreshing change. It was the day of "The Crate Climb." This was a competition where everybody in turn who had nominated themselves, had the chance to find out how high they could climb, stacking beer crates on top of each other whilst continuously standing on them. It was a very difficult manoeuvre to perform, but it could be done. There was scaffolding with steps built into them on either side of the climbing area, where some guy would follow the person climbing, for the sole reason of keeping the competitor safety harnessed at all times. These people could pile up to fifteen crates on top of each other whilst standing on them, which was an unbelievable fete. When the crates collapsed the count was over.

Yogurt chimed up, rubbing his palms together and laughing at the same time, "I'm going to have a go at that!" I didn't think for a minute that he'd become a threat to the experts around, that regularly turned up every time there was a session, but I was wrong. He started off very cautiously, crate by crate, but, gaining confidence by the second, speeded up. When it got to about ten crates he was becoming a threat, but when he reached the count of fifteen he was really pissing them off.

He shouted across to us, "I'm nearly there. I'm going to show them all who's the king around here!" At level eighteen the crates eventually collapsed. His score hadn't been touched for years. Yogurt had done it again, and didn't they know it. He never stopped bobbing about all that afternoon. We went back to Padiham with a photograph of him doing the business, and we had to listen to him for hours, bragging to everyone about it. Wasn't he just chuffed. He needed a boost of ego because he was rapidly loosing interest in everything around him. Not the Yogurt I used to know.

Now Kelly had it in her mind that Nicola was gunning for her because she was spending too much time with me, so I arranged for us all to get together at Nicola's home to prove her wrong, which she was apprehensive about at first but finally consented.

The first words that Nicola came out with was, "Don't be a madhead Kelly. I'm sure you and Kirsty know me better than that. In fact I think we should all make a point of partying out together now and then. What do you think?"

"Why not. Let's go for it, heagh Kirsty?" Kelly blurted out.

"Sounds right to me," Kirsty answered.

The night went well and although we all had decided to go out together before I received my driving ban, it was very difficult to arrange because up to press, I'd always stood in for Nicola whilst she went out. She wasn't happy about leaving her young baby with anyone else but me, but she eventually managed to come up with a suitable arrangement. It gave us a chance to hit the Orange Tree in Halifax again for another round, with reinforcements this time, which really destroyed the patron's brain cells. Kelly must have upset someone on the way out because as we were departing down the main road, a guy rushed out of the pub throwing empty beer bottles at us. Fortunately we were out of range. Kelly, poking her head out of the back passenger window yelled back at him, "What a wanker you are!" Not very nice at all, but whatever had happened he'd most likely have deserved it. A "Padihamer" was definitely a name he'd never forget.

Whilst the car was still available, we all decided to hit the pleasure beach at Blackpool. Kelly was dressed up to kill in her sexy schoolgirl's St. Trinian's gear. "I'm laying the orders down today," she insisted.

"Go on then. Go for it!" roared Kirsty always backing her up. Nicola never spoke a word.

"First we'll all take a ride in "Valhalla" without any protective clothing,." she commanded. And we all trudged on. The water was pouring onto us from every direction, drenching us to the bone. But it was just one big giggle to them. But the "Pepsi Max" was something else. She gave us specific instructions to hold our arms up in the air throughout the full extent of the ride, which scared the shit out of us all, especially descending the initial steep section. But if that wasn't enough, all three of them took their tops and bras off, holding them in their hands to blow in the wind, trying to dry them out a little, but also obviously for a good photograph on the automatic cameras. Nicola couldn't keep a hold of hers, they were rather large, the wind blowing them into the face of the guy behind us, who daren't let go of the bar. So they stuck there until the end of the ride when Nicola apologetically retrieved them. What a laugh we all had. Those were the times that none of us will ever forget.

The time eventually came when I was to appear in court. I had arranged to represent myself and needed Ernie as a witness. He'd agreed to back me up, so we both went to court together.

The magistrates were sat in the centre of the courtroom, I stood in the prosecution box to the right, whilst Ernie, my key witness. stood in the witness box to the left. Between Ernie and me, in front of the magistrates, was a youngish lady acting as clerk of the court passing documents from one to the other. I wasn't paying much attention to her. Everything was very formal and correct. Suddenly she looked up bemused, staring at me, checking some documents in her hand at the same time.

Letting out a shriek, she shouted across to me, "Haydn, it's you isn't it?" There was some distance between us. Being disguised in all her court regalia, and my eyesight was not the best in the world, especially in dimly lit surroundings, I was rather puzzled at first as to who she was. She came running past the magistrates, and threw her arms around me, giving me a passionate kiss.

I knew who she was then alright. A lass called Ingrad that I'd associated with at the "Starving Rascal," one of Eric's pubs, where I first met him years ago during the period I was homeless. She'd fallen in love with me having to unwillingly abandon her when I started living with Carol again at the house in Hebden Bridge, never to set eyes on her again up to that moment.

Now, as if that wasn't bad enough to upset the whole court protocol, Ernie chimes up, shouting across the court room to me, "What the fuck's happening across there? Come across here you Bitch, I want part of the action!"

I'll never forget the look on the magistrates' faces until the day I die. It was one classic moment. But consequently it goes without saying, I got a year's ban. So from then onwards, only Kelly and Kirsty went to Longley Hall with me. On the bus would you believe. We used to arrive there evening time and stop the whole of the night, singing and drinking, leaving around lunchtime the following day.

Yogurt wasn't happy about the situation, because he wasn't the sort of man to be catching buses, needing everything put on a plate for him. He was really losing it. He was making me feel so guilty for not being able to do anything about his situation. It was times like these that I sometimes wished I had never set eyes on the town, because then he wouldn't have had anything to compare his present situation to. Watching him slowly deteriorate was heart rendering to me.

Anyway it wasn't long before Sue came stampeding down into the main hall one morning, screaming at us, "Stop this noise now and would you all please leave and never come back." I could read her like a book, and it wasn't just a question of the noise. I think she was jealous of me having such a magnificent time with my two sexy girlfriends.

In my opinion, the place needed livening up drastically anyway, and to be honest with myself, I couldn't face living back there on my ownsome ever again. Padiham had definitely spoilt me for options.

So after a few insulting comments all round, the three of us took off on foot down the open fields heading for Sowerby Bridge, which was about two miles down the valley.

Kelly and Kirsty were cheekily holding their skirts high in the air whilst asking me, “Can you help us over the these dry stone walls so we can get into the next field?” And as I did so, they were purposely sticking their backsides into my face, the sexy creatures, wearing tongs only, just to make me feel uncomfortable. Then they'd dance along the tops of the dry stone walls, laughing and chanting at the top of their voices over and over again, “Rita, Sue and Bob too.” and you don't have to be that clued up to know what they were on about.

We had some fun together the three of us, without a shadow of a doubt. But being without a driving license definitely slowed the job down, so for the next eight months we just had to play about in Padiham. There wasn't an option.

There was one funny time (well to everybody except John's girlfriend Julie) when we all were invited to John's birthday at her home. It was a wonder he was alive to have a birthday that year because when pissed at my place, he'd be forever walking into this full size mirror thinking it was the way to the toilet, or he'd turn right instead of entering the door in front of him, falling ten feet down an hole in the floor where the new staircase was going to be fitted. In the end I had to pile a load of garbage bags there to break his fall every time he went down.

Julie had just bought a new white carpet with a crimson ring pattern to show the place off for the occasion. There was a lack of seating so Ernie and I sat on the floor resting our backs on the side of the settee. As the night went on and Ernie became more inebriated, I noticed to my shock, one of the crimson rings in the pattern of the carpet was one inch deep of snubbed cigarettes. He'd been using it as an ashtray. It was so stupid I just had to laugh.

"What's so funny?" Julie asked. I was splitting my sides.

"Just look at your new carpet," I replied. "It's totally ruined," pointing to the burnt mess beside Ernie. Well, by her expression, believe me, she didn't take it well at all. Ernie realising what he'd been doing tried to apologise to her, but it was too late for apologies, and we all got thrown out together. So much for John's birthday party.

I always remembered that night in particular because when I returned back to the club I received a telephone call from Eric.

"The club's been sold Haydn I'm afraid, and they want to start work on it in five days time, so you've only got five days to find another place to put your head down." Just like that!

"A bit short notice, isn't it, considering I've nowhere to move to."

"I can't do anything about it Haydn. I'm sorry but that's how it is."

"Thank you very much for your consideration towards me Eric," I thought baiting my breath.

Slowly replacing the receiver, I experienced an isolated moment of complete confusion, turmoil and disbelief. "Could this really be the final week I will be spending here?" was one of the many thoughts flitting through my mind, colliding into each other. Thoughts about the people I would be letting down, wondering how they would react to the devastating news? What would happen to me, and where would I be heading next? How would I survive and with whom?

So many questions and no answers. I thought I was prepared for this moment, but it seemed I had been kidding myself. Facing the unknown can be so terrifying at times. But what had to be done, had to be done, and remaining strong at heart, I had to hold my head up high and laugh in the face of adversity once again, not forgetting that I still had my friends this time.

"Be thankful Haydn that you're alive and healthy, but for the grace of God I could have been one of those more unfortunate people. You have no entitlement whatsoever to feel sorry for yourself. For once in your life Haydn, put yourself first for a change, to survive your immediate future trials, giving you another day to play again. If you can't help yourself you definitely can't help other people." Pouring myself a large stiff drink and sitting down with all these thoughts swirling around in my head, I decided it was time to get totally pissed, eager for the fog to engulf me, putting me in a place where you don't have to see what you don't want to, and I'd face the music tomorrow, giving me time to come to terms with the situation.

It was an unexpected shock to everyone concerned, but it was out of my hands now, there was nothing I could do about it, so I just had to accept the situation and depart gracefully. Thankfully Sharon volunteered to put me up until the time I could reorganise myself. But a strange thing happened that week. Ernie had been out of town for a short while, whilst I was in the process of leaving, and on returning found his house had been broke into and totally wrecked. So Sharon volunteered to put him up as well and the three of us all lived together for a short while in reasonable comfort.

"I'll tell you what Ernie," I commented, "I wouldn't mind living in one of these apartments myself."

"Yeah, I was thinking the same," replied Ernie gazing out of the window,

"Just look at that view of Pendle Hill, it's fantastic." He wasn't exaggerating. The unhindered view ten miles in every direction was superb, helping to calm the restless mind of anyone who set eyes on it.

So It was not long afterwards that her landlord Jeff was kind enough to sort us out with separate apartments on the same block. Steve, John and Mervin followed, living in their own individual apartments in the same complex. Although the Padiham saga had finally ended, it was like I had moved part of it with me. They told me Padiham had died a slow death after we left. What a sad, shameful ending to such a bustling town. The Padiham inspector got his way in the end establishing peace to the town. But only because there was nobody left to cause any trouble.

I lost touch with Yogurt for a while. His drinking habits had increased fourfold, trying to ease the effect of a totally boring and meaningless existence. When I last saw him whilst swimming in Clowbridge reservoir that day, he'd lost his door keys and a ten pound note in the shallows, and hadn't the strength to retrieve them. Steve, who was also with us at the time, offered to recover them for him. That was not the Yog I knew, but I thought he was just having a bad day.

Hillis's son came out of prison with a heroin addiction, which was passed on to Hillis and in turn to Yogurt. When I was eventually brought up to date with the situation I could have cried on the spot I was so upset. But there was nothing I could do about it anymore.

Hillis died first of a heart attack at the end in Feb 2006, on the same day that a guy, who ran his young grand daughter down, killing her outright, was jailed for only twelve weeks. I think Hillis just gave up on life. It was too painful.

But before he died, he took my car yet again for the last time whilst I was visiting friends in Padiham, to visit his girlfriend at Huncoat, leaving the windows wide open. Consequently my passport and Australian visa, which I had just acquired that day to attend my mother's funeral were stolen from the glove compartment of the car, rendering it impossible for me to go because of him. How bad was that? I had to settle for a photograph of the coffin. So it could be said that he got one up on me big style in the end.

It was only a year after Hillis died that Yog died also. I think Hillis's death attributed to his final downfall. His body just closed down under the intense pressure placed on it, and he died a lost soul searching for the things that he had once experienced being part of the club, that had been unfairly taken away from him. Lost through no fault of his and lost due to no fault of mine. But to this day I do believe the indirect blame rests on some arsehole's head still out there.

My mother's casket

Dwarling

John & Julie

Ernie

Chapter 10 The final day.

A number of days had passed since Nicola's whirlwind visit to my place with the heartbreaking news of Yogurt's unexpected death. And although I had slowly convinced myself of the reality of the situation, the formalities that I would have to experience on the day of his funeral in order to pay my final respects to him, I knew, were going to be devastating to me.

Lots of us had arranged to meet at Ernie's place and all make our way together to St. Leonard's Church, Padiham, situated on the main through road, about a hundred yards higher than the club, where we had experienced so many great times together. The time set for the funeral was 1.30pm.

I was restless and uneasy with the whole situation and I felt compelled to visit Pendle Hill by myself, to the exact spot where Yogurt and I had spent so much time discussing our lives over a few cans, in the peace, solitude and beauty of the setting sun over the distant hills. When I reached that special place I pondered for a while as tears welled up in my eyes.

"If Yog's soul is anywhere," I thought to myself, "this is the place it would be, waiting to make that final journey into eternity." My anomaly of life and death, not being a religious person, was that the human body was nothing but a sophisticated machine, and like all machines had a given lifespan. But the pure energy that controlled each individual being was the actual person within. It is a proven fact of physics, that energy can take many different forms, but cannot ever be destroyed. So now that my friend Yogurt had died, I believed that his energy was being released into the atmosphere, transforming itself into part of the environment surrounding him. The wind, the rain, the resulting vegetation, and every other element of nature were now partly Yogurt. It was so pleasing for me to think that the whole of Yogurt's dissipated energy could now have found its way onto these meandering hills, and had made a minute impression on the picturesque countryside that he loved so dearly. I just stood there, shoulders back, breathing in the clear air, looking around wondering, probing the space surrounding me, wanting desperately to believe that my whole countenance really did amount to something. It was a moment of sheer nostalgia and I felt so focused. I don't know to this day if it was my imagination, but I could definitely feel my dear friend's presence enveloping me.

St Leonard's Church, Padiham

"Yog!" I shouted out at the top of my voice, "are you listening to me?" My voice waves rolled down the side of the hillside in front of me, "I haven't give up on you yet! Just here to say Hello. I've been missing you. I'll be up here frequently to keep you updated on this book I am about to write. So hang about for a while will you mate?" A gentle breeze started to build up around me, rattling the long discarded cans that Yogurt and I had thrown there so many years before. I picked up on it and shouted, "Is that you Yog. Missing your lager already?" There was a final rattle and everything went still and quiet again. Whether he was trying to contact me on a different plane or whether it was just coincidence, I shall never know. But I do know that certain moments in time can sometimes be very frustrating. Yet taking everything into account, all Yogurt's and my discussions, all the laughs and tears we'd shed together, although he had no use for them anymore, I knew he had placed the accountability of preserving them all onto my shoulders. They were my responsibility now as long as I live. I felt very strongly that our vibrations must have caused some minute tilt to the way of the world as we first knew it. It just must have.

I slowly made my way back to the Padiham church, reflecting all these thoughts, and was amazed to witness the vast amount of people who had turned up to offer their last respects to the man that was. Not only was the church chocker block, but every inch of the pavements within a hundred yards in either direction was crammed. The entire town had turned up to pay their last respects. It could have been mistaken for a royal occasion. I kept catching glimpses of faces of most of the women he had associated with, scattered throughout the crowd. Lorretta, his last associate when the club eventually closed for good was on the opposite side of the road, directly in front of me, trying to gain my attention, whilst Maureen, Yogurt's girl when I first took the club over was at the side of me, giving me a nudge of acknowledgement. Yogurt and my solicitor Phil, who had looked after us both in many ways throughout that period was also present. He came over the minute he spotted me, to solemnly shake my hand in respect.

"It's a grim day today Haydn. Isn't it just. I had no alternative but to take the afternoon off to swill a last pint down in his name. Are you joining me for one?"

"Sure," I replied. "See you in the King's afterwards." I then started walking towards the main entrance of the church to beat the cortege that was due to arrive at any moment. Inside, I silently sneaked to the pew where Ernie and other friends were gathered. Glancing at them, they all looked so forlorn and silent, in their impeccable formal dress. Although in the name of respect, they fitted the situation perfectly, I could hardly recognise them. I'd never seen them dressed that way before, and to me it definitely wasn't them at all. The pew was full, but after a bit of a shuffle, I managed to find enough room, just before the cortege arrived. Suddenly the church doors opened and Paul, (Yogurt's brother) Callum, (Nicola's son) and two others, appeared at the rear of the church carrying his coffin. Nicola was a few rows in front of me, in a separate section with her mother and immediate family. She was dressed in black formal attire, her face covered by an expensive lace veil, making it impossible to read her facial expressions. But I knew from the way she was nervously fidgeting, that she was totally out of her depth with the situation. There was sadness everywhere. Not the sort of atmosphere that Yogurt would have wanted to participate in. He wouldn't have stuck around there long in such circumstances, which was a further reason why I firmly believed that whilst all this was happening, his soul was elsewhere. But regardless of my beliefs the show must continue, if only for his memory.

Paul had tears in his eyes. A very unusual sight because he always portrayed himself as the hard, unfeeling character. A man of stone. But today he looked so humble, effortlessly carrying his brother's coffin into position. The line from the song, "He's not heavy, he's my brother," sang by "The Hollys" shot through my mind. The music cracked up echoing around the large open expanse of the church, giving the quality and depth required for such an occasion. Immediately the first note of the vocal cracked up, John took it on himself to start singing in his proud stage-like manner, his strong professional voice totally overpowering the vocal section already playing,

"When you're weary, feeling small,
When tears are in your eyes,
I will dry them all,"

The whole congregation turned to investigate who was singing, all wearing such mournful expressions on their faces. It was so emotional. John kept singing. More confident now,

"I'm on your side,
When times are rough,
And friends just can't be found."

It sounded so compelling and moving, the rest of us just had to have a go at the chorus, all being very cautious so as not to let our fellow associates down.

"Like a bridge over troubled waters,
I will lay you down.
Like a bridge over troubled waters,
I will lay you down."

Everyone did their utmost to sing deep from their soul. And as all this was happening Yogurt's coffin slowly made its way towards the altar. Handkerchiefs could be seen appearing in the congregation as tears were forming in most of their eyes. John cracked up again with the second verse,

"When you're down and out.
When you're on the street,
When evening falls so hard,
I will comfort you."

Nobody else in the church uttered a sound. They just watched and listened in awe, whilst secretly wiping their tears away. John carried on,

"I'll take your part,
When da..arkness falls,
And pain is all around."

And again feeling right, we were all in for the chorus,

Like a bridge over troubled waters
I will lay you down.
Like a bridge over tro..oubled waters,
I will lay you down."

The combined results sounded so moving that virtually all the congregation were now crying their eyes out. We definitely turned a few heads that day, Yogurt would have been proud of us. Nobody could believe that such a sound could come from the likes of us. That was what it was all about. Each one inspiring the other to do their spontaneous utmost under difficult circumstances.

The coffin reached the altar and the music stopped, but those previous few minutes were one of those unforgettable moments. I thought to myself,

"We only live once. Best make the most of it whilst we can because nobody gets a second chance," although there were times throughout my life at the club, that I thought I could have been one of those exceptions to the rule.

The vicar started his sermon, but didn't tell me anything I didn't know already, quoting him as a honourable rogue that everybody loved, except for telling the congregation that he started practising his bridge jumping from Padiham bridge into two feet of water. Although being an accomplishment in itself, at that moment it was just another one of those irrelevant pieces of information that I never knew.

The coffin left the church whilst Janice Joplin's "Fast Cars" was playing, which brought many memories flowing back to me of the both of us happily riding the Trough together.

A thought occurred to me as I witnessed the hearse slowly departing. "If Yog could have his own way at this moment in time for his final journey he'd be doing a hundred mph down the road after listening to that music."

I wasn't present at the graveside. I left that for the immediate family, for the same reason that I didn't visit the garden of rest. I wanted to remember Yogurt as he was, full of life and energy. And that is how I still remember him. I called at his graveside weeks after to read the inscription on his headstone that had just been recently laid, which read,

Robert Coulson. Yogurt.
Dearly loved son and brother.
Born 29th Jan 1965
Died 29th Jan 2007
In our thought you'll always stay,
Till we meet again somewhere, someday.

And as I read it, I thought to myself, “Why should life be so harsh to such a worthy person? He didn't deserve the treatment he received. All he was guilty of was trying to make people feel happy with themselves, and because he tried, he died.”

Epilogue April 2010

Reflecting on everything that has happened to me during my time in Padiham, there is one person that reigns above everyone at this present moment in time. His name is Brandon, Nicola's son, born one month before the final club fire.

He is not my son, and at the time of her pregnancy I was far from amused with the situation presented to me, but now we are so insurmountably close to each other, it's uncanny. He was born with Cerebral Palsy, and had a twisted right leg, a very weak right arm and a serious speech problem. But he had one great advantage in life. He had Yog's blood and energy in him.

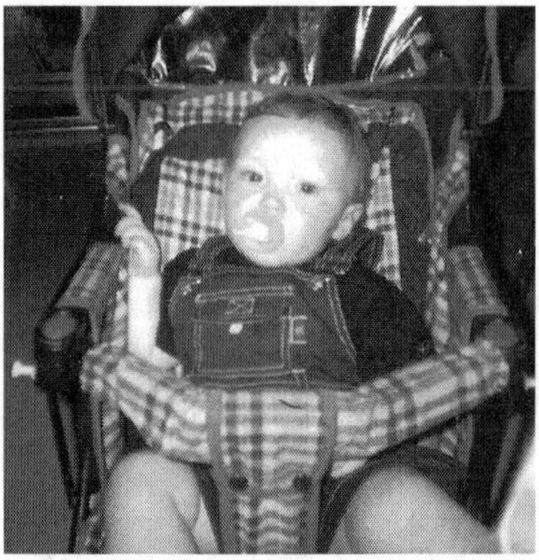

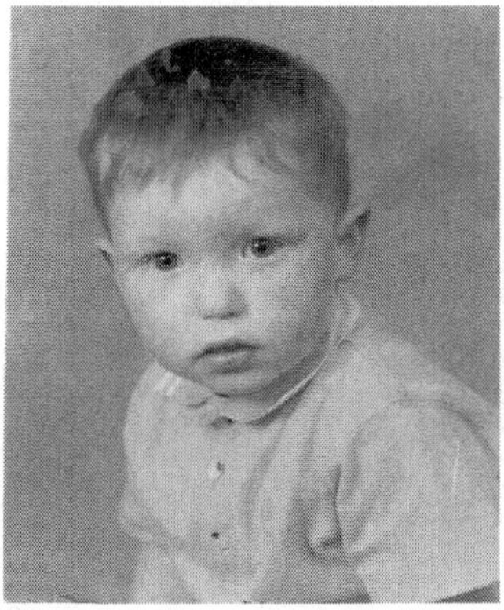

Brandon

Brandon and I have done lots together. Things like swimming, climbing, ice-skating, football, skiing, sledging, even tennis. And as a result, his body has straightened and strengthened. He has the same drive in life as Yogurt had, and although he has always been very intelligent, he is determined, because of his disabilities, not only to be as good as his friends, but to be better than them in everything he participates in, so nobody can ever laugh at him for his disabilities. And with my continuous help, at the age of nine, he has come through with flying colours. He reminds me so much of the Yog I knew. He is nearly cured now and has turned out to be a very needed person, with attitude. I place him above everyone, and rightly so. That was my promise to Nicola's father, Bob, that New Year's Day so long ago. And fulfilling it has given me much joy and belonging.

Myself & Brandon

And if Brandon were the only person that came out of this Padiham saga, it would have been well worth every minute spent there. He helped to dull the pain from the children I lost. Then there is Nicola. She wouldn't think or speak Yog's name for ages afterwards. It gave her too much pain. She is still one of my best friends, and considering I was warned initially that she'd suck me in and spit me out within the week, I don't think we've done too badly, it's been thirteen years now that we've known each other. It wasn't that long ago that she asked me to accompany her to get her nose pierced, being slightly wary of the procedure, needing someone to hold her hand. I finished up having to get mine done as well before she could build up enough courage to go for it. That's Nicola, just as mad now as she always was.

She visited my flat one evening and suddenly realised her taxi was pulling out of the car park below. Shooting out of the door, for some strange reason, she launched herself off the balcony, landing on her head ten feet below. What a mess she was in, taking a week or so to recover, surviving luckily with no noticeable scars. She must have still thought she was a vampire or something thinking she could fly, was the only explanation I could come up with. She definitely looked like one with blood dripping from her mouth when I scraped off the front lawn.

Ernie is still plodding on. He's always there for me if I need a helping hand. Nothing changes. I recently spent a little time with him and Keith in Cairo. Keith booked separate seating arrangements for the three of us, resulting from the cheapest possible prices for the Egyptian flight. I thought it was very unusual at the time, considering Ernie would need a wheelchair. We got to the luggage check-in at Heathrow Airport and Keith complained that the seating arrangements were totally impractical for a crippled man, his carer and hand luggage helper. We all needed to be together. They passed us to International customer care, who in turn informed the gate check-in of some last minute cancellations. We were immediately upgraded to executive class with caviar and champagne thrown in, all for no extra charge. So we got the best seating arrangements for the cheapest possible price. Pretty good, heagh? Street-minded is not the word for it, knowing a way round everything. But it was slightly embarrassing when Ernie struggled to his feet to obtain something from the luggage compartment, and lost his shorts in the process, doing a mooney to all the executive class patrons. He did get a cheer from a few people passing through to the toilet, though.

Tony died of a drinking related disease, a lonely man. There were only four people at his cremation and Yog and I were two of them. How sad is that.

"I hope this is not how we are going to finish up?" Yog whispered to me during the ceremony. Well Yog got sent off in style, thank God, but I don't know about me yet, and I hope I don't find out for a long time to come.

John still swears by Elvis, and given any chance to sing, he's always in first.

Steve's still drinking, but hasn't died yet and I hope he doesn't before this book comes out, as he is my principle defence witness. Joking apart, we are still great friends, and he is patiently waiting for me to pull something out of the bag to divert his drinking habits.

Leanne has a little boy and both are doing well. She is living with Ryan, the guy who stole my sound equipment back for me for £20. It's a small world we live in. We are still in close contact with each other.

Andrea and Paul eventually got married and divorced, but are still good friends. I do see Andrea occasionally.

I have never seen Tracey to this day.

Carol is still living in the same house in Halifax which I left so many years ago, whilst my step-children, Jennifer, Amanda, Kathleen and Leon still occasionally look me up. I recently received an invitation to Amanda's wedding, which I am more than eager to attend.

Lorraine, sadly, died of lung cancer shortly after taking me on the cruise, poor lass. I was at her side when she died.

My friendship with Eric survived it all and we have never been closer. He's doing fine, but even now I have to watch him when it comes to money matters. He's still a bit dodgy.

Gloria and my children, Rachel and Georgina have never been seen since she left Morecambe. Maybe one day I will bump into them again. One never knows what's waiting around the corner.

Paul, Yogurt's brother, is a very close friend of mine now. Yogurt's mother Rita is also close to me. She invited me to her place last Christmas for dinner and I gratefully accepted.

I did unintentionally bump into the retired police chief

Inspector, who was in charge in the club's hay day. He was giving a speech in Blackpool, on drinking and violence related to Padiham, myself being one of his pupils. I didn't recognise him at first but he recognised me alright, asking me to verify every point he was making. We had a few laughs together, reminiscing over the good old times, which gave me a buzz, him still remembering me after all this time. He's a good man.

As for Dwarling, he hasn't changed one iota. As I mentioned before, Eric approached him with a proposition to make up for his static caravan financial loss. There was a pub in Hebden Bridge called "The Shoulder of Mutton" that one of Eric's friends owned running under unsuitable management, and consequently wasn't a financial attribute.

Eric asked Dwarling to take over in an endeavour to increase the turnover. His intention was to get Dwarling to build the business up and then sell it on for a profit without Dwarling realising until it was too late. But Dwarling was too canny to be taken in by Eric.

One morning, Eric dropped Dwarling outside the pub, instructing him to do the business……just like that! He then disappeared off the scene, not wanting to get involved. I witnessed the spectacle as I passed on my way to Halifax. Dwarling, feeling totally abandoned, was slightly perturbed, but not put off. With an air of confidence he walked inside, a total stranger and demanded the keys to the establishment and an accurate inventory of stocks. The staff just stared at him dumbfounded, having that authoritative air about him. They were half expecting it and luckily for them, they had alternative living accommodation in the village. Dwarling eventually, convinced them to leave amiably on condition that he took care of a great dane they owned until such time that they could find enough room to house the poor thing. Feeling relieved that he had managed to get through the morning successfully, he contacted a mate of his, Gay John, asking him if he was willing to run the place with him. He then rang me later that afternoon, asking me to call in on my way back to Padiham, which I did. Within four hours of being there he knew every landlord in Hebden Bridge, taking me out on a tour of the pubs to introduce me to them. They were treating him like he'd been there forever.

Dwarling asked me, "Why don't you stop a week or so Haydn? There's a room for you, adjoining the main bedroom. Go up and have a look. Gay John had arrived and was watching from a distance. I went upstairs and opened the bedroom door. It was pitch black inside so struggling to find a light switch, I suddenly locked onto this large weird pair of green eyes staring down at me from above. Chills ran down my spine, nearly taking a fit. I backed off, running down the stairs, my feet hardly touching the floor screeching, "What's the fuck's in that bedroom?!" What a panic I was in. But looking around, they were bursting their sides laughing at me. They'd sent me up on purpose, the twats.

"Oh, we forgot to tell you. We've inherited a great dane," Gay John remarked. Immediately calming down and taking a deep sigh of relief, I went back upstairs to make friends. Well, I normally have a way with dogs, but there was this monster, crouched on a double bed, with its bulbous head nearly touching the ceiling, glaring down at me. I didn't know whether to go and stroke it or run a mile. Fortunately for me it turned out to be a soft old thing, thank God, although you wouldn't have thought so when you saw it taking Gay John for a run every morning.

Until Dwarling and Gay John arrived, the pub was empty and business was zero, but then the situation changed rapidly. They were both extreme exhibitionists and put together they couldn't lose. Within a week, people were coming from miles around to experience their company. The place was packed at all times, a complete reversal of affairs, turning it into a little gold mine. They were both artistic in their own right but they also hired a pretty young barmaid, who performed cartwheels and back flip-flaps when serving the punters. Very unusual indeed. They turned the pub into another one of those mad places……great!

Then came the crunch. They had been there about five

weeks and one special day Eric came demanding his cut, and ordering the rest of the weekly take to be deposited into the appropriate account. Instead, Gay John and Dwarling did a runner with the takings, never to be seen again in Hebden Bridge. So instead of Eric leaving Dwarling high and dry, Dwarling got one up on Eric, and with a profit to boot. Since then, Eric has been watching out for his special moment, which hasn't happened yet, and very likely never will.

Longley Hall was sold off behind my back, and I was forty grand poorer in the process, but that's another.

I have never set eyes on Kelly since I left Padiham. She moved to Haslingden with a guy and started a family. By all accounts she is doing well. I intend to visit her in the near future.

Kirsty on the other hand was not so lucky. She started seeing Hillis's son and it was her little girl who was killed. So tragic. But I see her knocking around and she seems to be surviving alright. We are still good friends.

Larry was the next to drink himself to death. At the very end he sent a message out for me to get there fast, but I didn't receive it in time. I still keep it as one of my prize possessions.

Then finally there's me. Ever since I arrived in Padiham, situations just mount up around me, and this was no exception.

Sharon had come into some money and had arranged to take her sister and mother for a month's holiday in Kusadasi, Turkey. But on the day of leaving, Sharon's passport hadn't come through on time, so her mother and sister left without her, her mother having all Sharon's money in her bank. The next day, her passport arrived, leaving me no alternative but to rebook a flight for her to join them, which Sharon's mother promised to repay, but just as expected, had no intention of doing so, and never did.

The last words Sharon came out with at Manchester airport as she made her way to the international lounge was, "Haydn, please come to see me for the last week, even if you have to come on your own. You'll have a really, really good time!" before disappearing through the doors. At the very last minute I decided to take her up on her offer, so with my rucksack on my back I took off for Turkey, impulsively. I was supposed to meet her in the harbour at a given time, but she never turned up, much to my disappointment, finding out later that her mother and sister, who hated my guts, getting wind of my unexpected visit, had moved hotels some twenty miles out of town to stop her seeing me. So there I was at the Hotel Atli, Kusadasi for a week on my ownsome.

"What could I possibly do to pass the time?" I thought to myself. And after much thinking I decided it was an ideal time to begin formulating this book of mine, being well overdue. So, getting to work with a vodka in my hand, lounging in the sun next to the swimming pool, I suddenly heard a voice beside me,

"You writing to your girlfriend?" I looked up to a young Turkish waiter who was standing there.

"I don't think so," was my answer, being a little pissed off with women at that moment in time.

"You a writer?" he asked me.

Now although I had never written before, I was definitely writing now, so I replied, "Yes, I am a writer."

Forthwith he asked, "I can speak and read English. Can I translate a part of it to my fellow waiters in Turkish?"

Getting a little perturbed with his continual interruptions, I answered, "Go on then, but a small random section only, and make it fast." He called his friends over and read a paragraph out to them.

One of them spontaneously screamed out pointing to the page, "Aghh……..Shameless!"

Thinking he meant it was like the series which was doing great at the time on English Channel 4, from the book written by Paul Abbott, I replied, "Yes. That is correct. Shameless." For the next two days everybody in the hotel was sending me drinks across, and one or two of them offered me to accompany them on nights out. Nobody would let me contribute in any shape or form.

I thought, "What a great set of people these are." Then on the third day I realised by one of their comments, that they all thought I was the script-writer for Shameless. It was too late to back down, considering all the alcohol they had been buying me, so I went along with being treated like a star for the rest of the week, whether I liked it or not, just to hold face.

I was finding it difficult to answer some of their continuous questions, so I decided to ring Dwarling to fill me in on a few details, his family being friends with the Abbot family. When he realised the position I had got myself into, and what he was missing out on, if there had have been enough time left, I think he would have joined me.

On the last day, whilst everyone was being hustled into transit buses to be taken to the airport which was sixty miles away, I was offered a lift in the hotel owner's Mercedes, and as we were pulling out of the hotel grounds, a Channel 4 camera crew were pulling in to film a documentary about young Turkish men and older English women, would you believe.

"Your friends are arriving," he blurted out. "But I am deeply sorry, we just can't stop, or we shall be late reaching the airport."

"Fair does," I replied. "It's alright. I'll catch up with them another time," thinking to myself, "Get me out of here fast! It could turn into a very sticky situation," and off we drove. Saved again. And what an unexpected end to such a brilliant week.

My Final Thoughts

Thinking back, remembering everybody I met and all that happened, taking into consideration the promises I made and fulfilled during those seven unforgettable years in Padiham, trying to weigh up what life was all about, I came to the conclusion that in the very end, I didn't have a frigging clue. What I can feel, is that writing this manuscript has given me a sense of closure to the whole affair and I am now ready to move on before it's too late.